THE

TYCOON

THE

TYCOON

GEORGE ALEXANDERS

PaperJacks LTD.

TORONTO   NEW YORK

PaperJacks

THE TYCOON

PaperJacks LTD

330 STEELCASE RD. E., MARKHAM, ONT. L3R 2M1
210 FIFTH AVE., NEW YORK, N.Y. 10010

Donald I. Fine, Inc. edition published 1987

PaperJacks edition published May 1988

U.S. ISBN 0-7701-0888-1
CDN. ISBN 0-7701-0890-3

TO ELENA

CHAPTER ONE

Was there anything in my background that made me different from other lads in our village? The only thing I can think of to set me even remotely apart was that my mother was from Crete.

My birthplace was the village of Drakopoulata on the island of Cephalonia, the largest of the Greek islands in the Ionian Sea. My father, Leonidas Sthanassis, was born there, as were his parents and grandparents. As far back as anyone could remember, the Sthanassis family had made its home in Drakopoulata or its neighboring towns and villages.

It was not a large village. Its stone, tile-roofed dwellings bordered olive groves that rose on terraced steps up a sheltering fold of a mountain valley. The valley creased its way inland from the stretch of sea that separates Cephalonia from its close neighbor, the island of Ithaca. At the time of my birth, Drakopoulata housed about one hundred families. I doubt that its population ever exceeded five hundred.

Our house was close to the western edge of the village. Through the cypress and olive trees, we gazed down on the checkerboard fields of the valley floor. To the north, the gray and treeless dome of Mount Kalon smiled down on us. To the east, beyond the olive tree- and scrub-mantled downward slope, were the roof tiles and church bell tower of the small harbor of Aghia Efimia — and beyond the harbor, the blue water of the strait and the steeply rising mountains of Ithaca.

Drakopoulata was my father's whole world. The two-and-a-half-kilometer journey to Aghia Efimia he avoided if at all possible. To proceed another ten kilometers to the port of Sami at the end of the bay was even less to his liking. How then did he come to meet and marry a girl from an island as distant as Crete?

In his late twenties, my father was conscripted into the Greek Army. In 1879, the year following the short-lived Russo-Turkish War, my father served in some sort of clandestine operation in Crete, then still under Turkish rule. During the course of the operation, he was wounded in the thigh and hospitalized in the Cretan port city of Chanea. My father has always been vague about the details of the mission and how he received his incapacitating wound. It is unimportant. What matters is that he *was* in Crete, *was* wounded and ended up recuperating in a Cretan hospital in which my mother, then seventeen, was a nurse's aide. Her maiden name was Maria Metaxis.

They fell in love, became betrothed and, following my father's recovery, were married in Chanea. To the union, my mother brought a small dowry provided by a well-to-do uncle who resided in the faraway American city of New York.

My father's brief period of military service at an end, the couple journeyed to Cephalonia to make their home in Drakopoulata. This was somewhat complicated by the fact that my father's mother, his younger brother, Alexander, and Alexander's wife and four-year-old daughter occupied the Sthanassis cottage. Since my mother was already with child, the accommodation would soon be strained beyond its capacity.

The dilemma was eventually resolved to everyone's satisfaction. Alexander had long had in mind a business venture in the Black Sea port of Odessa in czarist Russia. By pooling the family resources — including my mother's dowry — enough was accumulated to finance Alexander. He and his family left to take up residence in Odessa.

Childbearing did not come easily to my mother. In May of 1880 she gave birth to her first child, my older brother, Stefano. Thereafter, though she quickened four times over the intervening years, she lost each child through miscarriage until going to term with my eldest sister, Georgiana, in 1895. Three years later, she gave birth to Penelope. I arrived on the scene two years later, the last of her four children.

My mother had anticipated that the twentieth century and I would make our debuts simultaneously. Such was not the case. Obstinately, I clung to the security of the womb. Howling in protest, I finally put in an appearance at two o'clock in the morning of January 4, 1900.

I was christened Constantine, which promptly was shortened to the affectionate diminutive "Kostas."

My earliest recollections of family life revolve around my mother, my sisters and, to a lesser extent, my father.

My brother Stefano was nineteen when I was born. Before my first birthday, he had gone to Odessa to take employment with my Uncle Alexander, who, by that time, was prospering in his business venture in Russia. I never knew Stefano, other than through hearsay, and have no mental image of him whatsoever.

I recall my father as a man of stocky build and medium height. His hair was gray. He was swarthy of complexion and blue-jowled, even when freshly shaved. At home, he seldom smiled and rarely laughed. He was a forbidding figure who walked with a pronounced limp. The major problem between us was one of age. He was fifty at the time of my birth — a span of years difficult to bridge.

I cannot say that my childhood association with my sisters was one of harmony. To Georgiana, to whom often fell the responsibility of looking after me in my early years, I was a burden that kept her from more interesting pursuits. Penny, closer to my age, was fiercely protective but resented the attention paid me by my mother.

My sisters were not attractive girls. Penny, less attractive than Georgiana, had a narrow face, a sallow complexion and a rather large nose. Her one redeeming feature was a lovely smile, but it was something she rarely employed.

My fondest memories are of my mother. She was thirty-eight at the time of my birth. I recall her from my early years as a handsome woman, almost as tall as my father. Her hair was chestnut brown. She wore it long, combed back from her face. Her eyes — dark brown, with flecks of gold — were her most attractive feature. A smile seemed always to hover at the corners of her lips. At least in those days, I remember her as being unfailingly in good spirits.

Why did I suggest that the fact that my mother hailed from Crete might have set me apart from others of my age in our village? There were, I believe, three reasons.

The first of these was that the stories she spun for me during my most impressionable years — while they ranged the whole gamut of Greek myth, legend and history — included wondrous tales of the past glories of Crete. Without doubt, I one day would have read about the time when the Minoan civilization flourished and the naval might of Knossos controlled maritime trade, bringing fabulous wealth and power to the Minoans. However, since my mother was Cretan, this information came to me at an age when it impressed itself indelibly on my mind. I am convinced now that, even in childhood, I equated wealth and power with ships and seafarers thanks to mother's stories of the naval supremacy of the Minoans. If only subconsciously, this must have influenced some of my actions and decisions in later years.

The second reason was that my mother had acquired more education than was normal in our village. She was determined that I would have the benefits of at least a secondary education, an opportunity denied my brother due partially to his lack of interest but more to the family's financial circumstances at that time. To this end, mother borrowed books from Father Damianos, the priest who ministered to our diocese. During the dreary winter months, when heavy rains kept me indoors, mother taught me to read and write. It opened up a whole new world for me. By the time I was seven, I was devouring all the books mother could borrow. I so outdistanced my schoolmates that Father Damianos arranged for me to receive special tutoring in English and Italian.

The last, but by no means the least, reason was my mother's uncle, Nicholas. He left Crete when in his teens and became a wealthy man in the distant American city, New York. It was he who had contributed to mother's family support — much as my Uncle Alexander and brother Stefano were now contributing to our well-being. It was her Uncle Nicholas who had provided her with a dowry. Mother was not quite sure how her uncle had acquired wealth and substance, but she assured me that he was fabulously wealthy. In a borrowed atlas, mother pointed out to me both Odessa and New York. In a geography test, I read about New York and America. Since there was nothing available that gave much information on Russia or Odessa, it is only natural that, of the two cities, New York became firmly fixed in my mind as a fabled realm of golden opportunity.

Undoubtedly, those three factors influenced me in the years that lay ahead, but during my childhood they fell into the category of dreams. Like every other boy of the village, my head was filled with fancies and fantasies in which I imagined myself in heroic mold and form — in turn, such mythical heroes as Odysseus, or Jason, triumphing against overwhelming odds. But in my case, I think my mother's influence provided me with broader horizons and more vaulting ambitions.

CHAPTER TWO

Ours was a poor village. The olive groves, fig and almond orchards and most of the vineyards in our valley were owned by absentee landlords and administered through overseers. The villagers of Drakopoulata, as did the inhabitants of nearby villages, simply worked the orchards, groves and vineyards on a share basis. The share was small. The only things we actually owned were our homes, vegetable gardens, small herds of goats and a few sheep.

Poverty is relative, though. Since everyone in our village lived at subsistence levels, to get by with very little seemed a natural way of life. I don't recall ever thinking of our family as being impoverished. I never went hungry. Of course, by the time I was four, remittances from Uncle Alexander were arriving on a more or less regular basis, which put us in a better financial position than many of our neighbors. While I cannot remember experiencing much in the way of hardship, Georgiana recalls an earlier time when mother had to measure in grams from our hoard of food to insure the supply would stretch through the winter months and that each had his or her fair share.

As one would suspect, winter was the most difficult time in our village. Like all the wives of the village, my mother made and cured feta cheese — not only for food, but also to be used as an item in bartering with the boatmen during the lean time of the winter months. To this day, I can still smell the rich, tangy odor of the curing cheeses every time I taste feta. It is a conceit of mine that my mother made the finest, most flavorful feta ever produced.

Actually, I came to look on the monthly trading journey to the harbor at Sami as not a duty, but an adventure. I whiled away many a happy hour listening to the boatmen's tales of their islands and the mainland. I heard wondrous — often, I now know, grossly exaggerated — stories about the delights of Greece's second largest port, Patras. I was told much about Lefkas, rich in history, and of Zante, the southernmost of the Ionian isles, where the climate is said to be eternally springlike.

I listened with rapt attention to the boatmen, believing everything they told me. Well, almost everything. There were differences of opinion between many of the boatmen, and often violent arguments arose. As an example, I recall that there were some from Lefkas who claimed vehemently that Lefkas, not Ithaca, was Odysseus' native land, quoting archaeological finds at Nidri as proof of their contention. Quite naturally, those from Ithaca hotly contested this blasphemous claim. Both sides of this argument could agree on only one fact — that it was in the "Marble Cave," Marmarospilia, that Odysseus buried the gifts given him by the Phaeacians, a treasure that to this day awaits discovery.

Would it not be wonderful if, in one's youth, one could sip of some secret elixir and stay young and carefree forever? Despite the fact that life was relatively harsh in our village, the years I spent there until mid-adolescence were, without question, the happiest of my life.

Ours were simple pleasures. When, as a child, I went with my sisters on the journey to Sami, every step along the way was sheer delight. The scene always seemed to change in a most marvelous way.

The ideal time to make the trek was in the spring, when the almond trees were dusted with pale blossoms, or in the summer months, when the oleanders were a riot of white, pink and red blooms. In those days, there was no road joining Sami and Aghia Efimia. A donkey track threaded its way along the rocky coastline, skirting on one hand the blue sea and on the other the olive groves on the rising slopes. There, just across a narrow strip of sea, fabled Ithaca drowsed in the sun. The soft warm dust curled between my toes. The air was laden with the scent of grass and flowers. I gave myself over to daydreams. They were heroic dreams of adventure in the Homeric mold.

As I neared Sami, the dreams would fade, replaced by excitement. Surely on this visit, there would be a letter at the post office from Uncle Alexander. Since Stefano always included a few lines with my uncle's missives, a letter from Uncle Alexander meant word from Stefano as well.

All the way through the town the excitement mounted, even

though the possibility was strong that no letter would be there. Generally, correspondence from Uncle Alexander was spaced six months apart. Imagine then how my heart leapt with joy on those occasions when I was rewarded by the postmaster. On my return to Drakopoulata, the letter clutched tightly in my hand, my feet fairly flew over the ground.

Mother was deeply religious. She devrived much comfort from her faith. We were raised in strict adherence to the tenets of the Greek Orthodox Church.

As for me, even though I wandered from the faith in later years, it always remained an essential part of my being. With my sisters it seemed to make a deep impression. There was a time when I thought, from their praying and devotion, that they were becoming religious fanatics. If either had indicated a desire to make the church her calling, I would have accepted such devotion as normal, but neither did.

When I was thirteen, mother, my sisters and I journeyed to the monastery of Agio Gerasimos, the patron saint of Cephalonia, to attend the saint's festival and to observe the all-night vigil on August 15. It was then, following the vigil and the next day's ceremonies and festivities, that Penny confided in me the reason for what seemed to me her excessive devotion. She and Georgiana feared, above all else, spinsterhood, and their common supplications were an attempt to secure divine assistance in their quest for matrimony.

I really had not given their plight much thought until then. When I thought of the money supplied us by Uncle Alexander and, to a lesser extent, Stefano, it had always been in terms of *my* needs. I had thought of the money as being put aside to cover the expenses of my higher education in preparation for the bright future in some far-off land. Of course, my mother had mentioned dowries for Georgiana and Penny, but I had not thought much about what that meant to them. It came to me on that saint's day that, unattractive as both were, dowries for my sisters were a matter of vital concern. To them, the letters I brought back from Sami meant more, much more, than just improving the family's finances. To Georgiana and Penny, those letters spelled the difference between a life of fulfillment and one of sterile frustration. At thirteen, however, it was hard for me to grasp the full significance of their dilemma since, at that time, although the juices were starting to stir in my loins, marriage was the farthest thing from my mind.

How did I see myself as a boy and youth? Of course, in my fantasies, I assumed heroic stature. The reality was somewhat different. I was of about average height and weight for my age, although I thought myself too thin. I could hold my own in a brawl, but I didn't go out of my way to pick a fight.

In appearance, I was unlike either my father or mother. My hair was a lighter shade of brown than that of any of our family — I must have had some Dorian ancestors somewhere in the past. My eyes, behind drooping lids, were slate gray verging on blue. I thought my aquiline nose too large for my face.

Like Penny, I had a smile that lit up my face. It was a disarming smile. At an early age, I learned to use it to good advantage. I had but to flash that smile and most people would accede to my wishes.

I did not consider myself particularly handsome or particularly ugly. Frankly, my appearance was the least of my worries — although I must admit I have always wished I were an inch or two taller.

My years of growing up in Cephalonia were carefree, but for Greece it was a time of turbulence. This was hardly a new condition. Throughout its recorded history, Greece has been plagued by internal strife and been in almost constant conflict with its neighboring states.

For close to four centuries, until it achieved independence in 1821 under the sponsorship of the Great Powers — Britain, France and Russia — Greece had been held in thrall by the Turkish sultans of the Ottoman Empire. Lingering Greek grievances concerning the annexation of Crete and the status of the northern regions of Macedonia and Thrace were continuing root causes of friction with the Turks.

The Greek king, George I, and the astute Cretan prime minister, Venizelos, brought together Bulgaria, Serbia and Greece to form the Balkan league. In 1912, they embarked on the Balkan Wars. The armies, under the command of Prince Constantine, were victorious against the Turks on all fronts, and Crete was formally united with Greece. Sadly, though, Greece mistrusted her ally, Bulgaria, and formed an alliance with Serbia and Russia. In 1913, the Bulgars were decisively defeated in a continuation of the briefly recessed Balkan Wars. On March 18, 1913, King George was assassinated in Salonika and succeeded by Prince Constantine.

I am making it sound as though I was aware of what was taking place as it transpired. At the time, though, it had little direct impact on my life. War was not being waged in the Ionian isles. Life in Drakopoulata and its neighboring villages went on pretty much as usual. About the only indication of the distant conflict was the conscription and departure of many young men, a development which, to Georgiana and Penny, was traumatic.

The gods of ancient Greece are portrayed as a capricious lot. It is almost as though our family came to their attention, and they decided to take a hand in our affairs.

What befell us was a severe blow. It reached us in the form of a letter I brought back from the post office in Sami. The letter was from Uncle Alexander, written in October 1914, but we did not receive it until February 1915. Its contents came as a stunning shock to all of us.

Uncle Alexander related much we already knew — that Russia, in alliance with France and Britain, was at war with the Central Powers, Germany and Austria-Hungary — and a distressing fact we didn't know — that Stefano had been conscripted into the army of Grand Duke Nicholas and was serving with the Russian Second Army somewhere in East Prussia. Since we had heard of the disastrous defeat of the Russian Second Army, we wondered: had Stefano survived? We had no way of knowing.

The rest of the letter dealt with the state of Uncle Alexander's business affairs. Apologetically, he stated that, until the Allies won the war and Russia settled down, he doubted that he would be able to send any money. Not only was business bad, but also he had been cut off from many of his sources of supply. Moreover, heavy taxes had been imposed to finance the Russian campaign against the Central Powers.

This was indeed sobering news. It altered the family's financial picture dramatically. We had come to rely on the remittances from Uncle Alexander and Stefano. From these monies, mother had set aside savings to underwrite our future plans for my education and my sisters' marriages. But what if the war dragged on? What if Russia were defeated? We would have no option but to dip into our savings. How long would they last?

It was in April of that year that my father took me aside and spoke to me seriously.

"Kostas," he said solemnly, "much has changed. Your mother's wish has been that you go to Patras to continue your education. Even though I have felt for some time that you are too bookish . . . that your head has been in the clouds . . . I have not disputed your mother in this wish. But now we cannot afford further education for you. When I was your age, two years younger, in fact, I was helping support my family by taking salt on a donkey to the nearby towns. It is time, I feel, that you should start to earn your way and contribute to the family."

For some weeks I had been thinking along the same lines. My problem was that there seemed no way I could find employment in, or close to, Drakopoulata.

"You are right, Papa," I agreed, "but Greece isn't in the war. There are more young men seeking jobs than there are jobs to go around. Where can I find work here?"

My father nodded. "That is so. The king wants to keep us out of the war. The prime minister wants us to fight with the Allies. While this indecision is with us, jobs are scarce. I have heard, though, that there are jobs to be had in Corfu."

"What jobs, Papa?"

"I understand they are short of fishermen. It is time you learned a trade."

"Yes, Papa," I replied dutifully, yet with a sinking heart. All my dreams were collapsing. Corfu, the second largest of the Ionian isles, was hardly my idea of a place where fortune awaited me.

CHAPTER THREE

Early in May 1915, I, a youth of fifteen on the threshold of manhood, stepped off the ferryboat at Kerkyra, the ancient seaport and
capital city of Corfu. I was wearing my only suit. Unaccustomed
as they were to shoes, my rock-hardened feet felt cramped and
uncomfortable. In my pocket were a few drachmas. Wrapped in
a small cloth bundle I had feta cheese, half a loaf of bread, some
dried figs and a bottle of Robola, the famed white wine of
Cephalonia. I hadn't the vaguest idea where to look for either a
place to live or a job.

For the rest of that afternoon, I wandered the streets of the city,
gazing at the sights in wonderment. I was to learn a good deal about
Kerkyra and its illustrious past under a parade of foreign overlords
in the months and years that lay ahead, but my first impression
was that it was a strange city with narrow streets, wide boulevards,
large parks and squares and a bewildering mixture of architectural
styles.

When the sun was sinking behind the forest-mantled hills in the
west, I retraced my steps to the harbor. I was no closer to finding
accommodation and had no concrete thoughts about employment,
but if I was going to find work as fisherman, as my father had
suggested, I should not stray too far from the sea.

In the gathering dusk, I sat on the quay at the water's edge,
munching bread and cheese washed down with swallows of Robola.
The weather was mild. Corfu was indeed a marked change from
Cephalonia, but I was not dismayed. I was confident that something
would turn up in the morning.

That night I stretched out on the grass of a small park, my head
pillowed on my small bundle of provender. I had no fear of being
robbed. With the exception of my almost-new shoes, I had nothing

worth stealing. My first night in Corfu, I slept peacefully beneath the stars.

The slanting rays of early-morning sunshine in my eyes awakened me. I sat up and stretched. It took me a moment to adjust to my surroundings, to remember that I was a stranger in Corfu and that today I must actively seek some kind of employment. On my left, I noted a number of fishing boats entering the harbor after their night's work at sea. They converged on a long stone jetty. I picked up my small bundle and headed in that direction. Thinking back on that morning, I recall that I was filled with confidence. I was on my own. Adventure beckoned. This was not the bold beginning I had imagined, but Corfu would be a stepping stone to the fulfillment of my dreams.

The boat was white with dark blue trim. The weathered fisherman was lifting wooden buckets containing his night's catch onto the jetty. I stepped to the edge of the quay and took the laden buckets from him as he handed them up to me. When his boat was unloaded, I squatted on my haunches and smiled disarmingly down at the grizzled fisherman.

"Tell me, sir," I said, "do you know where I could find work as a fisherman?"

He looked up at me quizzically, then his lips twitched in an answering smile. "What's your name?" he asked.

"Kostas, Kostas Sthanassis. I've just arrived from Cephalonia. Work is hard to find there."

"I see. What do you know of the trade?"

"Very little," I said, still smiling, "but I am willing to work for my keep to learn its secrets."

The fisherman's smile broadened, displaying some broken teeth. "Well said, lad. If you are a willing worker, I think I can use you on those terms. You can begin this very minute by helping me take my catch to the market."

His name was Spiridon Papas. Frankly, I could have found no kinder employer. He did not make his home at Kerkyra, but in a cove some eight kilometers to the northwest, near a village of Kontokali. When we returned to his boat after marketing his catch, Spiridon and I cast off and set sail.

I removed my shoes, rolled up my trousers and helped get under way. Happily, while inexperienced as a fisherman, I was no stranger to boats and sails. Spiridon said nothing, but he grinned when he looked at my calloused feet and nodded approvingly as I went about coiling and stowing the ropes and lines.

Gouvion Cove opens westward behind sheltering headlands. We rounded the southernmost headland and altered course toward a shallow bay at the southeastern extremity of the cove. There a number of fishing boats rode at anchor or were tied alongside the rickety wooden jetties. Huddled on the shore were some tile-roofed, lime-washed cottages, one of which Spiridon pointed out as his. Behind these huts the wooded land rose steeply.

We made fast to a jetty jutting out into the rocky-bottomed, seaweed-cloaked bay. I helped Spiridon unload the nets and spread them out to dry on a packed-earth terrace fronting his cottage. That done, we entered the modest dwelling.

There I was introduced to Spiridon's wife, Katarina, a cheerful, motherly woman of middle years, who promptly fixed for us a satisfying meal.

At the conclusion of the meal the discussion between Spiridon and Katarina revolved around where I should stay. Their house was small. It had only two bedrooms, one theirs, the other occupied by their daughter, Danai, whom I had yet to meet. Obviously, their quarters were cramped, but, since I was to work for my keep, some compromise would have to be found. The solution was simple.

There was a toolshed to the rear of the enclosed garden at the back of the house. This we cleared of garden implements and potted plants, and a borrowed cot, a low table and a rush-bottomed chair were found to provide me with Spartan, but adequate, quarters.

I met Danai at the evening meal. She acknowledged the introduction politely. I gazed into her eyes — blue-green like the sea over a shelving beach of white sand — and was struck dumb. I thought I detected a glint of amusement in her eyes, but her lovely face remained expressionless. At last, I found my voice and mumbled something. She lowered her lids demurely.

All through the meal, it took a supreme effort on my part to keep from staring at Danai. She was the most beautiful girl I had ever seen. Her features were finely molded and of classic beauty. What sprang to my mind was the myth that the gods and goddesses of old often were wont to appear as mortals. It must be true. Surely the raven-haired vision of loveliness seated opposite me was Aphrodite incarnate.

Danai was going on seventeen. There was no adolescent gawkiness about her. She was every inch a woman. There is no doubt that, from the moment I laid eyes on her, I was hopelessly infatuated. For the first time, love had entered my life. It made me acutely conscious of my fancied faults and shortcomings. In her presence, I felt gauche and awkward. What made it worse was that she seemed barely to acknowledge my existence.

For the next few weeks and months, my waking thoughts were on little else than Danai. What complicated the situation was the fact that we saw little of each other during the summer months. During the day, Danai worked as a salesgirl in a shop in Kontokali. I, on the other hand, went out with the fishing fleet at dusk and didn't return until the next morning. I slept during the day. So about the only time I saw Danai was during the evening meal.

For me, those months were agony. In an attempt to put her from my mind, I worked myself to exhaustion during the day, yet, often, as I lay on my cot sweltering in the afternoon heat, my erotic fantasies made me groan aloud.

Spiridon was a good teacher, and I an apt and willing pupil. I was anxious to please him. I learned quickly.

There is nothing very complicated about setting the net and bringing in the catch. Where the skill comes into it is knowing where and when to place the nets in the offshore waters. We fished at night, using kerosene lanterns to lure the fish alongside our craft. Yet, for all the skill and local knowledge at Spiridon's command, there were many nights when our labors were rewarded with little more than a few squid and octopus.

When the catch was good, we put first into Kerkyra in the early morning hours to market our harvest. But when the catch was poor, we proceeded directly to Gouvion Cove at daybreak.

Our return to the tiny bay did not signal the end of our working day. The boat had to be scrubbed and inspected for leaks. From time to time the paintwork had to be touched up, the bottom scraped clean of marine growth and sprung strakes recaulked. Often the sails needed patching, and the standing and running rigging had to be renewed. Then, when the nets had dried, they had to be carefully inspected and mended where necessary.

I welcomed the long working day for two reasons. Not only was

I anxious to find favor in the eyes of Danai's father, but, as the summer progressed, I was given a share of our earnings and, in consequence, was able to send some drachmas back to my family.

I learned one thing that astonished me. Although Spiridon had spent more than forty years at his trade, he had, incredible as it might sound, never learned to swim. It was a good thing, he said laughingly, since it provided strong incentive to keep one's craft afloat regardless of what mischief Poseidon, or Triton, might visit on the unwary seafarer.

Once the nets are set, fishing is largely a matter of patience. During the long night hours, Spiridon and I talked of many things. He was fond of singing, and, when I learned the words, I would join in his lusty or wistful refrains. At other times, he whiled away the hours by telling me stories about Corfu.

Spiridon claimed that Corfu appears in Homer's *Odyssey* as Scheria, homeland of the Phaeacians. It was here that the shipwrecked Odysseus met the lovely Princess Nausicaa and her charming young girl companions.

Corfu, he contended, was first settled by Eretreans and then, sometime in the seventh century B.C., became a colony of the Corinthians. However, he stated, then as now, the Corfiotes valued above all else their independence and rebelled against the mother city. In 435 B.C., a quarrel with Corinth brought matters to a head and Corfu requested assistance from Athens. This alliance resulted in the Peloponnesian War.

Over the ensuing centuries, Corfu, with its commanding position guarding the entrance to the Adriatic Sea, was a much-sought-after prize. Successively, from the second century B.C. onward, it came under the domination of the Romans, the Byzantine emperors, the Norman kings of Sicily, Genoese pirates, Naples and then the Venetian mercantile empire. The latter held sway for a full four centuries. Thereafter, Corfu was governed by the French until they, in turn, were expelled by the British during the Napoleonic Wars. It remained a British protectorate until, in 1864, along with the other Ionian islands, it was ceded to Greece.

Sunday was normally a day of rest for us. Spiridon suggested that I should take advantage of this free time to explore the city of Kerkyra.

I did as Spiridon suggested, though I confess that my heart was not in sightseeing or delving into Corfu's past. I would have much preferred to spend my free time with Danai, exploring the present. But this was denied me. Each Sunday, after Mass and a noonday meal, she would go off by herself, taking with her a small cloth bag. I imagined that her destination was a tryst with a lover. Dejectedly I would set my face toward Kerkyra.

This unhappy state of affairs continued until late in August. Then one Sunday, I screwed up my courage and followed Danai at a safe distance.

She took the footpath that followed the southern curve of the cove before it cut westward to Kontokali. However, at the southernmost point of this path, Danai took a track that branched sharply northward, which I knew led to some private estates on the high ridge of the headland.

I was so far back that I almost missed the moment when she turned and disappeared into a screen of foliage. When I reached the spot, I located a faint path all but hidden by the thick brush and tangle of vines.

Following this track, I pushed forward as quietly as possible. I feared I would stumble upon Danai in the embrace of her lover.

It is well that I proceeded slowly. I pushed through a screen of branches to find myself standing on the lip of a cliff. Below me, almost hidden from view by a rocky ledge, was a tiny cove of seaweed-darkened rocks and coarse pinkish sand, whitened at its rim by pulverized seashells. As I looked down from this vantage point, I saw Danai cross the crescent of beach and disappear from view beneath the overhang.

Well, I thought miserably, I had discovered her trysting spot. I was about to turn away from the edge of the cliff, when, when I saw Danai, her nude body aglow in the afternoon sunlight, run lightly across the coarse sand and plunge into the limpid blue-green sea. I waited. No one followed behind her. My heart lifted. Evidently she came to this hidden cove to enjoy the privacy it afforded.

CHAPTER FOUR

During the week following my discovery concerning Danai's Sunday outings, I could think of little else. How could I contrive to join her? I don't know why I didn't simply consider asking her if she wanted company.

The following Sunday, Danai, as usual, left the cottage, carrying her cloth bag. I waited about twenty minutes before setting out to follow her.

As I pushed into the bushes toward the cliff's edge, my heart pounded in my chest and sweat beaded my brow. Just how was I to explain my presence when I came upon her?

From my vantage point at the top of the cliff, I viewed what I could see of the beach with alarm. Danai was nowhere to be seen. Still, much of the tiny cove remained screened from view by the overhang. She could be sunning herself in some spot not visible to me from where I stood. The obvious course of action was to descend to the beach.

As I picked my way down the faint path around an outcropping, I hit upon what I considered to be an acceptable excuse. It was weak — but it was better than no excuse at all.

As I scrambled over a weathered boulder near the base of the cliff, I saw Danai, her evenly tanned body breathtakingly beautiful in its nakedness, walking slowly down to the water's edge. From the shadow of the rocks, I watched her as she waded in up to her thighs, hesitated a moment, then lowered herself and stretched out to let the wavelets caress her firm, upthrusting breasts.

My breathing became ragged. Blood pounded in my ears.

After a moment's hesitation, I walked across the pebbles and stopped at the water's edge. "Danai!" I called out hoarsely, betraying my agitation.

Startled, Danai turned onto her stomach and stared at me in

bewilderment. "Kostas!" she exclaimed, her voice indicating disbelief, as if I'd materialized out of thin air. "What are you doing here?"

Involuntarily, I stepped forward into the ankle-deep water.

"Please, Kostas!" she exclaimed. "Don't come nearer! I beg you!"

I stopped where I was, and said in as natural a tone as I could muster, "Your mother and father were looking for you. They thought you were going with them to visit friends in Gouvia. When they couldn't find you, they left without you. They asked me to let you know where they had gone so you could join them on your return."

Danai looked at me intently for a moment before answering. Then a ghost of a smile touched her lips as she asked, "How did you find me?"

I saw at once the glaring flaw in my lie. I could only have found this place by following her. I felt my cheeks grow hot and flushed in embarrassment.

"I . . . ah . . . ," I stammered.

Danai laughed delightedly. "Never mind! I'm glad you're here."

She pushed herself backward into deeper water and rose to her knees facing me. Her wet hair hung down over one shoulder and fanned out across her breast. The other breast glistened with clinging droplets, the taut nipple and pink areola just clear of the lapping water.

Having been raised with two sisters, the female figure was no mystery to me. But this was different. Very different. I stared in open wonder at her perfect body, the shimmering curve of her hips clearly visible beneath the still water.

Danai colored slightly, but when she spoke her voice was steady, though softly subdued. "Kostas, you are too much by yourself, you spend too much time in thought. Don't you ever bathe in the sea? It would do you good, relax you. Come swim with me."

I was surprised, but I didn't question the invitation. I stepped back onto the shells rimming the water's edge, peeled off my shirt and quickly stepped out of my rolled-up trousers. Dropping my clothing in a heap on the beach, I waded into the sea as naked as the day I was born.

At fifteen, I was already physically well-developed. The hair on my chest was not as thickly matted as it would become in later years, but it was a respectable growth that extended in a thin line downward over my flat belly to join the thick bush of my crotch. As I waded toward her, Danai's frankly appraising scrutiny shifted downward. When they focused on my pendant manhood, her eyes widened. Even then, I was well-endowed, and, at that moment, my penis must have been partially swollen in hopeful anticipation. Danai's cheeks flamed as she quickly averted her gaze.

I joined her in waist-deep water. Hand in hand, we waded into deeper water where we splashed and played in joyful abandon. She swam away from me with a strong stroke. I churned the water as I flailed in pursuit. I had almost overtaken her when her rounded rump gleamed in the sunlight as she dived. Treading water, I scanned the depths, trying to determine the direction she had taken.

Laughing, she broke surface behind me. I swung around. She placed her hands on my shoulders, grinning impishly.

"The sea is a tonic," she said. "It keeps my body firm and draws the tiredness from my limbs. All during the week I so look forward to Sundays. I am happy that you have found it too."

I grasped her narrow waist and pulled her toward me until her firm breasts were pressed against my chest and our bellies flattened against each other. We did not speak. Her lips parted slightly. I kissed her hungrily. Crushed against her swelling mound, my penis quivered as though imbued with a life of its own.

Taking Danai by the hand, I led her toward the shore. She followed unresistingly.

As we stepped onto the crescent beach, I drew her to me roughly. She struggled in my arms.

"No . . . no!" she said. My heart plummeted — until she added in a voice close to a whisper, "Not here, Kostas. Not here."

Then she took me by the hand and led me up the beach and behind a projecting triangular rock. There, in an indent protected from the breeze — and the prying eyes of any who might chance upon the cove — her towel lay spread. She sank to her knees on the towel and drew me down into a fierce embrace. Hotly, insistently, her tongue darted between my lips. The blood pounded in my temples. I heard myself moan aloud.

We thrashed around on the towel like two animals locked in mortal combat. Then my wildly stabbing thrusts found their mark and I was pushing into her warm, wet receptacle.

"No! Oh, no!" she gasped, but her buttocks lifted to meet my plunging thrust and her fingers raked my back as she drew me even

closer. Then her voice changed to a hoarsely rising crescendo, "Yes
. . . Yes . . . Oh, God — *Yes!*"

I felt as though my groin had exploded. Gasping, groaning in
ecstasy, I continued to pump my juices deep within her. Then, spent,
I sagged limply upon her, my breath rasping raggedly in my throat.

For a while, we lay in each other's arms as the sweat cooled and
dried on our bodies. We said little, but our fingers lightly explored
the wonders of each other's bodies.

Her fingers twined in the hair of my chest, Danai tilted her head
and kissed my neck. "Kostas," she murmured in a small voice.

"Yes."

"It was good."

"Yes," I agreed, and I moved my hips to touch hers. "It was
wonderful."

Her hand slid slowly down across my belly and groped until it
found my penis. In her grasp, it stiffened with renewed life.

We made love twice more that afternoon. It was not the fiercely
brutal coupling of our initial lovemaking. I was more gentle and
slower until we neared the climax.

As the afternoon shadows lengthened across the beach, we
cleansed ourselves in the sea, dried each other with her towel and
reluctantly donned our clothing. We climbed the cliff and, hand
in hand, walked slowly in the direction of the cottage.

As we walked, guilt assailed me. Finally I said, "Your parents
didn't visit Gouvia . . . at least not that I know of. They didn't
send me to look for you."

Danai smiled softly. "I know," she said.

Why, after all these years, do I remember that afternoon in such
vivid detail? Danai was the first. It was she who introduced me
to manhood. It was a wonderful introduction to the joys of sex
— and the anguish of first love. She will remain enshrined in my
memory always.

How we kept it a secret from Spiridon and Katarina Papas I will
never know. It was not my doing, since I'm sure my love for Danai
showed on my face and in my actions. I was careful to treat her
as a casual friend — but it was she who was the gifted actress. She
seemed barely to acknowledge my existence when we were in the
presence of her parents. To be truthful, there were times when I

thought she had tired of me and was displaying her displeasure. It indicates how well she played her role.

Every Sunday, until inclement weather forced us to abandon the meetings, we would rendezvous at her secret cove and make passionate love in that hidden recess behind the shielding rock. When the rains of late autumn and the chill of winter embraced Corfu, we were reduced to the occasional furtive meeting in my makeshift quarters. All during that rain-drenched winter, I longed for the coming of spring as never before.

There were obstacles in the path of our clandestine romance.

One natural phenomenon was Danai's menstrual cycle. At those times, we either skipped our outing to the cove, or we would rendezvous there and spend the afternoon in earnest conversation.

A more serious problem was the risk of pregnancy. On our second meeting at the cove, Danai instructed me in this regard. The following week, when Spiridon was at the Kerkyra fish market, I excused myself and, with a good deal of embarrassment, purchased rubber contraceptives at a nearby apothecary shop. The embarrassment lessened with each successive purchase.

Most serious of all was the constant fear that our sexual activities would be found out. I was under no illusion on that score. If Spiridon had discovered that I was making love to his beloved daughter, he surely would have killed me. It was a compelling reason for me to exercise guile and caution — and, for other reasons no less compelling, for Danai to be discreet.

I am certain that, over the three-year course of the affair, Spiridon remained blissfully ignorant of our conduct. I am not so sure, though, about Katarina. I have reason to believe that she suspected what was going on between Danai and me.

Did I feel guilt concerning my betrayal of my benefactor's trust? Certainly. I was living under his roof, was partaking of his bread and was treated by him as a son. I would have been less than human had I not felt pangs of guilt. Nevertheless, my remorse was not strong enough to deter me. I stilled my conscience with the firm belief that I would, one day, openly declare my love for Danai and thus put matters to right with all concerned.

On looking back on that distant love, I now appreciate that its furtive aspects actually added spice to the adventure.

What of my dreams of seeking fame and fortune in distant lands? Did that resolve lessen during my years in Corfu?

At the beginning of our romance, I told Danai of my dreams to seek, meet and rise above the challenges in far-off places. I mentioned both Russia and America as possible destinations. She listened sympathetically, but without comment or encouragement. At the time, I didn't give it thought, but I realize now that, while she confided other things, she did not mention any dreams or aspirations of her own. She was the more practical. I am sure that, even in the beginning, she knew how the affair must end.

Naturally, I wanted to lay the world at Danai's feet, but as my love deepened I could not bear the thought of being separated from her, and adventure in foreign lands began to look less appealing. Of course, I fully appreciated that I would make no fortune as a fisherman in the Ionian isles. But I began to think in terms of owning my own boat and marrying Danai, and, once we were established and Uncle Alexander's interrupted flow of money resumed, I would take Danai with me to seek our fortune together in Odessa or New York. The dreams didn't die. I simply modified them to fit the changed circumstances.

What made this accommodation of my ambitions easier to accept was a subtle change I experienced that I didn't recognize until some years after I'd left. I don't exactly know what it is, but that verdant land has a peculiar influence on one. The Corfiotes are relaxed and easygoing, and, after a time among them, a certain waking sleep envelops one, each day melting into the next. There is a softness to the life that dulls ambition.

It may be just as well that things worked out as they did.

CHAPTER FIVE

The stalemated war in Europe seemed curiously remote. Notwithstanding pressures brought to bear by the Allies, Greece remained neutral due to the determination of King Constantine. The Liberal Party, under the leadership of Venizelos, advocated wholehearted participation on the side of the Allies. This resulted in a political polarization between Greek royalists and republicans.

Spiridon was pro-Venizelos. I could not fault his logic, since both Turkey and Bulgaria, traditional enemies of Greece, had thrown in their lot with Germany and Austria-Hungary. And even if the Western Front was bogged down in trench warfare, the Balkan Front was an increasingly active theater of combat. Spiridon claimed bitterly that the only reason Greece remained neutral was because King Constantine was married to a German princess.

Because of Stefano, my specific interest in the war was how Russia was faring. She was not, in fact, doing well at all. Russian losses in killed and wounded were staggering. Frankly, I feared that Stafano had been killed in the debacle that had overtaken the Russian Second Army in East Prussia in the early months of the war.

Strangely, Danai was royalist in her sympathies. Her contention was that far too many Greek youths had been killed in the Balkan Wars of 1912-13. Why should more Greeks be sacrificed to satisfy the greed of the great powers?

In 1917, things looked bad for the Allies, in spite of the fact that, in April, the United States had abandoned her neutrality and entered the war in support of the Allies. On the Eastern Front, the Russian forces were reeling and faced the total collapse that was to overtake them in September. In October, Lenin's Bolsheviks ousted Kerensky and, by December, had concluded a peace with Germany.

Of more immediate concern in Corfu, however, were developments in Greece. Venizelos had set up a government-in-exile in

Salonika in opposition to the king. The Allies, their patience worn thin, demanded that Constantine leave Greece. This he did in early June, turning over the monarchy to his second son, Alexander. Venizelos returned to Greece as prime minister, and, by the end of June, Greece declared war on the Central Powers.

Danai was distraught by this turn of events. I was elated, but I allowed her to persuade me not to volunteer for army service until the end of the summer. As July gave way to August, our lovemaking had about it an odd sense of urgency.

Then everything changed dramatically.

It happened one night in mid-August, or, to be more accurate, in the gray half-light of predawn.

I was rigging the loose-footed sail when I was startled by a surprised yell from Spiridon. I have no idea how he lost his footing, but I turned toward him just in time to see him go over the side. In a flash, I remembered he'd never learned to swim.

Grabbing a loose end of the mainsheet, I struggled aft through a tangle of nets and slippery fish. I saw Spiridon's head bobbing astern, his arms thrashing the water in panic. The end of the line clamped between my teeth, I dived in and swam out to him.

His face was contorted with fear as he slipped below the tossing waves. In a shallow dive, I caught him by the shoulders and brought him to the surface. I had to hit him as hard as I could to stop his frantic flailing. It was with some difficulty that I passed the mainsheet around his chest and secured it in a bowline. Getting behind him, I slid my right arm across his chest and beneath his chin to keep his face clear of the water. I hauled in on the line with my free hand.

When I got him alongside, I scrambled into the craft and, grasping him at the armpits, hauled him aboard.

He had taken in a fair amount of water. I manhandled his waterlogged body onto a thwart, and, astride his back, I went to work giving him artificial respiration.

He could not have taken on that much ballast. In response to my pumping, water bubbled out of his mouth. Soon he was coughing, sputtering and struggling to sit up.

I scrambled awkwardly down from my pearch on the thwart. As I did so, my foot caught in the tangle of net, and I lost my balance. I turned to break my fall, but, as I did so, my leg came down heavily across the loom of an oar. Cursing, I twisted around and tried to rise. With a gasp of pain, I fell back into the fish-choked bottom of the boat. Stupidly, I gazed at my right foot still caught in the net and canted at an odd angle. I had broken my leg.

When he had sufficiently recovered, Spiridon set sail and steered for Kerkyra.

Once we were alongside the quay, Spiridon's call for assistance was promptly answered. Two fishermen lifted me out of the boat. With them supporting my weight, and me hopping along on my good leg, we finally reached a clinic where the break could be attended to. A doctor set my leg and applied a plaster cast. On a borrowed pair of crutches, accompanied by a worried and solicitous Spiridon, I made it back to the boat.

It was well into the afternoon before we arrived at Gouvion Cove.

I was treated royally by both Katarina and Danai. The latter, now that I was incapacitated and could not be suspect of romantic transgressions, showed her affection for me more openly — which was all the reward I wanted. And she voiced something that, until she mentioned it, had not crossed my mind. At least for some months to come, I could abandon all thought of military service.

To my consternation, it also meant that negotiating the steep cliff to and from our trysting place was out of the question. I soon came to look upon my broken leg as a curse visited on me by the jealous and vindictive gods.

It was a bad break — a compound fracture that mended slowly. While I soon could hobble about with the aid of my crutches, I couldn't go out in the boat. My activities were confined to mending the nets and sundry other chores not requiring the use of my leg.

We were well into December before the cast finally came off. In response to my questions, the doctor said he saw no reason why I couldn't return to fishing, providing I favored my weakened leg. As for volunteering for army duty, he said I would not be considered fit for military service for another few months.

It was mid-afternoon, I should have been sleeping. I assume that Spiridon and Katarina thought I was in my garden shed, resting. In fact, I had been restless and was seated on a low bench protected from the February rain by the overhang of the eaves. The bench was directly beneath the kitchen window. I didn't intend to eavesdrop yet couldn't help overhearing the conversation between Spiridon and his wife.

"Petros' parents have agreed to the match and consider the dowry, small as it is, adequate," Spiridon said.

"I should think so," Katarina said. "Where would Petros find a girl as lovely as Danai in Gouvia — or even Kerkyra, for that matter."

"Well," Spiridon said, "we musn't lose sight of the fact that Petros owns three boats outright. He has an assured future. He is a good catch. I'm surprised that he hasn't married before this."

I would have liked nothing better than to tear myself away from this conversation, but I sat transfixed, hunched forward in misery, hanging on every dread word. Good God, they were talking about Danai. *My* Danai. It sounded as though they had already arranged a marriage for her. And with *Petros Koulouris!* Mother of God, he was over thirty . . . *an old man!*

"Kostas is nearer her age," Katarina said, as though I had spoken my thoughts aloud and she had heard me. "I think they are fond of each other. I know he has no money, nor much in the way of prospects, but I feel they are well suited to each other. He is certainly much more handsome than Petros. I have thought for some time that Kostas would make her a good husband."

Spiridon snorted. "Have you taken leave of your senses, woman? They are more like brother and sister. Don't misunderstand me. You know how much I like Kostas. He is like a son to me. And I owe him a debt I can never repay. But he is not for Danai. He is a good worker — a hard worker — but his heart is not in fishing. His thoughts are always leagues distant. Often at night I have heard him talking to himself. Only his body is with us . . . his soul is somewhere else. And, what is even worse, he is not a sociable lad. He prefers his own company to that of others. Haven't you noticed that he shows no interest in girls? At times he worries me."

I'll say this for Katarina, she didn't give up easily. "All that you say may be true, but I still say he is fond of Danai. *That* could well be the reason he doesn't chase after girls. Has that not occurred to you, Spiro?"

"It's possible . . . but I doubt it," Spiridon said. "Still, even if what you suggest is true, I would oppose the match. Kostas is too young for her. She needs a more mature man. She is strong-willed and needs a firm hand. Of all those who have displayed an interest, Petros is the most acceptable. He is of good stock, as you will agree. We know his family. We know nothing of Kostas. Besides, I've talked to Philip and Maria. They would be most happy to have Petros marry Danai. Philip has even agreed to give them that small house he owns near Gouvia as a wedding present. I can't think of a more suitable match."

"It seems you and Philip have settled this between you," Katarina said, "and that I have nothing to say in the matter. So be it. I hope for Danai's sake you are right. I have only one more comment."

"What?"

"I think you should arrange for the wedding to take place without delay, before Danai loses her virginity. If that happens, Petros might change his mind. It wouldn't be the first time a man has backed out of a marriage commitment on such grounds."

There might have been more to their conversational exchange. I don't know. I had heard more than enough already. Sick at heart, I moved away from the window.

I just couldn't picture my beloved Danai as Petros' wife. The thought of her making love with a man of his advanced years nauseated me. She would cook his meals, wash his clothes, yes, even bear his children — all those things I had pictured her doing for me. It wasn't right. It just didn't make sense. Yet threading through my somber thoughts was one I couldn't escape: Petros had three boats. His family was prepared to give the couple a house of their own. Compared with that, what had I to offer but my youth and my love? Although I felt Spiridon was being terribly unfair, I could find no fault in his attitude.

I shrugged dispiritedly. If I didn't want them to suspect I'd overheard their discussion, I'd have to act as though nothing had happened. It was time for the evening meal. I had better return, even though I no longer had an appetite.

The following Sunday, Spiridon and Katarina went to Gouvia directly after the noonday meal. Although they hadn't said why they were going, I naturally assumed it was to discuss plans for the forthcoming wedding. I went directly to my quarters. I had plans of my own to make. I had decided that I had no choice but to leave. I must think up some plausible excuse for doing so.

I was seated in my chair, staring moodily at my cot, when a shadow fell across the floor. I looked up to find Danai standing in the doorway.

"Kostas," she said, a worried frown on her face, "what's wrong? You've scarcely spoken two words to me all week. Have I done something to offend you?"

Offend me? Sweet Mother of Jesus! She was going to marry another, knowing full well of my love for her. I looked at her bleakly without answering.

"Kostas," she said more sharply, "what *is* the matter with you? Are you ill?"

"No," I said. "A few days ago, by accident, I learned of your plans to marry Petros. Do you expect me to be happy about that? Why, when you know how I feel about you, have you deceived me?"

The puzzled expression left her face. Tears glistened in her eyes. "I had no wish to deceive you. It was only settled a week ago. I was going to tell you. I've been trying to find the right moment."

"Well," I said, "this seems as good a time as any. What happened to your promise to wait for me . . . to wait until I could offer you a secure future?"

Her lips quavered. "Kostas, I made no such promise. You took my silence for assent. I love you, Kostas. I will never love another as I have loved you. But, wonderful as it has been, love is not enough. I must think of my future, and my parents' future. Surely you must see the sense in that."

To be perfectly honest, I *did* see logic in what she said, but I wasn't going to give her the satisfaction of admitting it. "But Petros . . . he . . . he's almost old enough to be your father. How *can* you marry him if you don't love him?"

Her lips trembled, but this time with a hint of a smile. "He's not *that* old, Kostas. He's only thirty-three. Not much more than twelve years older than I. And, though it would be nice to love one's husband, I don't think it's that important. He is a kind man. I like and respect him. He claims he loves me . . . and what he offers is security. Without that, Kostas, love can quickly wither and die. I don't love Petros — at least not as I have loved you — but I will make him a good wife."

My chest felt constricted. I think until that moment I hadn't really believed that she would marry someone else. But I no longer could delude myself. It was settled, and there wasn't a thing I could do about it.

"When are you getting married?" I asked.

"I'm not sure. Papa is making the arrangements today. Sometime early next month, I believe."

"It doesn't matter," I said. "Unless it was in the next few days, I'd miss it anyway."

"Kostas," she said, "why? What are you planning to do?"

In fact I had reached a firm decision only a few minutes before her arrival. Now I committed myself to that decision. "Tomorrow I intend to volunteer for army service."

Danai looked at me searchingly. "Is this decision because I'm getting married?"

"No," I lied. "You know it has been my intention for some time. My leg is mended now." Then I added maliciously, "If Petros is as youthful as you say, why isn't *he* fighting for his country?"

Danai's expression was one of sadness. "I don't know. I only know I'm glad he isn't . . . and I wish you would change your mind."

I started to protest, but she moved closer and took my face tenderly between her hands. "Let's not argue on the last chance we have to be together. There shouldn't be bitterness between us. Come, make love to me."

We made love, but what she asked of me was impossible. It would be a long, long time before the bitterness ebbed from my soul. I have always thought that she used me — and betrayed my love and trust.

CHAPTER SIX

That I did not join the army as intended was not due to any weakening of resolve. It was through force of circumstances.

It had been my practice to visit the post office in Kerkyra once each month, not because I expected mail from home but to send a money order to Drakopoulata. When I went into Kerkyra to join the forces, I went first to the post office to send off my accumulated savings. To my surprise, a letter from my mother had been sitting there for two weeks.

The letter advised that my father had been stricken with a serious illness. Mother requested that I return home as soon as possible.

At least for the moment, I abandoned all thought of enlisting. The following morning, I embarked on a ferryboat bound for Patras. From there, I would take a smaller craft to Sami.

My father had suffered a seizure that had left him almost completely paralyzed and unable to speak. He lay helpless in bed, his eyes following one's movements. With great difficulty, he could swallow food and drink that mother or Penny fed him. The doctor called it a stroke and held out little hope for recovery.

It was then late in February 1918. Spring was just around the corner. I would have to take over father's duties in the olive groves, orchards and vineyards. The preceding year, Georgiana had found employment as a waitress in Patras and was no longer available to lend a hand. This meant that I would have to help mother and Penny tend the goats, the sheep and our small garden.

The months sped by.

Greek troops saw action in Macedonia in May and played a significant role in the final offensive on the Balkan Front in September. By November, the Central Powers had been brought to their knees. In that month, an armistice was signed, bringing to an uneasy end the conflict known to history as "The Great War."

That I had taken no part in the war bothered me for a time, but any qualms of conscience I had soon were stilled by the troubles that continued to plague my family.

Gradually father wasted away before our eyes, yet he clung to life. His sixty-ninth birthday that September was no joyful occasion. Finally, in January 1919 — almost a year to the day since he'd been struck down — he gave up the fight. By then, his passing seemed a blessing to us.

Father was laid to rest in the Sthanassis family plot in the village churchyard. It seemed for a time that his death had brought us respite from trouble, but the gods were not yet finished making sport of us. The seasons followed one another until next winter was upon us. Then the next blow came.

For close to two years — ever since the Russian revolutionary government concluded a separate peace with the German High Command in December 1917 — mother had expected to receive a letter from Uncle Alexander or from Stefano. She clung to the hope that, even if wounded and made a prisoner of war, Stefano had survived the grim conflict on the Eastern Front. Even when, in 1918, we learned that Russia had sustained almost unbelievable casualties — nine million men — during the three years she had been engaged in the struggle, mother still clung to that hope. Her only comment was "No news is good news." I withheld comment. I feared the worst. Nonetheless, when confirmation that my fears had been well-founded reached us in October 1919, it came as a shock even to me.

The letter that finally reached us came from neither Uncle Alexander nor Stefano. It was signed by someone named Adam Hause, who stated that he had been a neighbor and close friend of both Alexander and Stefano Sthanassis. It was from Uncle Alexander that Mr. Hause had obtained our address. He had promised Uncle Alexander that, if and when he was able to do so, he would communicate with us on Uncle Alexander's behalf. Hause's letter, written in September and mailed from Constantinople in October, discharged his obligation.

The letter was written in English. Falteringly, I translated it into

Greek for the benefit of mother and Penny. I would have spared them its contents had mother not insisted that I translate it word for word.

The letter dealt first with Stefano. In 1917, Uncle Alexander had learned from a returning prisoner of war that Stefano had died in a German prison camp the preceding year.

Then the bald account moved on to give us the tragic news concerning Uncle Alexander and his family. In 1917, during the winter of extreme hardship, Uncle Alexander's wife had died of influenza. Early in 1918, Uncle Alexander had learned that his daughter and her husband had met death at the hands of a revoluntionary tribunal. Beside himself with grief and rage, Uncle Alexander had ignored the wise counsel of his friends and denounced the Bolsheviks as being murderous beasts. For this, Uncle Alexander had been imprisoned as a capitalist traitor. All his property had been confiscated by the state. Several months later, he had been sentenced to death and summarily executed.

For some minutes after I read the letter, no one spoke. Penny sobbed brokenly. Mother's face bore no expression, but her eyes were bright with tears.

It was mother who broke the lengthy silence. "It is better," she observed, "that we are kept no longer in suspense . . . that we know the worst. May God rest their souls."

That night, when Penny had gone to bed, mother and I sat by the embers of the kitchen hearth.

"Kostas," mother said, "now that Stefano has been taken from us, you are head of our house. There are some things we must discuss seriously. I had hoped against hope that all would be well in Russia, and that your Uncle Alexander would resume his obligation concerning financial assistance. That is not to be. We are cast entirely on our own slim resources. Your father's illness and funeral have all but exhausted our savings."

It came as no surprise to me. "Is there enough for dowries for Georgiana and Penny?" I asked.

"For one . . . perhaps. But not for both," mother answered. Then she added, "For Georgiana, it may already be too late. She will soon be twenty-five. I fear she is resigned to spinsterhood."

I pondered what she had said. Actually, it had been on my mind for some time. It would not be enough for me to work only on the land. I must find some means of supplementing my income.

It was as though mother had read my thoughts. "No, Kostas, you cannot earn enough working as your father did. Without the benefit of the higher education denied you, I doubt that you can make much money here, nor in Greece, for that matter. I have given this much thought. You must not remain tied to the land. You are intelligent and industrious. You can do well . . . but not in Drakopoulata."

"Then what do you suggest?" I asked.

"That we use what remains of our savings to send you to New York, to Uncle Nicholas. There, I am convinced, you will do well."

"But," I protested, "that means sacrificing Penny's dowry."

"Yes. But for the best, I think. When you are established you can send for us. In America, I have heard that dowries are not considered important."

What mother said might be true, but without dowries I doubted that Georgiana's and Penny's chances would be improved. I didn't voice that doubt. I saw only the opportunity of which I'd dreamed opening up before me. Nonetheless I felt constrained to question mother on one remaining important point. "It might take me some time to get established . . . even with the help of Uncle Nicholas . . . even in a land of opportunity such as America. How can you and Penny get by without my earnings?"

"We will survive," mother said.

Before the month was out, I was a passenger on a Greek freighter bound for Mediterranean ports — and New York. I was armed with a letter of introduction to my great-uncle and little more. That did not worry me. Life and adventure beckoned.

CHAPTER SEVEN

There it was.

Its base obscured by swirling mist, it materialized out of the veil of sifting snowflakes in dull green splendor. I stared at it in fascination. It looked even more impressive in reality than it had in Father Damianos' textbook.

The Statue of Liberty! It was a dream come true that stood there proudly against the backdrop of a leaden sky. I suppose the fancy that struck me — that she held aloft her torch as a gesture of personal welcome — was one that must have been experienced by countless new arrivals who had preceded me. Nevertheless, on that January morning, that was my fond impression. It was like meeting an old and trusted friend.

It was bitterly cold in the eye of the forecastle. There was no wind except for the breeze stirred by our forward motion at half speed, but the morning air had about it the chill of the grave. My hands pushed deep into my trouser pockets, the collar of my jacket turned up, a borrowed muffler wrapped around my neck and my cap pulled down over my ears, I stood up forward, shivering uncontrollably. Yet I was resolved to stay where I was until the skyline of New York came into view.

At last my vigil was rewarded. Satisfied that I finally had reached my destination, I scurried aft to seek the warmth of the small cabin I shared with three other passengers.

It was about ten in the morning when the freighter that had been our cramped and musty-smelling home for more than ten weeks berthed at a dock upriver from the heart of the city. The seventeen passengers, most of us Greeks and the rest of us Italians and French the boat had picked up along the way, were assembled in the small drab saloon to await the boarding of customs and immigration officials. By the time they came aboard, disappeared into the captain's cabin for drinks and lunched with the ship's officers, it was well into the afternoon. By the time our papers had been checked and we had been cleared to land, it was almost dusk. I suddenly found my confidence ebbing. I slept on board that night and disembarked the following morning.

It was just as well that I had taken the precaution of writing my great-uncle's address on a piece of paper. When I went ashore and made inquiries in English, I found that those I talked to had difficulty understanding me, and, while I knew they were answering in English, I couldn't for the life of me follow but a few words. But when I brought out the piece of paper, the faces of my informants brightened. I was directed to a tramway built above the street, one of several such elevated railways, some distance east of the docks. I was told it was the Second Avenue El.

The closer we got to the heart of the city, the taller were the buildings. I had never seen anything to equal them. I stared upward in open-mouthed awe — and down on the passing soot-grimed, snow-fringed streets bustling with pedestrians, horse-drawn vehicles and crawling motorized traffic — in growing dismay.

I recall my mixed feelings of wonder and fear. I had never seen such buildings or so many people. It was overpowering. It made me feel suddenly very small and insignificant. I was beset with doubts. Was this the city of golden opportunity I had set out with such confidence to challenge and conquer? It looked like a formidable undertaking.

As I had been instructed, I got off the train at Canal Street. I descended the iron-railed stairway to street level and stood in the shadow of the elevated track, shivering and totally confused. I accosted a passerby, showed him the paper and was directed toward my destination. Eventually, although I was only a few blocks from the address I sought, I found my way to the corner of Mott and Hester streets and had the tall, narrow-fronted, smoke-blackened brick dwelling pointed out to me. My heart sank. To be perfectly honest, this building did not look like the residence of a man of wealth and high standing in the community.

The woman who answered my knock I judged to be not much older than myself. She was a girl of Junoesque proportions, large of breast with ample, spreading hips. She had a pleasant enough face, but she looked at me suspiciously.

"Yes?" she said, in a surprisingly small voice. "What do you want?"

When I think back on it, I can hardly blame her for looking at me askance. Coatless, cap pulled low, my chin submerged in a muffler — my only purchase since leaving the ship — and clutching a battered suitcase, I stood at the top of the steps leading up to the entranceway. Chilled to the bone, practically blue with cold, I stood there shivering. I must have presented a sorry spectacle indeed.

"Kaliméra," I said politely, through chattering teeth. Then, because her expression didn't change, I switched to English. "I would like to see Mr. Nicholas Metaxis, please."

"He is at work," she said.

"Oh," I said. I took the envelope containing my mother's letter from the inside pocket of my jacket and held it out hesitantly. "I have a letter for him," I said, adding, "It is from his niece, Maria Sthanassis . . . my mother."

The girl's expression changed. Her eyebrows lifted in surprise. "From Greece? Is that where you've come from? What's your name?"

"Kostas. Constantine Sthanassis."

"Then," she said, not unkindly, "I suppose that makes us second cousins. I'm Phoebe Metaxis, Nicholas Metaxis' daughter." She took the envelope and added, "Come in, cousin Kostas. You look half-frozen."

Nicholas Metaxis was a very tall, very thin man with close-cropped gray hair. He was over two meters in height, but his stooped shoulders made him look somewhat shorter. Not so his son, Sofoclis, who had returned from work with Nicholas that evening. Sofoclis was taller than his father — a full head taller than I. There was nothing thin about Sofoclis. His thick neck sloped into broad shoulders. His chest reminded me of a wine barrel, and his arms, when he removed his coat and jacket, looked like tree trunks. He was a giant of a man. I don't believe I have seen a larger, more muscular man before or since. I always found it hard to believe that he was but a few months older than I.

If Nicholas was at all happy to meet his great-nephew, he did an excellent job of hiding it. He read my mother's letter with a deepening frown on his face.

"Hmmph!" he snorted, shooting me a penetrating glance. "Well,

I suppose we can put you to work doing *something*. For the time being — until we can make a more satisfactory arrangement — you can stay in the spare room on the third floor."

Sofoclis put down the newspaper he was reading, grinned broadly and winked at me.

I had a job, even if it wasn't much to my liking.

In those days, Metaxis & Company was situated on Lafayette Street between White and Walker streets. The building faced Lafayette. The front portion, by far the minor part of the business, was given over to a retail outlet. Most of my activities were confined to the large warehouse to the rear, opening onto Cortlandt Street. It was from here that the wholesale business was conducted.

I don't know why I had assumed that my great-uncle's business was confined to the importation and distribution of Greek products. That was far from being the case, though Greek products were represented. The imported products came from Greece, Italy, France and — though importation had been temporarily suspended during the Great War — Germany. Along with imported products, Metaxis & Company handled fruits and vegetables from upstate New York, New Jersey and states even further afield.

Initially, I was assigned the job of assisting Sofoclis in picking up imported goods and produce from the uptown docks in a district known as Harlem, from the docks along lower South Street and from the railroad freight yards. When I wasn't transporting goods to Cortlandt Street, I was delivering orders to customers throughout the city or wrestling barrels, crates and boxes somewhere on the four floors of the vast warehouse. Any spare time I had was devoted to trimming and cleaning fruit or vegetables and packing them neatly into shallow boxes for display purposes. It was backbreaking and thankless work I soon came to detest.

The pickups and deliveries in which I was involved were conducted by means of horse-drawn drays. As soon as I had learned how to handle the horses, had become familiar with the city and was considered to have mastered enough English in the local dialect to make myself understood, I was deserted by Sofoclis. Now it was I who drove the dray; my surly, uncommunicative helper was a muscle-bound Negro named Joe. If he had a surname, I can't recall ever hearing it.

In the year of my arrival, 1920, motor vehicles in New York far out-numbered horses. In the company stables-cum-garage there were motorized vans, as well as two touring sedans and a smart runabout. But it would not be until I was well into my third year at Metaxis & Company that I was allowed behind the wheel of anything so valuable as an automobile. Even then, it was due to necessity rather than privilege.

Uncle Nicholas never missed an opportunity to remind me that he was doing me a favor by allowing me to work for him. In every sense, he treated me as a poor relative whose presence was barely tolerated. I worked long hours for a mere pittance after deductions to cover my room and board in the Metaxis' Mott Street residence.

I was being exploited. I knew it. But until I could find a place of my own — and employment at a decent salary — there wasn't a damn thing I could do about it. And I was allowed so little time to myself that there wasn't much of an opportunity to seek another job. I was beginning to despair of ever being in a position to send for mother and my sisters, and had made up my mind to quit and look for a better job, when something happened that substantially bettered my position. I had Sofoclis to thank for this change in fortune. It came about in an unexpected way.

If I make it sound as though Sofoclis and I were on friendly terms, I am guilty of overstating the case. During the first two years of my employment, I saw very little of Sofoclis once he had discharged his chore of familiarizing me with drays, draft horses and routes I had to follow to and from our suppliers and wholesale customers. There was good reason for this. I worked during the day; he worked a good deal in the evening. So I rarely saw him, even at home.

Sofoclis' attitude toward me was nothing like the patronizing approach Uncle Nicholas adopted. Despite his formidable size and forbidding jut-jawed countenance, Sofoclis was of amiable disposition. In the early years of our association, however, he tended to ignore me. Some time later I discovered that he appreciated that his father was not treating me fairly, and, because Sofoclis felt somewhat guilty about this, he was uncomfortable in my presence.

The only one of the family who treated me as a human being from the outset was Phoebe. I think she felt sorry for me in the beginning. Later a somewhat different relationship developed between us. Had it not been for Phoebe, I would have sought other accommodations sooner than I did.

In all fairness to Uncle Nicholas, I don't suppose I could have arrived on his doorstep at a more inopportune time. The brief postwar boom had petered out and there were signs of an economic downturn. Chain stores such as Safeway and Piggly Wiggly were growing more and more popular with housewives and taking business away from the corner groceries that were the mainstay of Metaxis & Company. But almost simultaneous with my arrival an event occurred that Uncle Nicholas had dreaded and knew not how to counter. It is safe to say that Uncle Nicholas was a harried man. He probably looked upon me as a crown of thorns added to the cross he already had to bear.

That doesn't excuse his treatment of me; however, as I was to learn from Phoebe some months later, there was more to it than economic uncertainty. Nicholas Metaxis had arrived in New York at the age of nineteen, in 1868, a penniless immigrant speaking not a word of English. He had started out as a street-corner peddler and, from that humble beginning, had slowly built the profitable business that eventually became Metaxis & Company. He evidently saw in me a reflection of himself as he had been at my age. Unfortunately, however, the disparities in that reflected image stuck in his craw.

I learned from Phoebe that the command of English I'd displayed on my arrival in America — thanks to my love of books and Father Damianos' patient tutelage during my boyhood — was a source of annoyance to Uncle Nicholas. That I had enrolled in night classes to improve my written and spoken command of English he considered a waste of time and money. Nothing, Phoebe assured me, would sway him from that opinion. Thereafter, I adopted the practice of conducting what little conversation I had with Uncle Nicholas in Greek.

Other aspects of my presence apparently irritated my uncle. He seemed to find it particularly irksome that my mother, whom he remembered only as a snot-nosed child in Crete, should take it for granted that he would find employment for me immediately upon my arrival in America. Had he not done enough for his relatives in Crete? Had he not, in fact, scrimped in order to provide my mother, his only niece, with a dowry? Did his family in Greece believe him to be made of money?

The latter, I told Phoebe shamefacedly, was my mother's mistaken impression of her uncle. Phoebe laughed at my remark. Her father, she assured me, *was* a wealthy man. His wife, who had died ten years earlier, had brought a good deal of money to the marriage

— money that had enabled Nicholas, with the help of his in-laws, to expand the business considerably. Had her father so wished it, they could well afford to live on the fashionable Upper West Side — or even in a house overlooking Central Park. There was no need for them to live on Mott Street or to go without servants, except that her father was by nature miserly — and preferred to live in this neighborhood, which was predominantly Greek.

Without question, Uncle Nicholas was miserly. Still, I think he might have treated me with more charity had not my appearance on the winter scene been so ill-timed. I don't believe he actually meant what he told Phoebe — that his first inclination on reading my mother's letter had been to send me packing.

These were the circumstances. My twentieth birthday passed unnoticed by all but me on board the SS *Ganymede* eight days before we raised the Ambrose Lightship in the predawn hours of January 12. It was the thirteenth before I disembarked and found my way to the Mott Street address. Three days later the Eighteenth Amendment to the Constitution of the United States became law. This didn't catch Uncle Nicholas unaware. He, like everyone else, had had ample warning. But, like almost everyone else, he had hoped for a last-minute reprieve.

Why was the Eighteenth Amendment, and its accompanying National Prohibition Act — known familiarly as the Volstead Act — of such concern to my great-uncle? Foreign wines, liquors and liqueurs were among the most lucrative items imported and distributed by Metaxis & Company. Now, by a stroke of the pen in the nation's capital, the Volstead Act made it illegal to manufacture, import, distribute, sell or consume alcoholic beverages. I cannot blame Uncle Nicholas for being upset.

How could such idiocy be legislated into law? I don't pretend to understand such an excess of puritanism. I didn't then. I don't now. Surely there must have been many forward-thinking politicians who could have foreseen the results of attempting to deprive the public of one of its pleasures. To me, having been brought up with wine and liquor as part of my life, making their consumption illicit made absolutely no sense. Making drinking illegal would only make it more appealing. And that, of course, is exactly what happened — ushering in an era where the law was more or less openly flaunted and lawbreakers acquired an aura of respectability. I doubt if there has been any period in American history when its populace consumed so much alcohol on a per capita basis as it did during the life span of the abortive Volstead Act.

Uncle Nicholas was a shrewd businessman. Why could he not foresee the trend? Metaxis & Company should have been in a position to cater to the sharp rise in demand for the alcoholic beverages it had purveyed legally until the onset of Prohibition.

The simple fact was that Metaxis & Company didn't stop supplying wines and liquor. That aspect of its business simply went underground and operated outside the law. In short, the highly respected importing and distributing house of Metaxis became an efficient bootlegging establishment as well. But this phase of its business operated without the knowlege of Nicholas Metaxis. I did not become aware of it until I was well into my second year in the company. Uncle Nicholas, whether he knew it or not, had never before had it so good.

It was only when I stumbled across the company's clandestine bootlegging activities and, through force of circumstances, became involved in that illicit aspect of the business that both my financial picture and lifestyle underwent a radical change.

My dreams of wealth and power — prematurely, as it turned out — flared anew.

CHAPTER EIGHT

It had not originated with Sofoclis, but once it had been suggested to him by Omeros Kalandris, a close friend of the family, Sofoclis had been quick to see the possibilities and potential. He readily agreed to join Kalandris in the undertaking. Both agreed that Sofoclis' father, at all costs, must be kept ignorant of the operation.

There was good reason for the secrecy. Nicholas looked upon America as the land that had smiled upon him and brought him fortune. Even though he stooped to sharp practice in his business dealings and was not above cheating his customers, when it came to his relations with the state and federal governments Nicholas was almost obsessively law-abiding. He would not dream of circumventing regulations or cheating on taxes. Thus, to expect Nicholas to participate in anything that smacked of breaking federal law or defrauding the government was expecting too much.

The scheme was complicated and called for a good deal of organization. It was Sofoclis who contacted the suppliers and made arrangements, well before Prohibition became law, for an uninterrupted flow of liquor from Mexico and Canada by van and from the Caribbean islands by boat. Later, when law enforcement agents tightened up border crossing points, supply by sea became the favored method. Still, even from the beginning, power boats, trucks, fast automobiles and out-of-the-way storage facilities were required, together with trusted men — sometimes difficult to find — to handle each phase of the operation. It is a credit to the organizing ability of Omeros Kalandris that they were able to resolve these problems and were ready to swing into action the moment Prohibition was imposed on the thirsty nation.

How did Kalandris do it? Into the picture as equal partners he brought a Sicilian, Vittorio Martinelli, and an Irishman, Sean O'Flaherty. The former was a mobster with powerful connections;

the latter was a genial rogue who was a political force to be reckoned with in the Irish community of the Lower West Side. Both were men of sufficient vision to appreciate the money to be made from circumventing the new laws. And both had at their command manpower in the form of ready-built organizations in the rackets and political wards.

The manpower situation taken care of, Sofoclis and Kalandris turned their attention to transportation, storage and distribution. Kalandris advanced money for the purchase of fast boats and a number of trucks — fleets that would be expanded many times over within a comparatively short space of time. The manning of these boats and vehicles was handled by Martinelli and O'Flaherty, neither of whom trusted the other for a second.

Sofoclis made available space in warehouses leased by Metaxis & Company in Brooklyn and New Jersey, locations his father had not visited in some years. In short order, those facilities would be strained beyond their capacity, necessitating the leasing of additional storage space in other areas.

The distribution to bars and saloons — soon to become known as speakeasies — engaged in the illegal sale of alcoholic beverages was left to Martinelli's and O'Flaherty's henchmen. Deliveries to an established list of trustworthy individual customers were effected by pickup from Kalandris' flower shops, where a stock of liquor was secretly stored to meet that private demand.

It was a cash business. The boat skippers paid cash at the point of pickup from supply craft — fishing boats, coastal freighters and steam yachts — that arrived at designated rendezvous points outside the three-mile limit. At the off-loading docks or beaches, the boat skippers were paid in cash by truck drivers who, in turn, were paid off on delivery at the warehouse. Delivery to the saloon and private club speakeasies was made sometimes by motorized van but more often by private automobile. In each case, however, the drivers had to pay cash for the merchandise, for which they collected in cash from the customer on delivery. At each step along this route the price included a profit markup.

In discussing the bootlegging business with me some years later, Sofoclis admitted that neither he nor Kalandris had envisioned the staggering profits that would accrue, nor the myriad headaches they would encounter as their business grew by leaps and bounds.

At first, it had been ridiculously easy. The federal agents employed to enforce the new law were not as well organized as the lawbreakers. Nor had the Feds counted on the almost total lack of support they encountered from the average citizen. Public sympathy was with the violators.

The Feds struck doggedly to their unenviable task, and, while their numbers were never sufficient to achieve rigid enforcement of the unpopular law, they began to enjoy a measure of success as they learned the tricks of the 'leggers' own trade. Fast patrol craft plying the waters within the three-mile limit disrupted that supply line. Tips from informers resulted in ambushes at shoreside pickup points and along highways. Raids on warehouses and "speaks" became more and more frequent as time wore on and the Feds became better informed and more ingenious in the subterfuges they employed.

By far the greatest danger, however, came from within the 'leggers' own ranks. With the profits involved, Sofoclis stated ruefully, it could hardly have been otherwise, and he and Kalandris should have foreseen the trends that would develop. Their awakening, unfortunately, had been slow in coming.

The first indication of trouble came through complaints speakeasy customers made concerning the quality of liquor being supplied. Sofoclis had made it his policy to purchase only name brands. His first suspicion was that he was being cheated by his suppliers. When random checks at the warehouses and flower shops substantiated the suppliers' protests of fair dealing, the answer was obvious. The liquor was being adulterated after warehouse pickup. Both Vito Martinelli and Sean O'Flaherty denied the charge that they were cutting the liquor. Sofoclis and Kalandris knew both men were lying, but, short of putting together a distribution system capable of taking over from the Martinelli and O'Flaherty organizations, Sofoclis and Kalandris recognized that their hands were tied. The adulteration continued, becoming only marginally less apparent as competition became more fierce.

Competition hadn't taken long to manifest itself. It started with hijacking and rapidly deteriorated into outright gang warfare. Both Martinelli and O'Flaherty were prepared for this contingency. The drivers and their helpers were supplied with armed escorts. Even Sofoclis and Kalandris, after Sean O'Flaherty was gunned down in a Lower West Side tobacco store in late 1923, were assigned Martinelli triggermen as bodyguards.

It was a dog-eat-dog world of cutthroat tactics. There were few, if any, of the bigger 'leggers and gangland bosses who didn't walk in constant fear, not from the law, but from each other. The gang rivalries, Sofoclis told me, were not confined to outside competitors. There were internal rivalries arising from ambition and greed, often resolved with crude — but effective — ferocity. Cold-blooded murder fast became the rule rather than the exception.

Sofoclis stated matter-of-factly that, in the formative stages of the operation, strong differences had developed between Martinelli and O'Flaherty over the territorial division of the Lower East Side. Although he had no way of proving it, he was convinced that O'Flaherty had been bumped off on orders from Martinelli.

By the time Sofoclis and I had this discussion, I had acquired knowledge of the bootlegging operation through firsthand experience, yet some aspects still puzzled me. For example, Sofoclis claimed that his father, even though ignorant of and a nonparticipant in the operation, derived a share of the profits. How? As Sofoclis explained it, he had opened a number of bank accounts — some of them in his father's name — into which he funneled the profits. Sofoclis' chief concern was that those accounts were becoming so swollen that they soon might attract unwanted attention.

I advanced this suggestion: why not divert cash earnings and funds siphoned off from the accounts into the purchase of buildings and property in the names of dummy corporations or trusted nominees? Sofoclis followed my advice, which, as it turned out some years later, proved to be sound advice. In fact, it's how I ended up with several brownstones in my name in the West Seventies just off Riverside Drive. As luck would have it, he put several properties in Phoebe's name as well.

As for Uncle Nicholas, he died quietly in his sleep in the summer of 1924 at the age of seventy-five, without ever knowing of the profit Sofoclis made for him. For his peace of mind, it is undoubtedly just as well he died when he did.

How did I, a poor relative from the Old Country, get involved in the bootlegging game? As I have indicated, it came about by accident.

One rainy day in the autumn of 1921, I returned to the Cortlandt Street stables soaking wet and in a foul temper. I had no sooner started to steam myself dry by stacking crates and boxes than the warehouse superintendent approached me with a request. He asked me if I would mind taking over for him until closing time. There were, he said, no further deliveries expected that afternoon.

Half an hour later, a truck drew up at the entrance. The driver, accompanied by a tough-looking helper the size of a gorilla, said he had a load to deliver — and some money to collect.

Two things were wrong with his announcement. According to the superintendent, we weren't expecting any deliveries, and, even if we were, I knew enough about the routine to know that we signed for deliveries from our suppliers. I had never seen anyone paid off in cash. "Load of what?" I asked.

"Hooch. What else?" he said.

Liquor? We didn't handle the product. "There must be some mistake," I said.

"Not if this is Metaxis & Company. I was told to deliver to and collect from a guy named Sofie Metaxis. You him?"

"No. Mr. Metaxis rarely comes in in the afternoon. Have you got an invoice?"

"A loading list," the driver said, and passed me a sheet of paper. I glanced down at the list and raised my eyebrows in astonishment. The load consisted of more than three hundred cases of liquor. Looking at the address penciled in at the top of the sheet, I immediately knew the driver had made a mistake.

"It's not for here," I said. "It's for delivery to our Brooklyn warehouse. See?"

The driver, a frown on his face, snatched the checklist from me. Brow furrowed, he read the penciled-in address. "Yeah," he said. "You're right." Then, without any apology, he turned and stalked out, his apelike assistant at his heels.

Quite naturally, I was mystified. When it came to liquor, just about everyone was breaking the law in one way or another. But *three hundred cases!* That was a lot more than just bending the rules. Obviously, something was going on. Just as obviously, it involved my cousin Sofoclis. Well, it was none of my business. If Sofoclis wanted to explain the truck driver's mistake, he would do so. If not, I had just better forget the incident.

Sofoclis *did* want to explain the incident. He was most anxious to correct any mistaken impression concerning the truck driver's error. So much so that the following morning he departed from his practice of not arriving at the Cortlandt Street warehouse until sometime after ten and instead was there bright and early. As a matter of fact, Sofoclis was the first person I saw when I arrived.

Of course, he didn't know that I had substituted for the superintendent he wanted to see. It was only later, when he learned that I had been the one on duty, that he sought me out. He caught me as I was about to leave for the uptown docks, motioned me down from the dray and took me to one side.

"Tony tells me that you substituted for him yesterday afternoon," Sofoclis said, his expression betraying his anxiety.

"Yes."

"Then you were the one who directed the truck driver with the load of alcohol to take it to the Brooklyn warehouse."

"Yes," I said, rather enjoying Sofoclis' evident discomfort.

"I . . . ah . . . don't want you to mention it to Dad."

"Oh," I said. "Why not?"

"Well," Sofoclis said, obviously choosing his words with care, "it's like this. Ever since Prohibition came into effect, we've continued to supply doctors and prescription druggists — all those entitled under the Act to buy alcohol legally — with medical supplies. But you know how straitlaced Dad is. He thinks that even medical alcohol is an infraction of the letter of the law. So we've been meeting the demand from the Brooklyn warehouse and not telling him about it. Yesterday a new driver made a mistake and brought a shipment here. So far, Dad doesn't know about it. I'd appreciate it if you didn't say anything to anyone, in case it gets back to him."

Medical alcohol? Three hundred cases of name-brand liquor? Just how dumb did Sofoclis think I was? Nonetheless, even though his explanation only served to confirm my suspicion, it was none of my business. I went along with his explanation.

"Sure," I said, nodding. "Medical alcohol. I won't mention it."

Sofoclis' expression changed to one of relief.

A few days later, Nicholas summoned me to his office. "I'm told," he said, "that you've been doing good work. I've decided to give you a small raise and try you out in the retail store. Turn over your pickups and deliveries to young Ponti and start at the store tomorrow morning."

"Yes, sir. Thank you, sir," I said.

The suggestion must have come from Sofoclis. It amused me that I was being paid off for my silence — especially since I hadn't the slightest intention of saying anything anyway.

Had it not been for a peculiar twist of fate, the matter probably would have ended there and been forgotten.

I had a good deal on my mind that winter. I was glad to be working indoors, but when Uncle Nicholas had said he was giving me a *small* raise, he had meant just that. I was sending home all the money I could, but I was acutely aware that it was a far cry from what I had expected to be sending by this time. I *had to* send for mother and my sisters soon. I had been searching for suitable accommodations and was resolved to send for them no later than summer — even if it meant I'd have to borrow money to do so. With that pressing obligation almost constantly in my thoughts, it's a small wonder that the incident of the liquor shipment all but faded from my mind. When it cropped up again, it came as an almost total surprise.

CHAPTER NINE

It was only May, but for the past few days the weather had been unseasonably hot. Unable to sleep, I'd quietly dressed, let myself out the front door and gone for a walk. As usual, my mind was occupied by the inevitable financial concerns.

Returning homeward, I rounded the corner from Hester Street onto Mott Street. Glancing down the street, I saw an unusual sight for our neighborhood. Parked in front of the Metaxis house was a bright yellow Pierce-Arrow runabout. It was a two-seater, with the top down. As I drew closer, I noted that its occupants were two people: the driver, a bobbed-haired young lady, and in the seat next to her, a man. They appeared to be arguing.

The man got out of the car and slammed the door. The car drove off with a screeching of tires, leaving the man, weaving slightly, standing in the empty street. As I drew closer, I recognized Sofoclis. He appeared to be somewhat the worse for drink.

Sofoclis lurched toward the sidewalk. He stumbled at the curb and would have fallen had I not by then been close enough to step forward and assist him. What happened next was the last thing I expected.

His face contorted in anger, Sofoclis whirled on me. I thought at first he didn't recognize me, but I was mistaken.

"Kostas," he said. "Whacha doin'? Spyin' on me?"

"Shh!" I said. "You'll wake up the whole neighborhood."

I don't know what there was in that caution that galvanized him into action. But, without warning, he lashed out at me with a roundhouse punch.

Had the blow struck me squarely, it would have taken the head off my shoulders. It grazed my temple with sufficient force to send me reeling backward. My head spinning, tiny lights swirling before my eyes, I came to rest sprawling across the bottom two steps of the stoop. Dazed, I watched him advance toward me, his face a mask of fury.

I grasped the fact that reason would not prevail. As he let fly a left, I ducked beneath the swing and regained my footing. While he was still off balance, I hit him on his right cheekbone with all the force I could muster.

It is true that I wasn't well-balanced and was still in a state of shock, but my punch should have been more effective than it appeared to be. Sofoclis straightened, fists bunched, his determination unshaken. It came to me that if I couldn't find some way to blunt his attack, I could well be killed. Even with his senses dulled by drink and his reflexes slowed, Sofoclis was a frightening opponent. I wanted no part of this unequal battle, but I could see no way out.

I backed off a few steps, then ran toward him and, head lowered, launched myself toward him like a battering ram. My head caught him flush in the stomach. With a whoosh of suddenly expelled breath, he doubled over as the blow propelled him backward. He landed on the sidewalk on his backside, staring up at me in stunned disbelief. I stood warily a few feet back, waiting for his next move.

Supporting himself with his hands, he started to scramble to his feet. I didn't waste time. I kicked out viciously, my arching boot catching him on the neck just below the ear.

Sofoclis was projected backward and sideways by the force of the kick. He lay at my feet, sprawled on the sidewalk. If only temporarily, he was out of action.

I grasped him by the armpits from behind and dragged his inert form over to the steps. It wasn't easy. He weighed well over two hundred pounds.

I had hauled him up two steps and, gasping for breath, was wondering how I was going to get him all the way up to the top when the door above swung open. Phoebe, in a dressing gown, stood framed in the lighted doorway.

Without comment, she came down the steps and grasped one of Sofoclis' arms. Between us, we manhandled him onto the stoop and into the house. There was no point in trying to negotiate the stairs up to his second-floor bedroom. We dragged him into the sitting room and put him on the sofa.

Chest heaving from my exertion, I gazed down at Sofoclis. He was frighteningly still. Had my kick broken his neck? I found a vein on his neck and was relieved to feel a steady pulse beneath my fingertips.

"He isn't dead," I said to Phoebe. "Just out cold."

"What happened?"

"Don't know. He's drunk. A girl drove him home. I think they were having an argument. He stumbled over the curb. I tried to help him, but he took a swing at me."

"*You* did this to him?"

"It was either this . . . or get killed," I said.

Phoebe laughed. "Oh, I have no doubt he deserved it. He's usually as gentle as a lamb, but when he gets riled he's a terror. It takes an awful lot to stop him."

She moved closer and examined the side of my face. "You're hurt," she said.

I shrugged. "Nothing to worry about."

"Come into the kitchen. I'll put a cold cloth on it. You're going to have a beautiful black eye."

"I'm okay. Your brother's the one that needs attention."

"Don't worry about Sofoclis," Phoebe said. "I'll see to him after I've looked after your eye."

I was trimming vegetables when Sofoclis walked into the store. He walked stiffly. He came over to where I was working and stood awkwardly by the display counter.

"Kostas," he said, "I owe you an apology."

"Forget it," I said, applying myself to stripping the wilted outer leaves from a head of lettuce.

Sofoclis grinned sheepishly. "It's not quite that easy. Anyway, I want you to drop what you're doing and come with me."

I looked at him. "Why?"

"I've talked to Dad. I want you to take over as super at the Brooklyn warehouse — at least temporarily. It means a substantial increase in salary. I'm sure you could use the money."

I certainly could use extra money, but there was something that didn't seem quite right about the sudden offer. "What's the catch?" I asked.

"No catch. I'm caught short-staffed."

I accepted his statement at face value, but I remained skeptical. I followed him out to the curb where a Ford sedan was parked.

"Can you drive?" Sofoclis asked.

"Yes."

"Then you take the wheel. You don't know it, but I came off the loser in last night's uncalled-for dustup. You managed to crack a couple of my ribs. Just moving is painful. In the future I'll know better than to take you on."

As we got into the car it was my turn to grin. Sofoclis moved slowly, gingerly. "What made you pick a fight?" I asked, as I switched on the ignition and adjusted the spark level.

"I don't know. It's all pretty hazy. I'd had too much to drink. Had a fight with my girl. Guess I was just looking for trouble. You just happened along at the wrong time. Sorry."

I got out and cranked the engine into life. Getting back into the driver's seat, I eased the Ford out into the morning traffic. "Where to? Brooklyn?" I asked.

"No. Head uptown. Fifty-seventh between Sixth and Seventh. There's something I have to talk over with Omeros Kalandris before we drive over to Brooklyn."

We drove for several blocks in silence before Sofoclis ventured a question. "Last October, when the driver tried to deliver a load of liquor to Cortlandt Street, you didn't believe my explanation the next day, did you?"

"No."

"Why?"

"I'd seen the merchandise checklist. Three hundred cases of liquor didn't strike me as medical alcohol."

"But you didn't mention the incident again. Why?"

"None of my business."

"What did you think?"

"That Metaxis & Company is 'legging hooch . . . unbeknownst to your father."

A chuckle rumbled up from Sofoclis' chest, then ceased abruptly as he winced with pain. "The company isn't involved. Not directly. Kalandris, me and a couple of other partners handle the business — but the warehouse staffs in Jersey City and Brooklyn *are* in on it. You've got to know this before you get involved. It's strictly illegal, of course. I'm telling you this to give you a chance to back out if you want — before we discuss salary with Kalandris. What'll it be? Do you want in . . . or to stay out?"

"The pay I'm getting now doesn't leave me much choice," I said. "I accept . . . but I have one question."

"Shoot."

"You know I've been trying to save up enough to bring my family over from Greece. You know the kind of money I've been getting. Why have you waited all this time to come up with the offer?"

Sofoclis, looking decidedly uncomfortable, hesitated. "Yeah, I know you've been getting a raw deal from Dad. To be perfectly honest, I didn't think you'd stick it out this long. I thought you'd go out and look for another job. Had you done that, I'd have come up with an offer. When you didn't I began to wonder about you. I figured you had no ambition . . . no guts. If there's one thing that 'legging calls for, it's guts."

"So what made you change your mind? Last night's scrap?"

Sofoclis grinned. "Uh huh. Whether I'm ossified or not, there aren't many who'd have the guts to go up against me. You could've turned tail. You didn't. You stood your ground — and handed me one of the worst lickings I've ever had. This morning I could barely move. I decided right then that it would be better to have you on my side than against me." His grin broadened, and he held out his hand. "Friends?" he asked.

I grasped his outstretched hand. "Friends."

I wondered idly what Sofoclis would say if he knew that one of the reasons I'd stayed so long in a job I detested, and hadn't made any effort to move from the Mott Street house, was that for many months I'd been making love to his sister.

Omeros Kalandris was a skinny littly guy with a head that seemed too big for his body. He wasn't a stranger to me. A bachelor, he spent many a Sunday at the Metaxis house, playing backgammon with Uncle Nicholas and staying on for dinner.

Kalandris was always immaculately dressed. He was a wealthy man, and he enjoyed advertising the fact. He had a big chauffeur-driven Packard and lived in a swank apartment on Riverside Drive. He was smart. How else could he have started with the flower shop he inherited from his father and built it into a chain of flower shops throughout the city and the state? He was the last person I would have suspected of being a bootlegger.

When I got to know him better, I found him to be more shrewd, and a lot tougher, than I'd suspected. It had been his idea to go into the bootlegging business, using his shops as retail outlets and the Metaxis connections as an assured source of supply and warehousing facility. It had been Kalandris who had brought Vito Martinelli and Sean O'Flaherty into the operation. And it was

Kalandris, not Sofoclis, who first had seen the trouble looming due to their mobster ties and who had counseled caution. It was Kalandris who was the brains of the partnership, and Sofoclis who took most of the risks. Since Kalandris was a man in his middle fifties and Sofoclis a young man my age, the division of responsibilities was only logical.

In any event, that particular morning it was as if I were meeting Omeros Kalandris for the first time. He was crisp and businesslike. The salary he suggested made my head spin, but I raised no objection. My duties? Those he would leave for Sofoclis to outline except that, from time to time, he reserved the right to call on my services.

From that day forward, my life underwent a startling change. Suddenly I found myself with more money than I had dreamed existed. I could afford luxuries I had thought beyond my reach — clothes, a car and money to burn on entertainment. I got to know a very different side of New York. I enjoyed every minute of it, but I wasn't reckless. I had been poor too long to feel at ease in this new element. And I had obligations to meet — obligations I suddenly was in a position to discharge.

In June, I sent money home to defray my family's expenses for the voyage to America. I rented an apartment on Waverly Place, just off Washington Square, which Phoebe helped me decorate and furnish. I didn't tell her the source of my newfound wealth, but I believe she guessed it.

What did I do to earn this money? At first, very little. I took over as superintendent of the Brooklyn warehouse, and, a month later, my duties were expanded to a sort of overseer for all our various warehousing depots. I moved up rapidly within the framework of the organization. By that autumn, while I wasn't by any means on an equal footing with Sofoclis and Kalandris, I was sharing in the profits.

Of course I was operating outside the law. This didn't concern me at the time. As a matter of fact, a successful bootlegger was, in a manner of speaking, a respected — even sought-after — member of the social structure.

The reason I found it so easy to fit into the structure and rise within it as confidence grew in my ability was due to one very simple fact: fear. Omeros Kalandris and Sofoclis were getting in over their heads — and they knew it. They mistrusted Martinelli and

O'Flaherty. There were very few within the organization they *could* trust. They didn't know what was coming, but they suspected it wasn't going to be good. So, when I proved trustworthy, they gave me more and more responsibility. I don't think Sofoclis noticed it, but Kalandris moved more and more into the background. He was not only shrewd; he was a cautious man.

In any event, in October, when mother and Penny arrived, I was a young man of some importance. I was riding high.

I was also riding for a fall. I should have taken O'Flaherty's sudden and bloody demise as a warning.

CHAPTER TEN

In a young man, sexual drive may be subliminated or suppressed, but it cannot be ignored. The difficulty about examining such emotional responses in retrospect is that I find it next to impossible to do so with objectivity or clinical detachment. As the mental images form, dissolve and re-form, I live again the anguish and the ecstasy of those experiences.

There was a sort of innocence about my sexual awakening in my romance with Danai. When she rejected me on pragmatic rather than emotional grounds, I felt she had betrayed my love. I was sunk in bitterness, and my attitude toward women underwent a subtle change. What I could not appreciate at the time was that my love for Danai was not compatible with my dreams of attaining greatness. One — or the other — was doomed.

What if I *had* declared my love for Danai and been accepted by Spiridon Papas as a prospective son-in-law? I'm sure he would have helped me obtain a boat of my own. Danai and I would have been married. In short order, we would have started a family. The pattern of my life would have been set. I might prosper in a limited way, but I would be destined to remain a fisherman on Corfu until my death.

Would I have been content with such a life? I think not. The dreams of youth would have returned to haunt me. In time, I would come to resent Danai for having robbed me of a chance for fame and fortune. Dreams, unfortunately, can have more substance than reality.

I believe Danai knew this instinctively. I think her contention that material security made her favor an older, more settled man was only partially true. Women, I have found, place great store in emotional security. She knew from our many conversations of my vaulting aspirations. I doubt that she considered them other than youthful fantasies, yet, unattainable though she must have thought them, she understood me well enough to know they were very real to me. But they were dreams she did not share. All she could see was that my dreams would not die easily. Ultimately, they must become a barrier between us.

The fact remains that she chose Petros. I left Corfu convinced that my heart was borken — that I had lost the one woman with whom I wanted to share my life. And there was another consideration that added, for me, a sense of guilt. We had conducted our affair in secrecy, but it was no secret in the eyes of God. In His eyes, had we not sinned? Was her choosing another my punishment for our transgression?

On my return to Drakopoulata, I vowed to have no more to do with women. A life of celibacy was preferable to the pain they could inflict. I remained firm in that resolve for some three months — until my first visit to Sami following my return to Cephalonia.

She was a waitress in a small *taverna* close to the post office. I can picture her in my mind's eye — a vivacious little brunette with gray-green eyes who reminded me a little of Danai — but for the life of me I cannot recall her name. When she served me an ouzo, she smiled brightly. Regardless of my intentions to the contrary, I experienced strong stirrings in my groin. After all, I was a healthy young man. Desire overrode resolve.

When she got off duty that afternoon, we went to a small waterfront hotel. There was nothing tender about my lovemaking. Nevertheless, she gave every evidence of having enjoyed it. I justified my roughness with the belief that I was using this girl as I'd been used by Danai.

Over the next year, I returned to Sami a number of times when the pressure in my loins became too insistent to ignore. On most of these occasions, the waitress and I met at the small hotel and made love with varying degrees of violence. I believe that for her, as it was for me, it was simply a physical response and a release of tensions. Be that as it may, I came to look forward to the meetings and found myself making excuses to visit Sami more and more frequently.

Through force of circumstances, namely lack of money and, accordingly, a lack of opportunity, celibacy was forced upon me during the long sea voyage and my first few months in New York.

It was not a condition much to my liking. This was particularly true in New York, where I saw many attractive girls who set my pulse to racing. My moral code was much less rigid in this big, vibrant, crowded city than it was in the Ionian towns and villages to which I was accustomed. Shop girls and female office employees appeared to flirt quite openly. Later I was to discover that this forwardness by no means was confined to working girls. The conviction I formed was that American women were of loose moral fiber. It is perhaps just as well that my amorous activities during my introduction to urban life in New York were circumscribed by a lack of free time and a shortage of funds.

Phoebe was just about the only female company I had. My hours were such that I generally did not arrive back at the house until evening, by which time Uncle Nicholas had long since eaten and was either listening to the radio or already in bed. Phoebe kept my supper warm and slipped into the habit of joining me for the evening meal. It is only natural, then, that we developed a rather close relationship. It was based on mutual liking — and a need in both of us for companionship. It was some months before it went beyond that point.

It might never have happened at all had not Fate conspired to throw us together under circumstances almost impossible to ignore. Phoebe was a big girl, almost as tall as I. She was too heavy in the thighs, broad in the beam and thick of waist to appeal to me physically. I was growing fond of her, but it hadn't even crossed my mind that our relationship would go beyond friendship. Moreover, not only was I still carrying the torch for Danai, but also I had learned from sad experience the difficulties of carrying on an affair with the daughter of one's employer while living under the same roof. It was a mistake I didn't believe I would ever repeat.

Winter melted into spring, and, as the days lengthened, spring slid into summer. The heat hung heavily in the brick and concrete canyons of Manhattan. Whatever breeze tried to creep in from the Hudson and the East River was blocked and turned back by a solid wall of turgid, humid, exhaust-fume-tainted air. About the only good thing that could be said about a Manhattan summer was that it didn't last long.

One sweltering Saturday in late July, I returned to the Mott Street house at about seven-thirty in the evening, tired and sweat-soaked. Uncle Nicholas, probably to escape the heat more than for any other reason, had gone to spend the weekend with friends on Long Island. Sofoclis was in Chicago on business. Phoebe and I had the house to ourselves.

Phoebe greeted me with a cold beer from the icebox. She had gone to some pains to prepare dishes she knew I liked — Greek salad with plenty of feta cheese, and roast lamb. To my delight, and somewhat to my surprise, a bottle of burgundy graced the kitchen table. I hadn't the heart to tell her that the heat had all but robbed me of my appetite.

The cold beer went down well and somewhat revived my spirits. "Whew," I said, wiping my lips on the sleeve of my shirt, "It's a scorcher. Beer tastes good . . . but you'd better keep it out of sight in case a revenuer drops in on us." Nodding toward the bottle of wine, I added, "I didn't think your God-fearing, law-abiding father allowed alcoholic beverages on the premises. Where did you get it?"

Phoebe giggled. "Daddy isn't that bad. He likes an occasional beer, and you know he generally drinks wine with his meals . . . unless we have company. He just keeps it well-hidden. Mr. Kalandris keeps us supplied. Mr. Kalandris says he isn't going to change habits of a lifetime, no matter what the law says."

"Mr. Kalandris," I said, "is a wise man."

"Kostas," Phoebe said, "you're drenched with perspiration. Why don't you freshen up and change your shirt before we eat. If you want, you can leave your shirt off. There's nobody here to see you."

I grinned. "It isn't polite to sit around half-naked. But, if you'll excuse me, I'll change my shirt. It stinks of sweat and horses. I won't be a minute."

After supper I helped Phoebe with the dishes, then we went out and sat on the stoop, hoping to catch a breath of air. It was stifling, and I couldn't help but notice that her thin cotton dress clung to her ample breasts. She couldn't have been wearing a camisole. Her nipples, pressing against the damp fabric, were clearly visible.

Idly, I watched some children playing further down the street, and my gaze drifted to a young woman who rounded the corner and walked toward us. She had a good figure — a narrow waist and boyish hips that swayed provocatively as she walked. Her feet, what I could see of them beneath her long skirt, were encased in Russian military-style boots.

My eyes followed her as she passed and continued on toward Hester Street. "Keen," I said.

"Mmmm" was Phoebe's noncommittal response.

"I'll bet you anything you like she's got flasks of liquor tucked in the tops of her boots," I said, with a knowing wink.

"Kostas!" Phoebe exclaimed.

"I'm not kidding. Antonio, the super, assured me that the only reason Russian boots have become all the rage is that they provide a handy means of hiding hooch."

"Do you believe him?"

"Yes. He's a bachelor. He goes out a lot, and *seems* to know what he's talking about. He tells me that his best gal tucks a small flask under her garter when they go out on a date. She won't tell him which leg. He has to find out for himself before he gets a drink. He says that's half the fun of dating her."

Phoebe looked at me suspiciously, not sure whether I was pulling her leg. When she decided I hadn't made up the story, she frowned disapprovingly. "Good Lord," she said, "what's the world coming to? Girls today don't seem to know the meaning of modesty."

"Well," I said, "Antonio tells me that the fashion this fall is supposed to be shorter skirts, which will take most of the fun out of searching for the flask. His claim is that, if the trend continues, his girl will have only one place left to hide a flask."

Phoebe rose to the bait. "Where's that?"

I looked meaningfully at the cleavage of her swelling breasts and grinned broadly.

Phoebe followed my eyes, glanced down at her breasts and blushed.

I chuckled. "Antonio's problem is that his girl is flat-chested."

"Kostas!" she exclaimed again. "I don't want to hear another word. The things you men talk about." But she wasn't as shocked as she pretended. The flush ebbed from her cheeks, and her eyes glinted with amusement.

"What do women talk about? I'll bet it's about men."

Phoebe smiled. "Mostly, I suppose, but we don't discuss their anatomy."

The girl who had passed by wearing Russian boots seemed to have been a catalyst. My conversation with Phoebe had taken an unexpected turn. It was as though a chemical reaction was taking place. Beneath the bantering was an undercurrent of sexual awareness. I felt it not as an emotional surge, but more like a clinging mist slowly engulfing me. Heightening the impression was the deepening dusk, which softened our soot-coated surroundings and lent an air of mystery to them. At my side, her leg touching mine,

Phoebe underwent a subtle transformation. For the first time I was acutely aware of her as a woman. I had an odd tingling sensation where our legs touched. The warmth, which had nothing to do with the still heat of the evening, slowly spread to my abdomen and crept downward to my groin.

I hadn't expected anything like this. I looked at Phoebe quizzically. I sensed that she was experiencing a similar reaction. She looked directly into my eyes, and, as though in answer to my unspoken question, her leg alongside mine trembled slightly in anticipation.

I took her hand lightly in mine. Wordlessly, we rose to our feet, went inside the house and climbed the stairs to my third-floor bedroom. We undressed in silence, as though the smallest word would destroy the fragile magic of the moment.

Naked, we stood facing each other in the semigloom of descending night. I drew her close. Our sweat-filmed bodies met. Her firm breasts flattened against my chest. I was conscious of her hard nipples pressing through the mat of hair on my chest. My erect penis was flattened against the lower swelling of her abdomen. Her breathing was shallow and uneven. She trembled uncontrollably.

I eased Phoebe down onto the bed. She spread her legs, and, as my probing member forced an entrance, she gasped.

Despite the hunger of my loins, I restrained my impulse to take her violently. My thrusts were slow and even until the climax neared and my strokes quickened. Phoebe's groans of pleasure mounted to hoarsely rasping cries as, with explosive force, my pent-up juices spurted deep within her.

My passion spent, I sagged onto her breasts. Our bodies were slippery with sweat. The coverlet beneath her was wet.

When my breathing subsided, I got up from the bed and went to the bathroom. I dried myself and returned with a clean towel with which I gently patted the accumulated perspiration from her breasts and belly. She took the towel from me and dried her abdomen and between her legs. When she was finished, she examined the towel. It was marked near one corner with a stain of fresh blood.

"I'll have to wash the coverlet," Phoebe said, "but I suppose I can leave it until tomorrow morning."

I had tried not to be rough, but she *had* been tight at first. In some way I had injured her. "I . . . I'm sorry," I said.

Phoebe's lips twitched in a smile. "Why? I could have stopped you. I wanted you to make love to me."

"But," I said, "I've hurt you."

"No you haven't. It's to be expected . . . though I wasn't quite sure what it would be like. It was marvelous. It's just that this was my first time."

A virgin. Somehow that possibility hadn't even occurred to me. But it was so. The stained towel was mute evidence that I'd ruptured her maidenhead.

Thereafter, Phoebe and I made love an average of two or three times a month. We had to use caution. It was always Phoebe who took the initiative, coming to my room late at night when she knew Sofoclis wasn't likely to return unexpectedly and Uncle Nicholas was fast asleep in his ground-floor bedroom.

I enjoyed our lovemaking. I won't pretend that I didn't. To me it was like satisfying a hunger — or slaking a thirst. I was careful to make it clear to Phoebe that we were simply satisfying our physical needs. As far as I was concerned, our relationship had nothing to do with love. I treated Phoebe, I am now ashamed to say, more as a convenience than anything else. That her feelings might differ from mine didn't concern me. I freely admit it was an insensitive attitude for me to adopt. I looked on her as a friend — nothing more. I did nothing to lead her on, except, of course, to make love to her whenever the opportunity presented itself over a two-year period.

When I learned that Phoebe interpreted our relationship entirely differently, I must confess that it came as a complete surprise.

CHAPTER ELEVEN

Mother and Penny landed in New York in mid-October 1922. In spite of the fact that I had sent them more than enough to cover their fare on a passenger liner, they came on a Greek freighter. Why had they done so? It seemed all the more strange to me since mother had added to her savings through the sale of our property in Drakopoulata and since Georgiana — whose fare I had included in the money I sent — had elected to stay in Patras. Mother's response to my questions about her seemingly unnecessary frugality made sense. The reason was Georgiana.

Georgiana had turned twenty-eight that summer. She had abandoned all hope of marriage. The idea of starting life afresh in a strange country had not appealed to her. On the other hand, she'd had little desire to continue indefinitely being a waitress. Then she'd had an opportunity to buy an interest in a small gift shop. By effecting economies in areas such as transportation for herself and Penny, mother had been able to give Georgiana enough money to buy into that modest business.

After all, mother observed sadly, a dowry at this stage was unlikely to improve Georgiana's marital prospects. A business partnership, as a means of securing Georgiana's uncertain future, had seemed to mother a logical investment in lieu of a dowry. I couldn't argue with that logic, but I expressed unhappiness that I had not been consulted in this family matter. I was, I pointed out rather testily, in a position to buy the gift shop outright had I known what was being planned.

Mother smiled indulgently. She stated she was happy to hear that I was doing well, but that the impression she had received from my letters over the past couple of years, and from the money I had sent, was that I'd not been making out financially as well as I'd expected. She and Penny had had no wish to exclude me from a family decision. They merely had not wished to impose on me by adding any additional burden.

Mother and Penny were delighted when they inspected the Waverly Place apartment. They were impressed, and more than a little overwhelmed, by the display of affluence. I had told them I owned the Ford in which I'd driven them to Waverly Place. They had been suitably awed. Then, when they'd had a chance to explore the apartment, mother and Penny had lapsed into subdued silence. It must have registered on them that I was the man of substance I claimed to be. Why disabuse them? At that point, they would not have understood installment purchasing.

Mother was sixty, going on sixty-one. She did not adjust easily to so much that was new and novel. That water flowed freely out of a tap was a source of constant wonder, as was the fact that she didn't have to rely on the sitting-room fireplace alone to heat the apartment in winter, since each room had a steam radiator. Although she lived in fear that the gas stove would blow up in her face, she mastered its use. The refrigerator and the phonograph she eventually accepted as wonders of a new age, but it was her claim that the washing machine did not really get clothes clean. She refused to use it, and she frowned on Penny's approval of it as a timesaving device.

The major drawback to the apartment was its location. I should have thought of that. It was situated about four blocks from an Italian-speaking neighborhood, and a good thirteen long city blocks from Uncle Nicholas' Mott Street home on the fringe of the Greek community. In the two-and-a-half years she lived in New York, mother — who spoke no English and only faltering Italian — ventured no further from the apartment than the Greek-owned corner grocery, unless accompanied by either Penny or myself.

It had not been my intention to move into the Waverly Place apartment. I had planned, once I had the family safely installed and settled, to find a bachelor apartment for myself. Mother wouldn't hear of it. Since Georgiana had not accompanied them, there was a spare bedroom. Mother insisted that I move in and assume my place as the male head of the family. I did so in late November. Uncle Nicholas, I am sure, was glad to get rid of me.

Phoebe, while she was loathe to have me leave, appreciated and respected my mother's wishes in the matter.

For me, the move was far from being an ideal arrangement. My hours were sufficiently nocturnal to preclude what my mother considered to be a normal home life. How could I explain to mother what my employment entailed? I gave her a vague explanation that my duties involved supervising warehouses where the bulk of the deliveries, due to long-distance haulage and daytime traffic congestion, took place at night.

There were other drawbacks. Head of the family I might be, but my mother treated me more as a child than as a man. Then, as well, I was deprived of Phoebe's occasional company in bed. Frankly, by that time, this didn't concern me much. Already I was straying afield. What *did* concern me was that I had no place of my own in which to entertain obliging young ladies with whom I'd established satisfying relationships.

When mother and Penny arrived on the scene, Uncle Nicholas took it upon himself to welcome them with a dinner party in his home. It amused me. No such welcome had been extended to me when I had appeared on his doorstep. The circumstances, however, were now very different. Uncle Nicholas was under no financial obligation toward my mother and my sister. He could afford to be expansive.

It was a gala evening. For once, Uncle Nicholas had spared no expense. Instead of leaving all the work to Phoebe, he had had the dinner prepared and delivered by a nearby Greek restaurant.

Aside from the young Italian girl Sofoclis brought as his dinner partner, it was an all-Greek affair — and even she spoke Greek. And except for her and Mr. Kalandris, we were all related.

Mr. Kalandris seemed much taken with Penny. They spent a good deal of the evening talking with each other. On our return to Waverly Place, Penny triumphantly informed mother and me that Mr. Kalandris had offered her a job in his 57th Street flower shop. She had accepted the offer.

I must say that Penny surprised me. Prior to coming to America she had devoted two years studying English. On her arrival she was reasonably fluent, and she improved rapidly. That alone would have surprised me, but there was more to it than her mastery of the language. Where mother was cowed by New York, Penny was exactly the reverse. New York seemed to act on her like a tonic. She put on some weight, which she needed. She displayed a flair for fashionable dress that I'd never suspected. She adapted readily to local custom. She smiled often, which softened the severity of her features. In short, she became a changed woman in so many ways that I was hard put to recognize in her the same ill-tempered, sour-faced sister I'd known from childhood.

I don't mean to say that Penny suddenly blossomed into a beauty. I still thought her unappealing to most men. But, obviously, Omeros Kalandris was not "most men."

I suppose Kalandris was attracted by her youth. Also, she retained a good deal of her Old Country submissiveness even as she changed in other ways. Kalandris, used to less-reserved women, must have found her deference an appealing quality. But whatever it was, she definitely appealed to him. Before many months had passed, he was escorting her regularly to movies, the theater and social functions — including wining and dining her both at the most expensive clubs and in gin mills of lesser repute. By the end of 1923, she acted as his hostess when he entertained at his Riverside Drive apartment.

That was very well for Kalandris, but what could Penny possibly see in a man thirty-two years her senior? I suppose she was flattered by his attention. Without doubt, she thoroughly enjoyed the social life and the expensive gifts Omeros showered on her. I imagine that for a young woman who had foreseen nothing but bleak spinsterhood ahead, all this must have been pretty heady stuff. I was not particularly happy about their association, but I made no move to interfere in it.

It was not long before Penny learned I was involved with Kalandris in bootlegging activities. Knowing from whence I earned my salary didn't shock Penny; on the contrary, it seemed to amuse her. But we rarely discussed it. She felt as I did that mother would disapprove and entered into a conspiracy with me to keep her ignorant of the facts.

There was another relationship that Penny formed at this time about which I was unenthusiastic, but to which I could not object. She became a close friend to her cousin Phoebe.

How were my fortunes advancing during this period? Slowly, but surely, I was securing a position of authority within the organization. In my capacity as overseer of the warehousing operations,

I set about streamlining some of the more haphazard procedures. In addition, I introduced precautionary measures designed to make us less vulnerable to possible detection and surprise raids by the Feds.

There was not much I could do about the odd hours at which we received truck deliveries. The drivers were at the mercy of unpredictable elements such as last-minute changes of beach off-loading locations, suspected roadblocks and tip-offs about hijacking attempts. We had to leave it up to the drivers' ingenuity to circumvent such hazards. It wasn't *when* they arrived that concerned us so much as *if* they arrived at all. The only innovation I brought into the picture in that area was to increase the number of trucks so that the individual loads could be reduced in size. It meant added expense in vehicles and personnel, but it reduced the risk involved from the loss of one or more trucks during hours of darkness. During the winter of 1922-23, we had a rash of losses through trucks hijacked or apprehended, and the wisdom of my spreading the risk became immediately apparent and stilled the objections raised due to added costs.

An area more readily amenable to remedial action was that of warehouse pickup. Both Martinelli and O'Flaherty had been in the habit of expecting us to fill individual orders, no matter how small, at any hour of the day or night. The steady stream of automobiles arriving at the warehouses focused unwanted attention on this phase of the operation. The action I took was the institution of a staggered time schedule for pickups. This generated strong objections from our distributing partners, but it was finally accepted, even though with bad grace.

Ostensibly to ease the tensions, but in reality to have our liquour inventory spread over a wider base, I set up what I called "emergency stock points." These consisted of a number of small neighborhood stores that I persuaded to carry limited stocks of the more popular brands of liquor on an impress basis. It was pointed out to both O'Flaherty and Martinelli that their drivers could draw upon these stocks to restock if, for any unforeseen reason, they missed their scheduled pickup times or needed to fill emergency rush orders. True, tapping these emergency stocks would entail a small added cost, but this could be passed along to the customers to dissuade them from ordering at the last minute. My stock decentralization was seen as a conciliatory gesture by our mobster associates — exactly the impression I'd intended to impart.

By early September, I had advanced to junior partner. I attended all meetings involving policy decisions, and, more and more, my suggestions were accepted with little argument.

A factor that worked very much in my favor was that Sofoclis, once he had offered his hand in friendship and I had accepted it, trusted me implicity. In most things, he accepted my advice without question. In one aspect of his conduct, however, I could not influence him.

Ours was the least visible end of the business. It was our gangland associate who was bathed in the glare of publicity. While it was a temptation to me to act the part of a big cheese, I took my cue from Omeros Kalandris, who cloaked his bootlegging activities in secrecy. Kalandris, of course, already a man of wealth and a well-known figure in New York society, was under no complusion to alter his lifestyle. I, on the other hand, was an unknown. I thought it best to keep it that way.

I drove a modest Ford roadster. As I have already said, until November I continued to live with the Metaxis family and, thereafter, lived with my own family at Waverly Place. I did frequent a number of the better speakeasies and, as a concession to my elevated status, dressed quietly but expensively. I embarked on discreet affairs with showgirls, but I didn't flaunt my newly acquired affluence. Like Kalandris, I preferred to keep as much as possible in the background.

Sofoclis, on the other hand, thoroughly enjoyed the role of big shot. He dressed the part. He was seen frequently in the company of ranking mobsters. For the most part, the girls he squired were flashy gold-diggers and socialites. He spent money like water.

I remonstrated with Sofoclis about this, pointing out that his flamboyance attracted unwarranted attention, but to no avail. Sofoclis shrugged, grinned boyishly and stated that, because of his size, he stood out in a crowd anyway, so there wasn't much point in trying to hide his light under a bushel. He had a point, but the light he made no effort to conceal was like that of a runaway forest fire.

CHAPTER TWELVE

The bad blood between Vito Martinelli and Sean O'Flaherty went back a long way. Their uneasy alliance with Sofoclis and Kalandris did nothing to improve their attitudes toward each other. There were unmistakable signs, in fact, that the situation between them was steadily worsening. By the time I joined the organization, it had reached a point where Martinelli would not attend any meeting that included O'Flaherty. Martinelli adopted the practice of sending his trusted lieutenant, Alfredo Rubio, as his representative, whether or not O'Flaherty was in attendance. This didn't seem to bother O'Flaherty in the least. It should have.

Although I saw Martinelli at a distance on a number of occasions — in such night spots as the Club New Yorker, Club Vendome, the 21 Club and Leon & Eddie's — I didn't actually meet him until late in November 1923. At this time, the occasion was our first policy meeting after Sean O'Flaherty's funeral. Of course, Vito was much in evidence at the funeral itself, but it was an event I had purposely missed. The police and the Feds made it a practice to check up on those attending the funerals of prominent underworld figures.

How and why was O'Flaherty bumped off? The "how" was a matter of public record. O'Flaherty always went to the same tobacconist on Greenwich Street to buy his cigars. It was a morning ritual with O'Flaherty, known to all who knew the bluff Irish gangland boss.

On a Wednesday morning in late October, two men entered the shop behind O'Flaherty and riddled him with machine-gun slugs. The tobacconist was caught in the spray of bullets and seriously wounded but lived to tell about it. Neither the tobacconist nor anyone else who witnessed the shooting could give more than vague descriptions of the killers.

The "why" of the slaying was more obscure. Those who knew

the reasons weren't talking. Speculation was rife, but nothing conclusive in the way of evidence ever came to light.

I agree with Sofoclis that it was Martinelli who ordered the killing. It is my belief, though I have no proof, that O'Flaherty was muscling in on the Lower East Side, territory Martinelli considered exclusively his.

O'Flaherty's killing caused a flurry of excitement in mob circles but scarcely raised an eyebrow among law enforcement agencies. I can't say I blame the police for what many claimed to be a callous attitude toward gangland slayings. Lawlessness was rife, and it was increasing at an alarming rate. Trying to enforce the Volstead Act was a thankless and all but hopeless task. It must have galled the Feds and the police that gangsters were becoming folk heroes. So, when a gangland execution took place, the police merely shrugged. In fact, they probably heartily welcomed the thinning process.

At a later date, I'd have good cause to be thankful that the police conveniently lacked diligence when it came to gangland activities.

At the November 1923 meeting he attended, Martinelli blamed the O'Flaherty execution on Owney Madden's gunmen but offered nothing more by way of explanation. He advised us that business would continue without disruption since he was taking over O'Flaherty's territory. Then, claiming we might face trouble from Madden or "Big Frenchy" de Mange or, even more probably, some of the late Sean O'Flaherty's disgruntled lieutenants, Vito announced that he was assigning bodyguards to Sofoclis and Kalandris as a precautionary measure. At that point, Vito subjected me to a long, searching scrutiny then, with a fleeting smile, said he felt two bodyguards would suffice. Evidently, at that stage of the proceedings, he didn't consider me important enough to worry about.

By Christmas, Kalandris had persuaded Vito that his bodyguard was an unnecessary encumbrance. Sofoclis, who evidently thought that his bodyguard, Angelo, enhanced his image, raised no objection. Angelo, a lean, silent shadow, was never far from his charge's elbow.

At first I watched the performance with amusement. As the weeks wore on, however, I noticed that Angelo, even though he said nothing, seemed to take a keen interest in Sofoclis' business affairs. My suspicions aroused, I kept a close eye on Angelo. I came to the conclusion that Angelo was more a watchdog than a source of protection. Vito Martinelli trusted his partners no more than they trusted him.

Uncle Nicholas' death came without any warning the following July. True, he was in his middle seventies, but he hadn't had a day's illness for as long as I'd known him.

When the will was read, Sofoclis inherited Metaxis & Company, lock, stock and barrel. The house and all its contents went to Phoebe. The balance of the estate, consisting of personal savings, securities and paid-up life insurance policies, was divided equally between Sofoclis and Phoebe. Phoebe was right. America had been good to Nicholas Metaxis. He died a very rich man.

For me, there was an unexpected outgrowth attached to Uncle Nicholas' death. It was Penny who broke the news to me.

The day of the funeral had been a trying one for mother. On the way back from the cemetery, I had treated mother and Penny to dinner. On our return to the apartment, mother had pleaded exhaustion and gone right to bed.

Penny and I were in the kitchen drinking coffee and sipping Greek brandy.

Penny sighed heavily. "Mama just can't get used to life over here. It's *so* hard for her."

"It's partly our fault," I said. "We humor her too much. Maybe if we weren't catering to her all the time she'd make more of an effort to fit in. She hasn't any friends. If she only half-tried to, she could make some friends right here in the building."

"Who? There aren't any Greeks in this building . . . and precious few in the neighborhood."

"She speaks enough Italian to get by. There's no shortage of Italians here. But she just won't make the effort. For God's sake, Penny, she refuses to wear anything but widow's weeds. Today is about the only time she's been properly dressed for the occasion since she stepped off the ship almost two years ago."

"Leave her be," Penny said. "It's a mark of respect for Papa. She's worn black ever since his death. I respect her for it."

"That's fine in Cephalonia," I said, "but this is New York. Customs differ. There's no need for her to mourn Papa's death until the day *she* dies."

"She doesn't see it that way. It's what she wants. But I do worry about her. What will she do when I leave?"

"When you leave — ? What do you mean? Are you thinking of going somewhere?"

"Not right away. But Omeros has asked me to marry him. I've accepted his proposal."

I stared at Penny in stunned disbelief. I don't know why her news jarred me so, but it did. When at last I found my tongue, I said, "Is it what you want, Penny?"

"Yes."

"It's not his money . . . his social position?"

Penny's teeth flashed in a smile. "No, Kostas," she said, "it's not his money. But I will admit that security has a strong appeal to a woman from Drakopoulata."

I nodded. I knew exactly what she meant. "Does Mama know?"

"Not yet. I'll tell her soon. So far, I've told only Phoebe . . . and now you."

"When do you plan on getting married?"

"We're not going to hurry it. He wants me to have lots of time to back out should I change my mind. I won't. I'd say sometime next spring. But that doesn't stop me from worrying about Mama. Omeros says she can live with us, but I don't want to start our marriage that way. Am I wrong? Am I being selfish?"

"Hell, no. You can't just move Mama in. You'll need time to adjust. It won't be easy. He's been a bachelor a long time. No, I think you're right."

"Then what are we to do? Mama can't be left on her own, and you can't spend much time with her."

"Maybe Georgiana could come over this fall, or perhaps next spring. I'm sure she'll want to be here for the wedding."

"For the wedding, yes. To stay here, no. You know she bought the shop with the money you sent her. Now she's opened a second shop in Kerkyra. She doesn't want to leave Greece. It wouldn't be fair to ask that of her."

"I suppose you're right. We can't ask her to sell out and come over here because of Mama." I poured more cognac into my glass, swirled it slowly, looked at it thoughtfully — then I brightened. "Well, it's something we'll have to think about," I said, more confidently than I felt. "Your not planning on getting married until the spring gives us a lot of time to figure it all out."

"One solution suggests itself," Penny said.

"What's that?"

"You could get married, and have your wife move in here."

I laughed. "Who do you suggest?"

"Phoebe. She'd marry you if you asked her."

I looked at Penny to see if she was joking. She wasn't. She was deadly serious. "Damn it," I said. "You *can't* be serious. Phoebe and I are good friends . . . but that's all. Whatever makes you think she'd marry me if I asked her? Besides, we're cousins . . . so that kills *that* bright idea."

"Second cousins. That doesn't rule out matrimony. She'd marry you because she's in love with you."

"Well," I said, "I don't love her. She knows that. Let's change the subject."

"You may have told her you didn't love her, Kostas, but she didn't believe you. You made love to her — not once, but many times. You are the only man she's ever had. Women attach a lot of importance to that. If you don't love her, you must convince her of that for her own good."

"How?" I asked.

"*I* don't know," Penny said. "That's up to you. *Your* lust and selfishness created the situation."

I was embarrassed. I was also angry. By her own admission, Phoebe's loss of virginity had been as much her doing as mine. Phoebe had taken the initiative in our lovemaking, coming to my bed unbidden and when it suited her. Never, even in the heat of passion, had I told her I loved her. On the contrary, I had gone out of my way to make it clear that there were no strings attached to our relationship. Why, suddenly, was everything *my* fault?

And Penny — what right had *she* to censure me? Had I not been struggling to save money to bring the family to New York, and depriving myself of life's pleasures in the process? And here she sat, putting all the blame on me.

I have never been able to understand — and I suppose I never will understand — the emotional responses a woman's mind calls "logic."

I couldn't think of any satisfactory way to explain my feelings to Phoebe. I avoided her as much as possible. Eventually, I think it was Penny who convinced Phoebe it was hopeless to carry a torch for me.

CHAPTER THIRTEEN

Nineteen twenty-four was an eventful year.

It was a presidential election year. The Republican Administration seemed solidly entrenched in an era of general prosperity. Calvin Coolidge, who had succeeded to the presidency on the death of Warren G. Harding the previous August, was running on the Republican ticket and, in November, was elected president in his own right.

The economy was booming. Sofoclis was putting more and more of his profits into real estate holdings. So, on a smaller scale, was I. And both of us had succumbed to the lure of the stock market, our broker assuring us that vast fortunes were to be made through adroit speculation.

It was a yeasty period. Everyone seemed to have money — at least in New York — although that, I imagine, was an illusion strengthened by the fact that Sofoclis and I moved largely within a monied circle.

There was a restlessness to society, with everyone seeking new thrills and methods of personal expression that manifested itself in devotion to peculiar cults and fads, with individuals striving to outdo each other in inanities such as the flagpole-sitting craze set in motion as a Hollywood stunt performed by Sailor "Shipwreck" Kelly. It was the era of tabloid journalism and fabricated heroes. Radio was coming into its own. The movie palace was an established institution. Increasingly, Hollywood was dictating social trends. The matinee idol was part and parcel of the cult culture.

There is nothing to be gained by pretending that I was immune from these infections. As much as anyone, I devotedly followed the journalistic sensationalism. As for the movies, whenever I had a chance, I sneaked off to take in a matinee. In turn, I fancied myself madly in love with Pola Negri, Gloria Swanson and Greta Garbo.

The antics of the sad little tramp, Charlie Chaplin, brought tears to my eyes and laughter to my lips. As for Rudolph Valentino, before I gave it up as a bad job, I parted my unruly hair in the middle and did everything I could to get it to stay stylishly plastered to my skull. But Valentino, I reluctantly concluded, I was not.

As Antonio, the Metaxis & Company's Cortlandt Street super-intendent, had forseen, women's skirts were creeping higher. By 1924 they had reached a point between the ankle and the knee — a harbinger of the unheard-of, provocatively above-the-knee levels they would attain a few years later.

Everything was changing at a dizzying pace. In Manhattan, new skyscrapers seemed to sprout up overnight, like mushrooms after a warm rain. The automobile had evolved from a canvas-topped vehicle little protected from the elements to a solid-sided conveyance. The new Ford I bought that year afforded me the luxury of protection from the weather — but it was a far cry from the custom-built Packard limousine sported by Vito Martinelli. His car was chauffeur-driven, with ample space in its velvet-upholstered interior for Martinelli and his entourage of bodyguards. Reputedly it had bulletproof windows. While I never rode in Vito's limousine, I often saw it parked outside one of the Harlem nightclubs during the small hours of the morning.

Popularized by a series of Broadway shows with Negro casts, jazz was all the rage. Like the faithful making a pilgrimage to Mecca, socialites, celebrities and racketeers and their women descended on such Harlem revue-boasting gin mills as Barron's Cabaret, Connie's Inn and the Cotton Club in the after-midnight hours. That such unsavory citizens as Owney Madden and George de Mange were part-owners of the Cotton Club probably enhanced, rather than detracted from, the club's appeal.

Just why gangsters should have ranked as celebrities along with the great and near-great of the silver screen and the world of sports has always been a mystery to me. Without exception, the mobsters I met and associated with were a brutish, vicious collection of thugs who had clawed their way up from the gutter. For the most part, they were men of limited vision who were normally and culturally bankrupt. Their approach to social and business problems was simplistic — murder. Yet many of these captains of crime were accorded fawning adulation. I wonder if this popular acclaim would have come about had it not been for the advent of Prohibition. Somehow, I don't think it would have. I believe it to have been an aberration of that era of flux and uncertainty.

Were Kalandris, Sofoclis and I any better than our mobster associates? I think the answer to that would have to be in the negative, regardless of our opinions of ourselves at the time. Since in our end of the illicit business we were a step or two removed from the competitive violence, we considered ourselves superior to the criminal element. We weren't. Regardless of the methods employed, all our profits derived from the same source. And, I must confess, many of the lessons I learned through my exposure to and association with mobsters I would put to good use in the years to come.

On a more personal level, 1924 was a year of change and shifting viewpoints.

In January, much to my relief, Phoebe announced her intention to move to California. Quite frankly, I was happy to see her go. I didn't consider myself at fault with respect to her feelings toward me, but it was a constant source of embarrassment.

I was kept busy during the waning months of winter and into the early spring with a reorganization of our warehousing setup. Sofoclis, now that his father was no longer a factor, wanted to shift some of the liquor storage to the Cortlandt Street warehouse. In fact, he wanted it to become our major distribution facility due to its central location. It was with some difficulty that I dissuaded him that this would be a sensible move.

For some time, I had been concerned about the position of Metaxis & Company in our bootlegging operations. While the legitimate business conducted by the company provided us with a screen behind which we could cloak our illegal activities, there was an ever-present danger that a crackdown by the Feds on the latter would place the former in jeopardy. With Sofoclis I argued the case persuasively that, far from thinking of a transfer of liquor stocks to Cortlandt Street, he should be thinking of divorcing bootlegging from Metaxis & Company altogether.

I argued that he had inherited a thriving legitimate business. Why endanger both the company and its lawful income? Bureau of Internal Revenue agents were becoming better informed and more of a threat to us each day. Sooner or later, they were bound to descend on Metaxis & Company, and, when that day came, the company should appear to be above reproach. Moreover, thanks to his legacy, he was now wealthy enough to retire from the rackets and devote all his time and energy to increasing his legitimate corporate earnings.

In all but one respect, I was able to persuade Sofoclis. He saw no reason why he should give up 'legging. That was all very well, except that in the process of separating the lawful from the unlawful aspects of the business, he was of next to no help. During that period, he was too engrossed in acting the part of gentleman mobster to pay attention to much else. If, as I suspected, Angelo's real function was to report back to Vito on Sofoclis' activities, there was precious little information concerning Sofoclis' business dealings to impart.

To me, then, fell the task of divorcing Metaxis & Company from the 'legging name. I leased additional warehouse space and started to transfer stock to new locations. I had all but succeeded in the separation when I ran into stiff opposition. Sofoclis — at the urging of Martinelli, though I didn't find this out for some time — wanted the Jersey City operation to continue untouched. Since, as Sofoclis stressed, it was out of New York's jurisdiction and used only occasionally by Metaxis & Company for overflow storage purposes, I gave in to his wishes, even though not entirely happy with the situation.

Then, in May, a disturbing element entered the picture. It was a repeat of a problem that had plagued Sofoclis and Kalandris before I became involved. I began to hear complaints about the quality of liquor being supplied to our customers through Martinelli. Evidently, having eliminated O'Flaherty and secured a virtual monopoly over the Lower East Side, Vito had reverted to the practice of adulterating the liquor somewhere between the warehouse pickup and point of delivery.

Concerned and angry, I convinced Kalandris that a meeting should be called to discuss and resolve the situation. The meeting took place on a Tuesday evening at Kalandris' apartment. Kalandris, Sofoclis, Martinelli and I were there.

Kalandris stated the reason for the meeting without advancing any suggested remedial action. Martinelli calmly admitted that the liquor was being adulterated, but only with first-grade grain alcohol, and no more so than were the stocks of our competitors. All the 'leggers were doing it to increase profits — profits sorely needed in view of the spoiling tactics of the Feds. Why shouldn't he adopt the same policy since, after all, his boys were the ones running all the risks?

Sofoclis and Kalandris seemed to accept Vito's explanation. I didn't feel so inclined. In previous meetings, I'd held my tongue. Not so this time.

"Mr. Martinelli," I said, "I see no reason why these risks you speak of shouldn't be spread more evenly. If the Feds are hampering your end of the operation to the detriment of profits, I suggest we consider an across-the-board price increase to cover any losses. I think that would be preferable to reducing the quality of the product delivered to our customers."

Martinelli's expression didn't change, but he stabbed me with a penetrating glance before turning his attention to the others.

"It sounds reasonable," Kalandris said. "If, as you say, all the suppliers are guilty of adulteration, our customers should not object to paying a bit more for uncut liquor."

Sofoclis nodded his affirmation.

"Maybe," Vito said, "you guys would like to take over the distribution."

"That hasn't been suggested," Kalandris said.

"Okay," Vito said. "I'll jack up the price to our regulars, give 'em good stuff and see how it goes." After a significant pause he added, "For a while."

A unilateral price increase by Martinelli was not, to me, an acceptable alternative. "What I suggest," I said, "is that we put the difference between our present warehouse price and the increases we agree upon into a fund that can be drawn upon wherever we encounter losses through disruption — such as if any of Mr. Martinelli's boys need bail money, or legal fees, or if we need to absorb losses incurred by confiscation by the Feds or through hijacking anywhere along the line. That's what I meant when I suggested an across-the-board price increase to spread the risks more evenly. I fully agree with you, Mr. Martinelli, that you shouldn't be expected to assume the lion's share of the risk without adequate compensation."

Vito looked at me from beneath drooping eyelids. He knew damn well that I was using blocking tactics, but the logic I had presented was hard to refute. For a full minute, he debated his answer. From his lack of expression, it was impossible to read his thoughts, but I could almost see the wheels turning in his head. If he didn't choose to go along with my suggestion, what the hell could we do about it? Sofoclis was the one with the contacts with the offshore suppliers. What we *might* do was reduce the inflow. If Vito couldn't meet the demand, whether with adulterated or unadulterated product, he would be opening the door to inroads by his competitors. As his response indicated, he must have considered that possibility.

"Yeah," Vito said, "a pool fund to cushion losses. Not a bad idea, kid. Wonder why none of the other mobs have thought of it. Okay, we'll play it your way for a few months to see how it works in practice."

I was under no illusions. The adulteration would continue in supply to all but the biggest and best customers — the ones big enough to voice complaints. At best, I had won a Pyrrhic victory. I had brought myself to his attention by serving notice that we were not as submissive as he'd thought. But he was far from happy with this development. I hoped I hadn't pushed too hard.

Penny was married to Omeros Kalandris in June. The Greek Orthodox ceremony was attended only by family and a few close friends. Phoebe came out from Los Angeles to act as maid of honor. Sofoclis was best man. I gave the bride away.

Following the ceremony, there was a reception at Omeros' Riverside Drive apartment. Omeros had wanted to hold it at the Waldorf Astoria, but Penny had vetoed the suggestion. She wanted it to be a more intimate gathering. As it was, it was a pretty splashy affair.

I stood a bit apart, surveying the scene. Penny, I thought, for all her plainness, made a radiant bride. Georgiana, who had been brought over at Kalandris' expense, and who would be staying at our Waverly Place apartment until a sailing booked for September, was beginning to put on weight but looked chic, though wistful. I caught much the same expression on Phoebe's face. Both of them must have been thinking that if Penny could find a man, there was hope for them. Mama, proud as punch that at least one of her daughters was safely married, looked absolutely queenly. How, I thought, was it possible for such a handsome woman as mother to produce such plain female offspring?

A good many of the guests were socialite friends of Kalandris, and strangers to me. Then I caught sight of an all-too-familiar face — that of Vito Martinelli. At his side was a petite, stunning blonde. She couldn't, I thought, be more than eighteen. She looked oddly out of place with Vito.

A short time later, I found myself standing close to Vito. He was seated in a corner by himself. He was engaged in clipping the end off a cigar with a gold cigar cutter. Glancing up, he saw me and smiled. "Quite a blowout," he said, letting his gaze slowly sweep the room. "The bride is your sister, isn't she?"

"Yes."

"Cigar, kid?" he said, holding out a pigskin cigar case.

"No, thank you. I don't smoke."

"Smart. My croaker tells me I should lay off 'em."

"Can I get you a drink?" I asked.

"Not at the moment, kid. The doc tells me that's also bad for me" — then, smiling broadly — "even the good stuff. Not easy advice to follow when you're in the business. I've already had a couple . . . and I'll down a few more. Feel a little out of place, not being Greek and not speaking your lingo."

"There aren't too many of us here that are Greek," I said.

"Enough," he said. "Damned if I know how a Sicilian ended up with so many Greek associates."

"At least," I said, smiling, "we're from the same general area."

"Yeah, that's right. So we are. Understand you came over from the Old Country only a couple of years ago."

"Four-and-a-half years ago."

"It didn't take you long to get the hang of things over here. What do you want?"

"What? I don't understand," I said.

"What're you aiming for? Everyone's got to have a goal in life."

I thought about it for a moment, then said, "To return to Greece one day . . . a rich and respected man."

Vito looked at me for a moment, his face expressionless. "You're smart, kid. You just might make it . . . if you don't try to move too fast."

At that moment, the blonde girl joined us. Vito favored her with a fond smile and rose to his feet. "My dear," he said, "I'd like you to meet a young associate of mine, Constantine Sthanassis. Mr. Sthanassis, my niece, Teresa Martinelli."

"Pleased to meet you, Mr. Sthanassis," she said, melting me with a smile.

I was flustered. Not only did her doll-like beauty unnerve me, but I was surprised that Vito knew my name. "My pleasure," I said awkwardly.

As I had guessed, Teresa was eighteen. She was an only child who lived with her parents in Brooklyn. Her father, Salvatore Martinelli, was not connected with the rackets.

It was some months before I learned all this — and not until October that we went out on our first date.

CHAPTER FOURTEEN

In September, Sofoclis came to me with a bright idea. Why not open a speakeasy of our own? By not being in on the retail end of the business we were letting an awful lot of profit slip through our fingers. After all, Martinelli and practically every 'legger and gangster in the business had interests in one or more clubs. Why not us?

Why not? But shouldn't we include Omeros Kalandris in the project? Sofoclis said that, since Omeros and Penny were enjoying a European cruise, we couldn't very well ask his opinion. Why not go ahead on our own and invite his participation on their return? It sounded like a sensible approach. I agreed to go ahead on that basis.

The location we picked was a brownstone in the East Fifties. It happened to be a property owned by Sofoclis, but in my name. We set about extensive remodeling and decorating. We spared no expense. What we had in mind was a ritzy establishment catering to the upper crust of New York society. The name I decided on was in keeping with our background. It was called the Apollo Club.

There was a lot more to getting the club ready for its opening than simply remodeling, decorating and hiring staff and entertainers. Little details like paying off precinct officers and cops on the beat and bribing the Feds to turn a blind eye had to be attended to. Before we were ready to open our doors — or, to be more precise, our peephole-installed, basement-level door — to a select public, the Apollo Club had become a very expensive operation.

We had an advantage over many club owners. Apart for meat, poultry and fish, all our foodstuff was provided by Metaxis & Company at cost, enabling us to offer superb cuisine at reasonable prices. And, of course, being in the business, we were assured of ample stocks of the finest wines, liquors and liqueurs.

Although Sofoclis made it a point to keep Vito advised of our progress, I was convinced there was no need for this. Angelo, I am sure, supplied that information on a regular basis.

By mid-December, the Apollo Club was ready for business. We threw a gala opening night for invited guests — all food and drink on the house. The timing was good. We were fully prepared for the holiday season rush. It surpassed our most optimistic expectations. The Apollo Club was an immediate success.

I was not so busy during those autumn months that personal matters escaped my attention.

Well before Georgiana's departure, I employed a young Greek girl named Aletha — a recent arrival from Lefkas — to act as mother's companion. She took over the bedroom Penny had vacated. Mother was delighted to have someone with whom she could gossip in her own tongue and treated Aletha like a daughter.

Teresa was much on my mind. Our meeting had been brief, but still she'd made quite an impression. To be honest, I don't quite know why she should have. Up until then, all the women to whom I'd been attracted had reminded me in one way or another of Danai. Between Teresa and Danai, there was no similarity whatsoever. It may have been that Teresa's dainty fragility brought out the protective instinct. It could have been — a lingering suspicion I didn't discount altogether — that she was Vito's niece. If there was one thing I was sure of, it was that Vito would not approve of me, a Greek bootlegger, as a potential escort for anyone of his blood. It presented me with a challenge.

It took me quite a few weeks to find out about Teresa. I learned, through various sources, where she lived, about her family background and, more through luck than enterprise, that she was an aspiring actress and was taking dancing and singing lessons. The unwitting source of this latter information was Angelo. On several occasions, he had had to pick her up after classes and escort her home to Brooklyn. He considered this an imposition and had complained about it to Sofoclis in my presence. Armed with that information, I laid my plans.

I made it appear that the meeting was accidental. To my delight, she remembered meeting me at Penny's wedding reception. I invited her to join me for a cup of coffee. From that innocent beginning, it was a simple matter to arrange something of a more formal nature.

It wasn't as simple as I'm making it sound. Her father felt she was too young to date and, in any event, wouldn't have approved of other than an Italian with impeccable credentials. Her Uncle Vittorio had stated in no uncertain terms that she wasn't to go out with anyone in his line of business. Discretion was called for. Deception was necessary.

I suggested a Broadway show. It was Teresa who evolved the scheme. She would say that she was going to the show with friends from her dancing class as part of the instructional program. I could meet her at the show, after which we could slip away for a quiet dinner before I sent her home by taxi.

It worked out well enough — at least from her viewpoint. On my part, I must admit it wasn't too satisfactory. But, at any rate, it was a beginning.

Thereafter, on one ingenious subterfuge or another, we managed to meet on a more or less regular basis. What kept my hopes alive was that, in the coming year, when she turned nineteen, her father had promised her more freedom — but reserved the right to pass judgement on her escorts. There were, we felt, a number of ways of getting around this sanction. Frustrating as it was, I was enjoying the game. I had yet to make love to her, but the promise was in her eyes and her hungry kisses. I was impatient, but I could wait.

Everything was running smoothly. The precautionary measure we had adopted had discouraged hijacking. It had been, up to late February, an easy winter. Our supply flow hadn't been disrupted by the weather or undue attention from the Feds. Martinelli's organization seemed to be immune from interference from law enforcement agencies. Kalandris' flower shops were bringing in a steadily increasing income as liquor outlets. The Apollo Club, under the able management of Emilio Traglatti, was coining money. All the indications were that 1925 was going to be our best year yet.

In the second week of March, the roof caved in.

It was a Wednesday night. Teresa and I had taken in a movie. I had driven her to within a few blocks of her house. We had done some heavy petting in the parked Ford before she had broken away with a gasp as she discovered how late it was. Humming a show tune, I had driven back across the bridge and uptown to the Apollo

Club, making one stop along the way, at the Côte d'Or on East 50th, to sip a quick drink and count heads to see how the competition was faring. The Côte d'Or was faring reasonably well, considering it was not yet twelve and the biggest crowds generally didn't start hitting the gin mills until after midnight. If the Apollo was doing this well, it would be a good night, and Wednesdays were normally slow.

The Apollo Club was doing better.

I settled myself at the table reserved for me on the raised semicircle facing the dance floor. Across the floor, I noticed Sofoclis, in evening dress, hosting a party of about eight or ten. I smiled thinly as I saw Angelo, seated by himself at a small table to the rear and slightly to the side of Sofoclis' table. Sofoclis appeared to be drunk. Undoubtedly Angelo was cold sober and, as usual, bored. As if to confirm that, he looked at his watch — and did so once again a few minutes later. It wouldn't do him much good to check the time. It looked as though Sofoclis was making a night of it.

I ordered a beer. When it arrived, so did Emilio, his normally bland face wearing a worried frown.

Emilio eased himself onto a chair at my side. "I don't like it, Mr. Sthanassis," he said.

"Don't like what?"

Emilio nodded in the direction of a table on the dance-floor level. I recognized Captain Rafferty and Lieutenant Betz of the local precinct. "Cops are human," I said. "Don't worry about them. They're on the payroll."

"Neither one of them has set foot in the place before tonight. I just don't like it."

I was beginning to feel Emilio's uneasiness. "Are they drinking?"

"If you can call it that," Emilio said. "They've been nursing two beers for the last half hour."

"How long have they been here?"

"Since just before midnight."

"Any other strange faces in the crowd?"

"Plenty . . . but none that didn't come in as guests of customers with membership cards."

Emilio and I both knew that didn't mean a thing. The cross-section of our so-called membership covered a broad spectrum. Their guests could be anyone — including federal agents. I nodded thoughtfully. "Okay, Emilio, *just in case* there's trouble brewing, start moving our best customers quietly out the back way. Tell 'em there's a possibility of a raid, but don't panic 'em. Whatever they've had up to now is on the house. And take all the waiters you can spare to shift the liquor stock to the cellar next door."

Emilio moved to set these precautionary measures in motion. I sat staring glumly at the two police officers some tables away.

On his return from his honeymoon, we had offered Kalandris part-ownership in the club. He had declined. What he had said at that time came back to me now: "Why be greedy? Owning and operating a speakeasy puts you right out there in the front lines. You're inviting touble. Not only do I not want *in* . . . I'd strongly advise you two to sell and get *out!*"

As I sat there, watching Emilio moving among the tables and getting an orderly exodus under way, Kalandris' words took on the ring of dire Delphic prophecy. His had been sound advice that, of course, we'd not heeded. Well, I thought, struggling with resignation, it was a bit late in the day to think of that. And there was a good possibility that Emilio — experienced clubman that he was — was overreacting to the presence of the two off-duty police officers.

Only Emilio hadn't overreacted — and Rafferty and Betz were not off duty.

I had left my table and sauntered over to a vantage point close to the entranceway end of the bar when trouble struck with a capital "T." I'll have to admit that it was all done smoothly.

Two men at the checkroom, ostensibly picking up checked coats and hats, turned abruptly and stood blocking the small foyer. Another man walked calmly onto the stage. Taking the microphone from the master of ceremonies, the man announced that this was a raid and that everyone should avoid panic and stay where they were. Among the tables men, obviously agents, stood and began issuing crisp orders. I counted eight of them, including Rafferty and Betz. In the foyer, one of the men guarding the exit opened the door to let in a stream of uniformed cops.

Then all hell broke loose at the table where Sofoclis and his guests sat. It happened so fast that, even though I had a relatively unobstructed view, the details are still vague.

I heard Sofoclis bellow with rage. I saw a man, I think it was Betz, fall backward over the low railing and land sprawling among the diners below. Several men moved in to pin Sofoclis' arms to his sides. Then there was the unmistakable sound of a gun shot. One of the men attempting to restrain Sofoclis slumped to the floor. I caught a glimpse of Angelo, a smoking automatic in his hand

and a look of grim satisfaction on his face. Then the club erupted into a babble of shouts and screams as people milled about in confusion.

There wasn't anything I could do about the situation, so I took advantage of the confusion to slip behind the hanging drapes, go to the elevator we'd installed, ride up to the third floor and, through the back of a closet in one of the bedrooms, escape into the vacant adjoining brownstone, which was also registered in my name.

Through a grime-filmed upstairs window, I watched the scene unfolding in the street below. Patrons of the club, club staff and entertainers were being unceremoniously herded into the police vans parked alongside the curb. I had no difficulty identifying Sofoclis, but nowhere could I locate Angelo.

When the police drove off and the crowd of curious spectators had been dispersed by cops left behind to make sure the club stayed closed, I groped my way downstairs in the darkened brownstone and let myself out into the alleyway.

CHAPTER FIFTEEN

The maid let me in on the fourth ring. I paced the floor in the sitting room until Omeros, bleary-eyed, tousle-haired and unmistakably annoyed at having been wakened from a sound sleep at two o'clock in the morning, joined me. He became considerably more alert as he listened to my recap of the proceding hour's events.

Omeros uncrossed his matchstick-like legs and pulled the dressing gown closer around his knobby knees. "By now," he said, "Sofoclis will have contacted his lawyer. However, just in case, I'd better put through a call to make sure someone's on hand to post bail. What worries me, though, is his hitting a policeman — that, and the senseless shooting."

"Goddamn him," I said. "From the look on his face, I swear that trigger-happy Dago enjoyed shooting that cop."

"Are you sure it was a policeman?"

"That, or a Fed. What's the difference?"

"It could make quite a difference. Was he killed?"

"I didn't stick around to find out."

Omeros trotted off to his study to make the phone call. On returning, he said, "We won't be able to get Sofoclis out until morning. He faces an assault charge and is being held as an accessory in an attempted murder. From that, I gather the victim wasn't killed. We can thank God for that. But it looks like quite a mess, killing or no killing. There's a warrant out for your arrest."

"My arrest? I haven't done anything!"

"You own the house. The club's in your name. You'll be charged with running an illegal drinking establishment. Apart from that, they know you were in the club and want you as a material witness. My advice is that you not return to your apartment. Check into a hotel under an assumed name. Then phone me to let me know where you are."

I registered at the Iroquois Hotel as Stanley Constantine. Not very imaginative but, in my agitated state, it was the best that came to mind. I telephoned Omeros to let him know where I was, steamed myself in a hot bath and turned in. It was close to dawn when I finally dropped off into a troubled sleep.

I was still asleep at eleven-thirty when a knock on the hotel room door awakened me. For a moment, I didn't know where I was. Then memory flooded back, and I sat bolt upright. "Yes," I said, "who is it?"

A muffled reply came through the door. "Omeros."

I let him in. He was alone. He was carrying a suitcase that I recognized as one of mine. He placed it beside the door and seated himself facing the bed.

"How's Sofoclis?" I asked.

"Fine. They released him on bail a couple of hours ago. He'll have to stand trial, but the lawyer is sure he can get him off with a stiff fine."

I breathed a sigh of relief. "That might teach the big ape a lesson. Make him cut down on his drinking and keep his fists in his pockets. What about Angelo? I hope they locked him up and threw away the key."

"If they could find him, they might do just that. During the melee in the club, he got away. He's disappeared."

"Jesus," I said. "How could they let the one really guilty party in this mix-up give them the slip?"

Omeros shot me an odd look. "They did. But I have more bad news. Last night the Feds also raided the Metaxis warehouse in Jersey City. The Apollo Club is padlocked. They confiscated the liquor found on the premises in Jersey City, and the warehouse is closed pending Bureau of Internal Revenue investigation."

"I warned Sofoclis," I said, holding my head in my hands. "Damn him. He wouldn't listen."

"I know. He told me this morning that he should have listened to you instead of Vito."

"Vito? How does he figure in this?"

"I'm very much afraid that he is the key figure," Omeros said. "The raids weren't launched to get at Sofoclis or me. They were out to get *you*. The police and the federal agents acted on information supplied by an informant. The informant was Vito. The shooting in the club last night was no accident. Angelo was acting on Vito's orders. The idea was to make the club look bad, to lend weight to the charges brought against you as owner of the club. Frankly, when you described the incident to me this morning, I was suspicious. At that range, if he'd been shooting to kill, Angelo couldn't have missed. By the way, it was Rafferty who was wounded. Nothing serious. A flesh wound. But having a police officer shot in a club registered under your name is something that can't be lightly shrugged off. In short, Kostas, Vito was setting you up."

Mouth agape, I stared at Omeros in disbelief. "Why? How did you find this out?"

"As I said, it just didn't smell right. The Jersey City warehouse raid convinced me that there was more to it than just an attempt to close down the Apollo Club. So, this morning, I made some discreet inquiries. I have some pretty powerful friends in City Hall. Reluctantly, they gave me the answers I needed. I'm afraid, Kostas, that you're in deep trouble."

"How? I've kept pretty much in the background. Putting the club in my name was just a matter of convenience, since I owned the brownstone. As for Jersey City, it's a Metaxis & Company warehouse. I'm merely an employee."

"An employee who just happens to be in sole charge of warehouse operations. To keep the company from landing in serious difficulties, Sofoclis will have to claim ignorance of illegal activities and place the blame on your shoulders. He really hasn't much choice in the matter. You can see that, can't you?"

"Yes," I said. "So that makes *me* the fall guy. What can they do to me other than stiff fines?"

"You're forgetting one important detail. You're not yet an American citizen. Yes, you'll face heavy fines but, in addition, a prison sentence and deportation as an undesirable alien. Probably all three. Vito wants you put out of circulation for a long, long time."

"You haven't answered my first question. Why?"

"I think you know the answer to that. Vito found out that you've been dating his favorite niece. He's furious. To be perfectly frank, I don't know why he's gone to all this trouble to frame you instead of just having you rubbed out. I think the answer must be that it's better for you to appear as a deported criminal than a dead martyr. I think that consideration is the only thing that's saved your life."

"What can I do about it?" I asked.

"Sofoclis and I have discussed it. We believe that to give yourself up at this stage would be to invite disaster. We feel the best thing is for you to stay in hiding until things cool down . . . until we can talk some sense into Vito, if that's possible. You haven't gotten the girl pregnant, have you?''

"Hell, no. I haven't even made love to her."

"Well, in that case, when Vito simmers down, we should be able to bring him around to a more reasonable point of view. I certainly hope so, for your sake as well as hers. I imagine that life at home isn't going to be too pleasant for her."

"Okay. I'll accept your advice and keep out of sight as long as possible. But I can't stay cooped up here in this damned hotel room."

"That's true. Sofoclis is exploring an angle he thinks will solve the problem. He can't contact you himself. He's sure he's being followed by some of Vito's torpedoes. So far, we don't think the surveillance extends to me, but I'm sure it will before the day is out. I don't think that it will be safe to phone in or out through the hotel switchboard. Someone identifying himself with the word 'Apollo' will contact you personally when we have the details worked out."

"When is that likely to be?" I asked.

"I'm not sure. I hope no later than this evening. If not, sometime tomorrow at the latest. You can't afford to stay here *too* long." He nodded toward the suitcase. "Penny went over to visit your mother this morning. To explain your absence, and to keep her from worrying, Penny said you had to go to the West Coast on unexpected business. She picked up a few things she thought you'd need. And, in case you run short, there's an envelope containing some money tucked in under your shirts."

Omeros seemed to have thought of everything. It was comforting to know that I had him and Sofoclis solidly behind me.

All through the afternoon I fretted and fumed. I examined my predicament from every angle to see if there was something Omeros had overlooked. I couldn't think of anything — nor any alternative course of action to the one he'd suggested. And he was right. It was a miracle I wasn't lying at the bottom of the Hudson River, my feet encased in cement.

I phoned down and had dinner sent to my room. While I was toying with the food, my thoughts were on Sofoclis. Whatever trouble he was in stemmed from my idiotic infatuation. Well, he wasn't faced with anything like the dilemma confronting me. I wondered what sort of a scheme he had devised to protect me from the police — or Vito's — bloodhounds. I didn't have long to wait.

I had finished my meal and was pushing the table out into the hallway when I noticed a dapper little man several doors down the hall. He was peering myopically at the room numbers as he advanced toward me. When he reached me, he glanced at the number on my opened door, then brightened.

"Mr. Apollo?" he asked.

"Yes."

"I'm from the Panamanian Consulate. I was told to deliver this to you personally." He reached into his briefcase and pulled out a sealed manila envelope.

Then the little man scurried off toward the elevator. Examining the envelope curiously, I went back into my room and closed the door.

Inside the envelope was a letter of instruction from Omeros, another bulky envelope containing ten thousand dollars in greenbacks and an official-looking document certifying that Constantine Sthanassis was a fully qualified second officer in the Panamanian merchant service. It bore a photograph of me that I recognized as one that I had given Penny some months ago. It also bore stamps and seals of the Panamanian Consulate attesting to the certificate's authenticity.

The instructions were explicit. At nine o'clock sharp, a cab would be in front of the hotel to pick up a Mr. Apollo. After changing taxis twice at specified points along the way, I would find a speedboat waiting for me in a cove near Amityville. The speedboat would run me out beyond the three-mile limit to a waiting coastal freighter of Panamanian registry, the SS *Pandora*. The master of the *Pandora* would sign me on the ship's articles as second mate.

I glanced from the letter of instruction to the second mate's ticket. I chuckled. Trust Sofoclis to turn to his seagoing suppliers for a solution to my dilemma. Long before the dawn streaked tomorrow's sky, I would be safely out of reach of city, state and federal law enforcement agencies — yet still well within sight of Long Island.

CHAPTER SIXTEEN

The captain's name was Timothy Driscoll. I was taken directly to his cabin as soon as I'd boarded the *Pandora*.

He examined my Panamanian second mate's certificate perfunctorily, then laid it on the cluttered top of his rolltop desk. "At least," he said, "it's your photo. For twenty dollars, that greaser would issue a deep sea certificate to an Airedale."

I smiled, but the captain's next question removed all humor from the situation.

"I suppose," he said, "it would be asking too much to expect you to have any of the qualifications this ticket implies."

"I . . . ah . . ," I mumbled, then lapsed into embarrassed silence. It hadn't even crossed my mind that seagoing experience might be expected of me.

"Thought not," he said. "A bloody passenger. Too bad. The supply of qualified deck officers falls far short of the demand. The mate and I have been standing watch-on and watch-off for over six months. Bloody tiring."

"I've put in three years on a fishing boat in the Ionian Sea," I said.

The creases at the sides of the captain's eyes deepened in mild amusement. "Better than nothing, Mister Sthanassis, better than nothing. If you stay with us long enough, you might even earn that ticket."

I'd been so relieved at being snatched, as it were, from the clutches of the law that I hadn't been thinking clearly. I don't know what gave me the idea that we would remain near Long Island. Within half an hour of my embarkation, we were under way on a southerly heading, our destination Havana, Cuba.

It didn't strike me until the next morning that if Martinelli's objective had been to make me inaccessible to his beloved niece, he had achieved his purpose admirably. With each turn of the screw, the distance between Teresa and me widened. Of course, as a member of the ship's company of a rumrunner, I could expect to lay off Long Island at relatively frequent intervals. The question was, when? Captain Driscoll had made mention of the fact that this time in Havana we would have to have engine repairs, a boiler clean and a general overhaul. He hadn't indicated how long this would take.

Captain Driscoll had been a mariner since boyhood. He was a Newfoundlander from Port aux Basques. The chief officer was a quick-tempered Cuban, Francisco "Pancho" Lopez. The chief engineer, Andy McCurdy, was a Canadian, hailing from Yarmouth, Nova Scotia. All the rest of the ship's company — the seamen and stokers — were Panamanians, Colombians, Venezuelans, but mainly Cubans.

The language spoken on board the *Pandora* was, for the most part, Spanish. At the outset, this didn't concern me much. I didn't expect my stay aboard the vessel to be lengthy, and most of my conversations were with either Captain Driscoll or Chief Engineer McCurdy. Later, when it dawned on me that I would be aboard much longer than I had anticipated, I made an effort to learn Spanish. Being Greek and having a reasonable command of Italian, I found Spanish not too difficult to pick up — although much of the vocabulary I mastered was not exactly suited to polite society. It was more than adequate, however, to meet my shipboard needs and to serve me in good stead in the bars and whorehouses of Havana and Colón.

My position on board the *Pandora* was something of an anomaly. On the one hand, I was a paying passenger. On the other, I was signed on as second mate, if only to meet the requirements of the insurance underwriters. As time went on — as the weeks stretched into months — Captain Driscoll was as good as his word, and I became a deck officer in fact as well as fiction. Of course this didn't happen overnight. As he had said, I would earn my ticket. Not only that, but I also earned, and was duly paid, the salary that was shown on the books and, additionally, a share of the profits from each voyage. The latter was no mean sum. An offshore rumrunner operated at a handsome profit and at virtually no risk other than from the weather, providing he kept outside the three-mile limit.

When he had said that he and the mate stood watch-on, watch-off, the captain had been guilty of a slight exaggeration. The bosun, even though he had no watchkeeping ticket, stood most of the eight-to-twelve morning and evening watches. In consequence, even though I was being instructed in pilotage, navigation, rules of the road and cargo stowage by the captain and chief officer, during my mornings on the bridge I came to know the bosun. He was a Colombian named Enrique Ramirez. It was he who encouraged me to learn Spanish. In time, we became friends.

But, once again, I'm guilty of jumping ahead of myself.

Cuba game me an introduction to tropical climes. On the first visit, I had time to explore the countryside close to Havana, as well as to come to know something of the port city itself. The boiler clean, repairs and general overhaul occupied the better part of three weeks, during most of which the crew lived ashore while the vessel was in shipyard hands. Pancho Lopez, a native of Cienfuegos, took advantage of the layover to visit his family. I have no idea where Captain Driscoll stayed, but it couldn't have been far from the shipyard since he spent a good part of each weekday checking on the ongoing work. The crew, those who weren't Cuban, were billeted in a waterfront hotel. That left me more or less on my own. I had yet to be accepted by either the officers or the crew as one of their number — nor, at that stage of our association, had I any particular wish for the pleasure of their company.

I rented a room in a tourist hotel and settled down to enjoy what I considered to be a well-earned vacation. I made it a practice to wend my way to the shipyard every few days to check on the progress being made. Actually, I knew very little about what was being done, but it seemed to me that, whatever it was, the work was proceeding at a snail's pace.

My stay in the Cuban capital was enjoyable. After the hustle and bustle of New York, I found the leisurely pace of Cuban life a welcome change. The lissome mulatto women were a delight to the eye and the senses. One of my chief pleasures during that visit was to seek out the white-sand beaches and swim lazily in the warm waters of the Caribbean.

Had it not been for my uncertainty and concern over what was happening in New York during my absence, I would have found the weeks spent in Havana one of the most pleasurable interludes of my life. As it was, however, as the shipyard work was completed and the crew and officers returned to their shipboard quarters, I was increasingly anxious to be done with the cargo loading and be off. When at last, in mid-April, we nosed through the narrow entrance to the harbor into the open sea, I experienced a sense of relief and a thrill of anticipation.

Had I known then the news awaiting me, I might not've been so anxious to leave Havana.

After stops along the way to rendezvous with flotillas of small craft and to off-load cargo off the coasts of Florida, the Carolinas and Virginia, early in May we lay at last off Long Island. My suitcase packed, I waited impatiently in the waist of the vessel for word from shore, confident that I would slip ashore under cover of darkness the same way I had arrived on board. I had made my good-byes to Captain Driscoll and Andy McCurdy. That the former had given me a strange look had not registered on me as having any particular significance.

Shortly after nightfall, a boat came alongside, and I recognized the figure awkwardly climbing the swaying Jacob's ladder as Sofoclis. I hadn't laid eyes on him since that fateful night at the Apollo Club. I was happy to see him and immensely relieved that he hadn't ended up behind bars.

When he stepped aboard, I grabbed his hand and pumped it, grinning like an idiot. Then, as I saw his morose expression, my grin faded, and I released his hand. "What's the matter?" I asked.

"Bad news, Kostas. Is there someplace where we can talk privately?"

When we were in my cabin, Sofoclis sitting stiffly in my only chair and myself perching tensely on the bunk, I asked, "Well?"

Sofoclis cleared his throat. "It's not safe for you to come back to town . . . not yet. Omeros and I feel you should stay out of sight a bit longer."

"Why? *You* don't seem to be in trouble. Surely things have cooled off enough by now for me to go back to work — even if I still face questioning and possible fines. Surely, by now, Vito must know that Teresa's precious virginity remains intact. Why the hell should I remain in hiding?"

Sofoclis looked uncomfortable. "It isn't just Teresa, as we originally thought . . . although Vito is still mad as hell about that. It's something more serious."

"To a Sicilian," I said, "what could be more serious?"

"Business."

"What the hell are you talking about? I haven't stepped on Vito's toes in any business dealings."

"You have, but you might not remember it. It's about the Apollo Club. When Omeros got back from his honeymoon, do you remember the policy meeting we had, the one Vito attended?"

"Yes."

"It was you who proposed that we supply the club directly from warehouse stock, instead of going through Vito's distribution setup."

"Sure. We had an argument about it. He calmed down when I assured him he would still get his cut from the warehouse price. I guaranteed that we would not undercut any pricing he quotes to gin mills in which he has an interest. He agreed to that arrangement."

"He agreed, but he didn't like it. Then, sometime in January or February, he heard something that angered him so much he still can't talk about it without getting red in the face. You told someone that dealing directly with our warehouse instead of going through Vito was the only way we could be assured of receiving unadulterated liquor at the Apollo Club."

I stared at Sofoclis in astonishment. That had been my chief reason for wanting to supply our club directly. But, to the best of my recollection, I had never discussed that aspect with anyone other than Sofoclis and Omeros. If anyone had let slip a remark of that nature, it was much more likely to have been Sofoclis than me. Still, if Vito believed the statement had been mine, there was no use protesting my innocence — and nothing to be gained by accusing Sofoclis of the indiscretion.

"So," I said flatly, "he took the rumor as a personal insult. Is that it?"

"Yes. He wants you out . . . all the way out. He admitted to us that if Teresa hadn't been mixed up in it, he'd have had you put out of the way permanently. As a matter of fact, neither Omeros nor I am convinced that if he feels it can be kept from Teresa, he still won't have you bumped off. That's why we feel you should stay out of sight and keep as far away from the operation as possible."

"Am I supposed to rot away on board this stinking tub?"

"Well . . . for a while it seems like the best hideout. Yes, I think you should stay here until we can think of something else. Can you think of a better place?"

"No," I said, "offhand I can't. Okay, I'll stick it out here for another few months. But what about you? What's been happening while I've been away?"

"The club's been shuttered for good. I'm trying to sell the fixtures. I've unloaded the liquor stocks and most of the furniture, but we took a beating. I've paid off the fines, which were pretty heavy. As for you, thanks to Vito's unrelenting political pressure, you're still very much wanted by the police. As for the Jersey City warehouse, I paid a fine and squirmed off the hook by blaming you for any illegal activities that took place there without my knowledge or approval. Omeros said you were already in so much trouble with the law that making you the fall guy wouldn't make much difference."

I nodded. "You did the right thing. But I suppose that means that, when I *do* get off this ship, I haven't got a job to go back to. Vito wanted me out, so I'm out. Is that it?"

"Not exactly," Sofoclis said. "We can't show you on the books of Metaxis & Company — and you certainly can't put in an appearance at any meeting including Vito — but, as far as Omeros and I are concerned, you're still entitled to your share of our profits. While you're away, your share will be deposited in your bank account."

"Generous of you," I said, then changed the subject. "Omeros was of the opinion that life would be difficult for Teresa because of me. Have you heard anything about that?"

Sofoclis brightened. "In return for her promise that she wouldn't see you again, Vito agreed that you wouldn't be harmed. Last month, when she turned nineteen she and her mother went to Los Angeles at Vito's expense. He's using his influence to get her into the movies."

I snorted. "I lose out all down the line."

Sofoclis made no comment.

"How are mother and Penny? Penny is going to have to invent a better story than she did to explain my lengthy absence."

"Penny's okay," Sofoclis said, "but your mother hasn't been so well."

Alarm gripped me. "What's wrong?"

"We had a cold snap at the end of March — it lasted almost a week. Somehow, your mother picked up a bad cold that turned into bronchitis. She still has a bad cough, but now that we're into spring weather, Aletha and Penny feel she should improve rapidly."

"Look, Sofoclis," I said, "It's all very well for me to keep out of circulation for a while, but I want to know what's happening. There must be some way I can be kept informed of things like mother's illness. The *Pandora* has a ship's radio. She has regular ports of call in the Caribbean and Nova Scotia. If there's anything you feel I should know about, for God's sake keep in touch by letter or, in an emergency, contact me by radio.'

In a way, I'm sorry that I brought radio communication to Sofoclis' attention. We were well out to sea, about midway between Boston and Yarmouth, Nova Scotia, when the message reached me that mother had developed pneumonia and been rushed to the hospital but had died a day later.

There was absolutely nothing I could do about it. I couldn't even attend the funeral. Could I have done anything to prevent the tragedy had I been on hand in New York? I imagine not, but that did little to ease the guilt I felt at the time.

CHAPTER SEVENTEEN

If, when I joined the SS *Pandora* in March 1925 with my meaning-less, though authentic, seafaring credentials, anyone had suggested that I would remain a ship's officer for close to five years, I would have scoffed at them. Had someone told me that I would become almost as fluent in Spanish as I was in English and ultimately assume command as the master of the vessel, I would have thought he had taken leaves of his senses. Yet that is exactly what happened.

She was a sound ship, admirably suited to her purpose. She was a small coaster of fifteen hundred tons' burden, built in Holland in 1908. Prior to the advent of Prohibition in the States, she had been engaged in interisland trade in the Caribbean. Then, when supplying liquor to the thirsty country loomed as a lucrative enterprise, she was purchased by a group of American businessmen, refitted and put into service as a rumrunner.

Her clanking reciprocating engines could, if pressed, deliver upward of eleven knots. For the most part, we rarely exceeded a cruising speed of eight knots. As long as we remained on the high seas — outside the territorial limits of United States' waters — the vessel was immune from seizure and had no need of a greater turn of speed. Of course, if we were foolish enough to venture inside the three-mile limit, the ship was subject to seizure and her crew to arrest.

As Captain Driscoll informed me, the *Pandora,* like all vessels engaged in similar activities, was well-known to the U.S. Navy and U.S. Coast Guard. At least her officer complement, if not her individual crew members, was on a list of wanted men. From the moment I signed on as second officer, this distinction applied to me. So, not only was I wanted to face charges for operating an illegal club and for storing contraband in the Jersey City warehouse, my problems were compounded by this additional felony. The moment I set foot in the United States, I would be a fugitive from justice.

At first this caused me a good deal of concern. I had gotten myself exiled from the land of opportunity of my youthful dreams. Gradually, however, my concern diminished. I consoled myself with the knowledge that the money I had earned was safely banked in New York, and if Sofoclis and Omeros were protecting my interests as Sofoclis had indicated, my bank balance would continue to grow. In the booming American economy, my investments in property and securities were increasing in value with each passing day. And my wages as a ship's officer, together with the bonus share I received from the profits, were not to be sneezed at. As matters stood, I had little reason to complain.

New York no longer attracted me now that mother was gone. Even Teresa, who might have lured me back, was no longer there to tempt me. I missed New York and its exciting vitality, but not nearly so much as I thought I would. From times of misty antiquity, we Greeks have been drawn to the sea as to a magnet.

Timothy Driscoll was a crusty old sea dog of very few words. Taciturn and demanding though he was, I found myself drawn to him, and a bond of mutual trust and friendship developed between us.

From the beginning, he devoted a good deal of time to teaching me the mysteries of navigation and pilotage. I think that much of his interest in me stemmed from the fact that he knew, as I didn't, that my stay aboard his ship would be longer than I thought. Then, too, I spoke English and, like him, had served my apprenticeship as a fisherman. As a boy, he had learned his trade on a Grand Banks fishing schooner.

I learned a good deal more from Captain Driscoll than a mastery of navigation, pilotage or indeed, ship-handling, seamanship and the stowage and working of cargo. My introduction to the sea had been in the relatively sheltered waters of the Ionian Sea where storms, though often violent, bore little relationship to those of the restless North Atlantic. Driscoll knew, loved and had a healthy respect for this sometimes peaceful, but more often threatening, ocean. From him I learned to share that respect and to face the raging sea, if not without fear, at least with the confidence of the capabilities of both myself and my ship. He taught me neither to underestimate nor to overestimate either quality.

To Driscoll, the *Pandora* was a good deal more than an object crafted of iron, wood, steel and brass. She was a living creature who should be pampered, cajoled and, sometimes under severe stress, subjected to harsh discipline. He looked on the sea, as well, as a living being of many moods and tempers. I've never forgotten his words: "A man who loses his fear of the sea and treats it with contempt is a fool who will not long survive its wrath." Or yet again: "A man is never closer to God than he is when facing the fury of the elements. A man who does not pray during a storm at sea is a man doomed to damnation and a watery grave."

Driscoll lived by his code. Often, during a storm, when the mountainous waves devoured our bow, thundered over the break of the forecastle, crashed against the bridge housing and rushed aft in frothing torrents, he would take over the helm himself. Hour after hour he would stand there, legs spread wide to brace himself against the roll, eyes slit, a half-smile on his lips, his hands firm on the spokes of the wheel and the muscles of his forearms knotted. At times, when we plunged into a yawning trough, or rolled almost onto our beam ends, I would see his lips move in silent prayer. But his face never lost its calm. At such times, I tasted fear — but I doubt that he did.

When he sensed from the feel of the helm that the storm had eased, the captain would return the wheel to the helmsman, fish his pipe from his pocket and light it, then leave the bridge without a word.

Had we simply plied the coastal waters between Cuba and Nova Scotia, a distance of some two thousand miles, we could have completed the return voyage in about three weeks. However, we often called in at the Bahamas and Bermuda to take on additional cargo, and our off-loading stops were frequent and time-consuming. Rarely did we complete a return voyage in less than six weeks, and then only when we had consistently favorable weather.

Very often we would have to sit offshore at a rendezvous point for days on end, waiting for the seas to moderate so that the small craft could come alongside and take on cargo without fear of being swamped or losing the cargo through mishandling. We rigged scrambling nets and hand lines along the cargo-working side, the lee provided by working our engines at dead slow speed to keep us broadside to the wind. We provided rattan fenders at the waterline. Our seamen were skilled at lowering the laden cargo nets. But this exercise, at best a difficult operation, was made all the more complicated in that it had to be carried out in the dark, or in the half-light of dawn or dusk. It was exhausting work for all hands aboard the *Pandora* and dangerous work indeed for those who manned the craft taking on the cargo.

To me, it seemed a minor miracle that so little cargo was lost due to accidents. But this, I was to learn, did not hold true for most rumrunners. On the *Pandora,* we refused to allow a boat alongside until Captain Driscoll judged the conditions to be such that they afforded a minimum of risk. Other rumrunners, less particular or experienced, worked cargo under hazardous conditions, often resulting not only in the loss of cargo but also in the loss of boats and men as well. It was a matter of pride to Captain Driscoll, and at a later date to me, that the *Pandora* enjoyed an enviable safety record and a bare minimum of cargo loss.

That I rose from an unqualified seaman to master of the *Pandora,* even given the shortage of experienced officers, was something of a miracle.

At Captain Driscoll's insistence, I had sat for and passed my qualifying exams for chief officer, in Halifax, Nova Scotia. At that time, I was not considering the sea as a career, nor did I expect to remain on board the *Pandora* much longer, even though I had long since ceased to be a paying passenger and had been, for close to two years, a fully employed and accepted ship's officer. Sofoclis had written to advise me that the charges against me with respect to the Apollo Club had been dropped, though I still would have to face charges concerning the Jersey City operations. Also, Teresa, under the screen name of Tess Martin, had had a minor role in a recent motion picture and her name was being linked romantically with that of a prominent actor. If, Sofoclis had stated, she had been a virgin on her arrival in Los Angeles, the odds were heavily stacked against her being one now. The only major stumbling block, then, to my returning to New York was my present status as a ship's officer of a rumrunner. There must be, I thought, some way to overcome that problem. So it had been more to humor Captain Driscoll than through any desire to advance myself in the merchant marine that I had sat for the Board of Trade's exams.

When I had joined the vessel, by any standard one cared to apply I was already a wealthy young man. Since then, my savings had increased by the money I had deposited in my account with the Havana branch of my New York bank. The wise thing to do now would be to liquidate my holdings, withdraw my savings and invest in a business of my own. If I was barred from the United States, did it really matter? There was nothing to prevent me from establishing myself in business elsewhere.

Actually, though I had mentioned it to no one, I had been thinking about this for several months and was in the process of exploring several attractive propositions in Cuba. One was the purchase of a controlling interest in a small rum distillery. A second was a sugar plantation. A third was a chance to buy a coastal freighter that was coming up for auction. She would, if I could swing the deal and cover the cost of a refit through borrowing, be well suited to rumrunning. If I was going to stick with the sea, it might as well be as a shipowner, even one whose vessel was mortgaged to the gunnels. The latter was a risky proposition, but I knew the profit to be made in this business.

It was while I was debating which project to pursue that the Fates stepped in to postpone my final decision.

It took place in a bar-cum-brothel a few blocks from the Prado. It was a favorite haunt of many of the *Pandora*'s crew members, including myself.

To this day I don't know how the fight started. Ramirez told me later that someone had insulted Pancho Lopez' lady and that Pancho had reacted, as he usually did, violently. All I know for sure is that one minute I was sitting sipping my beer and that the next minute I was hit behind the ear and was sprawled, stunned and bleeding, at the feed of Mercedes, my current mulatto mistress.

My memory from then on is confused. I remember staggering to my feet, dodging a knife thrust and ending up with my back to the bar, a bottle in my hand. I recall seeing Lopez off to my left, shouting as he went down in a welter of thrashing bodies. Then, I must have smashed the bottle against the edge of the bar because I remember holding it, jagged fragments extended toward the knife-wielding assailant who lunged toward me.

I have a vague recollection of the arcing knife-blade catching the light, and a much clearer vision of the broken end of the bottle slashing into a face. Then someone, or something, struck me from behind, and I went blank.

When I came to, I was in Mercedes' room. A doctor was working on my scalp wounds. While I had still been unconscious, he had attended to the stitching and dressing of the knife wound that had laid open my face from cheekbone to jawline.

I must have been a sorry sight. Although I don't recall having been struck there, one eye was swollen and almost shut. I was swathed in bandages from the neck up. Blood matted my hair and had soaked my shirt and trousers. I found out later that Ramirez had helped Mercedes get me up to her room and then had gone to fetch the doctor. Then he had made his way back to the ship to break the news of my injuries — and to advise the captain that the barroom brawl had cost Pancho Lopez his life.

Since by then I was qualified in all respects to fill the billet, I moved up to the position of chief officer. Enrique Ramirez was elevated to acting second mate and was confirmed in that rank three months later when he sat for, and passed, his qualifying exams.

Although I had not changed my mind about following a career at sea, I served as first mate of the *Pandora* for nineteen months and, during that time, again at the prompting of Captain Driscoll, sat for and passed my Board of Trade qualifying exam as ship's master. On the face of it, if I had not altered my intention to go into business for myself, that doesn't make much sense. But to me, at that particular time, it seemed the most sensible course to adopt as a temporary measure. In all honesty, however, I'm not quite sure how I defined the "temporary" qualification.

It was a matter of vanity. I looked upon the knife scar on my left cheek as an intolerable disfigurement. The scar itself was bad enough, but what I found even more disturbing was the fact that the wound had damaged some facial muscles. The disarming smile on which I had so long prided myself had acquired a sinister quality.

I should not have been so sensitive about my appearance. The fact remains that I was and, when ashore, was convinced that people were staring at me. It was a feeling that persisted long after the scar had healed and the discoloration had faded to a thin white line running from just below the outer corner of my left eye to a point just below the left side of my mouth. So, for some time, I spent very little time ashore. On the ship, the crew regarded my scar as a badge of honor.

Quite simply, I used my disfigurement as an excuse to put off venturing into uncharted waters. The *Pandora,* already a sanctuary from prosecution, had become a refuge for my wounded pride.

I suppose it is one of the reasons that I accepted Captain Driscoll's suggestion to study and sit for my master's certificate — even though I never expected to command a ship of my own.

Of course, when Driscoll made the suggestion, I had no way of knowing what he had in mind.

CHAPTER EIGHTEEN

It was a hot morning in early June. We were in Barbados topping up cargo with rum. Capless and stripped to the waist, I stood by the hatch combing, keeping an eye on the stevedores stowing the cased rum in the semi-gloom of the tweendecks. I didn't hear Ramirez approach.

Ramirez tapped me on the arm. "I'll watch the thieving *hijos de putas*," he said. "Cap'n wants you on the bridge."

"Problems?"

"Don't know. Just said he wanted to see you."

Captain Driscoll was on the offshore wing of the bridge. He turned to face me, but his expression gave me no clue as to the reason for his summons.

"You wanted to see me sir?" I asked.

"Aye, Mister Sthanassis, that I did. I have some news that I think will interest you. I've just received word from the agents that the owners have accepted my resignation . . . and agreed to my recommendation that you assume command."

I received the news in stunned silence. It was totally unexpected. At no time had he as much as hinted of any such plans. My astonishment must have been evident.

"You're wondering why I've said nothing about my intention to retire."

"Well . . . yes. I'm afraid you've caught me off balance."

Driscoll smiled. "Why do you think I nagged and prodded you into getting a master's ticket?"

True, he *had* pressured me, but it simply hadn't crossed my mind that he was contemplating retirement — or had me in mind as his successor. "Your suggestion was that, even if I never commanded a ship, a master's ticket was a valuable asset. It didn't enter my head that you could have had any other reason."

"Hmm. Maybe I *should* have said something sooner, but it's long been a superstition of mine that discussing plans before their fulfillment is to tempt fate and invite disaster."

"Your recommendations must carry a good deal of weight with the owners," I said. "They know me only through what you've told them. I've never met any of them . . . at least not that I know of."

"Nor have I," Driscoll said, to my surprise. "Not the present owners, that is. Since they bought the *Pandora* from the Duarte family seven years ago, my only communication with the new owners has been through our Havana agents, Rodriguez y Cia. Still, there's no reason why they shouldn't accept my advice with regard to the ship or its complement. We've earned them a tidy profit over the last few years. My suggestion was that, under your command, they could expect the *Pandora* to show better profits than any of their five other rumrunners."

We were fortunate. In Halifax, a young officer who had apprenticed with a British shipping company signed on the *Pandora* as second mate. So, when I took over command in late July in that Canadian port city, we weren't shorthanded, as I'd feared would be the case.

Captain Sthanassis. It had a nice ring to it. I was proud, and I had every reason to be. At twenty-nine, I had a seagoing command. True, in terms of tonnage the *SS Pandora* was a relatively small vessel. But she was a well-found ship with an experienced crew. She had proved her worth in the trying weather of the North Atlantic. She enjoyed an excellent reputation — and I, Kostas Sthanassis, enjoying the confidence of her owners, was her master.

It is difficult to describe the feeling of pride I felt on taking command of the *Pandora*. Before joining the vessel under clouded circumstances, I had earned respect and enviable status in a highly competitive line of work. Already I had put together a sizable fortune. I took pride in those achievements, but it was nothing compared to the euphoria I felt when I moved my gear into Captain Driscoll's recently vacated cabin.

We were due to sail on the morrow. I was in my cabin attending to some paperwork when I came across a file of miscellaneous documents Driscoll had left me. He had mentioned it only as a file containing information I might find useful. Now, with a few minutes to spare, I absently scanned its contents.

It was the second sheet in the file that caught and held my attention. It was a list of the names and addresses of the ship's seven owners. The name at the top of the list was that of Alfredo Rubio. It struck me as having a familiar ring. Alfredo Rubio? Where had I run across that name? Then it came to me. Wasn't "Alfredo" the Christian name of "Big Al" Rubio, Vito Martinelli's right-hand lieutenant?

Sweet Jesus! Was it possible that the Alfredo Rubio listed here as a shipowner was Vito's man? If so, what of the others? Of the other names on the list, only one, G.A. Carniello, seemed at all familiar. I thought I recalled a Gino Carniello as having been one of Vito's torpedoes. If I was not mistaken, Gino had been killed in a mob shootout back in '23. It was difficult to think of Gino Carniello as a deceased shipowner.

I had to face it. There was a damn good possibility that *all* of the people named on the list were, in one way or another, connected with Vito Martinelli. They did not represent, by any standard, the cream of gangland's hierarchy. The idea that such men had banded together to purchase a number of ships was ludicrous. For them to be listed as shipowners could mean only one thing: They had been fronts used to hide the identity of the real purchaser or purchasers. If what I was beginning to suspect was true, the owner of the *Pandora* and the other ships Captain Driscoll had mentioned was Vito Martinelli, or a group in which he was the dominant member.

It was a numbing thought, but I couldn't escape it. My conclusion was that, from the moment I'd set foot on the *Pandora,* Vito had known exactly where I was and what I was doing. In fact, no matter how indirectly, for the past four years I had been working for Vito — and still was. Through application and ability I'd earned the right to command this vessel, but the authorization had come from Vito. In the name of God, why? Vito was not a forgiving man, and I was certain that, even though four years had passed, he bore me nothing but ill will. Then why would he approve Driscoll's recommendation? The only reason that sprang to mind was that while, as a ship's officer, I was a wanted man in the States, as the *captain* of a rumrunner I would warrant special attention from the Bureau of Internal Revenue should I ever be fool enough to venture into United States waters or set foot on its soil.

Was I letting my imagination run away with me? Were the names

I thought I had recognized nothing more than coincidence? Well, there was one way to find out. If I had been the victim of deception, Sofoclis, wittingly or unwittingly, had been party to the act.

That afternoon I went ashore and sent a telegram to Metaxis & Company, advising Sofoclis that it was imperative he meet me in Havana on, or shortly after, August 15. In case he was in league with Vito, or still subjected to the scrutiny of a Martinelli-appointed watchdog, I explained that I wanted to meet to discuss the disposal of the Manhattan properties still registered in my name.

Wearing a white linen suit and a Panama hat, Sofoclis towered above the shipping agent and the uniformed customs official. The trio stood on the quayside as I nosed the *Pandora* into her berth. From the wing of the bridge, I grinned down at Sofoclis and flipped him a mock salute. It had been four years since I'd last seen him, but he seemed not to have changed at all. Even if he had been party to having me shanghaied onto the *Pandora,* I was delighted to see him.

I rang off engines and descended to my cabin, where my steward was setting out bottles and glasses to welcome our visitors.

We had drinks all around. When the formalities had been attended to and the agent and customs official had departed, I shrugged out of my uniform jacket and suggested to Sofoclis that he would be more comfortable if he took off his suit coat and loosened his tie. I freshened our drinks.

Nothing would be served by beating about the bush. Handing Sofoclis his drink, I said, "Was it your idea, or Vito's, that I be fixed up with rigged credentials and placed on board this ship?"

Sofoclis' face sagged, but, to his credit, he made no attempt to evade the question. "Vito's," he said.

His answer confirmed my suspicion. "Did you know that Vito owns — or has a big interest in — this ship?"

Sofoclis' eyes widened. "No. I didn't know that."

I shrugged. "It doesn't matter." I paused to take a sip of my drink, then added, "But you *did* know that the *Pandora* wasn't the safe hiding place you and Omeros led me to believe. You knew that Vito was using the ship as a means to put me out of circulation. Were you and Omeros in on the frame-up from the beginning?"

Notwithstanding the breeze wafting in through my cabin portholes, Sofoclis was sweating profusely. "Neither of us had any idea that Vito was going to frame you," he said, "and Omeros still thinks the ship and Panamanian papers were my brainchild."

"Knowing full well you were banishing me from the States . . . and putting me where Vito could lay his hands on me whenever he wanted. Why did *you* go along with it, Sofie?"

Sofoclis looked so utterly miserable that I found myself feeling sorry for him. "God, Kostas, what could I do? Vito swore that if I didn't get you onto this ship within forty-eight hours, sacred oath or no sacred oath, he'd see to it you became a corpse . . . and me along with you. He said that if I breathed a word about the plan to you, or anyone else, I was a dead man. What's more, he said that if you returned to the States, he'd have us both killed. He isn't one to make idle threats."

"So, to save your skin, you had me shanghaied," I said.

"To save *both* our skins. For God's sake, Kostas, what would you have done in my place? Besides, I didn't dream you'd be out here this long."

"Okay," I said, "in your place I'd more than likely have done as you did. But what beats me is why in hell Vito hasn't lifted his edict. For Christ's sake, it can't have anything to do with his precious niece. If he placed that much store by her chastity, he'd have to bump off half the leading men in Hollywood. I don't get it. As you can see, I'm now in command of the ship, a promotion he had to have played some part in approving. It almost looks as though he's rewarding me for being a good boy . . . but that sure as hell isn't like Vito."

"No," Sofoclis said, "it isn't. Whatever reason he had, it wasn't to reward you. It must have been to make damn sure you stayed on the *Pandora*. It's some kind of fixation with him."

"I still don't get it. Why?"

"I think I can answer that . . . at least partly. About a year ago I mentioned to him that Omeros and I would like to have you back running the inventory side of the operation. He blew up. He wouldn't hear of it. He even told me why. He said that you were too damn smart, too damn ambitious and had grown far too big for your boots. He said he'd see you dead before he'd let you anywhere near the business again. He told me he'd learned from Angelo that the Apollo Club had been your idea, and the club had been cutting into business in his territory. I told Omeros about that blowup. In his opinion, Vito fears you."

"Vito's afraid of me? You've got to be kidding!"

"No. It makes sense. The way Omeros sees it is that Vito is undisputed boss of his territory. No one dares challenge his authority. No one but you has done so within the last eight to ten years and lived to tell about it. Then you had the crust to start dating his niece. What it all adds up to, according to Omeros, is that Vito sees you as a real threat to his unchallenged authority. What astonishes Omeros is how in hell Teresa got Vito to promise you immunity. Up to now, he's abided by that promise, but I wouldn't give you a plugged nickel for your chances if you put in an appearance anywhere in the United States."

"He's screwy, out of his head," I said, "but if that's his attitude, how come he doesn't object to my share of the profits at your end?"

"He doesn't know about it. Your share comes out of Omeros' and my profits."

My thirty pieces of silver, but I didn't say so. I changed the subject. "How's Omeros? In her last letter, Penny said he was suffering from asthma and that they were thinking of moving to Arizona."

"They did. They moved to Phoenix last month."

CHAPTER NINETEEN

Cargo holds all but empty, we were off the coast of Florida south-bound for Havana on that fateful October 29 when share values nose-dived on Wall Street. I did not learn of the financial debacle until we berthed in Havana on November 4.

When news of the market crash reached me, I was not particularly concerned. Why should I have been? Had I been in New York prior to the crash, like most speculators I undoubtedly would have had substantial holdings bought on margin and been caught in the squeeze as the stocks tumbled. But I hadn't been in New York. So what if my securities suddenly had depreciated in value by forty percent? I'd acquired them before 1925. By my reckoning, they were still worth twice as much as when I'd bought them.

It did cross my mind that I'd given my broker wide discretionary powers, but I didn't entertain for a minute the suspicion that he would exercise those powers to my detriment. Unfortunately, that is exactly what he *did* do. During that period of frenzied trading, he liquidated my holdings to meet margin demands for himself and some of his clients. I suppose he had every intention of making good on the "borrowed" securities. The road to Hell is paved with such intentions. He blew his brains out in the bathroom of his Bronxville home.

It was, however, some weeks before I learned of my broker's reprehensible conduct. By the time that news reached me, in a letter from Sōfoclis, matters of more pressing urgency were weighing on my mind.

If the stock market crash wasn't of immediate concern to me, a concomitant financial disaster came as a staggering blow — although I remained blissfully ignorant of the fact until November 17. The bearer of these ill tidings was the shipping agent's representative. This distraught individual arrived on board on the morning of the seventeenth. I received him in my cabin.

The substance of his story was that Rodriguez y Cia. had received a sight draft from the owners, money intended to meet salary and bonus payments and current operating expenses for the *Pandora* and two other vessels not presently in port. A couple of days before, Rodriguez y Cia. had sent the draft to its bank for collection only to be advised that, that very day, the New York bank on which the draft was drawn had closed its doors. It was true. The Havana branch of that bank was also closed and no one could say when, or if, it would resume business. Alarmed by this turn of events, the company had cabled the owners. This morning, they had received a reply that the owners hoped to be able to honor the draft by the end of the month. This, the representative assured me, had placed Rodriguez y Cia. in a *most* difficult position.

I didn't immediately see the difficulty. As for the payroll and bonus payments, if the draft wasn't honored by the time we sailed, I could always meet the commitment from cash received as we disposed of cargo on our coming voyage. As was the practice, we had paid cash in advance for the cargo now being loaded. I had also paid cash for the coal we'd taken on. Specifically, I wanted to know, how was the *Pandora* affected by this delay in payment?

The representative enumerated the outstanding accounts — stevedoring, stores, provisions and a rather large bill for repairs. There was, he stated, only enough cash on hand to meet the berthage, harbor dues and pilotage fees, providing we sailed no later than the twenty-first, four days hence. He pointed out that the owners had said that they "hoped" to honor the draft by the end of the month. What if there was further delay? Under normal circumstances, creditors didn't mind waiting for payment. But the financial situation in New York was so chaotic that if the bills were not met promptly — or if there was the slightest suspicion that they might not be paid — the creditors might have the *Pandora,* or any other ships belonging to her owners, detained or seized.

What, I asked, did he expect me to do about it? He said that they had radioed the other ships expected to arrive before the end of the month to delay their arrival until otherwise advised. As for the *Pandora,* even if it meant sailing without my full cargo, they wanted me to clear the harbor on — or preferably before — the twenty-first.

I assured him I would do so and would do everything possible to complete loading within the next two days. Then, more from curiosity than from suspicion, I asked the name of the New York bank that had folded. His answer hit me like a blow to the solar plexus.

Every penny I had saved, both in New York and in Havana, was in the vaults of a bank that had struck a financial reef and foundered.

So, when Sofoclis' letter advising me of the actions of our mutual broker arrived two days later, it didn't come as the blow it might have. I was already in a state of shock. I don't know how many speculators were wiped out by the crash of 1929. All I knew was that one man, Constantine Sthanassis, had been effectively obliterated.

I laid the blame for all my misfortunes on Vito Martinelli. Had it not been for Vito, I would have been in New York to personally attend to my investments. Had it not been for Vito, I would not have become the captain of the *Pandora* and, by now, would have withdrawn my savings and invested in a business of my own. And whatever I still owned in the world in the way of property was beyond my grasp due to Vito's vindictiveness.

Vito would be made to pay. What I had in mind might be called grand larceny by a court of law, but I looked on it as a collection of a long-overdue debt. I had settled on a rough plan even before receiving Sofoclis' letter. All his letter did was make me impatient to settle my account with Vito. My impatience caused me to alter my plan.

Originally I'd planned that, once we had disposed of our cargo on our northward run and reached Nova Scotia, I would turn command of the *Pandora* over to Enrique Ramirez. I would leave him with enough cash to meet the crew's requirements and immediate operating expenses. But, instead of contracting for a cargo of liquor for the return voyage, I would simply pocket the money and make myself scarce. The change I made in the plan was its destination. Once clear of Cuba, I would alter course southward. In Colón, in the Republic of Panama, I knew people who would take the entire cargo off my hands at a substantial discount.

That change proved to be my undoing, but it had one beneficial outcome. It prevented me from adding barratry to the list of crimes for which I was wanted in the United States.

We had cleared the Yucatan Channel and were well south of the

Cayman Islands when the hurricane struck. There had been nothing on the ship's radio to alert us that a tropical storm was brewing. Nonetheless, we were forewarned by unmistakable signs that a violent storm was shaping up and did everything possible to prepare our vessel for the onslaught.

The glass started to fall in the middle watch. Day broke, with the barometer still dropping. It was dead calm. A glasslike sea had a burnished appearance in the pale morning light. A high, thin haze gave a brassy hue to the sky. During the morning watch, we went about securing everything above and below decks in wary anticipation of heavy weather to come.

Before noon, we were rolling in slow cadence to a long, low, easterly swell. By the time we had laid off our noon position, a line of ragged black clouds had appeared on the southeastern horizon. The bank of dark clouds grew menacingly as it advanced toward us. An advance guard of wind sent cat's-paws chasing each other across the swells. Then the clouds raced overhead, and the storm engulfed us.

To this day I do not know how we survived ill-tempered Poseidon's wrath. Never before or since have I encountered winds and seas of such unfettered violence. The slashing rain and raging sea seemed to emerge into one vast, impenetrable wall enclosing us on all sides. We were tossed about like a cork and buffeted by shrieking winds that registered, at times, well in excess of one hundred knots. It seemed as though all the Furies had been launched against us.

I took over the wheel at 1300 hours and stayed at the helm for nine hours. I reduced speed and strove to keep head to the tumultuous seas and the howling wind, fine on my starboard bow. Hour after hour, we rose to the tops of mountainous waves, hung for a moment on the wind-whipped crests, then plunged sickeningly into the yawning troughs.

I might have appeared outwardly calm as I fought the wheel to compensate for roll, pitch, yaw and sudden lurches, but in my heart I was afraid. I freely admit that I prayed silently, promising God all manner of reforms if he would see us through. I was grateful for one mercy; at least we were in open seas.

Beneath and around me, the *Pandora* groaned and creaked in agony. I doubt she had ever been called upon to weather such a storm. I had a strange feeling that she and I were one and that we alone were battling the elements in unison. And I thought of her mythical namesake, the original woman bestowed upon mankind by the vengeful Hephaestus. Poor Pandora. Zeus had given her a jeweled box, cautioning her not to open it, yet knowing full well she would be consumed by curiosity and unable to resist temptation. As the gods had known she would, she had opened the box and released all the evils that have plagued mankind from that day forward. Yet Hope, caught by the lid, had remained in the box. Hope, then, had not abandoned the *Pandora* and me in our hour of severest trial.

I lost all track of time. I don't know exactly when it was that I noted the wind was backing. To me, this meant that the hurricane was on a northerly course and that the eye of the storm had passed to port of us. I eased the helm to place the wind on our port bow. Some time later, I thought the fury of the storm seemed to be slackening. I turned the wheel over to the bosun. In the charthouse, I wedged myself wearily into a corner of the settee, every muscle aching.

Somehow I managed to drop off to sleep. When I awoke, dawn was streaking the eastern sky. The rain had ceased, though the sky was still leaden. The wind had slackened to gale force, and the seas had moderated considerably.

I was joined by Enrique and, together with the bosun, we ventured out on deck to survey the damage. Neither the ship nor its crew had come through the hurricane unscathed. In the forecastle, I discovered that three of the crew members had sustained broken bones. The vessel had also been damaged.

Atop the bridge wheelhouse, the monkey island and its binnacle had been carried away — as had happened to all but a ragged stump of the funnel. The port wing of the bridge had been badly damaged. Nothing remained of the seaboats but a few scraps of wood swinging from the davit blocks.

Wind, sea or both had ripped the battened tarpaulin from the for'ard hatch and denuded it of hatch boards. During the storm I had watched tons of water pour into the gaping hatch as wave after wave broke over the forecastle and washed aft. So I had ordered the pumps started.

Now, Enrique, the bosun and I stared down into the hold. It was a shambles of broken crates, casks and bottles. It reeked of rum. We would have to wait until an accurate count could be made, but I estimated that we had lost about one-sixth of our total cargo.

Shifting cargo had given the *Pandora* a pronounced port list. My fear was that we could have sprung some of our below-water plates. I ordered the bosun to sound the bilges once every half hour and report his reading to the bridge.

Apart from keeping the pumps working, there wasn't much, at the moment, I could do. I returned to the bridge and went into the chartroom.

To continue south to Colón was out of the question. Not only were we in need of repairs, but also I had crewmen who required medical attention. In addition, I needed a marine surveyor to accurately assess the damage for the benefit of our insurance underwriters.

The Fates, it seemed, had conspired to protect Vito Martinelli's interest. I laid off a course for the closest harbor I could find in the area.

CHAPTER TWENTY

On November 25, listing heavily, the *Pandora* limped into the small Honduran harbor of Trujillo.

I reread the report I'd written to Rodriquez y Cia. and signed it. The gist of the report was to explain the *Pandora*'s presence in these Caribbean waters when, by rights, we should have been somewhere off the Virginia coast. I had stated that, in view of the distressed financial picture, I had, on my own initiative, decided to proceed to Colón, the *Pandora*'s Panamanian port of registry, to procure a loan against the vessel and its cargo. I then had intended to return to Havana to pay off any outstanding bills and complete the loading of cargo interrupted by our early departure.

I was confident that this explanation would satisfy the agents. Not so Vito Martinelli. I was sure he would correctly conclude that I had been intent on defrauding him. Fine. I'd been quite prepared to accept the consequences of my action once I'd extracted my pound of flesh. It was galling to know that I was now inviting his retributive action without having fleeced him of so much as a penny.

Until a few days ago, I had been a wanted man in the United States. Now I was sure I was a man marked for execution by Vito Martinelli. For the moment, it wasn't a matter of concern. Vito had a long arm, but I doubted that it extended to Honduras. So, for now, I was safe, but I doubted that would hold true for long. Vito, I was quite sure, would spare neither effort nor expense to have me tracked down and killed.

Absently, I ran my thumb along the scar on my cheek. What would my next move be?

Once I had disposed of the cargo in Colón, my plan had been to put a good deal of distance between myself and New York. South America appealed to me as a likely sanctuary. Initially, I had settled on Colombia as my immediate destination.

Why Colombia? I had Enrique to thank for that. Time and again he had sung the praises of his country and its fabled riches. In particular, one of his stories had gripped my imagination.

According to Enrique, he had a fabulously wealthy cousin, Carlos Ramirez, who lived in a town named Tunja in the mountains of Boyacá. This region was famed for its emerald mines. As Enrique told it, his cousin knew the location of a secret mine somewhere in the mountains near a town called Chiquinquirá. I must admit that I thought the story a lie until Enrique showed me a green-flecked stone he assured me was emerald matrix from Carlos' mine.

So Chiquinquirá had been my intended destination. From Enrique's description, it was off the beaten track, an unlikely place to look for a Greek sea captain. Not only would it serve as a haven until things cooled down, but also I could put my time to good use prospecting for emeralds.

Until two days ago, that had been the script. It had been predicated on my slipping out of Colón with a suitcase stuffed with greenbacks. Unfortunately, the hurricane had written a dramatic change into the script. The only money I could lay my hands on now would be the one thousand dollars in the cash box of the ship's safe.

I examined the situation. It was hardly what I could term reassuring.

Ten years ago to the day, I had been a passenger on a freighter out of Piraeus, bound for New York. A lot had happened to the kid who had stepped off that ship at Manhattan's Harlem docks.

I'd learned a good deal about the commodity and produce importing and distributing business. I'd learned a good deal more about the bootlegging business.

From Omeros Kalandris, I'd learned the value of keeping in the background. From the Apollo Club experience, I'd learned the folly of fronting a business venture as vulnerable as a speakeasy. And from the part Sofoclis had played in having me shanghaied onto the *Pandora,* I'd learned that even blood relatives are not to be trusted and that there is little room for sentiment in the grim game of survival.

Thanks to Timothy Driscoll, I'd risen from a falsely qualified second mate to a bona fide master mariner in his first command. Thanks to Vittorio Martinelli, it was likely to be my last command, and, if I didn't move swiftly, I wasn't likely to see my thirtieth birthday.

What I had to figure out now was how far I could go on one thousand dollars and what I was going to do when I got there.

The idea of going to the Colombian town of Chiquinquirá still appealed to me. Not only were there emerald mines in the vicinity, but also Enrique had spun yarns of Chibcha Indian treasures of gold. Surely, with all this wealth to be had, some of it would find its way into my pockets.

It would have been helpful to have had a letter of introduction to Enrique's cousin, but I decided no one on board must know of my intentions. Still, if Carlos Ramirez was the man of wealth that Enrique claimed, he shouldn't be too difficult to locate once I reached Tunja.

When, in response to my summons, Enrique arrived in my cabin, he wore only khaki shorts and a pair of scuffed sandals. "If you want a cheap drunk," he said, "try going down into number one hold."

"How's it going?" I asked.

"Slowly. The lower hold is awash with rum. We'll have to let it air out before we can work down there."

"Any idea about our losses?"

"Not an accurate count. There was some breakage in number two, but not as much as we expected. On the other hand, number one looks even worse than we thought. Offhand, I'd say we've lost about one-quarter of the cargo."

"Are we still taking water?"

"Yes, but the pumps are coping with it. I think we've lost rivets, or sprung a plate or two below the waterline at number one. If we find it, and can lighter off some of the cargo, we may be able to check the leak."

"There's not much we can do about it here, other than temporary repairs. We'll have to go into dry dock in Colón." I nodded to the report on my desk. "I've written the agents a full account of the storm, and the damage as we know it without a survey . . . and explained why I was heading south in the first place."

"Why *were* we bound for Colón?" Enrique asked. "You never did tell me . . . or say why we left Havana without a full cargo."

"The agents had reason to believe that the owners were in temporary financial difficulties because of the collapse of a New York bank. They were afraid that if we stayed any longer, creditors might detain the ship. I set course for Colón because I know bankers there who I thought would advance us a short-term loan. Now, of course, we have a different situation on our hands. One which involves an insurance claim."

"We'll need a proper survey. Can we get one here?"

"The harbormaster told me there was a Lloyd's surveyor available in Puerto Barrios, in Guatemala. I'm going there this afternoon to make the necessary arrangements. From Puerto Barrios I'll go by train to Guatemala City. From there I'll contact both Colón and Havana, then, depending on Havana's instructions, I'll either return here or go directly to the Canal Zone to arrange for dry-docking in Colón. In the event of the latter, I'll get a radio message through to you."

"What then?"

"When the survey's completed, and you're satisfied the ship's sufficiently seaworthy again, bring her south to Colón. I'll join you there."

I watched Enrique's departing figure. I *would,* as I'd stated, secure the services of a Lloyd's surveyor in Puerto Barrios. It was the least I could do for the ship that had served me so faithfully and so well. And I was leaving her in good hands, even if Enrique didn't know he had just inherited her command.

I felt a twinge of guilt at leaving Enrique holding the bag. He had been a staunch friend. But I wasn't too worried about the fate of the *Pandora*. Enrique was a resourceful man, and the *Pandora* was too valuable an asset for her owners to abandon. I wondered idly if I would ever see him again — in this life, or the next.

To my delight, the cash box held more than the one-thousand-dollar petty-cash float. With all the things that had crowded my thoughts over the past week, it had completely slipped my mind that I had put close to three hundred Canadian dollars of my own money into the box for safe-keeping.

I couldn't help making a comparison. Ten years ago I had arrived in New York filled with hope, armed with the address of a great-uncle I'd never seen, a few drachmas in my pocket. Now I was a far cry from the wide-eyed Kostas Sthanassis who had first set foot in the United States, but my position was remarkably similar. Once more I was venturing into the unknown, virtually penniless. The difference was that I was now a marked and wanted man, a fugitive.

And this time, at the end of my journey I had no one to turn to for assistance. Which might not be entirely true. I had a name — Carlos Ramirez — but no address, no letter of introduction and no ties with him other than a friendship with a cousin he had probably forgotten.

As the heavy iron door of the ship's safe clanged shut, I was acutely conscious that the hollow sound marked the closing of a chapter in my life. What lay before me was in the hands of the capricious gods.

CHAPTER TWENTY-ONE

I finally located Carlos Ramirez — not in Tunja but in Chiquinquirá, and in circumstances vastly different from those Enrique had led me to expect.

My introduction to Colombia was through the Pacific port of entry, Buenaventura. I can't say that I was favorably impressed. It's a tropical city, a green-and-white commercial center that's unbearably hot and insufferably humid.

When I had cleared through customs and immigration, my seaman's papers providing identification, I took a ramshackle bus to the center of town. Not wishing to spend any more time there than absolutely necessary, I asked directions to the railroad station, where I bought a tourist map at a newsstand. The map indicated that Tunja was unreachable by rail. I was told I would first have to go to Bogotá, the capital, and from there take a bus north to Tunja. As a train left for the interior every night, I bought a ticket to Bogotá and waited in the station restaurant for its departure.

If Buenaventura had failed to impress me, the train most certainly did. The coach was jammed to overflowing with fat women, squalling infants, screaming children, cackling hens and drunks who sang loudly off-key throughout most of the trip. The least offensive of my fellow travelers were the sad-eyed Indians who sat in stoical silence.

It was a harrowing journey. The train crawled along a perilous roadbed that threaded its tortuous course through two mountain ranges of jagged, threatening peaks and yawning chasms. To compound the misery, at one point, either where the rail line had yet to be completed or where a section had been obliterated by some catastrophe, we disembarked, spent most of the night in a barracklike hotel, then were herded into buses and driven to where another train awaited us. It was my introduction to train travel in the Andes, an acquaintanceship I cheerfully could have foregone.

We did not arrive in Bogotá until the morning of the second day. I was exhausted and in foul temper. The Colombia I had seen and experienced up to that point fell far short of Enrique's lyrical descriptions.

I found an inexpensive hotel not far from the railroad station. After a bite of lunch and the luxury of a bath, I turned in and very nearly slept around the clock. When I arose the following morning, both life and Bogotá had taken on a more pleasant aspect.

The Bogotá I was exposed to during my brief visit in 1929 bore little resemblance to the metropolis it has now become. Then it was little more than a large town. At the time I recall thinking that, in the four centuries since its founding by a Spanish *conquistador*, Gonzalo de Quesada, it should be a more imposing city, particularly if there was truth to Enrique's claims about the country's fabulous wealth. I was finding it harder and harder to believe in the proud stories Enrique had told me about Colombia and was beginning to have serious doubts about the wisdom of having journeyed to this remote backwater.

In one aspect, though, Enrique hadn't erred in his description. Bogotá was, as he had said, situated in an upland valley ringed by Andean peaks and, at its 2,600-meter altitude, canopied by an almost-constant cloud cover. He had described it as being mild by day, pleasantly cool by night. Hell, I found it downright chilly come evening, especially after my recent exposure to the Central American republics and tropical Buenaventura.

One thing was abundantly clear: My clothing was not suited to this mountain climate, so the first thing I did was shop for warmer clothing at prices that would not make too great a dent in my dwindling hoard of dollars.

As I lunched that day, I mentally reviewed my position.

The cost of living in Colombia appeared to be such that I could sustain myself for several months on my remaining funds. So, for the time being, money was the least of my worries.

The language barrier wasn't the stumbling block I'd anticipated. I spoke Spanish with a decided Cuban accent, but I was finding little difficulty, after only three days, in understanding the Castilian Spanish spoken by the Colombians. Nor was I having much trouble making myself understood, despite my accent and limited vocabulary. No, the language barrier didn't appear to be a problem.

My chief concern was Vito's bloodhounds. By now they must have made contact with the *Pandora*. Since my only travel document was my seaman's identification, and since I bore a distinctive facial scar, I shouldn't have been too difficult to track, at least as far as Panama. What then?

I reasoned that whoever was stalking me would waste valuable time checking out Colón before eventually concluding that I must have gone somewhere by sea. They would waste more time in checking shipping before arriving at the fact that I had taken passage south from Panama City. Eventually the trail would lead to Buenaventura — but just how long was "eventually"? Under the worst conditions I could imagine, with everything favoring the tracker or trackers, I must by now be at least a week ahead of my pursuers.

But suppose my pursuers *did* reach Buenaventura a mere week behind me? My description as a man with a scar on his face would no longer be helpful. On leaving Guatemala I had started to grow a beard, which was now sufficiently full to hide the scar. Even if they concluded that I had gone inland, and if by some miracle it was discovered that I had spent two nights at Bogotá's Hotel Carib, from there my trail would grow ice-cold. By tomorrow morning I would be just one more bearded man wearing a soiled raincoat, riding a northbound bus.

The voluble little man seated beside me in the bus was a compulsive talker, a fount of unsolicited information. My contribution to the one-sided conversation was smiles, nods and monosyllabic grunts registering everything from appreciation to mild disbelief.

He volunteered that his destination was Bucaramanga. When he asked where I was headed, I confined myself to one word, "Tunja."

Ah, yes. He was familiar with the Boyacá region in general, and Tunja in particular, although he hadn't stopped off there in some time. Fine town. Fascinating history. But, then, I must know all about that. When I responded with a nod indicating that I didn't, he launched into an account that would have done credit to a tour conductor.

I learned that Boyacá was, before the coming of the Spanish conquerors, an Indian empire of unbelievable riches. The fertile valleys yielded crops that sustained a large native population. The mountains yielded wealth of a different kind — gold and emeralds. Deeply religious, the Indians fashioned idols of gem-studded gold to grace their magnificent temples to the sun. Tunja had been the administrative and religious capital of this ancient civilization. Even with the coming of the Spanish and the conversion of the natives to Catholicism, Tunja had retained its position of religious preeminence. If I was not familiar with it, I should make it a point to visit the cathedral in Tunja, dating from 1598.

The names of Spanish *conquistadores* rolled off his tongue as though he'd known them personally. The names meant nothing to me, nor had I the slightest interest in the seminaries and churches he described so enthusiastically. Only when his ramblings included accounts of treasures in gold and gems did my interest quicken. It began to look as though Enrique hadn't been guilty of gross exaggerations and that I was pointed in the right direction to exploit these riches.

Only half-listening to the running monologue, I turned my attention to the scenery outside the bus window. I could see what my traveling companion had meant when he'd said that this broad upland valley was fertile. The gently undulating fields were green with new plantings of vegetables and grain, or golden with ripening crops. Cattle grazed on rich grassy pasturage. Windbreaks of lofty blue-green eucalyptus dotted the landscape. In the middle distance, encircling mountains I estimated at standing no more than two or three hundred meters above the valley floor were thickly forested with evergreens, their peaks grazing the underside of the cloud cover.

Through breaks in the overcast, sunlight slanted into the valley, sending bright patches chasing shadows across the valley floor. Not too far off, the scene was misted by gently falling rain. The combination of altitude, cloud cover and intermittent rain and sunshine had blessed this highland paradise with a climate of eternal spring. How different it was from Cephalonia, where the lack of rain and the relentless summer sun burned the landscape to a crisp. It was little wonder that ancient civilizations had flourished here and that the region had so strongly appealed to the Spanish colonizers.

My companion, noting my preoccupation with the scenery, broke into my thoughts with a comment, "Wonderful thing, the invention of the motor vehicle. When I was a young man, it took days to make this journey by coach . . . and, in the mountains, we faced the danger of being set upon by *bandidos*. In my father's day, before the completion of the railroad, a trip from the Caribbean coast to the capital involved both riverboats and coaches and could take weeks. We've come a long way since those days."

I made no comment. To me, the rattling bus — and the swaying train that had transported me from Buenaventura to Bogotá — didn't represent much in the way of advances in transportation. I think I would have preferred to take my chances with lurking bandits.

How wrong I was.

I arrived in Tunja in the late afternoon. As it seemed too late in the day to start looking for Don Carlos Ramirez, I rented a room in an inn near the church of San Ignacio, dined at a nearby restaurant and retired early.

The next morning, after eating a light breakfast, I sought out the police station and launched my inquiry concerning Don Carlos' whereabouts.

The young policeman stared at me uncomprehendingly. "Don Carlos Ramirez?" he repeated.

"Yes," I said, controlling my impatience. "I understand he is an important man in the community."

At the far end of the room, a sergeant standing with his back to us searched the contents of a filing cabinet. A chuckle came from that direction as the sergeant, some papers in his hand, turned toward us. *"El Borrachín,"* the sergeant said, addressing his remark to his colleague.

The young policeman's face cleared. He laughed, but, noting my expression, he sobered and said, "Yes, I know the Señor Ramirez to whom you refer. He now resides in Chiquinquirá. When last I heard, he was staying at an inn called *La Posada de los Andes.* He may be there still. If not, the innkeeper can surely tell you where to find him."

I thanked the policemen for their help and, with troubled mind, left the police station.

El Borrachín — The Drunkard! Hardly a flattering nickname to give an important man. Still, one never knows. Many wealthy men drink to excess. Yet there had been derision, not amused respect, in the sergeant's use of the nickname. Well, there was little to be gained by speculation. The answer awaited me in Chiquinquirá.

Chiquinquirá, I was told, was some fifty kilometers almost due west of Tunja. The difficulty was that no direct road between them had as yet been completed through the rugged terrain. I could, if I wished, go part of the way by muleback and the rest by horseback, but the best route would be to return by bus the way I had come to a junction leading to Zipaquirá and change there to a bus for Chiquinquirá. Admittedly, the distance was close to four times greater than by cutting due west, but, in the long run, the longer route would save time and much discomfort and reduce to a minimum the risk of being accosted by brigands.

I was beginning to appreciate why Bogotá had slumbered through the centuries virtually unchanged. Travel to and from the Colombian interior was a difficult and perilous undertaking.

The bus deposited me in the central plaza in front of an imposing basilica I felt excessive for a village Chiquinquirá's size. A number of balconied inns fronted the central square; *La Posada de los Andes* was not one of them. I found it a few blocks away.

Although it was probably an unnecessary precaution, I registered as Señor Ricardo Lopez. By the time I had unpacked, washed off the surface dust from my journey and returned to the tiny entrance hall, the innkeeper was nowhere in evidence.

I roused the drowsing *portero* and asked him if Señor Ramirez was a guest at the inn. When he stared at me blankly, I added, *"El Borrachín.* Does he stay here?"

"Oh . . . *that* Señor Ramirez! No, señor, he has not lived here for more than three years."

"Has he an address in Chiquinquirá?"

"He has no address, señor. The street he lives on has no name. The houses have no numbers."

"Can you direct me to his house?" I asked.

"Sí, señor. It is not far from here. When you leave the inn, turn left. Walk two blocks to Calle Santa Marta, then turn left again. The first street you come to on your right is the one you want. It is a dead-end street. The last house on your left is where you will find Señor Ramirez."

Officially, the narrow, dead-end street, little more than a dusty alley-way, bore no name, but to the local residents it was known as Calle de las Putas — Street of the Whores.

CHAPTER TWENTY-TWO

Chiquinquirá is at a lower altitude than Bogotá and Tunja and is considerably hotter during the daytime. A fierce afternoon sun blazed down from a cloudless sky.

The one-story, whitewashed, boxlike dwellings lining the narrow street were more like market stalls than houses. The shutters of the single windows, and the wooden doors, were opened wide to provide ventilation. In some cases, the windows were partially screened by flimsy curtains, affording the occupants a small measure of privacy. For the most part, however, a passerby had an unobstructed view of the interiors and the activities within. The occupants on display, and the action in progress, left no doubt in the mind that these cramped dwellings were prostitutes' cribs.

In the street itself there was little activity at this hour. Halfway down the street, a man stood lighting a cigarette. A second man emerged from one of the houses and stopped to relieve himself against it, then walked toward me, nonchalantly buttoning his fly. Near the end of the street, a group of children were playing.

Myself excepted, no one seemed even mildly interested in the spectacle of upraised legs, rhythmically heaving buttocks and intertwined nude bodies, nor in the accompanying medley of grunts, moans of feigned delight and creaking of bedsprings.

Filled with misgivings, I neared the end of the alleyway. The last house on the left was, like all the others, a one-story structure, but it was slightly larger. Its doorway was screened by a curtain of bamboo segments. I stood in front of it, unsure of my next move. A boy, the closest to me of the four or five children playing at the end of the street, eyed me curiously.

I didn't bother using Ramirez' surname. Nodding toward the curtained opening, I asked the boy, *"El Borrachín?"*

The boy grinned, displaying gaps where teeth were missing. *"Sí,"* he said, then, losing interest in me, rejoining his boisterous playmates.

I hesitated a moment, then parted the curtain and stepped into the interior's semigloom. When my eyes adjusted, I beheld a scene of such squalor that I very nearly stepped back out into the street.

Most of the floor was taken up by a bare mattress. Sprawled full-length on the mattress, lying on his back and naked from the waist up, was a fat man I judged to be somewhere in his late fifties. His face was covered with a gray stubble of several days' growth of beard. Saliva, or vomit, trickled from one corner of his half-opened mouth. The crotch of his frayed, once-white trousers and the mattress beneath his buttocks were dark and wet with urine. His bare feet were grime-blackened. He was snoring discordantly. Scattered around the room was a jumble of cheap, broken furniture, and it stank of piss, stale sweat and rum fumes.

The figure on the mattress stirred, and the fingers of one outstretched hand opened and closed clutchingly close to a nearly empty bottle of rum that sat on the floor.

A wave of nausea swept over me. This obese, rum-soaked, piss-drenched caricature of a man was Enrique's fabulously wealthy cousin.

Anger surged up in me. It was all a cruel joke at my expense. I had been cheated.

Walking over to a table, I filled a pitcher with water from an earthenware jar that sat on the floor. Then, turning, I poured the water onto Ramirez' upturned face.

Gasping, coughing and sputtering, Ramirez roused from his drunken sleep and struggled into a sitting position, water streaming from his head and shoulders. His first act, even before his eyes opened, was to grope for the rum bottle, which, with the toe of my shoe, I pushed well beyond his reach.

When his groping fingers found nothing but air and bare floor tiles, Ramirez opened his eyes. His gaze focused on the rum bottle. Mumbling something I didn't catch, he leaned toward it. I put my foot against his chest and pushed him none too gently back into a sitting position. It was only then that he seemed to become aware of my presence.

Looking up through bloodshot eyes, he mumbled, "Who th'hell're you?"

"A friend of your cousin, Enrique," I said.

Carlos looked at me. "Enrique?" Then memory stirred. "Oh . . .

Enrique! But I haven't seen him since he was a boy. C'n barely remember him."

"He hasn't forgotten you," I said. "He speaks often of his rich, respected cousin, Don Carlos Ramirez. You are an inspiration to him. Thank God he can't see you now."

Carlos ran his hand across the stubble on his cheek. He straightened slightly. "Before illness overtook me, señor," he said, "I was all he said I was."

"Was," I said, "must have been a long, long time ago."

This time, when he leaned forward to reach for the rum bottle, I made no move to stop him. He put the bottle to his lips and gulped greedily. Then he was seized with a fit of coughing. When he put the bottle down, it was all but empty.

After his coughing had subsided, he said, "Why did you seek me out? Did you come alone . . . or is Enrique with you?"

"I am by myself. I came to look for emeralds. From what Enrique told me about you, I had hoped you would help me. On Enrique's recommendation, I have come a long way to find you. It looks as though it was a wasted journey."

At the mention of emeralds, Carlos seemed to shrink before my eyes. With a shaking hand, he brushed at dirt streaking his belly. He sat with downcast eyes without speaking for so long that I thought that what I'd said hadn't sunk in. But it had. When he finally looked up, he eyed me with suspicion.

"How do I know you're Enrique's friend? What proof have you of that? You haven't even told me your name."

"Lopez," I said. "Ricardo Lopez. If I didn't know Enrique, I wouldn't have come all the way from Central America to look for *you.* As for his being my friend, you will just have to take my word for that."

My answer seemed to satisfy him. Some of the suspicion ebbed from his face, but his bleary eyes still regarded me warily, "Señor Lopez," he said, "I could take you to a place where, with a little luck, you could find emeralds the size of your fist. I could . . . but I won't. Years ago, emeralds brought me wealth. They also brought me much suffering. I have been robbed and beaten, not once, but many times. I have been tortured and left for dead in the mountains. As you can see, I am old and sick. Emeralds have been my ruination. I want no more to do with them. My advice to you is that you give up your quest for them and go back to wherever it is you came from."

Apparently exhausted by this lengthy speech, he again reached for the bottle, lifted it and drained it in a single gulp. Then, pushing the empty bottle away from him, he shouted, "Juana!"

The curtains at the rear of the room parted and a shapeless old mestiza of uncertain age stepped hesitantly into the room. "*Sí,*" she said.

"More rum," Carlos ordered.

Later I sat at a candlelit table in the local *cantina*, quietly sipping a beer, my thoughts concentrated on the dilemma before me.

To go back where I'd come from, as Carlos Ramirez had advised, was impossible, nor was I prepared to abandon all thought of prospecting for emeralds. On the other hand, I couldn't stay in Chiquinquirá doing nothing until my money ran out. And I couldn't go looking for emeralds without the help of someone who knew where to look and how to mine them. If not Ramirez, then who else could I find in this godforsaken village to help me?

I wasn't prepared to give up on Ramirez just yet. At the moment, he was in no condition to do anything but drink himself into the grave. Yet by his own admission he knew where emeralds were to be found. Given time, I might be able to pry enough information from him — perhaps even get him to draw me a map — about such matters as what rock formations to look for and how to mine the gemstone to make feasible an expedition on my own. It was worth a try.

It was a question of how long I could hold out before my funds had dwindled to where I would have to return to a port city and seek employment as a ship's officer. Absorbed in this mental calculation, I didn't hear anyone approach my corner table. The first intimation that I was no longer alone was a soft voice — nor, for a moment, did I realize it was I who was being addressed.

"Señor Lopez?" the voice repeated.

With a start, I realized it was I who was being questioned. "Yes," I said, turning my head toward the questioner.

Then I froze in my chair. It must have been a trick of shadow and candlelight. For a moment I could have sworn that the young woman standing at my elbow was Danai. My mouth must have hung open in stunned disbelief, and, in my confusion, I must have looked odd indeed to the vision of loveliness gazing down at me.

Her lips trembled in an apologetic smile. My God, even her smile was Danai's. "May I join you, señor?" she asked.

"Yes . . . of course," I said, struggling to my feet and pulling out a chair for her.

Of course, it was not Danai, but the resemblance was truly remarkable. She had Danai's olive complexion and finely molded features. She wore her hair combed in the same style. But the most striking similarity was in the eyes. Her eyes were almost exactly the same shade of blue-green I had seen in no other woman except Danai.

Now that I examined her more closely, there were subtle differences. Her hair wasn't quite as dark as Danai's. A lift to the girl's cheekbones indicated mestizo forebears. And, of course, by now Danai would be thirty-two. This girl appeared much younger. But the resemblance was so pronounced that my heart pounded.

My intense scrutiny must have disconcerted her. She colored slightly. "If I'm intruding, señor, I will leave."

"No. I'm sorry. It's just that you remind me of someone I knew years ago. Forgive my rudeness. Will you join me for a drink?"

"*Gracias. Un guarapo, por favor.*"

I went to the bar and returned with another beer for myself and the fermented cane juice, *guarapo*, she had asked for.

"What's your name?" I asked.

"Josefa. Josefa Moreno. But most people call me Pepita."

"How did you know my name?" I was indeed curious on that score. I had been in Chiquinquirá but a matter of hours and had used the name of Ricardo Lopez only when registering at the inn and in introducing myself to Ramirez. I doubted that *El Borrachín* had been in any state to remember it.

"My stepfather sent me to the inn to find you. He thought that, since you were a stranger in town, you would like a girl to keep you company. At the inn, the *portero* told me I would find you here."

"That was considerate of your stepfather," I said, "but how did *he* know my name?"

"You met him this afternoon. Carlos Ramirez. Since my mother has lived with him for many years . . . since I was a child . . . I call him my stepfather."

Mother of God! Was that shapeless hag, the mestiza Carlos had called Juana, the mother of the exquisite creature beside me? It didn't seem possible.

At that moment, three men came into the *cantina*. They went to the bar and ordered *aguardiente* in loud voices. Then they turned toward us. Two of the men looked hungrily at Pepita. The third, a mean-looking tough, glared at us, his face suffused with anger.

"Did you notice the three men who just came in and passed by our table on their way to the bar?" I asked Pepita.

"Yes," she answered, without looking toward the bar. "One of them is my half-brother, Ramón. I do not know the others, but if they are with Ramón they must belong to a gang of thieves he belongs to."

"One of them," I said, "is staring at us as though he'd like to kill us."

"That's Ramón. It infuriates him to see me in public with a customer. It reminds him that he contributes nothing to the support of our mother. I could see when he came in that he was in an ugly mood. Come, let's leave before he makes trouble."

It was sound advice. I didn't want to attract attention to myself by brawling in a *cantina*, nor did odds of three against one appeal to me.

I left a few coins on the table. We stood up and walked out without a backward glance. I half-expected that the toughs would follow us, but they didn't. We reached the inn without incident.

CHAPTER TWENTY-THREE

I had been many weeks without sexual gratification. Pepita was skilled at her trade, and her responses, even if a practiced act, were convincingly passionate. For me, our lovemaking that night was deeply satisfying. Later, my hunger sated, she lay beside me, fitting herself into the curve of my body. Relaxed in mind and body, I dropped into a deep and dreamless sleep.

What awakened me at dawn was Pepita's hand gently coaxing my penis to rock-hard rigidity. Her eyes, looking into mine, were glazed with unfeigned passion. Her lips slightly parted, a soft crooning sound came from deep in her throat. I cupped one of her breasts in my hand. Our lips met in a hungry kiss, and her tongue, like a fiery probe, darted into my mouth.

She may have been acting the night before, but not when we made love with fierce passion that morning. Her whole body quivered as she pressed upward to meet my plunging strokes. As we neared the climax and my strokes quickened, she locked her feet behind my buttocks and raked by back with her fingernails. As I reached an explosive orgasm, I groaned aloud, the sound mingling with her own gasping, shuddering cry of ecstasy.

Propped up against the bolster, I watched Pepita, unabashedly naked, as she washed herself at the basin by the bedroom window. Her body was sculpted perfection. Her figure was very much like Danai's, or Danai's body as I remembered it. There was one difference. Pepita's firm, pink-nipped, out-thrusting breasts were, I thought, fuller than Danai's. Otherwise, in the flatness of the belly, the slimness of waist, the swelling curve of the thigh and the long well-formed legs tapering to slim ankles, their figures — the one enshrined in my memory, the other delighting my eyes this very moment — were remarkably similar.

It was strange. Last night, when I had made love to Pepita, as my passion mounted she had been oddly blended in my mind with Danai. Not so this morning. In the light of dawn, the woman I had possessed had been no one but Pepita.

To think that a creature of such beauty and passion was a *pulu* saddened me. It angered me to think of her selling such a lovely body to satisfy the lust of *campesinos* or roughnecks such as her half-brother Ramón's *bandido* companions. I wondered if, with such men, she ever exhibited the unbridled passion she had displayed with me this morning.

Suddenly I was struck by another thought. Whores were no strangers to me. The normal practice was to settle on a price and ask for payment in advance. A man with a hard-on is much more inclined to generosity than one whose desire had been satisfied. Yet, up to now, she had made no mention of money. This puzzled me.

Pepita toweled herself dry, then returned to the bed and handed me a damp washcloth. She climbed up on the bed and sat cross-legged beside me as I cleansed my thighs, crotch and limp penis. Her hair, still damp with perspiration, cascaded over her shoulders and splayed out over her breasts. On her lips was a tender smile.

"Pepita," I said as casually as I could, "what do I owe you for bringing me such pleasure?"

Her smile vanished. "For me, nothing, señor, but I was bidden to ask a favor of you."

"By whom? By Ramirez?"

"Yes."

I experienced a quick surge of anger. That bloated old bastard has used his stepdaughter to promote some kind of a swindle. My anger must have shown. Pepita, with a worried frown, leaned forward and gently touched my bearded cheek.

"Please do not be angry. Do not think ill of me. I should have asked the favor of you last night."

"Why didn't you?"

"I don't know. You are not like any man I have known. I . . . I should not have spent the whole night with you . . . but I wanted to. Was it wrong of me?"

My anger evaporated. "No," I said. "I don't think it was wrong of you. What was the favor your drunken stepfather wanted you to ask of me?"

"I do not know what passed between you yesterday afternoon, but, in some way, you shamed him. He asked me to tell you that he had reconsidered and will show you where emeralds are to be found. But he will need money to buy equipment. The favor I was to ask of you was that you advance him one thousand pesos to take care of the necessary expenses."

I could hardly believe my ears. "That alcoholic wreck can't even get up to piss," I said. "Do you expect me to believe that story? I don't feel like giving him money to keep him supplied with rum for the next six months."

Pepita's face registered concern. "Please," she said, "it is not as you think. He is not always as you found him yesterday. He told me to tell you that he will go to the hospital in Tunja, where the nuns will cure him of his sickness. He has done so before . . . although not for a long time. Once he is cured, he promises he will buy what is needed and guide you to a place where you should find the wealth you seek."

"I've known many drunks," I said. "Their promises aren't worth a damn. Why should I believe your stepfather?"

"Because," she said, "he is not lying to you. If you agree to his request, then you are not to be seen in his company. It would be too dangerous. There are people who would get suspicious and follow your . . . and his . . . every movement. They would follow you into the mountains and rob you. If you agree, I am to take the money to him. He will leave alone for Tunja this very day. You should be seen in and around the town today. He suggests that, to disguise your real interests, you make inquiries concerning the purchase of farmland. Tonight I will come here, but quite late so that no one will see me. Tomorrow, before sunup, we will leave together, and I will take you into the mountains. No one must see us leave. There are things you will need, but we will buy them along the way."

"If you know the region where I should prospect for emeralds, why do we need your stepfather?" I asked.

"But I do not know where to look for them," she said. "I know only the way to a *cabaña* in the mountains that in the past he used as a base camp. I am to take you there, where we will wait until he joins us in a week or two."

"Your mother," I asked, "does she know of this plan?"

"Yes, but she is against it. Once before, my stepfather was left for dead in the mountains. She fears that, if he goes in search of emeralds again, he will be killed. Then, too, as he is now, he is helpless and has need of her. I don't think she wants him cured of his sickness."

"But you do?"

"I would like to see him again the man he once was."

I thought it over. Preposterous as it sounded, it had about it the ring of truth. Certainly I could be being victimized, but if it was a confidence game it was a clever one. I didn't think that Ramirez, in his present alcohol-fogged state, could have contrived anything so complicated as a scheme to fleece me. Very well. I would take a chance.

When I told Pepita I would grant the favor Carlos asked of me, she clapped her hands together in delight. She scrambled down from the bed and quickly slipped into her panties and the thin cotton dress.

She came back to the bed and leaned over to kiss me. When she had done so, she hesitated before leaving.

"There is a question I have been wanting to ask," she said.

"What is it?"

"My stepfather told me you are from Central America, but I find you speak different from any Latin American I have ever met. And you speak Spanish with an unusual accent. Are you of Spanish extraction?"

I laughed. "No, I suppose you would call be a *gringo*. I have lived some years in the United States, but I hail from a distant land called Greece."

Her eyebrows lifted. "A *Greco*. You are the first I have met. If they are all like you, it is a land I could grow to love."

I must admit that, as the day progressed, the feeling grew in me that I had been neatly conned out of a thousand pesos. Nonetheless, as Pepita had suggested, I made some inquiries about land prices. In the evening, I settled my bill at the inn, letting it be known that I intended to go to Tunja on the morrow. After a late dinner, I returned to my room to await Pepita's arrival. As the hour grew later and later, I gradually convinced myself that I had been a gullible fool to have swallowed her story.

It was well after one o'clock in the morning that a soft knock on my door announced Pepita's arrival.

We traveled on foot, leaving the dirt road well before dawn and heading toward lightly forested rising ground. When Pepita had last made this journey eight years earlier, at fourteen, it had been on muleback. Appreciating that her memory would be hazy, Ramirez had provided her with a crude map and written instructions. The journey, which I estimated would have covered less than forty miles had we been able to travel directly to our destination, took us the better part of four days by the route Ramirez had laid out for us.

The things we needed — knapsacks, provisions and the woolen *ruanas* worn by mountaineering Colombians — we bought along the way, widely spacing our purchases.

The first part of the journey was not at all difficult. We climbed up a mountain by a well-defined trail at an easy angle of ascent. When we crested the ridge, we were on the lip of a rocky escarpment, gazing down into a farm-dotted valley far below. At the northern end of the valley, two mountains, their summits crowned with clouds, rose steeply. The furthermost of those mountains was our objective. The problem was that we had to descend into the valley and cross it without making our presence in the area known. At all costs, Ramirez had cautioned, we were to give a wide berth to the village at the base of the mountains, Villa de Leyva.

In the treacherous predawn light of the second day we worked our way cautiously down the escarpment, crossed the valley and spent the balance of the day hidden in the protecting folds of an eroded sandstone formation. At dusk we skirted the formation and made our way into a stand of pines on the lower flanks of the closer of the two mountains.

Starting at dawn on the third day, we circled the first mountain and started our ascent of the second. When darkness overtook us, we were high on the eastern face of the mountain.

The following morning, with Pepita stopping frequently to check our bearings, we ascended higher toward the peak; then, about noon, we started a descent that brought us to a tiny alpine valley tucked into a rocky cleft. There, in a forested and grass-carpeted hollow, hidden by an out-cropping and a rock overhang, was the *cabaña* we sought. Grass and brush-tufted rock shelved down to a small lake that mirrored the forbidding sheer rock face rising on its far side.

I couldn't think of a more ideal place for a secret base camp. The lake provided water. There was ample pasturage for mules. The pine forest was a ready source of firewood. And the cabin was safe from prying eyes until one was within only a few meters from it.

Don Carlos had chosen the site well. Gazing about at the looming cliffs, I wondered where his mining site was hidden.

The cabin was a solid structure of stone and cement. Its roof, one section of which had fallen in, was of thick thatch. From what Pepita had told me, Ramirez had abandoned it more than seven years ago, yet its windows were tightly shuttered and both the front door and the door to the storage shed at the back were shut and padlocked. It didn't look as though the cabin had been molested since Ramirez had deserted it. I doubted, in fact, if anyone, apart from Ramirez, Juana, Pepita — and now myself — knew of its existence.

Ramirez had given Pepita keys to the padlocks. The lock on the front door yielded readily enough, but I had to break the padlock on the storage shed. When I did, I found the shed a veritable treasure trove of tools — cement, window glass, tinned provisions, several boxes of ammunition and a rifle carefully wrapped in grease-soaked burlap. Ramirez, I concluded, hadn't abandoned the *cabaña*. When he had left it, he had fully intended to return.

I questioned Pepita about this. What she recalled was that, some months after she and her mother had accompanied Ramirez to the cabin and then returned to Chiquinquirá, he had stayed behind and, later, was to have gone to Tunja to deposit a two-year cache of emeralds in the bank. It had been on that journey that he had been ambushed by bandits, beaten within an inch of his life, robbed of his emeralds and his mules and left to die in a mountain pass. Had not some Indians found him, he surely would have died. He had returned to Chiquinquirá, broken in body and spirit. It had been then that he had taken to drinking heavily. Yes, she agreed with me, it certainly looked as though he had had every intention of returning. There was even, she pointed out, a supply of charcoal in the shed and firewood stacked at the base of the cliff. Who would go to such trouble if he intended to abandon the site?

Pepita and I stayed in the cabin for a full two weeks before Ramirez put in an appearance. Although I said nothing to Pepita, I was beginning to suspect that we had both been hoodwinked by the old drunk. Our supplies were running low, and I was on the verge of suggesting that we return to Chiquinquirá when Carlos — riding one mule and leading a second one heavily laden with supplies — arrived on the scene.

Our weeks of waiting were not idle ones.

One of the first things I did was to shave off the beard I'd grown. Not only did it itch, but also I felt it was camouflage I no longer needed.

The first thing Pepita did was to air the blankets and feather-stuffed tick of the cabin's single bunk. The first tasks to which I addressed myself were to repair the section of the roof that had fallen in and to replace the glass that had been broken in two of the windows. In less than two days, the cabin was as snug and shipshape as it must ever have been. And now, with a log fire crackling and sputtering in the stone fireplace, the cold nights at that altitude no longer troubled us.

It was a delight for me, when returning with a load of firewood or from stoking the charcoal pit, to hear Pepita singing as she went about her chores. But our greatest joy was when the evening meal was over. Then we would pull the mattress tick close to the fireplace and, naked in each other's arms, talk long into the night or make love passionately, or tenderly, as the spirit moved us.

CHAPTER TWENTY-FOUR

During our journey into the mountains and our waiting period in the alpine valley, Pepita and I came to know each other intimately. I don't think I have ever talked as openly with anyone, man or woman, as I did with Pepita. In turn, she confided to me details of her life so intimate that I doubt she had ever disclosed them to even her confessor.

I told Pepita of my boyhood in Cephalonia, my years in Corfu and my experiences, good and bad, in New York and Cuba and on board the *Pandora*. I talked about my father, mother, brother and two sisters. I told her of my romances with Danai and Teresa Martinelli — explaining that the latter had been nothing more than unrequited infatuation. Pepita smiled at my protestation of honorable intentions and said it sounded like the affair would have been consummated had not fate intervened.

Rather shamefacedly, I told Pepita of my affair with Phoebe and of fleeting affairs I had had in Cuba and Nova Scotia. I seemed to be under some strange compulsion to tell Pepita everything about my life to date and my dreams for the future. I even told her how I had intended to defraud the *Pandora's* owners. It had been that disaster, I said, that had led me all the way from Trujillo in Honduras to Tunja and, finally, all but penniless, to her drunken stepfather's doorstep in Chiquinquirá.

I freely admitted to Pepita that my only interest in emeralds was the acquisition of capital. If I was successful, I would see to it that never again would Constantine Sthanassis work for anyone but himself.

Pepita listened sympathetically to everything I told her. She expressed confidence that, with her stepfather's help, I would find the wealth I sought and that one day I would realize my ambition of returning to Greece a wealthy and respected man. She said she *knew* this to be true — that it was written in my stars.

In many ways, the story of Pepita's twenty-two years was a depressing one. The Fates had been against her even *before* she was born. She recounted the highlights of her life with stoical acceptance of this fact, but not complaint.

Her mestiza mother, Juana Maria Moreno, had been orphaned as a young child and raised as a charity ward in a convent. When Juana was young, Pepita said, she had been very beautiful. At the age of fourteen, while still in the convent, Juana had been sexually assaulted by a priest. She had run away from the convent to Bucaramanga, where she had drifted into prostitution.

At nineteen, Juana had given birth to a son, christened Ramón Julio Moreno. Two years later, she had given birth to a second, but stillborn, son. Then, three years later, Pepita, christened Josefa Maria Moreno, had been born — in Bucaramanga, as had her brother. Juana had not neglected her children and, in those days of youthful beauty, had prospered at her trade. As a child, Pepita claimed, she had lacked for nothing.

Then, when Pepita had been ten and Ramón fifteen, something had gone wrong. Pepita wasn't sure exactly what had happened but thought it had to do with the jealous wife of a public official. In any event, Juana had had to leave Bucaramanga. She had moved to Medellín.

In Medellín, Juana had met, in a professional capacity, a well-to-do widower, Carlos Ramirez. Two years later, Juana had taken sick and had appealed to Ramirez for help. He had paid her doctor's bills and hospital expenses and had advanced money for Ramón's and Pepita's care.

When, months later, Juana had been released from the hospital, what remained of her beauty had faded. Out of sympathy for her plight, Ramirez had taken her on as his housekeeper and accepted the responsibility for rearing her children. Juana and the children moved from Medellín to the house Carlos Ramirez maintained in Tunja.

What Pepita told me next shocked me. She told me that it was Ramón who had robbed her of her virginity when she had been but twelve and that, thereafter, he had frequently forced his attentions on her. It was something of which she was deeply ashamed, and, until she haltingly told me about it, it was a secret she had kept locked within her.

Don Carlos, I learned, had started to drink heavily some years ago when the family had still lived in Tunja. He had suffered financial reverses and had moved the family to a much smaller villa in Chiquinquirá. It was then that Ramón had left home to take up with a gang led by the notorious César Nuñez. Pepita had welcomed his departure.

Pepita had been fifteen when Don Carlos had returned from the mountains a broken man and had started once more to drink heavily. A year later, he could no longer afford the upkeep of his villa and had moved Pepita and Juana into *La Posada de los Andes*. They had lived there for close to three years before they were thrown out and had ended up living in the sordid little street where I'd found Don Carlos. It was then that Pepita had turned to prostitution as a means of supporting herself, her mother and her drunken stepfather.

"But," I protested, "surely there must have been some other course open to you. Couldn't you have married?"

"In a large city, I might have lived down the facts that I was the daughter of a well-known whore and that I'd been violated by my brother, but not in a pueblo the size of Chiquinquirá. No decent man would dream of marrying me."

"I thought you said you'd told no one of what happened between you and Ramón."

"That's true. Not even the priest. But Ramón must have boasted about it to his fellow *bandidos* because . . . as I discovered even before I became a *puta* . . . it was known to many."

"Well," I said, "there must have been *something* else you could have done."

"What?" Pepita shrugged with resignation. "Ramón didn't contribute so much as a peso. Don Carlos was helpless. Mama wouldn't leave his side. I was tied to the pueblo. In a village that size, there is little in the way of employment. I have little formal schooling. Prostitution was the only thing open to me."

"Then," I said, "Don Carlos and I have no choice but to succeed in our quest for emeralds so that you can leave Chiquinquirá and start a new life."

Pepita snuggled closer and hugged me tightly. "I pray that will be so," she murmured.

Don Carlos' arrival changed everything drastically. Pepita left the same day on muleback to go to Tunja by a roundabout route Carlos had mapped out for her. From Tunja, she would return to Chiquinquirá by bus.

I walked a short distance with her. When we were some distance from the cabin, I lifted her down from the mule, held her tightly and kissed her.

"Here," I said, handing her what money I had left.

"But, Kostas," she said, trying to give it back, "I can't accept this."

"You can. You will!" I said. "I don't want you going with men."

She looked up at me, her eyes bright with unshed tears. Her lips trembled. "*Amorcito,*" she said, "it would mean nothing. They would take only my body. They could not take my heart . . . it is yours. But it shall be as you wish. No man but you shall have me."

When I returned to the cabin, I found Carlos reassembling two stripped-down rifles on the tabletop. He glanced up. "You have grown fond of each other," he said.

"Yes," I said.

"Josefa is a fine girl. Don't let her down . . . as I have."

Embarrassed by his candor, I changed the subject. "Why such an arsenal?" I asked, nodding toward the rifles.

"We must go armed at all times," Carlos answered. "I'm pretty sure I wasn't followed, but bandits control this region. They buy off, intimidate or kill all who oppose them . . . police, army, civic officials. In this particular region, that devil César Nuñez behaves like a king. He thinks he's above the law. That is why I insisted that Josefa take the third rifle. She knows how to use it. God willing, she will not have to."

"For whose use is the fourth rifle?"

Carlos looked at me blankly. "What fourth rifle?"

"The one wrapped in burlap in the storage shed."

Carlos slapped his forehead with the palm of his hand. "*¡Por Diós!* I completely forgot about that gun. Well, it won't hurt us to have a rifle in reserve."

"When," I asked, "do we go to your mine?"

Carlos looked bewildered. "My mine?"

"Yes. Enrique told me you owned a lost Indian mine, a rich source of emeralds known only to you."

Carlos chuckled. "*Chico,* my fanciful young cousin has filled your head with nonsense . . . but, at least in part, I suppose I can be blamed for that. I must have told him tall tales of mines that the Indians had kept hidden from the early colonists for centuries. Probably I told him I had stumbled on such a mine, and, in a sense, that is true. But, like many people, I think Enrique had visions of bright, sparkling gemstones hanging in clusters from cave walls."

"But you do have a source of emeralds," I protested. "You said as much in Chiquinquirá. And this cabin. It must have taken you years to pack in the tools and materials and construct it. You didn't build it as a monastic retreat. Pepita called it your base camp. You boasted that you could lead me to emeralds the size of my fist. I can only assume that somewhere not *too* far from here you have a mine."

"*Had* a mine," Carlos said. "It wasn't a mine in the same sense as the world-renowned Boyacá emerald mines in Somondoco, or Chivor, or Muzo. It was a vein of beryl-bearing matrix. I worked the vein, on and off, for close to twenty years before it finally petered out eight years ago. As for emeralds the size of your fist, *chico*, I'm afraid that was the rum talking. Rough crystals of more than two or three centimeters in length are a rarity."

"If the vein is worked out," I said, "why the hell are we here?"

"Because, when the vein I was working ran out, I carefully examined the surrounding area. I think, from surface indications, I found another vein. I was going to come back here to prove it. For one reason or another, I didn't get around to it until now. If we're lucky, we'll come up with emerald-bearing matrix."

"And if we're not lucky?"

Carlos leaned one reassembled rifle against the wall and shrugged. "Then we'll have put in a few months of hard work for nothing."

And, I thought bleakly, I'll be a pauper.

When Carlos had said it would be hard work, he hadn't been exaggerating.

The site we worked was in a depression of a saddle between two soaring peaks. We reached the saddle only after a stiff climb that took close to two hours. Later, when I adapted to physical exertion at that altitude and Carlos regained much of his vigor sapped by heavy drinking and lack of exercise, we made the ascent in better time, but never in under an hour and a quarter.

At the site we labored with pickaxes, shovels, wedges and hammers, cutting into a stratified layer of gray-black bituminous limestone. As we cut deeper into the rock face, the layer widened and become mottled here and there with calcite nodules of lighter hue. As these calcite nests appeared, Carlos grunted in satisfaction.

Until our second week at the site, the calcite nodules, when broken open, yielded nothing but flecks of pyrites and quartz crystal. Then a day came when Carlos pried loose a calcite chunk with a greenish cast. He examined it closely, then broke it open with his hammer. Inside, some tiny crystals, roughly hexagonal in shape and smoky green in color, nestled in the nodule's coarse-grained center.

"*Chico*," Carlos said, "I was beginning to have doubts, but we're in luck. A lot of hard work lies ahead, but it won't be for nothing." Pointing to the greenish crystals, he added, "Those, my boy, are emeralds."

Carlos was right on both counts. We worked harder, and longer hours, than we had before, and our efforts did not go unrewarded.

As the weeks went by, we pried a small store of rough gemstones from their calcite nests. This tiny hoard of emeralds, ranging in size from no bigger than lentils to a few close to three centimeters in length, seemed pitifully small to me, considering the work we had put in over the past four months. When I mentioned this to Carlos, he smiled broadly. His estimated value of what we had accumulated made me gasp. If he was right, my half of the proceeds, translated from pesos to American currency, would exceed eight thousand dollars. And, according to Carlos, we had only scratched the surface of a rich vein.

The arrangement we had made before departure was that Pepita would return in four months with additional provisions. For the week prior to her anticipated arrival, I was jumpy and irritable. Carlos pretended not to notice, but from his quiet smile it was evident he knew what ailed me. Nonetheless, he said nothing. What he did say, however, the day before we expected Pepita, was that the cabin was getting stuffy. He suggested I take the day off to air the mattress tick and blankets. As for himself, he declared that he would take his sleeping bag down by the lake to sleep under the stars for a few nights, a gesture for which I was was properly grateful.

"You're sure you weren't followed?" Carlos asked.

"I'm almost certain I wasn't," Pepita said. "I backtracked several times like you told me to. I saw no one."

"My lengthy absence hasn't aroused suspicion?" Carlos asked.

"No. Everyone believes the story you circulated before leaving Tunja . . . that you were going to do some prospecting in the Coscuez region. But there *has* been speculation concerning the whereabouts of Señor Ricardo Lopez."

"Why should my presence, or absence, be of interest?" I asked.

"When we bought provisions in Pináculo pueblo, I was recognized, and the bearded man with me fit the description of the Señor Lopez who spent two nights at *La Posada de los Andes*. It was César Nuñez who came to question me about you."

"What did you tell him?" Carlos asked.

"I told him that Señor Lopez was an agricultural expert who was looking for the right condition in which to grow a valuable type of Asian cinnamon. He had paid me well to guide him into the mountains and to the eastern slopes leading down to the *Ilanos*, searching for just the right combination of altitude, soil, humidity and rainfall. On reaching the *Ilanos* foothills, I returned by way of Tunja. The story explained my absence of almost a month and the fact that I had returned with money."

Carlos nodded approvingly. "How," I asked, "did you manage to invent such a yarn?"

Pepita smiled. "Some years ago a *gringo* came to Tunja with just such a scheme. He hired Papa to guide him to the *Ilano* foothills. Isn't that so, Papa?"

"*Claro*, but it surprises me that you remember it. You had barely turned thirteen at the time."

After supper, Carlos yawned and said, "Think I'll turn in. I suggest you two turn in early, too, and get a good night's rest. Tomorrow I want you to start out for Bogotá. I want the emeralds we've collected safely stored in a bank. I don't want them here a moment longer than is absolutely necessary."

Pepita and I did go to bed early — but we didn't get much sleep that night.

CHAPTER TWENTY-FIVE

The route Don Carlos mapped out for us led almost due south before curving eastward to bring us to the highway well south of Tunja at a ranch belonging to a friend of his. We left the mules quartered at the ranch and caught the bus to Bogotá.

In Bogotá, we put up at a commercial hotel on the Avenida Ciudad de Lima, within easy walking distance of a number of banks and the address of the gem dealer Carlos had given me.

The following morning, I followed Carlos' instructions. First I rented a safety deposit box in a nearby bank. Keeping out only a few of the smaller stones, I stored the rest in the box. I sold the stones I'd retained to the gem dealer to raise money to cover our immediate expenses and to give us a small cash reserve. As Carlos had counseled, neither the quality nor quantity of the stones sold was such that they would cause a flurry of excitement in the gemstone market. The last thing we wanted at this stage was to attract undue attention to ourselves. From the indifference displayed by the dealer, there seemed little danger of that.

My business concluded, Pepita and I had nothing to do for a few days but to enjoy ourselves on a well-deserved vacation before once more forced to part company for months. When she left Bogotá, she would return directly to Chiquinquirá by bus. I would strike out in the direction of Tunja and get off the bus a kilometer or two from the *quinta* where we had left the mules. Leaving one mule behind for Pepita to pick up in August when she returned to restock us with provisions, I would ride the other mule into the mountains and back to the base camp.

Pepita and I spent five wonderful days, and five even more wonderful nights, in Bogotá. They were carefree days, and the nights were filled to overflowing with tenderness and passion. They sped by all too quickly.

I don't know exactly how to explain it. When I was with Pepita I felt complete, as though she gave me something that without her was missing. In mind and body, we seemed perfectly attuned. In all those days and nights together, I can recall only one difference of opinion between us.

I lay on my back, my head and shoulders propped against the bolster. Pepita lay within the circle of my right arm, her head on my shoulder, her body pressed close to mine. The fingers of her right hand nestled in the hair on my chest. Her right leg lay across my lower abdomen.

"I think," I said, gently stroking her hair, "that another seven or eight months should do it."

"Do what?"

"See us in a financial position where I can make plans for our future."

At my side, I felt her tense slightly. "What sort of plans?" she asked.

"Just as soon as I have enough money, I'll invest in a business more suited to my taste than mining, and we'll get married. I have no particular business in mind . . . but there are opportunities in Cuba, and I own property in New York."

She didn't say anything for almost a full minute. When, finally, she broke her silence, it was in a voice that was barely audible. "I cannot marry you, my love."

"Why not? We love each other, don't we?" I asked.

"Kostas," she answered, "I am your woman. Nothing can change that. I will go with you wherever you wish to take me . . . but I will not marry you. I have given it much thought. I am a whore . . . or was, until I met you. I have little schooling, I speak only Spanish and even that not well enough for polite society. With you it is different. You dream of greatness. You will achieve it. It is your destiny. As your wife, I would only hinder you. In time you would come to resent me . . . even hate me. That I could not endure. It is better . . . far better . . . that I remain your mistress for as long as you want me."

I shook her roughly. *"¡Por Diós!"* I exclaimed, "I don't want to hear such words from you! Not now! Not ever! If I succeed . . . as you are so confident I will . . . you will be at my side as my wife to share my triumph. You are the only woman I want to bear my children. They will *not* be born out of wedlock." I relaxed my grip on her shoulder and drew her close. My tone softened. "You will be *both* my mistress and my wife, *mi vida*."

She untwined her fingers from the hair on my chest, reached up and ran her finger lightly down the scar on my face. "If that is the way you want it, *amorcito*, and it is in our stars, then it will be so," she said.

It is an odd thing. At the time, it didn't strike me as strange. Now that I think back on it, until that night in the hotel in Bogotá when we had that conversation, I don't believe I thought at all about my former life in New York.

It must have been my mention of the property I still owned that triggered my memory. The next afternoon, after I had seen Pepita safely off on the bus, I returned to the hotel in deep thought. I suddenly felt it important to know the state of affairs in New York.

I was directed to a kiosk that stocked foreign newspapers. From it I bought copies of the New York *Daily News* and the *Daily Mirror* and returned to the hotel to digest their contents.

In general, the American scene as pictured in the newspapers was gloomy. Despite the reassuring predictions being made by economic experts in the Hoover Administration about good times just around the corner, the stock market crash and bank failures seem to have left the whole country in a financial mess. There were stories of businesses and factories closing down and ever-growing lines of the jobless. And reports from abroad indicated that economic conditions in Europe were equally unsettled and apparently worsening.

I derived wry satisfaction from the situation as reported. After all, I had been wiped out in the first wave of the disaster. It was gratifying to learn that I was not alone in my misery. But it was news of a different nature that caught and held my attention.

An editorial in the *Daily Mirror* stated that Prohibition had been an idiotic experiment and a miserable failure. Worse, it had spawned a wave of lawlessness that made a mockery of city, state and federal law enforcement agencies. It was not enough, the editorial said, that mobsters such as Chicago's Al Capone and New York's infamous Vito Martinelli had drawn stiff prison terms for income tax evasion. If there was any justice in the land, the editorial contended, gangsters like that should go to the electric chair for the murders they had ordered. Such men corrupted all they touched and should be stamped out like the vermin they were. The editorial went on to demand a repeal of the Eighteenth Amendment and a return to sanity and law and order. There was more, in a similar vein, but I'm afraid that once Vito's name caught my eye I paid little attention to the rest of it.

So Vito had been jailed. The editorial had mentioned a stiff prison sentence but hadn't specified how stiff. Was Vito still behind bars? If so, it was unlikely that he exercised enough authority from a prison cell to carry on his vendetta against me. Or could he? It was maddening. I needed to know.

That evening I wrote Sofoclis a long letter. The next day, when I checked out of the hotel, I said I was going to Barranquilla but would return in a few months. I said I was expecting some mail. The desk clerk assured me that they would hold any mail addressed to Señor Ricardo Lopez until my return.

When I told Carlos that I planned to marry Pepita, he didn't seem at all surprised, yet neither did he receive the news with any great show of enthusiasm.

"Has she told you of her mother . . . and of her own life in Chiquinquirá?" Carlos asked.

"Yes. What she was is not important. She is no longer a *puta*."

Carlos smiled. "I am glad to hear that. I hoped that Josefa had given it up, but lacked the courage to ask her about it. I must say, she has been a different person since meeting you. If you know of her unfortunate background and are prepared to overlook it, you have every chance for happiness together. But take care that, one day in anger, you do not throw her past in her face. She took to prostitution through no fault of hers. The fault was mine."

"I love her too much to hurt her as you suggest," I said. "And I'm well aware that the fault was yours . . . yours, and her mother's."

Carlos smiled again. "Love follows strange and often twisted paths, *chico*. Stick to your resolve not to give her pain."

It happened a few days before Pepita was due to rejoin us. I shall never forget the excitement of that moment.

Carlos had loosened a large chunk of grayish-green calcite from its limestone bed. I wasn't paying any attention when he broke open the nodule until his long, low whistle caused me to turn in his direction. He was staring into the rock's center, his eyes wide in astonishment. Gingerly he worked his knife blade until he extracted a rough gemstone that appeared more than four centimeters long.

"*¡Madre de Diós!*" he said wonderingly, staring at the huge rough emerald cradled in the palm of his hand. "It is magnificent. It is the largest stone I have ever seen."

He held it up toward the sun and squinted at the gemstone appraisingly. I moved closer to get a better look. "Is it valuable?" I asked.

"Valuable? Some of the emeralds you stored in the bank are valuable. A couple may be very valuable. But *this* one, *chico,* this is worth a fortune."

He handed it to me. I examined it curiously. Then, when I went to return it, he wouldn't take it from me. Instead, he closed my fingers around it. "It's yours," he said.

I protested. "We agreed to split fifty-fifty. It's as much yours as mine. I can't accept it as a gift."

"You can, and will," Carlos said. "Consider it my wedding present to you and Josefa. Had you not arrived in Chiquinquirá when you did, *chico,* I would still be a useless drunk . . . if not, by now, a corpse. Either way, this beautiful emerald would not have seen the light of day."

Carlos and I talked it over. The arrangement we arrived at was that, when Pepita returned, we would give her a few days to rest up, then all three of us would go to Bogotá by the route Pepita and I had taken on our trip three months earlier.

In Bogotá, as before, I would sell some of the smaller stones. Then, with Carlos acting as a witness, Pepita and I would get married. With my share of the emeralds, Pepita and I would go to the Ecuadorian capital, Quito. Carlos claimed that in Quito I would get a better price for the stones, and it would delay, if not prevent, unwanted speculation in the Bogotá gemstone market concerning the source of emeralds of such size and quality.

After Pepita and I left for Ecuador, Carlos would return to Chiquinquirá, collect Juana, if she would agree to go with him, and return to the mine by a devious route. He intended to work the vein for a few more months before leaving the site, if only temporarily. And, if things didn't work out for me as I anticipated, I could always return to the mine. It was, Carlos assured me, as much mine as his.

On the evening of Pepita's return, we walked hand in hand along the shore of the lake. I told her of the plans Carlos and I had made.

"Are you sure that is what you want, Kostas?" she asked.

Taking her face in my hands, I lifted it toward mine. I have no idea why, but her eyes were misted with tears. I kissed her eyes, the tip of her nose and then, lingeringly, her lips.

"Yes," I said. "It is what I want."

She circled my waist with her arms and placed her cheek against my chest. "Then it shall be as you wanted it. Your child will be legitimate," she said.

"My child?" I asked.

She looked up at me, her eyes shining. "It has been forming in my womb since our stay in Bogotá."

CHAPTER TWENTY-SIX

We had no reason to suspect that Pepita had been followed. As on her previous visit, she had exercised due caution and had seen nothing to arouse suspicion.

Whoever it was who had tracked her must have done so at some distance. Having discovered the location of our *cabaña*, the tracker must have returned to wherever his companions were encamped to recruit the raiding party that invaded us.

Pepita had been with us for three days. During that time, Carlos had gone up to the mine site each day in order, if possible, to add to our hoard of emeralds. I had stayed down in the valley to tend the smoldering charcoal pits and to lay in a stock of firewood against Carlos' eventual return from our visit to Bogotá.

It was dusk. I was returning, leading a mule heavily burdened with firewood, when I heard a shot ring out from the direction of the cabin. Dropping the halter, I raced stumbling through the brush, cursing myself with every stride for having neglected to leave the cabin armed.

Five mules stood in the coarse grass in front of the cabin, only one of which I recognized as ours. From the cabin came sounds of cursing and the noise of furniture being smashed.

When I reached a point where I could see through a window, I checked my headlong dash and, stricken, viewed the scene within.

Three men, one of whom I recognized as Pepita's half-brother, were ransacking the cabin. One of them was slitting open the mattress ticking. Ramón, on his hands and knees in front of the cupboard where we stored our clothing, was ripping shirts, trousers and woolen outer garments to shreds. As I watched, the third man swept earthenware pots and bowls off the shelf by the stove with the butt of his rifle. It was obvious they were searching for our store of emeralds. And it was equally obvious that Pepita, who knew they were buried in a cache by the lake, had not disclosed the hiding place.

The fourth man, who I guessed was the leader, stood beside Pepita, a long-barreled revolver pointed downward at her head. He was a swarthy-faced mestizo of more than average height, scowling darkly as he watched his men methodically tear apart the cabin.

Pepita was seated before the table. The front of her dress had been ripped open to the waist, exposing one breast. Her small hands were clenched into fists. Her expression was one of tight-lipped defiance, not fear.

A rifle lay on the floor at Pepita's feet. It was she, I realized, who must have fired the single shot that had alerted me. None of the brigands appeared injured, so I assumed she had had time only to fire the warning shot. From where I stood, I could see my own rifle in its rack above the fireplace. A lot of good it would do me there.

Where was Carlos, I wondered? It was getting dark. He should have come down from the mine before this. Well, if he had, he was nowhere in evidence. It was up to me to do something.

To rush into the cabin, weaponless, against four armed cutthroats was to invite sure death for me, and probably Pepita as well. What I had to do, then, was to make them come to me.

I looked around for something to use as a weapon. My frantic gaze settled on a pickaxe handle leaning against the wall. It wasn't much to use against knives, revolvers and rifles, but it was better than nothing. Armed with the axe handle, I could position myself by the door, club the first man to exit the cabin and, with luck, acquire a more effective weapon. Now all I needed was some ruse to get them out of the cabin.

Then a thought struck me: I *wasn't* without a weapon! I had completely forgotten about the rifle in the storage shed.

It took me some minutes to find the sacking-wrapped rifle, and more minutes to unwrap it, wipe off some of the outer film of grease and load it. Jamming a fistful of cartridges into my pocket, I worked my way around to the front of the cabin.

At the window, I paused. What I saw inside momentarily froze me in my tracks.

Pepita had been stripped naked. She lay stretched out on the floor. Ramón was holding her arms. A man on each side held her legs wide-spread. Between her legs, on his knees, was the tall mestizo in the act of dropping his trousers.

White-hot rage surged through me. I went berserk. My memory of the next few minutes is confused. Blurred. Out of focus.

I recall bursting through the cabin door screaming like a madman and firing my rifle as fast as I could work the lever. My target was the mestizo leader. How many shots I got off, I don't remember. Two. Possibly three. I'm not sure. Then, close to my face, I saw a rifle muzzle spit flame. Something seemed to explode in my head. A blinding white glare enveloped me. Then blackness.

When I regained consciousness, I was lying on the floor, my head cradled in Carlos' lap. I tried to sit up, but sparks danced before my eyes, and a searing headache struck me. I sank back with a gasp of pain.

"Take it easy," Carlos said. "I thought you were dead. They must have thought so, too. But the bullet just creased your skull."

I reached up and touched the side of my head. My hand came away wet with blood.

I moved my head cautiously to survey the room. It was a shambles of broken furniture and crockery. Torn clothing and feathers from the shredded mattress were strewn everywhere.

On the far side of the room lay a body sprawled at an awkward angle in a pool of blood. I recognized the corpse. It was that of the tall mestizo.

In the center of the room, next to the remains of the smashed table, an inert form covered with a blanket lay stretched out on the floor.

Carlos was seized with a fit of coughing. When the spasm subsided, I asked, "What happened?"

"I was late returning," he said. "Later than I should have been. I was on the far side of the rise when I heard a single shot. I started to run toward the cabin. When I got to this side of the rise, there was a rapid volley of shots. As I neared the cabin, I heard shouting and cursing. Then — " He was cut short by another coughing spell.

"Then what?" I prompted.

Carlos took a deep breath. "Through the window I saw Nuñez bandaging his thigh. You were slumped in the corner, your head a bloody mess. That piece of filth Josefa calls her brother was shouting and struggling with two men I've never seen before."

I think I knew the answer to my next question before I asked it. "Pepita?"

Carlos nodded mutely toward the blanket-covered form. When I started to crawl in that direction, Carlos put a restraining hand on my chest. I pushed his hand aside and moved forward on my hands and knees.

I wish now that he had had the strength to stop me.

When I lifted the top corner of the blanket, Pepita's sightless eyes stared up at me. Her mouth hung open. Her throat had been cut.

I shuddered, turned aside and vomited on the floor. But I still had not seen the worst. The blanket, which I still clutched in nerveless fingers, slid off to reveal her naked body and its gaping abdominal wound. She had been laid open from breastbone to crotch. A tangle of her blood-drenched guts had spilled out onto the floor.

I fainted.

I don't know how long I was unconscious. Probably no more than a few minutes. When I came to, Carlos had replaced the blanket. Nonetheless my eyes were drawn to the covered form.

"Who did it? Nuñez?" I asked.

"No. Ramón."

"Ramón! Her own brother! Good God! Why?"

"I don't know. I only know what I saw," Carlos said. "One of the bandits, his trousers around his ankles, was arguing with Ramón. It looked to me as though they had been fighting. Another of the bandits was hanging onto Ramón's right arm. Ramón held a knife in that hand. The knife, and his hand and forearm, dripped blood."

"Pepita," I said. "Where was she? What was *she* doing? You were armed. Wasn't there anything you could have done to save her?"

Carlos' face took on a stricken expression. "I . . . could only see her from the waist down. She was where she now lies . . . only her legs were spread wide apart. There was no sign of movement. I think . . . I'm almost positive . . . she was already dead."

"But you said it was Ramón who did . . . that!" I said, pointing with a trembling hand toward the blanket-covered corpse.

Carlos nodded. "He did. He broke loose from the man holding him and, screaming curses, dropped to his knees and ripped Josefa open with his knife. I couldn't stop him. I didn't have a clear line of fire. I did the next best thing. I shot Nuñez," he said, nodding toward the body on the opposite side of the room. "I guess that seeing Nuñez killed before their eyes panicked them. All three of them were out the door before I could get off another shot. I raced around to the front and dropped one before they made it to the mules. I think he's dead. I haven't checked. He's lying about twenty meters from the doorway. I started —'' Once more Carlos stopped in midsentence as he was racked with another coughing fit.

When his coughing subsided, I noticed for the first time that his lips were flecked with blood. His shirt was soaked with blood. Until that moment, I had taken it for granted that it was wet with my blood — not his.

''You're wounded,'' I said, regretting that, in my thoughts, I had been accusing him of timidity, if not cowardice.

''When I chased them, they gave answering fire. I was hit in the chest. It's nothing.''

It wasn't nothing. We both knew it. He could drown in his own blood if he didn't get medical attention. ''We'll have to get you to a doctor,'' I said.

Carlos wiped his mouth with the back of his hand. ''How? They took the mules.''

''All but one,'' I said. ''There's one still loaded with firewood not far from here. I'll bury Pepita . . . then get the mule.''

''No. Don't bury her. Burn the cabin. It's what I was getting set to do before I noticed you stir and realized you weren't dead. I never want to see this place again.''

Inside, the kerosene-soaked contents of the cabin blazed fiercely. Flames licked out through the door and windows. I turned my back on the crackling funeral pyre and did my best to concentrate on loading the mule with the bedrolls and provisions we would need for our journey. But it wasn't easy to concentrate. I had a splitting headache. Scalding tears blurred my vision. My fingers fumbled as I tried vainly to tie the knots.

Carlos approached from the direction of the lake. He had gone to the lakeshore to retrieve our cache of emeralds. I watched as he came into the circle of light cast by the burning cabin. His footsteps dragged. His face was haggard and drawn with pain. He would be lucky if he was still alive by the time we reached Chiquinquirá. He wouldn't have stood the slightest chance, making the journey on foot.

Then it came to me. Carlos had believed all the mules had been stolen. He had believed me dead, and himself as good as dead. Yes, he had been preparing to make a funeral pyre of the cabin — and he had intended to be in it when it burned. The emeralds? If I knew Carlos, they too would have been among the ashes.

With Carlos astride the mule, and me leading the beast, we started westward toward Chiquinquirá. Carlos did not survive the night.

CHAPTER TWENTY-SEVEN

I rode into Chiquinquirá late in the afternoon. The innkeeper was surprised to see me. He asked me if I had been successful in my quest for a suitable farming area in the eastern foothills. For a moment, I didn't know what he was talking about and stared at him blankly. Then I remembered the story Pepita had circulated and made some comment about it being too hot and humid in the *llanos* to suit my purpose.

I bathed, shaved and embarked on another sort of quest. I was prepared to find Ramón Moreno if I had to follow him to the ends of the earth. I found him, in fact, within an hour after my arrival in Chiquinquirá — at the same *cantina* where I had first met Pepita and first seen her glowering half-brother.

When I relive that brief scene, it always plays itself out on the screen of my mind like a film shown in slow motion.

Ramón was with two companions, neither of whom I had seen before. Ramón's back was to me as, knife in hand, I came up behind him.

"*Hijo de puta,*" I said, if a flat, hard voice.

Ramón reacted to the insult exactly as I had expected. His right hand flew to the revolver tucked into the waistband of his trousers as he whirled to face me. I grasped his right wrist with my left hand to prevent him from completing the draw, but it was a wasted precaution. When he saw me, the color drained from his face, and he swallowed convulsively. At that moment, I doubt that he was capable of completing the draw.

I didn't give him long to wonder whether he'd seen a ghost. I buried my knife to its hilt in his belly and sawed upward. The sound he made was an odd mixture of a grunt and a gurgle. He started to sag onto my upthrusting blade.

I released his wrist and, with my left hand, caught him by the hair as I withdrew the knife from his guts. I wrenched his head back.

"For Pepita!" I snarled, as I slashed his throat with such savage force that I came close to severing his head from his body. Blood spurted over me, the bar and the barmaid, who had witnessed the killing in open-mouthed horror.

I let go my grip of his hair. His eyes glazing in death, Ramón slid slowly down the front of the bar. I hastened his descent by kicking his legs sideways.

Nobody made any attempt to stop me as I stalked from the *cantina*. Neither the barmaid, Ramón's drinking companions nor the one or two others in the bar moved a muscle or uttered a sound.

I fully expected to be questioned by someone — police or army officials — concerning my role as Ramón's self-appointed executioner. Nothing. Neither that night nor the next morning was the incident so much as mentioned in my presence. As a matter of fact, when I climbed on board the bus at noon, a policeman in the dusty plaza grinned broadly and gave me a mock salute. I gathered that Chiquinquirá was more than happy to be rid of Ramón Moreno.

I should have gone to the house in Calle de las Putas and turned over Carlos' share of the emeralds to Juana. But I didn't. Had Carlos lived, he could have done what he wanted with his share of the proceeds. Had he wanted to, he could have given it all to Juana. But I had nothing but contempt for a mother who would encourage her daughter to become a prostitute and live off her daughter's earnings. I have never regretted for a single moment not having given anything to Juana. As far as I was concerned, she could starve to death.

CHAPTER TWENTY-EIGHT

Try as I may, I cannot clearly recall the period immediately following Pepita's death and my act of grim reprisal. It is like trying to fit together a jigsaw puzzle with some of the pieces missing.

Instinct overrode reason. Like a wounded animal striving to crawl back to its lair, I wanted to quit the Colombian uplands and make my way back to a more familiar environment: the sea. In my confused state of mind, the mountainous highlands represented pain and terror; the sea represented safety. But before I could respond to the sea's siren call, there were matters I had to attend to. Thankfully, while I performed these tasks mechanically, I did so rationally.

In Bogotá, recognizing there was no longer need for secrecy, I sold two of the larger gemstones. Even in my emotionally drained state, I had the presence of mind not to accept the first offer, but shopped around among the emerald buyers and determined the approximate worth of my accumulated hoard. To my surprise, excluding the large emerald I had decided not to part with, the total value exceeded the equivalent of forty thousand dollars.

I withdrew the gemstones from bank custody and added them to those stowed in the canvas money belt Pepita had made for me. That done, I checked out of the hotel.

I was leaving the hotel when the desk clerk dashed over to me. With profuse apologies for not having given it to me when I'd checked in three days earlier, he handed me a letter postmarked New York. I thanked the clerk and put the letter into the inside pocket of my jacket. There it stayed, unread, for over a month.

I don't recall much about the train journey to Buenaventura except that, as we descended from the Cordillera Occidental to the coastal plain, the moist heat hit me like a hammer blow.

In Buenaventura I checked into a first-class commercial hotel and had my money belt placed in the hotel safe. Thereafter, the picture becomes distorted and confused.

Perhaps, had I been able to obtain a berth on a ship as master or mate, it might have been different. Such was not the case. Due to the economic doldrums gripping the world, those who had seagoing billets were grimly hanging onto their jobs. I suppose I should have expected that condition, but it hadn't even crossed my mind. The sea was my sought-after haven, but its solace was denied me.

I hung around waterfront haunts of seaferers, drinking to excess. From time to time I checked with shipping agents, but without much hope or enthusiasm. Did I expect someone to come up to me in a bar or brothel and offer me a master's berth? Frankly, I can't say what I thought. I was so immersed in grief and self-pity that I made no serious effort to change the situation. I just drifted. This continued for some weeks before I woke up to the fact that I was going nowhere but downhill — fast.

I don't know exactly how it struck me, or why, but one morning, through the haze of a thumping hangover, I had a mental picture of Don Carlos as I'd first met him. It shook me. If I continued on my present course, *I* could end up a drunken derelict. By my present conduct I was not only letting myself down, but was also dishonoring Pepita's memory. She had been confident I would become a successful man. I sure as hell wasn't going to achieve much drinking myself into a stupor night after night in Buenaventura.

That was the turning point. Four days later I booked passage for the Ecuadorian river port of Guayaquil. It was when I was packing for that voyage that Sofoclis' letter fell out of the pocket of the jacket I hadn't worn since leaving Bogotá.

Before I relate the unexpected contents of Sofoclis' letter or record what befell me in Guayaquil, I should dwell for a moment more on the profound effect Pepita's death has had on my life and actions, not just at that time but also in the years that followed.

From the night I left the mountain valley with her dying stepfather, Pepita has occupied a special niche in my memory. I recall pausing briefly to look back at the flames leaping upward from the cabin's burning thatched roof. It did something to me.

I'm not sure what, but, from that moment, I placed Pepita in a sort of sealed compartment in my mind. The image of her that has remained with me through the years is as she was, young, lovely and radiant with happiness, in those last few days we spent together. I had no wish to share that memory. For years — far too many years — I could not bring myself to speak her name aloud.

It was not a good thing to keep her locked away in my heart and soul. I know that. I have known that for a long time. Nor would Pepita have wanted it so. Had I been able to talk freely of that romantic interlude I might have led a happier, fuller life and brought less pain to those who shared my life in later years.

I would have loved both Pepita and our child dearly and am sure we would have had other children. But behind those convictions lie thoughts I rarely probe. Had she lived, my life probably would have been very different. With Pepita at my side, I might not have felt driven to achieve such success. But, if the drive could not be dampened, I fear she *would* have proved the handicap she visualized — and I fear I would have, in time, resented her for this.

But those are thoughts that have grown slowly over the years. At the time, in Guayaquil, and as I moved on to broader horizons, I lived with an aching emptiness that goaded me to strive to attain the promise Pepita had seen written in my stars.

The news in Sofoclis' letter was startling. It had been written in October. However, even had it reached me sooner, or had I read it when the desk clerk gave it to me, it wouldn't have changed anything. On the other hand, had I known its contents in the early part of the year, it might have considerably altered my actions. The irony of the situation was that, all the time I'd been fleeing supposed pursuers, no one had been looking for me.

Vito had accepted my report to Rodriguez y Cia. at face value. It seemed that Enrique had added a rider to the report giving my courage and seamanship credit for having saved the *Pandora* and all aboard her from almost certain destruction. Having learned that I knew him to be the ship's owner, Vito had been impressed by my actions and stated intended actions. So much so, in fact, that he had told Sofoclis and Omeros that he would not oppose my return to the States.

Then, with weightier things on his mind, Vito had lost all interest in my movements or activities. Having been indicted on a number of charges ranging from implication in murder to bribery and tax evasion, Vito, on the advice of his lawyer, had pleaded guilty to tax evasion and was sentenced to ten years in Leavenworth. Not that Vito had served much of that sentence. In late August, Vito had been stabbed to death by an unknown assailant in the prison exercise yard.

Concerning my position, Sofoclis stated that all charges except that of rumrunning had been dropped, and Omeros was confident that he could get that charge set aside.

With respect to himself, Sofoclis advised that the market crash and bank failures had cleaned him out. He had had to borrow from Omeros and Phoebe to keep Metaxis & Company from going under.

The concluding line of the letter puzzled me. It read: "Aletha sends her love." When mother died, Penny had taken Aletha on as personal secretary. I had no idea why she would be sending her love. The mystery was not cleared up for some months, until a letter from Penny informed me that, on a trip to Phoenix, Sofoclis and Aletha had dated. Two months later, they had been married.

If now there was no real obstacle to prevent me from returning to the United States, why did I not do so instead of journeying to Ecuador? There were two reasons. One, I'd been told that my chances of obtaining an officer's berth in a merchant ship would be better in Guayaquil than they were in Buenaventura. Two, as Don Carlos had indicated, emeralds commanded a better price in Ecuador than in Colombia. The latter was fact, the former wishful thinking.

By the time I'd negotiated the sale of all but the one magnificent gemstone in my cache of emeralds, the lack of seagoing berths seemed relatively unimportant. By then, one disclosure in Sofoclis' letter had diverted my thoughts into other channels.

Ecuador was an exporter of agricultural products such as bananas and other tropical fruits. Sofoclis had managed to keep Metaxis & Company from foundering. Thus, Metaxis & Company represented a potential importer of Ecuadorian produce. All I needed to do was effect a marriage of those interests. Having arrived at that conclusion, I sought advice from the manager of the bank in which I'd deposited my funds and had vault-stored the large emerald for safekeeping.

"An assured market. It's an interesting proposition, Señor Sthanassis," the bank manager said. "I can see only one drawback."

"Which is?" I asked.

"You're a tourist. To own and operate a business such as you propose calls for resident status."

"How long would that take?"

"It's difficult to say. Even with connections it can be a lengthy process."

"Then you advise against the venture?"

"Not at all," the bank manager said. "Ours is not a rich country. The last thing we want to do is turn away capital investment."

I smiled thinly. "Have you an alternate suggestion?"

"Form a joint venture with an established local firm engaged in exporting Ecuadorian commodities. I'm confident your proposal will meet with enthusiastic response."

"Can you recommend such a company?"

The banker smiled. "*Claro*. Guayaquil Exportación, a reputable exporting concern and valued client of this bank. If you like, I can arrange a meeting between yourself and Fernando Alvarez, the owner of the company."

Alvarez, as well he should have been, was receptive to my proposal. Guayaquil Exportación had nothing to lose. At no cost to the company other than processing paperwork, it stood to gain access to what had been a virtually untapped market. The risk was entirely mine. My end of the bargain was to underwrite the purchase and shipping of the initial cargo. If the transaction proved profitable, I would have the option of buying into the company as a junior partner.

Although I did not recognize it as such at the time, my agreement with Guayaquil Exportación was the first stumbling footstep along the road that eventually would lead to the realization of my boyhood dreams of wealth and influence. Everything that had led up to that point could be termed my apprenticeship.

CHAPTER TWENTY-NINE

When I left Colombia I discarded my assumed identity of Ricardo Lopez and entered Ecuador as Constantine Sthanassis, using my seaman's identity papers. Once it became obvious that my seagoing career was in limbo, seaman's papers were no longer adequate. Through the Greek honorary consul I obtained a Greek passport and, now armed with this proof of citizenship, applied for and in due course was granted Ecuadorian resident status.

My correspondence with Sofoclis did not develop as I'd expected. In spite of the fact that my initial shipment to Metaxis & Company was on a consignment basis, he was reluctant to accept the cargo, advancing spoilage as his reason. He was, of course, under obligation to me and had little choice but to take delivery. Then, when the shipment was already on the water, he wrote suggesting it would be advisable to offer the produce at below-market pricing to insure quick turnover.

One thing I'd learned when working for Uncle Nicholas was that people will happily pay premium prices for quality produce; sacrifice pricing makes people suspicious of the product and normally inhibits sales. Sofie had spent most of his adult life in the importing and wholesale produce business. Surely he was conversant with this maxim of the trade. Granted, trading with Ecuador was something new for Metaxis & Company, but that, to my way of thinking, didn't excuse Sofie's trepidation. I answered his letter with a caustic reply that he need have no fears concerning the quality of Ecuadorian commodities and advised him to offer them to the trade at premium prices.

Thankfully, Sofie heeded my advice. The first shipment moved quickly. Our second shipment was on a letter-of-credit basis. From then on, orders increased in size and frequency. It was an even more profitable venture than I'd envisioned.

By the end of 1931, I'd acquired Ecuadorian resident status and become a full partner in Guayaquil Exportación. I should have been a happy man. I wasn't. I could see areas we were not exploiting to advantage and wanted to expand our operations.

Fernando opposed expansion. He was delighted with the increased business accruing to the company but lacked the courage to embark on what he considered risky ventures.

Early in 1932, exasperated by Fernando's lack of vision, I took matters into my own hands. Ostensibly I set out on a business trip to New York, embarking as a passenger on a freighter carrying one of our shipments as part of its cargo. My unspoken intention was to explore broader commercial horizons.

After transiting the Panama Canal, we tied up at Barranquilla to load coffee. During our brief stay in that port city I concluded an agreement with a Colombian coffee exporting firm similar to the deal I'd originally made with Guayaquil Exportación.

From Barranquilla we proceeded north to Havana to top up with bagged sugar. I found the Cuban city little changed from when I'd left it unceremoniously some two-and-a-half years earlier.

While the ship was unloading, I took advantage of my free time to visit several of my old waterfront haunts and made casual inquiries concerning the *Pandora*. I learned that the vessel had changed hands some eighteen months ago and was delighted to learn that her captain was Enrique Ramirez.

Havana was abuzz with rumors concerning the upcoming presidential election in the United States. Prohibition, it seemed, was a contentious political issue. If the Democratic candidate, Franklin Delano Roosevelt, won the election, repeal of the Volstead Act was sure to follow. In fact, as far as I could gather, regardless of who won the election, Prohibition's days were numbered.

I made a mental note of that prediction. It meant that the freewheeling era of rumrunning was about to become history. In that event, owners of a number of coastal vessels such as the *Pandora* would find it difficult to secure cargoes in competition with newer, faster merchant ships. The probable result would be a buyer's market for vessels like the *Pandora*.

I was acutely aware of an essential weakness in the trading positions of South American exporters in general and Guayaquil

Exportación in particular. Distance was our adversary — distance, canal transit charges *and* a lack of adequate sea transport. Europe was closer to New York than was Ecuador. Europe and North America were served by long-established maritime links sadly lacking between North and South America.

Procuring hold space for South American cargoes was an expensive proposition. The solution was obvious: more ships and regular schedules. And therein lay the snag. Based on the existing volume of trade, no shipping company would be able to justify the expense of increased service.

But what if ships could be acquired for a song and the volume of trade increased substantially? It *could* become a paying proposition. It would be a worthwhile gamble.

All of which brought me back to my starting position. More was involved than the purchase price of coastal cargo vessels; they would have to undergo conversion to bring them up to standards suited to the trade. These were costly considerations, which put the gamble beyond my reach.

I disembarked in the United States at New Orleans. If I was a wanted lawbreaker, immigration officials in New Orleans had no record of that fact.

From New Orleans I flew to New York. I recall it as a bumpy ride as the pilot of the twin-engine aircraft weaved his way between towering thunderheads over the Carolinas.

New York's skyline had undergone considerable change during the seven years of my absence. There were other changes — the mode of dress, the automobiles, the storefronts — but what struck me most forcibly was a more subtle change. It was one of attitude. In the mid-twenties, New Yorkers had displayed a carefree buoyancy. Now their faces wore worried frowns. The mood was one of troubled concern. Yet, oddly enough, I immediately felt at home. It was as though the city were welcoming me back as one of its own.

I didn't have time to dwell on my fancied homecoming, nor to visit many of my former haunts. My business was with Sofoclis.

In the three years since last I'd met him in Havana, Sofie seemed to have aged. It wasn't anything physical. It was more a matter of outlook. Where formerly he had been outgoing, he now seemed hesitant and reserved. Previously he had eagerly seized on suggestions I had advanced. Now his response was cautious, almost to the point of timidity.

He had turned a tidy profit on the commodities we'd shipped him from Ecuador, yet, despite this, he was markedly reluctant to accept the Colombian coffee already consigned to him. When I advanced the suggestion that Metaxis & Company should expand its operations to include West Coast markets already being serviced by Guayaquil Exportación, he refused even to consider the proposal.

I attributed Sofie's uncharacteristic hesitancy to the stagnant American economy. Some days later, when I visited Penny and Omeros in Phoenix, I received a different explanation.

Since mid-1929, when Omeros and Penny had moved to Phoenix, their visits to New York had been infrequent. Though they had seen little of Sofoclis and Aletha, they had kept in touch through correspondence. Omero said he would have severed his bootlegging connections entirely had it not been for a growing concern for Sofie. Omeros had feared that Sofoclis was being unduly influenced by Vito and had cautioned Sofie of the dangers involved in becoming too closely identified with mobsters. Sofie had scoffed at the warning.

When Vito had been indicted and sentenced to prison, Sofie had been shaken, yet he hadn't become truly frightened until Vito had been murdered. Only then had Sofie heeded Omeros' counsel, pulled out of bootlegging, broken with his former racketeer associates and devoted his attention to the legitimate side of the family business. And by then, as Sofie himself had informed me, Metaxis & Company had been in serious difficulties due to collapsing markets.

Omeros and Phoebe had come to Sofie's assistance by lending him enough money to stave off bankruptcy. Then I learned something Sofie had *not* told me, something which had direct bearing on his hesitant attitude. At the time he'd been forced to borrow, Sofie had secured the loans with corporate shareholding to the tune of sixty percent of the company divided equally between Omeros and Phoebe — *and the loans were still outstanding*.

Omeros apprised me of something else I didn't know. During my enforced absence, Omeros had taken it upon himself to pay the taxes on and collect rents from my New York property holdings. These monies were deposited to an account in my name in a bank that had *not* failed during the market debacle in '29. In short, instead of being wiped out by the crash, I found myself in a healthy financial position.

What I proposed to Omeros was that I repay the loan advanced to Sofie and that the shareholding he'd put up as collateral be transferred to me. When I explained what it was I had in mind, Omeros accepted my proposition.

Despite Penny's assurance that Phoebe would welcome my visit, I approached the meeting with apprehension. I need not have worried.

Phoebe's producer-director husband, Irving Goldman, was rotund, bald, half a head shorter than Phoebe and quite obviously adored her. Phoebe appeared to return his love measure for measure. I was happy things had turned out so well for her. It removed any lingering feelings of guilt I'd harbored.

Evidently Phoebe had told Irving about the affair we'd once had. He didn't seem to resent it and insisted I be their houseguest while in Los Angeles. I stayed with them for four days, during which time they threw a lavish party in my honor. While what newspapers were referring to as "The Depression" might hold most of America in thrall, the affliction didn't seem to have affected Beverly Hills.

When I told Phoebe what had transpired between Omeros and me and outlined my plans for Metaxis & Company, Phoebe was delighted and in full accord. Not only did she turn over her shareholding collateral to me but also generously insisted that I not repay the loan until it suited me to do so. She sincerely believed that what I intended was in Sofie's best interest.

On the eve of my departure for New York, the Goldmans hosted the party at which I was the guest of honor. It was a glittering affair. I met so many Hollywood luminaries my head was spinning.

My meeting with one star in particular was memorable. For that matter, considering what happened two years later, it might have been better had our paths not crossed at all.

It was Douglas Fairbanks, Jr. who steered the stunning blonde toward me. Flashing the engaging smile known to millions of moviegoers, he said, "Mr. Sthanassis, may I present someone who claims to be an ardent fan of yours?" It was a moment before I recognized her. "Teresa!" She laughed. "Tess," she said. "It's been a long time since anyone called me Teresa. I've often thought about you, Kostas. How have you been?"

I don't recall much of the rest of our conversation except that

I promised to contact her when next I visited the West Coast. She wrote down her unlisted phone number.

After the party, I questioned Irving about Teresa. I hadn't heard of her for some years. She seemed to have dropped out of sight completely.

Irving spread his hands in an eloquent gesture. "For a few years, she was big box office. Then, when the talkies were introduced in twenty-seven . . . blooie. With her Brooklyn accent, who could use her?"

"I didn't hear any Brooklyn accent when I talked with her tonight," I said.

"So she took voice lessons. But times and tastes change. The public is fickle. Look, she has great legs, small tits, a cute ass and a pretty face. In the cloche hats and short skirts of the mid-twenties she was terrific. But flappers have gone out of style, and she's been out of circulation too long."

"What does she do now?"

"How should I know? Working on her fourth husband — and the rumor mill has it she's trying for a comeback. I wish her luck . . . but not in one of *my* pictures."

I had wired ahead, reserving a suite at the Waldorf-Astoria. On my arrival, I took a cab from Grand Central directly to the hotel.

When I'd checked in at the reception desk and was walking toward the elevators, two men accosted me.

"Mr. Sthanassis?" one of them asked.

"Yes?"

"My name is Barker. This is Mr. Kowlaski. We're federal agents. We have a warrant for your arrest. I suggest we not make a scene . . . that you come with us quietly."

CHAPTER THIRTY

I put through a long-distance call to Omeros from the precinct station house. Within half an hour a lawyer appeared, and I was released and back in the Waldorf.

I don't know who he contacted, or how he did it, but Omeros didn't waste any time. He must have gone pretty high on the ladder — to a senior senator or congressman — but however he worked it, it was effective. I hadn't been in the hotel suite more than an hour when the phone rang.

The caller identified himself as Edgar Zimmerman of the Bureau of Internal Revenue. He apologized profusely for the mistake that had been made and any inconvenience it might have caused me. He hoped that I had been treated courteously and that this grievous error on the part of overly zealous underlings would not prejudice me toward the United States Government, nor reflect adversely in any business ventures I might be contemplating during my stay in America.

I assured Mr. Zimmerman that I bore his government no ill will . . . providing the error was not repeated.

When I cradled the receiver, I couldn't help but laugh aloud. The slade had been wiped clean. Whatever Omeros had told his contact, it had been laid on with a trowel.

What I had done through the cooperation of Omeros and Phoebe amounted to a takeover of Metaxis & Company. I held sixty percent of the shares, giving me effective control of the company. How would Sofoclis accept this situation?

I wasn't too worried. Unless marriage and fatherhood had changed him dramatically, Sofie was a man who shied away from responsibility. He enjoyed the prestige imparted by his position of authority but did not relish the obligations it imposed. Sofie was not a decision maker. In my opinion, he would be happy to be relieved of the responsibilities of corporate leadership.

I presented it to Sofie as a simple matter of capital injection. True, this made me the majority shareholder, but my Latin American interests would prevent me from playing other than a peripheral role in the company's corporate affairs. Sofie would continue in the capacity of president while I, in effect, would be a silent partner.

Now that the company was debt-free, it was in a position to go ahead with the West Coast expansion we had previously discussed. I told Sofie I'd explored that possibility in Los Angeles and advanced the names of two importing-distributing firms in financial difficulties that appeared admirably suited to our purpose both as operating companies and as tax write-offs. I added that, since these acquisitions would entail expanded administration, we should find a competent executive vice president to assume much of that burden. Sofie, who by this time was positively beaming, wholeheartedly agreed with this suggestion.

The intervention of Omeros on my behalf had appreciably altered my financial picture. I returned to Guayaquil by way of Havana to pursue an initiative I'd considered beyond my grasp.

My inquiries with Cuban ship brokers confirmed what I had suspected. A good number of small vessels were up for sale or auction. I discovered, to my delight, that the *Pandora* was one of the ships open for purchase bids. Contingent on favorable marine surveys, I entered bids on the *Pandora* and an eight-thousand tonner, the *San Cristóbal*.

The surveyor's reports were satisfactory. The owners accepted my bids. By using my New York real estate holdings as security, I borrowed enough to close the deals.

When the *Pandora* arrived in port, I instructed the broker to advise the captain that the new owner would come on board at ten o'clock the following morning to inspect the vessel.

At 0930, unannounced, I stepped into Enrique's cabin. He was at his desk, his back to me. When I cleared my throat, he swung around. When he recognized me, he jumped to his feet, a broad grin on his face.

"Madre de Diós!" Enrique exclaimed. "Where the hell did *you* spring from. Jesus! You might have given me some warning. Sit

down. Drink?''

I accepted a drink and fielded as best I could the volley of questions he threw at me. My explanation of why I had not been in Colón to greet him on the *Pandora*'s delayed arrival in December 1929 was that, having been cleaned out in the stock market crash, I'd had more pressing personal matters to attend to. I didn't mention then anything about going to Colombia. I felt it best I leave that to later. I turned the questions around by inquiring about the *Pandora* and her present employment.

Enrique's deeply tanned forehead creased in a frown. ''Actually, Kostas, I don't know where she'll be employed . . . or *if* she'll be employed . . . or if I'll still be her captain after today. She's just changed hands, for the second time since you walked off and left me in command. I haven't got any idea what the new owner has in mind for her.'' He glanced at the bulkhead-mounted clock above his desk and added, ''But I should have some answers soon. He's coming aboard to inspect her at ten. I'll have to leave you in a few minutes. Have to be on deck to welcome him.''

''I can satisfy your curiosity on most of those points,'' I said. ''The *Pandora* is going into shipyard hands for conversion to diesel. When she comes out, she's going into service running bananas from Guayaquil to American West Coast ports. Oh, another thing, the same owner is purchasing another ship, an eight-thousand tonner, the *San Cristóbal,* only she's being renamed the *Galatea.* She's to be the flagship of a new shipping line that's about to be formed. When her conversion from reciprocating engines to steam turbine is completed, the *Galatea* will ply between Barranquilla, Havana, American Gulf ports and New York.''

Enrique interrupted me with an impatient gesture. ''How in hell do you know all this? The agent didn't have this information.''

I chuckled. ''You didn't let me finish. There's more. You are going to be offered command of the *Galatea* . . . as senior captain of the new shipping company.''

Enrique stared at me in open disbelief. ''Where did you come by this fairy tale? You don't expect me to believe it, do you?''

''You should,'' I said. ''It comes straight from the horse's mouth.''

Enrique's eyebrows arched upward. ''The new owner? Do *you* know him?''

I laughed. ''Sure do. I've known him all his life. You don't have to be on deck to welcome him aboard. You're looking at him.''

I spent three days in Havana before embarking on a ship bound for Guayaquil. During my stay, Enrique and I mapped out the future of my infant shipping line. To that project we devoted the better part of the days. The nights we spent revisiting waterfront bars and brothels we'd known of old.

I told Enrique how I had gone to Colombia to look for his wealthy cousin, Don Carlos. I recounted how Carlos and I had worked a rich vein of emerald-bearing limestone in the mountains of Boyacá, and how we had been attacked by bandits. I related how Carlos had been wounded and later died in my arms, and that I'd buried him somewhere in a remote mountain pass.

There was much of the story I withheld from Enrique. It wasn't necessary to tell him of Pepita or Juana and Ramón. That part of the story was best left untold. Nor would it serve any purpose to tell Enrique that when I finally located his cousin in Chiquinquirá, Don Carlos was a lush derisively nicknamed *El Borrachín*.

During a two-day stopover in Panama City, I registered my newly formed shipping company. I called it the Kybernas Line. Two vessels didn't represent much of a shipping company, but, even then, I had a gut feeling that the Kybernas Line would one day take its place among the giants of the shipping industry.

From the very beginning, my relationship with Fernando Alvarez was one that could be described as uneasy. It's a wonder our partnership prospered as it did, since we rarely saw eye-to-eye on any issue. Both mentally and physically, we were poles apart.

Fernando was in his mid-forties when we first met. He was short and balding and getting a bit of a paunch. He sported a pencil-thin mustache. He was given to flashy ties, the latest in fashion and male jewelry. He was a ladies' man and, in spite of the fact that he had a beautiful wife, Nadine, fifteen years his junior, kept a mistress and generally had one or two girlfriends on the side.

I do not like to attract attention to myself. I dress conservatively. I considered Fernando's flamboyance to be in poor taste. His amatory pursuits I considered none of my business, my only unvoiced objection being to his publicly flaunting his latest acquisition.

Fernando was as shrewd as the next man when it came to business deals within his realm of expertise, yet, even there, he displayed little in the way of imaginative aggressiveness. He had inherited Guayaquil Exportación from his father. Under Fernando's stewardship, the company had prospered, but it remained relatively static until I entered the picture. That our profits had soared since we had started trading with Metaxis & Company delighted him.

Fernando took credit for what he termed an audacious gamble taken by Guayaquil Exportación, yet he knew full well the gamble had been mine and mine alone. He resented that fact. That may have been the reason behind his dogged opposition to almost everything I proposed.

Although I didn't advise Fernando that I'd committed myself to a deal with Colombian coffee exporters, I did inform him that I'd acquired an interest in the Kybernas Line, though I didn't disclose that I was the founder and sole owner of the shipping company. I had little choice in the matter. How else was I to explain the preferential freight rates offered us by the *Pandora?*

Another piece of information I withheld was that the U.S. companies in Los Angeles and San Francisco suddenly favoring Guayaquil Exportación with substantial orders were wholly owned subsidiaries of Metaxis & Company and that, for all practical purposes, I *was* Metaxis & Company.

Some months later an opportunity arose to purchase an Ecuadorian banana plantation at a sacrifice price. When I suggested that Guayaquil Exportación would be well advised to take advantage of the situation, Fernando strenuously objected on the ground that the producing end of the business was outside our field of competence and too risky a proposition. No amount of arguing would convince him otherwise. He lacked the vision to appreciate the benefits that could accrue from a vertical operation.

I ceased to argue the toss. What I did was have my lawyer in Panama City incorporate Metaxis y Cia. as a subsidiary of Metaxis & Company and conclude the purchase of the plantation through that corporate vehicle. Shortly thereafter, I arranged for Metaxis y Cia. to buy the Colombian exporting firm in which I had a financial interest.

I have chronicled only a few instances of the differences that kept cropping up between me and Fernando. The pattern that emerged was that, from the first year of our association onward, ours was a partnership in name only.

Fernando had no cause for complaint. As Metaxis & Company and its Panamanian subsidiary expanded, so did their dealings with

Guayaquil Exportacion. The Kybernas Line numbered five vessels in 1937. Two of these were assigned to the Pacific trade, and Guayaquil Exportación enjoyed scheduled deliveries at preferential freight rates. Moreover, Metaxis y Cia., during the same period, increased its Ecuadorian plantation holdings, thus assuring Guayaquil Exportación of an uninterrupted supply of produce.

Strangely enough, when the break came between Fernando and me in 1937, it was a personal rather than a business issue that brought matters to a head. We parted on a note of bitterness.

What I most regret asbout my dispute with Fernando was that it generated a good deal of unwanted publicity. In the newspaper coverage of charges and countercharges, many of my financial holdings were disclosed, and I was dubbed *El Greco Dorado* by the local press. Such labels have a disconcerting way of sticking.

In 1941, to my embarrassment, I found myself referred to in defamatory articles in the American press by the Anglicized version of *El Greco Dorado,* "The Golden Greek." By then it was a matter of record that I was a wealthy man, but it was a fact I didn't want advertised by demeaning publicity. If I was publicity-shy before those stories broke, I became almost obsessively so thereafter.

CHAPTER THIRTY-ONE

Looking back on that period, it seems that from the beginning of 1933 until mid-1937 I was almost constantly on the move. In all, during that period I don't believe I spent more than ten months in Ecuador. Ten months, however, was more than enough time to get myself into a difficult situation.

In the November elections of 1932, Franklin D. Roosevelt defeated Herbert Hoover. Unjustly, in my estimation, the Hoover Administration was blamed for the stock market crash of '29 and the economic chaos known now as the Great Depression. In the United States, I find most people ignored the fact that the Depression was global in character and that economic collapse in Europe in 1931 was probably the largest contributing factor to what was later dubbed the Hungry Thirties. Hoover could hardly be blamed for Europe's woes. Nonetheless the American people were in a mood for change — and they got it. When Roosevelt was inaugurated early in 1933, he assumed near-dictatorial power and resolutely moved to set the United States on the road to economic recovery.

The first task confronting me in early 1933 was to find an able assistant for a very harried Sofoclis. The choice I made was a young corporate lawyer, Gerald Welton. My selection was based on three attributes: Welton had proved his competency in three years as a junior associate with a New York firm of corporate lawyers. He was a good-looking young man of confident presence. But the deciding factor, as far as I was concerned, was that Welton appeared to be a man driven by ambition. That was a quality I could understand and turn to my advantage.

Welton worked as executive assistant to the president. Sofoclis held the titles of both president and chief executive officer, but Welton, from the beginning, knew that I was the major shareholder and the one who'd be calling the shots. I made it clear to him that, if he displayed the organizational and administrative abilities I was confident he possessed, within a few years he could expect to move up to executive vice president. And, when Sofoclis moved up to the position of chairman of the board, I could see no reason why Welton shouldn't step into the presidency. An ambitious man who believes he will rise to the top in an organization should do everything within his power to make it a corporate structure worth taking over.

Did I see no threat to my own position of authority? Certainly I did. As Welton gained power, I would have to guard my flanks. In my arrogance I welcomed the challenge he would one day represent.

Having provided Sofoclis with this essential backup, I was free to devote my attention to other matters.

In recognition of the fact that I would be spending a good deal of my time in the States in order to establish guidelines for Welton and to expand the company's activities on the West Coast, I first renovated a brownstone I owned on West 76th Street in New York, then turned my attention westward. My preference would have been San Francisco, but, since Los Angeles represented our major market, that is where I established temporary residence in a rented house in Malibu Beach. To resolve my commuting problem, I bought a Packard sedan.

Did the fact that Tess Martin owned a house in Malibu Beach influence my decision? There's no point in kidding myself. Of course it did. I'd not yet called the unlisted number she'd given me but had every intention of doing so once the pressure of business eased. I invented an excuse to make the call within a few days of settling into my oceanside home.

When the *Pandora* docked at Long Beach on her maiden voyage, it became readily apparent that I'd been guilty of a grievous error in judgment. Her conversion to diesel had given the vessel a reasonable turn of speed, but she lacked sufficient carrying capacity to meet a burgeoning West Coast market demand. For the expansion I envisioned, the *Pandora* would need backup.

I cabled Enrique in Barranquilla, instructing him to divert the

Galatea to Guayaquil and advised concerning the possibility of purchasing another vessel of comparable size. Ten days later he cabled that a ten-thousand-ton, steam-turbine-powered British merchantman, the *Cape Nevis,* was being offered for sale in Galveston, Texas.

I flew to Houston and drove to Galveston to inspect the vessel. She had sustained damage in a collision with a fishing trawler but otherwise was in sound condition. I learned that the reason the owners needed to sell was due to the fact that an Admiralty Court judgment had gone against the *Cape Nevis,* and the funds were needed to cover court costs and claims. I concluded a purchase agreement on attractive terms.

When repairs were effected, she was rechristened *Eos,* and her registration was changed from British to Panamanian. Sporting a gleaming white paint job with sky blue trim, she entered service as the new flagship of the Kybernas Line, Captain Enrique Ramirez commanding.

Although its formal demise did not come until December 1933 with the enactment of the Twenty-first Amendment, the death knell of Prohibition was sounded when Roosevelt was elected. Few mourned its passing.

Through his bootlegging activities, Sofie had maintained ties with wine and liquor suppliers of the pre-Prohibition era. It was now time to think in terms of reestablishing the trade along legitimate lines. To that end, Sofoclis, with Aletha, their son Nicholas and Nicholas' nurse embarked on a European cruise in August 1933. The trip was to be partly pleasure and partly business. My hope was that it would be chiefly the latter. Sofoclis was in a strong negotiating position with old and new suppliers alike. With the acquisition of the West Coast outlets and the market penetration planned for the southern states, the Midwest and the Pacific Northwest, Metaxis & Company was in a position to demand exclusive representation.

During the seven months of his absence, I would spend most of my time based in Los Angeles and quietly explore possibilities in San Diego and in the Pacific Northwest. Gerry Welton would hold down the fort in New York and explore other markets with my advice and assistance, where required.

I make no excuse for my eighteen-month affair with Teresa — if it could properly be called an affair. Nor will I accept any responsibility for the way it ended. As I said earlier, it would have been better had our paths not crossed again. But our paths *did* cross. Nothing could change that. Nor, I suspect, could what eventually happened have been avoided.

The understanding between Teresa and me was that our relationship would remain on a strictly physical plane. I made it clear from the beginning that there would be no question of marriage. I was not going to repeat the mistake I'd made with Phoebe by leaving room for doubt. Yet, even with those guidelines firmly established, our relationship developed along rather unusual lines.

Of course, from the outset, I felt a deep sense of obligation for the part she'd played in keeping me from harm — possibly death — at the hands of her Uncle Vito. This caused me to give in to demands that, under other circumstances, I would have rejected out of hand. Then another factor crept into our relationship. When I got to know Teresa — and believed I understood her — I felt sorry for her.

From what she told me, she had never wanted to be an actress. That had been her mother's doing. Her mother had been obsessed with the idea of having a movie star for a daughter. From the age of six onward, Teresa had been carefully groomed for an assault on Hollywood. Uncle Vito's connections guaranteed that Teresa would get favorable consideration and, if nothing else, a few minor roles.

The Martinellis, mother and daughter, appeared in Hollywood just when the era of flaming youth and flappers was being exploited. Teresa, her name changed to Tess Martin, was ideally suited to the parts being cast. Like Clara Bow, and for much the same reasons, Tess Martin zoomed to stardom, enjoyed a few years of fame and fortune, then faded from the scene when talking pictures became the norm.

Somewhere along the line, Tess had submerged Teresa. Basking in the glare of popular acclaim can be heady stuff. It was for Tess Martin. She hungered for that adulation now that the spotlight no longer shone on her. She had gone to a great deal of trouble and expense to rid herself of her Brooklyn accent. Now her one desire was to make a comeback.

It was not the rise and fall of Tess Martin that made me feel sorry for Teresa. It was something else, something she revealed to me hesitantly and shamefacedly. It turned out that about 80 percent of the well-publicized affairs she'd indulged in had absolutely no basis in fact. They'd been invented by studio publicity departments. And three of her four marriages had been little more than staged productions. I'm afraid I wasn't too sympathetic about the tinsel character of this sexual extravaganza. It still left one valid marriage, and 20 percent of the affairs she was reputed to have had, to be accounted for. It was when I commented on this that she confessed to something she claimed she'd never revealed to anyone. She enjoyed intercourse, but it had never lifted her to the peaks of ecstasy it was supposed to bring. Neither as Teresa Martinelli, nor as Tess Martin, had she ever experienced an orgasm. Yes, she admitted to having a number of affairs, vainly hoping that each new one would bring gratification. None had. That, she said sadly, included her present affair with me. But with me, she felt she was coming close to the cherished goal.

I'll say this for Teresa: she tried. God how she tried! She taught me positions I didn't believe existed outside an acrobatic act. She may not have reached a climax, but I emerged from a weekend session feeling like an orange that had been squeezed dry. Petite she may have been, but there was nothing small about her sexual appetite.

In November of '33 Teresa came to me with a script she wanted me to read. She was excited about it. It was a sophisticated comedy called "The Marriage Mill." I couldn't see Teresa in the part, nor did I find the screenplay particularly amusing, but I didn't have the heart to tell her so. For one thing, I felt she had started drinking to excess. I felt she needed something like this to divert her energies into useful channels. So, against my better judgment, I agreed to finance the production, providing my name didn't enter into the project in any way.

I should have known better. Nothing in Hollywood remains a secret for long, as I discovered when Phoebe invited me for dinner a few weeks later.

"How could you?" Phoebe said. "It's bad enough that your name is linked with hers in all the gossip columns . . . but to back that little tramp in a film . . . Jesus, Kostas, you must be mad."

"If it wasn't for her," I said, "there's a good chance I wouldn't be sitting here tonight. I owe her a favor I can't begin to repay . . .

but this will help square the account."

Phoebe's eyes widened. "You believe that? You really believe an eighteen-year-old schoolgirl could have swayed Vito Martinelli sufficiently to save your hide?"

"That's what Sofoclis told me. He claims he got it from Omeros."

"My dear brother has a knack for getting things ass-backward, but I don't suppose he can be blamed too much in this instance. That was the story someone fed to Omeros. I only found out what really happened a couple of years ago when I met Teresa's father, Salvatore Martinelli. He's a bit on the naive side, but a sweet guy. When he found out you were my cousin, he told me what went on back in twenty-five. Are you interested?"

"Of course," I said.

"Somehow, her mother learned that Teresa was secretly dating you. Mama felt that if it got around that her darling was going out with a Greek bootlegger it might hurt her chances in Hollywood. So Mama asked her dear brother-in-law to discourage you from seeing Teresa. Vito said it would be a pleasure, adding that he'd been planning to have you bumped off anyway. Mama was horrified. If it leaked out that Teresa had been connected with the victim of a gangland execution, she could kiss a movie career good-bye. So Mama made Vito promise that, regardless of how he stopped you from dating Teresa, it wouldn't involve your getting hurt."

"Well," I said, after taking a moment to digest what I'd just heard, "at least Teresa was *indirectly* responsible."

"You *could* put it that way," Phoebe observed.

"How come her mother had that much influence over Vito?" I asked.

"Have you ever seen her?" Phoebe countered.

"No."

"You should. She has almost as many filmland scalps to her credit as Tessie. At the time we're talking about, Mama was about forty . . . and must have been a knockout. My guess is that Vito was humping her on the side. Under such circumstances, as you should know, it's hard to say no to a favor asked."

CHAPTER THIRTY-TWO

I've heard it said that a man who has a million in cash is a poor millionaire. A rich millionaire is one who owes that amount to banks. That being the case, by mid-1934 I was a very rich millionaire. I owed staggering amounts to banks in Los Angeles, New York, Havana, Panama City, Bogotá and Guayaquil. I had book value assets to cover those loans and an almost inexhaustible line of credit, and I was acquiring new assets at an astonishing rate.

What struck most people as strange about this was that I was becoming fabulously wealthy during the economic doldrums of the Great Depression. There wasn't anything strange about it. I was dealing chiefly in commodities in demand despite depressed conditions, and my sources of supply were countries where labor was cheap. Given those conditions, how could I fail? Moreover, for someone with capital and the willingness to take a chance, there were properties, businesses and capital goods to be picked up at sacrifice prices. I was certainly not the only one taking advantage of the situation. What *I* found strange was that there weren't more of us.

True, I was taking grave risks, but it seemed that I just couldn't go wrong. About the only really questionable investment I made during those years was backing "The Marriage Mill." But even there I spread the risk. Metaxis & Company, Metaxis y Cia., the Kybernas Line and I were partners in the undertaking. If the venture failed, the losses could be written off against taxes. If by some miracle it showed a profit, I stood to gain directly and indirectly. Sadly, that miracle was granted me.

The film went into production in December 1933. At the time, I was in Galveston for the commissioning of the *Eos.* I went to Barranquilla with her on her maiden voyage and then proceeded by passenger ship to Guayaquil. In February, when I returned to Los Angeles aboard the *Galatea,* the shooting was nearing completion.

Everyone connected with the film was enthusiastic. By then, however, I'd learned more about the movie industry. It deals in illusions and feeds on self-delusion. I sought an unbiased opinion from someone not connected with the production, Irving Goldman.

"It stinks," Irving said.

"Can it be salvaged?" I asked.

"Doubt it. I don't think putting the best writers in the industry onto it could have made it a good property. Even with top stars, which it ain't got, I think it'd be a loser. But don't quote me. This is a crazy business. Who knows? It might break even. It might even make a buck, but I doubt it. I just hope you aren't the sole backer."

I grinned. "Don't worry. I'm not."

In March I went to New York to welcome Sofoclis on his return from Europe. To my delight, I found that he had exceeded my expectations. Not only was Metaxis & Company back into wine, liquor and liqueur importation in a big way, but also most of the representations were on an exclusive basis.

I saw an opportunity to be seized. The Kybernas Line could profit from expanded trade with Europe, but to do so I would have to enlarge my fleet by at least one more freighter. It was time I made a trip to Europe to look over the situation, but first I had some loose ends to tie up on the Coast.

I returned to Los Angeles at the end of March, intending to spend no more than a week. Because of Teresa, I stretched my stay to eighteen days.

The film was being edited. Teresa had free time on her hands. She moved in with me, dividing her time almost equally between my bed and my bar. Her mood, when she wasn't drunk or nursing a monumental hangover, was one of forced gaiety.

I knew something was desperately wrong. I suspected that it had to do with the film, although Teresa would neither confirm nor deny this. I am convinced that she knew — almost five months before it was released — that the picture would be a disaster. And I think she had already decided what she would do if her comeback failed.

In mid-April I went by train to New York and, from there, by passenger liner to England. In all, I spent four months in Britain and on the Continent, sounding out the commodity markets and visiting shipyards in Ireland, Scotland, Sweden and Holland. In Rotterdam I contracted for the construction of a turbine-powered, twelve-thousand-ton freighter. Delivery was scheduled for July 1935.

"The Marriage Mill" was released in August. Even if I had had a mind to do so, I couldn't have attended the premiere. At the time I was at sea, en route from London to Havana.

The news reached me in Cuba, where I was negotiating the purchase of a sugar plantation, refining mill and distillery. The film had received scathing reviews and, as Goldman had predicted, was playing to empty houses. But that was the least distressing part of the news.

On Labor Day weekend, Tess Martin had thrown a large party at her beach house. Sometime after midnight, most of the guests had indulged in nude bathing. Later some of them recalled having seen Tess wading out toward the breaking surf.

At dawn, Tess Martin's nude body was discovered washed up on the beach about a mile from her house.

There was an investigation. Witnesses testified that she had seemed in excellent spirits. Yes, she had been drinking, but not to excess. Her death by drowning was labeled an unfortunate accident. I knew better.

Teresa's dramatic exit, and the morbid publicity following it, spurred interest in her last film. For a while "The Marriage Mill" played to packed houses. I ended up making a small profit on the venture. I sometimes wonder if Teresa knew that would be the result of her suicide.

Had I been in Los Angeles when Teresa took her life, I might have been more deeply moved than I was when the news reached me in Havana. It was a shock, but I must confess that I actually felt a surge of relief. As far as I was concerned, our affair had ended in April. I was sorry that she had taken her life, but it meant that she could no longer make emotional or physical demands of me. I will admit that sounds callous, but I didn't think so at the time, nor do I now. I believe that tortured girl was better off out of her misery.

I didn't blame myself for having financed the film in which her attempted comeback had failed so miserably. Sooner or later she would have found a backer and been brought face to face with the fact that her leap to stardom had been due more to her Uncle Vito's influence, and to happy accident, than it had been to her acting ability. I believe she already suspected that.

There may have been another factor that contributed to her decision to take her life, but I didn't learn of it until some years later. An autopsy had revealed that she had been three months pregnant at the time of her death. The police had not ruled out foul play, even though they had called her death an accident. It was a lucky thing for me that I hand't been anywhere near Los Angeles that fateful Labor Day weekend, and an even luckier thing that I hadn't had any contact with Teresa for the preceding five months. Otherwise I well could have become a prime suspect on a murder charge.

As it turned out, however, there was, for me, a series of disturbing sequels to Teresa's tragic exit from the scene.

The first of these occurred shortly after my return to New York. I had no further need for the beach house in Los Angeles. So I transferred the title on the house and the ownership of the Packard to Metaxis & Company. Unfortunately, a Hollywood gossip columnist got wind of the fact that I had gotten rid of them.

The way it appeared in the scandalmongering press was that Tess Martin's secret lover, Constantine Sthanassis, the wealthy Greek shipping magnate who had financed Tess Martin's last film, was so overcome with grief at her accidental death that he had sold their Malibu Beach love nest at a considerable loss and given away his Packard limousine, vowing never again to set foot in Los Angeles. That should have been the end of it. It wasn't. The incident was resurrected during the war years and came back to haunt me at a time when I least needed to be in the limelight.

Over the years my brother-in-law had been a good friend to me. I had learned to accept his counsel without question. That autumn, when I visited Penny and Omeros in Phoenix, he gave me some sound advice and did me a great service.

"When you and Sofoclis offered to include me in your Apollo Club misadventure," Omeros said, a suggestion of a smile on his thin lips, "do you recall why I rejected the offer?"

"You felt we were asking for trouble by becoming too visible.

You were quite right. I haven't forgotten that lesson. I learned it well."

"If anything," Omeros said, "a bit *too* well."

I couldn't see what he was driving at. "What do you mean?"

"Over the last couple of years, I've watched your maneuvering with a good deal of interest. You've managed to keep your involvement with Metaxis & Company adroitly hidden from public view. You've learned the value of anonymity. But —"

"I know," I interrupted. "Nobody regrets the publicity given my affair with Teresa more than I do."

"I wasn't going to make reference to that," Omeros said. "I agree that was unfortunate . . . but no great harm done. Public memory is short. Besides, you were identified only as a foreign shipowner, a fact you make no effort to cloak in secrecy. No, I was referring to another lesson you should have learned from your Apollo Club experience. Of course, I don't know how you're operating in Ecuador, Colombia, Cuba or overseas. I'm basing my criticism only on how you appear to be operating here."

"I don't follow you. The Apollo Club incident is past history. What other lesson should I have learned that has present application?"

Omeros answered my question with one of his own. "How, when you were operating outside the law, did you keep the club in operation?"

"You know how," I said. "By paying off the cops, the Feds and damn near everyone in City Hall."

"Exactly. That's the other lesson you should have learned . . . but appear to have forgotten."

"But," I said, "now I'm operating within the law."

Omeros chuckled. "Strictly speaking, yes. And it doesn't hurt, your not being an American citizen. Establishing residency in Ecuador was a shrewd move . . . as was setting up Metaxis y Cia. as a Panama-based holding company. Your shipping company is also based in Panama. You aren't evading taxes. Where possible, you're simply avoiding them. There's nothing illegal in that. But at the rate you're expanding Metaxis & Company, you're bound to attract attention to your operations . . . and your position within the corporate structure. The day will come when you will need friends in high places. As far as I can see, you don't have any, at least not in this country. To operate successfully within the law,

Kostas, the best way is to be in a position to bend or shape the laws to suit your purpose.

"Are you suggesting that I should have state and federal legislators on the payroll?"

"Not exactly. You select your civic, state and federal politicians carefully. You want only the most influential. Those you entertain and contribute to their campaign funds and their pet projects and charities, and you arrange employment for their idiot sons and nephews. In one way or another, you make them obligated to you against the day when you need to call on them for a favor. I've operated on that principle throughout my entire business career. It's effective . . . as you should know from your brush with the authorities when you returned to the States. I couldn't have fixed that without friends in the federal government. What I'm suggesting is that you will need such connections . . . and probably much sooner than you think."

Omeros was right. It was an area to which I'd paid little heed, both here in the States and elsewhere. I'd recognized that the exercise of power calls for strong alliances within the political structure but had naively assumed they would follow naturally with the acquisition of sufficient wealth. That didn't appear to be the case. As much as I disliked social activities, it looked like I was going to have to alter my view and entertain selectively. But where to start?

It was as though Omeros were reading my thoughts. He chuckled. "Don't look so worried. When you have the money, the easiest thing in the world is the acquisition of friends that are long on influence and short on cash. It's much more difficult to get rid of them when they've outlived their usefulness. Anyway, to get you off on the right foot, I've invited a few people from Washington down for the weekend."

By the time I returned to Guayaquil early in 1935, I had established connections in Washington that were to stand me in good stead in years to come. I had done a few other things as well. Figuring it was best to consolidate our gains, I temporarily called a halt to further Metaxis & Company expansion. I had another reason. Before we embarked on more expansion, I wanted to change Metaxis & Company to a public company, yet retain my uncontested position of control. What I sought were the advantages of corporate taxation and expanded financing capabilities through stock issues. I consulted a corporate lawyer, who advised that I incorporate in a state where the existing shareholding could be converted to preferred shares and where only the preferred shares, not the common shares, held voting rights. Without discussing the matter with either Sofoclis or Welton, I instructed the lawyer to investigate the legal position and state laws and taxation structure and advise me accordingly on my return from South America.

On my arrival in Guayaquil in February, I was mindful of my need to establish strong connections with influential political and military figures, both here in Ecuador's commercial and financial center and in the republic's capital, Quito. Heretofore, in the slightly more than four years I had resided in Ecuador, I'd done little entertaining and was virtually unknown outside financial circles. There was every excuse for this, since I'd spent very little time in the country since 1932. When in Guayaquil I had always operated out of a suite in the Humboldt Hotel.

I needed a permanent residence in which to entertain. However, with Omeros' timely warning in mind, I couldn't use my lack of one as an excuse. I had my secretary prepare a list of the most important military and political figures. Selecting discriminately from the list, I embarked on a series of lunches and small dinner parties at the hotel. I soon discovered that Omeros was quite right. For a man of wealth, establishing influential contacts is ridiculously easy.

There were several reasons why I had absented myself from Guayaquil as much as I had over the past few years. For one thing, I found it difficult to adjust to the equatorial heat and humidity. For another, I found the city most unattractive. Earthquakes and termites had taken their toll, and most of the mold-mottled buildings appeared depressingly decrepit. Last, but by no means least, while Guayaquil is an excellent deepwater port, it is a river port situated some eleven nautical miles upstream from the mouth of the Guayas River. The river is chocolate colored, a far cry from the clear blue-green waters of my beloved Ionian Sea. For that reason I have never been able to bring myself to like river ports, and Guayaquil, with its ever-present smell of tropical decay, is the least attractive port I can recall.

Understandably, then, I started house-hunting without much enthusiasm. As it happened, I didn't have to look very hard. One of my newfound contacts, a general, put me in contact with the widow of a former military colleague. She owned a mansion located on the river. She no longer could afford the upkeep or staffing of such a lavish residence and had moved to more modest quarters in the city. The mansion had been empty for several years and was in a sad state of disrepair. She sold it to me at a price I couldn't help but accept.

The rambling house needed repair throughout. Much of the interior woodwork was crumbling or had been reduced to dust by termites. In many places the plaster had fallen away from the walls and ceilings. Roof tiles needed replacing. All the stonework had to be acid-cleaned of mold and lichen. The extensive grounds, stretching down to the riverbank, were a tangle of neglected growth. The small jetty and boathouse would have to be rebuilt. On top of that, the mansion would need to be completely refurnished. And, in addition, I wanted to install a large swimming pool.

I estimated that it would be at least eight months before the mansion could be restored and ready for occupancy. Actually, it was not ready until late in 1936. In fact, the first night I slept in the master bedroom of my palatial Guayaquil dwelling was the morning of New Year's Day 1937.

CHAPTER THIRTY-THREE

In reviewing my business career, I would say that 1935 and 1936 were my most hectic years. I entered 1935 a multimillionaire — on paper — with a debt position that could have made it a fortune of the shortest duration on record. The slightest misstep spelled disaster. There is no question about it, I was dangerously overextended.

Why didn't my precarious position at the beginning of 1935 scare the hell out of me? That's a question I can't answer at this late date, even to my own satisfaction.

I suppose it had something to do with the arrogance of youth and the fact that I had survived a threat on my life, two murder attempts, the stock market crash, a hurricane that should have swamped my ship and a desperate mining venture in the blue mountains of Boyacá. Since then I had enjoyed success after success, which is heady fare. But I truly believe that my supreme confidence stemmed from a belief that Pepita's hand was in mine; that with insight into the future she was guiding me through the maze of the present. Nonsense. Ghosts don't shape one's destiny. Still, can any of us in the world of the living truly say what lies beyond the grave? Perhaps, during those crucial years, Pepita acted as my guardian angel. I know I thought so at the time.

But even at that, there came a time in 1936 when everything hung in the balance, and I thought my luck, and Pepita, had deserted me.

I'm confusing the issue. I'd better chronicle the events in their proper sequence.

Having set in motion the restoration of my Guayaquil mansion, I returned to the States in March 1935. My first act was to incorporate Metaxis & Company in the State of Texas.

Why Texas? Not only were its corporate laws suited to my

purpose, but its outlets in the Gulf of Mexico favored my Caribbean operations. I explained all this to Sofoclis, but I don't think he fully appreciated what I was doing. Gerald Welton, on the other hand, knew exactly how Texas worked to my advantage. He wasn't at all happy with the incorporation. He was somewhat happier when I gave him, as a bonus, 2 percent of the preferred shares, thereby giving him a voice in the corporate affairs.

In theory, Metaxis & Company was now a Texas-based corporate structure. In practice, however, we continued to be headquartered in New York.

In June 1935 I went by passenger liner to Europe. There I rendezvoused with Enrique Ramirez. We were on hand for the launching and fitting out of the vessel I had christened the SS *Hebe*. At the end of July, on schedule, we took over the vessel. She sailed, Captain Ramirez commanding, to load cargo in French, German and English ports. As much as I would have liked to have been on her maiden voyage, I had to stay behind to arrange financing through Swiss and English banks. I had contracted with the Rotterdam shipyard for the construction of a second vessel. This one, to be christened the *Artemis*, was even more ambitious than the *Hebe*. The *Artemis* was to be a seventeen-thousand tonner with a cruising speed of fifteen knots. She was to be fitted with refrigerated hold space and accommodations for twelve passengers, including an owner's suite. The shipyard estimated that the vessel would be ready for delivery by October 1936. When the *Artemis* made her maiden voyage, I fully intended to be on board.

I arrived back in New York early in November in time to attend the christening of Sofoclis' second son, Constantine Peter Metaxis. I was doubly honored — the child had been named after me and I was his godfather.

The christening of Sofoclis' second child brought home to me an awareness of the passage of time. It was now almost sixteen years since I had landed as a wide-eyed immigrant at New York's Harlem docks. Good Lord, so much had happened over those years it was difficult to believe. Sofoclis hadn't changed much, but I had changed a good deal. So, for that matter, had New York.

I had come on the scene at the beginning of an era now referred to as the Roaring Twenties. At least as far as New York was concerned, it had been a boisterous, permissive, freewheeling era of unparalleled prosperity. It had been a decade of changing values, the era of flappers, mobsters, speakeasies, hip flasks and rumble seats. Then the bubble had burst. The stock market crash of '29, followed by the European economic debacle of '31, had had a sobering effect. Prosperity had given way to economic depression. The mood had changed to one of doom and gloom. Now, however, almost three years of belt-tightening under the Roosevelt Administration appeared to be having a beneficial effect. The Depression seemed to have bottomed out. Confidence was returning. Spirits were lifting. Business was on the upswing, both in the United States and in Europe, which was a damn good thing for both Metaxis & Company and the Kybernas Line.

It was not only the mood of the city that was changing but its face as well. Of course, having been removed from the scene for seven years and now being absent for months on end, I probably noticed the changes more than Sofoclis did.

When I had first arrived, horse-drawn vehicles had been much in evidence. Now they were few and far between. The motor cars had undergone considerable changes as well, as had transportation in general. The city was going underground in both utilities and transport. Already the Sixth Avenue El had disappeared, and, when new subway lines under construction were completed, the Second Avenue and Ninth Avenue elevated railways were slated for abandonment and demolition. Streetcars were being replaced by buses. The skyline was in a constant state of flux. Under the flamboyant leadership of its new mayor, Fiorello La Guardia, New York was well on its way to recovery.

Metaxis & Company was soon to contribute in its small way to the changing face of the city. During that visit to New York, I authorized the purchase of an old building on lower Broadway. The building would be torn down. On its site, the Metaxis Building would soar majestically skyward.

I returned to Guayaquil in mid-December. Considering the steadily increasing volume of Guayaquil Exportación's business with Metaxis & Company, I expected to find Fernando in good spirits. The news I brought with me concerning my plans for the *Artemis* should have pleased him. I was wrong on both counts.

". . . Ecuadorian bananas are superior in quality to the African product now supplying the European market. Up to now, our problem has been spoilage. With the *Artemis'* refrigerated holds, we've solved that problem. I'm confident that by nineteen thirty-seven we'll have a solid foothold in that market," I said, concluding what I'd been telling Fernando about the vessel and my plan to enter the European market.

Fernando snorted. "Hmmph! What about supply from this end? Have you thought of that? I have enough trouble filling our orders as it is. You're a partner in this firm, you know. While you're dashing about the world playing with your damn ships, I have to sit here and do all the work."

I looked at Fernando in astonishment. He probably pushed out some correspondence and signed some shipping documents, but he didn't even have to do that if he didn't want to. His secretary and the firm's accountant could take care of those details. He had spent more than six months of that year in Buenos Aires. What the hell was he talking about? Thanks to Metaxis y Cia. we had no supply problems. Had it not been for the Kybernas Line granting Guayaquil Exportación favorable freight rates we would have found it tough to be competitive. Fernando was well aware of that. I didn't know what was eating him, but it sure as hell couldn't be the business.

Maybe Nadine, his wife, was playing around. I'd heard rumors to that effect. Well, there was nothing to be gained by making an issue of it. I let his criticism ride unanswered.

A few days after Christmas, the general who'd helped me house-hunt told me in strictest confidence about the tin-mining proposition in Bolivia. A rich lode had been discovered. The general had seen the assay reports. He assured me that they represented the most promising find in years. A company was being formed to bring the mine into production.

Put simply, the proposition was this. The general was in a position to acquire a six-month option on 45 percent of the company's shareholdings, provided he moved quickly. To ensure the option the general would have to come up with a total of three million dollars, and he said he could raise one million. He asked me if I would put up the remaining two million in return for two-thirds of the optioned shares. I told him I would think it over and give him an answer within forty-eight hours.

The proposition was tempting. I reasoned that the general was in too sensitive a position to be involved in something fraudulent.

Moreover, he was putting a sizable chunk of his own money on the line and must be confident he could raise the remainder prior to the expiration of the option. I decided to go along with his proposal.

At that point I was faced with a dilemma. I could swing the two million without difficulty, but what then? In financing the *Artemis,* I had borrowed heavily. What if, when the option expired next June, I was unable to come up with the eight million I would need to close the deal? In that event I'd forfeit the two million. I was running close to the line. Too close. If I lost the two million, where would I stand? It *could* bring everything crashing down around my ears, but, what the hell, if you gamble you have accept the risks.

Actually, raising the two million presented a problem. It entailed producing the huge uncut emerald as part of my collateral. It was the first time in five years that I'd held the gemstone in my hand.

I remember the moment well. It was an odd experience. As I gazed at the emerald, I fleetingly imagined I saw Pepita's eyes smiling gently from the stone's cool green depths.

The June meeting took place in my suite in the George V Hotel in Paris. There were three of us present: Señor Eduardo Williams, representing Bolivia's Cariño Mining Company; Monsieur Guy Fournier, the mining group's French lawyer, and me.

I was not in a good frame of mind. I'd just returned from Geneva, where I'd renegotiated one loan and had been refused an additional loan of four million dollars. In five days, my option on the Cariño shares would run out. I was still four million dollars short and needed more time to negotiate bank guarantees. I'd cabled Fournier, requesting that he contact his principals to arrange for a one-month extension of my option. This meeting, on the lawyer's initiative, was in response to that request.

Williams opened the discussion. "Under normal circumstances, Señor Sthanassis, we would be happy to grant you an option extension. However, during the last few weeks, the situation has undergone a change. Perhaps, Monsieur Fournier, you will be good enough to explain."

The lawyer cleared his throat. "We have received," he said, "a firm offer, backed by a Swiss bank guarantee, of twelve million dollars for the shareholding you have under option."

"I think you'll agree," Williams said, breaking in smoothly, "that this alters the picture. The additional two million dollars is not a sum to be taken lightly. Naturally, we are obliged to honor our commitment to you, but, under the circumstances, you can hardly blame us for not granting your request for an extension."

If they had a valid offer, I couldn't fault them, but instinct told me that this was a squeeze play. It was too neat, too pat. I didn't believe any such offer existed.

"You have a guarantee from me on the commitment," I said.

It was Fournier who replied, "We find that your guarantee is backed by ships, Monsieur Sthanassis, only two of which you own outright."

I saw it all now. They had known the shipping situation when they'd accepted the guarantee and granted the option. Since I hadn't posted a bank guarantee, they must have suspected — quite correctly — that I was overextended. At the very outset they had seen a good possibility that I would default and have to forfeit my two-million-dollar deposit. They'd watched and waited. Without doubt, they now knew that the Swiss bank had rejected my request for an additional loan. They must think they had me backed into a corner. So did I, but I wasn't going to give them the satisfaction of having me beg for favors.

"I see," I said. "I find it odd that you raised no objection to my guarantee six months ago."

"We do now," Señor Williams said. "You have just five days to complete the transaction."

I flew to London that afternoon. As soon as I was installed in a suite in the Savoy, I was on the long-distance telephone line to New York.

The next day, my lawyer returned my call. He had been successful in raising a million but could find no other ready source of cash. He told me he would keep trying, but he advised me not to build my hopes on his success. My broker was even less helpful. For him to liquidate holdings in the amount required would take at least a week, more likely two weeks. Hell, I already knew that. It had been the reason I'd requested the extension.

With less than seventy-two hours remaining, I put through a call to Phoenix. Omeros listened without comment as I outlined my predicament and my immediate need for solid bank-to-bank guarantees to cover a loan.

"How much do you need guaranteed?" Omeros asked.

"Three million dollars."

"What's your London bank?"

"National Westminster . . . Marble Arch branch."

"I'm not sure I can handle it," Omeros said. "I'll call you back in an hour."

On tenterhooks, I waited for his call. When it came through, I noted that my palms were sweating. "Okay," Omeros said, his voice sounding oddly metallic over the phone, "the guarantees will be in your London bank no later than tomorrow morning. I'm guaranteeing two million. Irving Goldman is taking care of the other million."

After I'd cradled the phone, I sat for some minutes before it fully registered on me that I'd won. By God, I'd won!

I ran my thumb down the scar on my cheek and started to laugh uncontrollably. I'd called their bluff — and emerged the winner.

I discovered later that it hadn't been a bluff. The twelve-million-dollar offer had been perfectly legitimate. The mining speculation was a highly profitable venture. Over the next few years I realized substantial returns in dividends. I sold my shareholding in 1948 for one hundred fifty million dollars. No wonder the mining group had been so eager to have me default on my option.

It goes without saying that the Ecuadorian general who was my partner in this venture was my friend for life.

CHAPTER THIRTY-FOUR

After my close brush with ruin in late June, the remaining months of 1936, while busy ones, seemed tame by comparison.

I spent July and August in England and Germany, soliciting business in the produce and commodity markets. I took time out to attend the XI Olympic Games in Berlin, which I found a magnificent but oddly disturbing spectacle. At the conclusion of the Olympics, I went to Athens. To my astonishment, I found I was rusty in my native tongue. I kept lapsing into English or Spanish during the first couple of days of my brief visit.

I had business to attend to in Athens, but my stay in Greece was limited because I had to be in Holland in time to take delivery of the *Artemis*. I'd cabled Georgiana, who was spending the summer and autumn months in Corfu, where her second boutique did a flourishing business during the tourist season, to meet me in Athens. She arrived the day following my arrival and spent two days with me in my suite at the Grande Bretagne.

It had been eleven years since I'd last seen Georgiana. I must say that she seemed to have improved in both appearance and temperament. She had put on weight, but I found her plumpness becoming. She was now in her early forties, successful in business, and seemed to have accepted spinsterhood with cheerful resignation. Actually, as I discovered during the course of our conversations, her contentment stemmed from the fact that she had a lover, an Italian antique dealer from Brindisi who, despite the fact that he had a family and a bedridden wife, still managed to spend a good deal of his time with Georgiana in Kerkyra and Patras. All in all, even though she lamented the fact that she was childless, I would say she'd made a satisfactory adjustment to her status and appeared to be enjoying life.

Captain Ramirez accepted delivery of the *Artemis* in Rotterdam. I arrived a day later.

I was seeing the vessel for the first time. She was beautiful — everything I had visualized. Her gleaming white hull and superstructure looked even whiter due to the three blue bands at the bow and the blue band on the funnel bearing on each side a white circle centered with a blue letter *K*. My heart swelled with pride.

We loaded cargo in a number of European ports. After a fast and uneventful Atlantic crossing, we off-loaded cargo at New York, New Orleans and Galveston before transiting the Panama Canal and steaming toward Guayaquil. It was a relaxing and thoroughly enjoyable voyage, during which I spent a good deal of time with Enrique. Old shipmates make excellent companions, and he still loses more often than he wins at gin rummy.

We arrived at Guayaquil on December 28. I had radioed ahead to my secretary, and she had sent out invitations to a New Year's Eve party to be held on board the ship. I was pleased to note that most of those invited had accepted.

It had been more than ten months since last I'd been in Guayaquil. When I'd left for New York and Europe, the renovation of my house on the riverbank had been a long way from completion. Now I was pleased to find that the old mansion looked like new. Of course the jetty, boathouse, swimming pool and poolside bar, terrace and changing rooms *were* new. The gardeners had worked wonders on the grounds and in the flower beds.

The house was fully staffed, thanks to my secretary's enterprise. I inspected the house and grounds on the twenty-ninth and found everything to my complete satisfaction. I could have moved in then and there but decided to remain in my quarters on board the *Artemis* until after the party.

The party was to get under way at nine o'clock, but, knowing Latin Americans' casual attitude toward time, I didn't expect guests until ten o'clock or later. I was surprised, therefore, when Nadine Alvarez came aboard promptly at nine. She explained to me that Fernando had been in Guayaquil to spend Christmas with the family but had had to leave for Buenos Aires on business the day after. It was common knowledge that Fernando had a mistress in Buenos Aires.

Nadine said that, knowing I was a bachelor, she had come early in case I needed someone to act as hostess. I thanked her for her consideration yet was anything but pleased. Had I wanted someone to act as hostess, there were a number of unattached young ladies in the city who would have been delighted to comply. Besides, I had made it a practice to keep Nadine at arm's length. On a number of previous occasions she'd made it abundantly clear that she would welcome my advances. She was a striking beauty of unquestioned physical appeal, but the last thing I wanted was to have an affair with my partner's wife.

Considering Fernando's flagrant infidelity, few people would blame Nadine for seeking sexual satisfaction outside the home. In fact, it was rumored that her not-infrequent trips to Quito were due more to a lover, or lovers, than to her excuse of escaping the oppressive heat of the coastal plains. If there was truth to those rumors, at least, unlike her husband, she conducted her affairs discreetly. Be that as it may, I had no desire to become involved.

Theirs was a strange relationship. Nadine was a White Russian Fernando had met on a trip to Shanghai in the early twenties. Her father, a former cavalry colonel in the czarist army, had escaped to China — Harbin, and then Shanghai — shortly after the Russian Revolution. He was the maître d'hôtel in Shanghai's Cathay Hotel — and a stateless person. The story was that Fernando had met Nadine working as a bar hostess and had gotten her pregnant. Her father had forced Fernando to make an honest woman of her. Another version was that the ex-colonel had paid Fernando a considerable sum to marry Nadine in order for her to acquire valid citizenship. I don't know which, if either, of those stories was based on truth. All I know is that Nadine was a sultry beauty with a slightly oriental cast to her features and that she had a handsome son, Miguel, in his early teens, and an indifferent husband who treated her more like chattel than a wife. It wasn't what I would have called much of a marriage. I sympathized with her unenviable position but had no intention of intruding into her and Fernando's peculiar domestic arrangement.

I couldn't get into the spirit of the party. For one thing, Nadine adopted a proprietary attitude toward me, which I found annoying in the extreme. I spent the better part of the evening doing my best to avoid her. I wasn't in the mood for drinking, which didn't help. Finally, shortly after one in the morning, I became bored with the festivities. I looked around and, not seeing Nadine anywhere, assumed she had slipped ashore with one of the male guests.

I located the deck officer and requested that the ship's launch be lowered and manned. I took the launch upriver to the jetty and spent my first night in the mosquito net-shrouded double bed of my master bedroom, cooled by the ceiling fan rotating noiselessly above the filmy canopy.

The next morning, after a leisurely breakfast on the balcony of my bedroom, I had my chauffeur drive me back to the port. When I boarded the *Artemis*, Enrique, looking crisp and cool in his white uniform, met me as I stepped on board. He frowned slightly.

"A woman spent the night in your sleeping cabin," he said.

I matched his frown. "I told the steward to keep my quarters locked."

"I know you did . . . but I wouldn't be too hard on him. She told Manuel she was your business partner's wife, and she *was* a bit drunk."

"So was just about everybody," I said.

Enrique grinned. "It was a great party. We served breakfast to those who still had an appetite . . . and didn't get the last guest ashore until about an hour ago. That is, all but one. Your partner's wife is still in your cabin."

"*¡Mierda!*" I exclaimed. "Well, I'd better rouse her and send her on her way."

When I entered the cabin, I thought Nadine was still sleeping. In spite of a cool breeze coming through the open porthole, she lay on my bunk stark naked. Her firm breasts, tipped with plum-colored nipples, rose and fell evenly with her breathing. She had a magnificent body. I recall wondering how in hell Fernando could treat such a woman with such casual indifference.

As I approached the bunk, her eyes opened, and a slow smile parted her lips. She ran her hand down her belly until her fingers entered the downy black bush of her pubic mound. She spread her legs wide. Her fingers parted her vulva invitingly. "Where the hell have *you* been," she murmured. "I've been waiting for you for hours."

All right, I know I should have made her get dressed and sent her home. But I didn't. What man with red blood coursing through his veins could have rejected such an invitation?

Nadine's sexual appetite seemed insatiable. Rarely have I encountered such pent-up passion, such an animal response to intercourse.

It was the next morning before she finally left the ship. It's a damn good thing I didn't have any appointments to keep or business to conduct that day. I was exhausted. I'd been squeezed dry of vital juices.

Maybe that was the answer. Maybe Fernando wasn't man enough to satisfy her demands.

CHAPTER THIRTY-FIVE

Fernando returned to Guayaquil in February, by which time the *Artemis* was on her way to Mediterranean ports, and I was in Barranquilla attending to Metaxis y Cia. business.

It's no wonder that what happened following the New Year's Eve party on the ship wasn't long in reaching Fernando's ears. Nadine might have exercised due discretion in her affairs in Quito, but there had been nothing discreet about the episode aboard the *Artemis*. I wouldn't have blamed Fernando for being incensed, but his reaction — and subsequent action astounded me. He could have accused Nadine of adultery. He had grounds for divorce, naming me as correspondent. Yet, for some reason I never learned, the last thing Nadine wanted was a divorce. The story she gave Fernando was that I must have slipped something into one of her drinks. When she had become dizzy, I had suggested that she use my cabin to rest until she felt better. She had done so and had passed out from the effects of whatever drug I'd administered. When she had regained consciousness, I'd been sexually assaulting her.

I don't know whether Fernando actually believed her story, but he acted on it as though it were gospel. He brought charges of sexual assault against me and was suing me for the equivalent of one million dollars in damages. My God! I was accused of raping my business partner's wife! When this news reached me in Barranquilla, I was dumbfounded but not unduly alarmed. I suppose that, when she told her story, Nadine hadn't known that I could produce any number of witnesses to attest to the fact that, at the time the steward let her into my cabin, I had been some miles away at home and in bed. Moreover, as it turned out, some of the crew members on deck had, unbeknownst to either of us, been spectators to a good deal of our lovemaking through the open porthole. They were prepared, if necessary, to produce depositions that, of the two of us, Nadine had been the most aggressive. I was in a position to prove that Nadine's version of the incident was a pack of lies.

To insist on proceeding in the matter, against the sound advice of his attorney, was madness on Fernando's part. He didn't have a leg to stand on. Nonetheless he continued to fly in the face of reason and press charges.

Why did he do so? That question has never been satisfactorily answered. For one thing, I believe he felt that, since he was an Ecuadorian and I a foreigner, the court would rule in his favor. He should have known better. By then I probably had more influential Ecuadorian friends than he did. It went deeper than that, much deeper. To be cuckolded had been more than just an affront to the macho image he sought to project; it had been the final straw that had enraged him to where he took leave of his senses.

As my attorney and others who knew what they were talking about described to me, far from being happy that Guayaquil Exportación had increased its business more than tenfold since I had entered the picture, Fernando resented it. Everyone in the firm, and most of the business community, knew that the company's spectacular success had been due to my initiatives. Fernando felt he had been made to look a fool. And in his heart he knew that the suggestions I'd advanced, and that he'd rejected purely out of pique and resentment, had been the right ones. His resentments had turned to bitter hatred. I doubt that he believed the story Nadine had told him, but I think he saw in the incident a way to force me out of the partnership. It backfired on him.

It took me several months to gather from the crew members of the *Artemis* the depositions I needed to build an airtight defense. In late April the case was heard privately in judge's chambers. The presiding judge cleared me on all charges.

I should have been charitable and let the matter drop, but then I thought differently. For one thing, I had been subjected to much adverse publicity. The Ecuadorian press had pounced on the incident, and it was at this time that I was dubbed *El Greco Dorado* and pictured as a womanizing lecher. I brought countersuit for defamation of character, claiming two million dollars in damages.

The case was settled out of court for considerably less than my asking figure, but for a sum large enough that Fernando had to sell his interest in Guayaquil Exportación. I offered to buy him out, which he, of course, refused. I then had Metaxis y Cia. come forward with a generous offer, which he accepted. It would have been a bitter pill indeed for him had he known I owned Metaxis y Cia.

What became of Fernando I don't really know. I know that he and his family moved to Buenos Aires in July 1937. I later heard that he had gone into the meat-exporting business. I heard as well that Nadine had run off with an Argentinian cattleman. I hope — for the rancher's sake — that he has the stamina of one of his bulls.

In October 1937 I was back in New York. I had decided to sell my brownstone on West 76th Street and had moved into a penthouse apartment with a commanding view of Central Park from its rooftop terrace. It was while I was moving that Penny called to tell me that Omeros had died during the night of a heart attack.

Omeros had been born in, and for the most part raised in, America. His father had come from Ermoúpolis, the principal city of the island of Síros, one of the Cyclades Islands in the Aegean Sea. When Omeros had completed his high-school education in New York, he had been sent to Síros for three years to perfect his Greek. He had fallen in love with the rock-hewn island, and his wish was that, after his death, he be cremated and his ashes taken there and scattered on the Aegean.

Sofoclis, Aletha and I flew to Phoenix for the funeral. After the service, attended by an astonishing number of American politicians and dignitaries, and the cremation, I stayed on for several weeks to look after the formalities and to help Penny adjust to her loss. I also made arrangements for the disposal of Omeros' ashes. The following May, when the Atlantic weather improved, Penny and I would travel to Piraeus to board the *Artemis*. There Georgiana would meet us, and the three of us would go by boat to Síros to carry out Omeros' last wish.

After a movingly simple ceremony in which Penny, Georgiana and I committed Omeros' ashes to the Aegean, my sisters — who'd not been together in thirteen years — checked into a hotel in Ermoúpolis for a much-anticipated reunion, while I paid a short visit to Drakopoulata for yet another funeral.

A distant relative of ours, Cousin Denisio, had died two days earlier, and on meeting me in Piraeus Georgiana had suggested that, since I was already in Greece, putting in an appearance might be the polite thing to do. In fact, the villagers expected it and had delayed the rites until I could be present.

"But what do I have to do with it?" I'd asked. "I haven't seen Cousin Denisio in years. And how in hell did they know I was due in Greece?"

"You're something of a local legend, Kostas," she'd said. "You know there are no secrets in Drakopoulata. They knew you were coming because everyone there follows your exploits . . . and it was reported that you and Penny would be coming to Greece this month. Besides, it's all arranged. I've hired a launch at Patras to take you directly to Aghia Efimia."

With no small amount of protest, I gave in to Georgiana and took the hired boat to Aghia Efimia, where the town dignitaries — an unsmiling, black-clad lot — solemnly met me on the quay. Except for the odd familiar face, I recognized no one.

From the quay I was escorted to Cousin Denisio's home, where I paid my respects to his family — two singularly unattractive daughters I'd never met — and later that afternoon, in a borrowed black suit, attended the funeral and took part in the procession to the cemetery.

I've attended many a funeral, before and since, but this one stands out in my mind chiefly because the waxen-faced cadaver in the satin-lined coffin was practically a stranger to me, yet the villagers couldn't get over the fact that I had come to the funeral. "How he must have respected his cousin!" I heard whispered. "To think he's come all this way!" "Such devotion is a rare thing these days!"

Led by the village priest swinging his smoldering censer, I with five others, carried the casket, a gleaming, black-lacquered mahogany affair with silver-plated handles. Behind us came the musicians, followed by Cousin Denisio's weeping daughters and the paid mourners, about fifty old women dressed completely in black and wailing loudly. Bringing up the rear were the men carrying the floral offerings. Georgiana had thought of everything, ordering in my name a wreath so mammoth that two men had to carry it.

With Cousin Denisio laid to rest, it was time to forget the dead. That evening, with food and wine in abundance, a party was held in the church hall. There was singing, dancing and much laughter.

I spent the night as a guest in the home of one of the town fathers.

CHAPTER THIRTY-SIX

The next morning, the last thing I wanted was an official send-off. So I got up early, let myself quietly out of my host's house and, in the gray light of early dawn, started walking downhill toward Aghia Efimia.

Dawn had broken by the time I reached the harbor and roused the skipper of the launch, but the sun was still hidden from view behind the southern peaks of Ithaca. At its widest point, which happens to be on a line of bearing almost due east from Aghia Efimia, the narrow deep-water channel that separates the islands of Cephalonia and Ithaca is slightly less than five nautical miles. So near, and yet so far.

During my boyhood on Cephalonia, the steeply rising western face of Ithaca, shadowed in the morning hours and boldly etched in grays, dark browns and shades of ochre in the afternoon sunlight, had beckoned me invitingly. Yet not once during those years had I crossed the short stretch of water to the fabled shore of the island that had been Odysseus' homeland. Since my youth, Ithaca had gripped my imagination and fired my fantasies. Since then I had traveled countless thousands of miles over seas and oceans and visited many foreign lands, yet Ithaca eluded me still. As the launch sped eastward into the sparkling sunshine, I resolved that Ithaca should no longer remain a mystery. I could spend at least a few hours ashore before returning to Patras.

At Ithaca's southernmost tip, Cape Ayíou Andréou, I instructed the skipper to change course, proceed up the eastern shore, then take me into the Gulf of Molou. The gulf slices Ithaca in a southwesterly direction, very nearly dividing it in two. Only a neck of land, less than a kilometer in width, at the western end of the gulf links the island's mountainous northern and southern halves.

A narrow fingerlike inlet, branching off the gulf in a southwesterly direction, leads to the sheltered harbor of Vathí.

My intention was to have the launch drop me at Vathí, then circle back the way we had come to wait for me in a shallow cove on the western side of the island. I would explore Vathí, then follow the road that skirted the southern shore of the gulf, climb over the connecting neck of land and descend to the western cove. In all, the distance I would have to cover on foot amounted to a mere eight or nine kilometers, whereas the launch would have to cover some sixteen nautical miles to reach the cove.

The moment I set foot on the steps of the stone quay of Vathí, I was flooded with a sense of well-being. Vathí, basking in mid-morning sunshine, was an enchanting small town fanning out in an arc at the end of the narrow inlet, rising on gently sloping ground amid vineyards and olive groves.

I didn't linger in the town but struck out along the roadway leading to the westernmost of the two ruined Venetian forts at the head of the inlet that had once made Vathí a nearly impregnable haven.

I hadn't proceeded much more than two kilometers from Vathí when I came to a neglected estate. The ground, sloping upward toward the base of the mountain, was stony yet had been terraced into gardens, vineyards and olive groves that were now overgrown and choked with weeds. Through a line of cypresses, I could make out a manor house in a state of tumbled disrepair. The estate appeared to have been abandoned for some time. It struck in me some sort of a responsive chord because it reminded me of my Guayaquil residence when I'd first seen it. I grinned. Why not? I was becoming something of an expert at restoring abandoned properties.

A short distance further along the road, I came to a stone farmhouse. In response to my inquiries, I was informed that the estate, which extended, in fact, down to the inlet's shoreline, had been unoccupied for more than ten years. I was given the name of the family, now residing in Athens, who owned the property.

Where the road neared the southwestern end of the gulf's embayment, it rose steeply toward the saddle forming the joining neck of land. A cart track forked off to the left. I took the left-hand fork and, as I crested the saddle, found myself looking across the sunlet channel to Aghia Efimia on the far shore. I hadn't descended far when I saw, well below me on the Ithaca shoreline, that my hired launch was nosing into the cove where we were to rendezvous. The skipper had made good time.

It was growing hot in the noonday sun. As I paused to shed my sports jacket, a voice hailed me. I glanced past a venerable olive tree. There, in a cypress-shielded hollow, was a small stone cottage I hadn't noticed. In front, beneath the fresh greenery of a grapevine-covered trellis, an old man sat in the mottled shadows. It was he who had called me.

"My son," he said, "it is a hot day. Come, refresh yourself with a glass of wine before you continue your journey."

He was seated at a low table on which rested a plate of coarse bread, a large chunk of feta cheese and a carafe of cloudy, staw-colored wine. Suddenly, the prospect of a glass of wine appealed me. "Thank you, father," I said, making my way toward him down a short footpath.

At my approach, the oldster smiled broadly in welcome, revealing the two or three yellowing teeth he still had. The thinning hair atop his head was snow white. His sun-browned face was creased and wrinkled. But his dark brown eyes sparkled good-naturedly, and, though he was older than I had suspected from a distance, his firm, deep voice did not betray his years. He moved over to make room for me on the bench and, reaching for the carafe, poured me a glass of wine.

The wine had the crisp, clean flavor of Cephalonian Robola. I nodded appreciatively and toasted his good health. Beaming, he responded to the toast and asked me to share some bread and cheese.

"Many thanks, father," I said, "but a boat awaits me in the cove below. They will have prepared a lunch for me."

The old man looked at me inquisitively. "Where do you hail from, son? Your Greek is of these islands . . . but your clothes are of foreign cut."

The old man was perceptive. I laughed. Nodding toward Aghia Efimia, clearly visible from our vantage point, I said, "You're right on both counts, father. I was born and raised over yonder in the Pylaros region, a scant few kilometers from Aghia Efimia. Were it for that headland, we could see it from here . . . Drakopoulata. But, as my clothing has advertised, I've been many years abroad."

"If you look closely, my son, you *can* see Drakopoulata from here . . . at least a few of its houses."

By God, he was right. The old man had lost none of his keenness of vision. I could make out some of the houses. With binoculars, I most likely could pick out the house in which I was born and raised.

"Do you follow the sea?" the oldster asked.

"Yes," I said.

"That is good. As a young man, I too went to sea . . . but that was in the days of sail. It is a good calling for a man. I fear there is not much future for a young lad in these islands. But have a care, son. While fortune may lie on distant shores, don't stay away *too* long. It is here, where the sea and sky are clean and clear, that one finds peace of soul."

When I returned to Síros, I fully expected to find Georgiana and Penny at the hotel. But they were not there. I was advised that they'd gone to visit friends on the island of Míkonos and weren't expected back in Ermoúpolis for two or three days. Unfortunately, I'd already dismissed my hired launch. I hurried back to the harbor, hoping to find it still there, but it had already left to return to Piraeus. I was standing on the jetty, debating my next move, when a voice from a yacht tied alongside the quay hailed me by name.

"Kostas! What in hell are you doing here in Síros?"

Shielding my eyes against the sun's glare, I looked at the luxurious craft. It was Philip Demitrios, a Greek shipowner I'd met on a number of occasions in New York and the Caribbean islands. I grinned. "I am," I said, "seeking peace of mind. You have just destroyed any chance of that."

Demitrios laughed and said, "You sure as hell aren't going to find much comfort moping about the docks like a lost soul. Come aboard and have a couple of stiff drinks. You'll be surprised how it improves the outlook."

The upshot of the chance encounter was that I dined on board Demitrios' yacht, and he persuaded me to join him at his home on the island of Andros for the weekend. We sent one of his crew back to the hotel to leave word for Georgiana and Penny, who were scheduled to return Sunday evening, that I would be on Andros until sometime Monday morning.

Phil Demitrios was a popular figure on Andros. His summer residence, perched precariously on the edge of a cliff overlooking the sea, was a gathering place for many of the wealthy shipowners and their wives who, through common interest, had chosen Andros as a site for permanent or semipermanent residence. Actually, Demitrios was not then in the exalted ranks of the illustrious names connected with the shipping industry, but he and his lovely wife Helen were gracious and well-liked. Over the course of that weekend, at one time or another, I met many of the most prestigious shipowners of the period. Demitrios' name would join their ranks within a few years — mine, not until more than a decade later, by which time some of the biggest names in the industry had passed from the scene. I must say it was an illuminating couple of days.

Among those men I recall meeting that weekend were well-known figures, some of them considerably older than I, such as Kouloukoundis, Goulandris and Livanos; some closer to my age, such as Vergotis and Embricos; and two even younger than I, but not as well-known then as they would become a few years later. Vergotis, already a name to be reckoned with, was the closest to my age and, like me, a native Cephalonian. Konialidis was, I would say, about four or five years younger than I but already making quite a name for himself. The youngest of those I met that weekend, and the one who impressed me a great deal, was the son-in-law of Livanos. He was in his early thirties. The world was to hear a good deal of him in the years ahead. His name was Aristotle Onassis. I sensed in him the same driving ambition that goaded me into accepting risks and challenges.

What particularly stands out in my memory is the serious nature of many of the discussions that took place. There was a good deal of banter as people kept dropping in and taking their leave after short stays, and there were the inevitable lighthearted exchanges between friends of long standing, yet, in most instances, the serious matters of business and the unsettling conditions prevailing in Europe often emerged from just beneath the surface. I fear that my preoccupation with the affairs of Metaxis & Company and Metaxis y Cia. and the unsettling differences that had arisen between Fernando and myself had caused me to pay less attention to the global picture than I should have. These men, however, had their fingers on the international pulse. I listened with a good deal of interest and much concern to what they had to say, but I was able to add very little.

What came under discussion were the warlike posturings of Benito Mussolini and his military thrust into Abyssinia, the ongoing civil war in Spain, the serious threat posed by Germany's growing military strength, the increasing pressure Japan was exerting in China and the Far East, and the ill-preparedness of Britain, France and the United States to counter these threats to world peace. The consensus of opinion was that, unless some miracle prevented it, war was inevitable in Europe in the not-too-distant future, and the chances were that it could spread to become a global conflict rivaling — or surpassing — the Great War.

There was good reason for concern on the part of these men, all of them shipowners. There was every reason why I should be concerned as well. War meant the movement of huge quantities of material. It posed serious threats to mercantile traffic. To both sides of any conflict, merchant shipping was a legitimate target.

One aspect of the movement of war material to which I had given little thought was the vital necessity of crude oil and petroleum products on which modern mechanized warfare was so dependent. There was a good deal of talk about the availability of tankers of adequate tonnage to meet the leasing requirements of the oil companies. I could add nothing to the debate on this issue, but I listened . . . and learned.

Penny's decision to stay on in Athens, at least temporarily, rather surprised me. Georgiana had purchased a large house in the Glifada beach resort suburb, which she proposed to share with Penny. Omeros had made Penny a wealthy widow. She was now forty and, while chic, was not what I would call an attractive woman. Still, wealth has a way of balancing odds in a woman's favor. Nonetheless, I felt she would stand a better chance of remarrying, if that is what she wanted, by returning to the States.

In the time remaining before the *Artemis* sailed to load cargo in Mediterranean ports, I contacted an estate agent and had him track down the owners of the abandoned estate I'd discovered on Ithaca. They were interested in selling the property. Before sailing, we concluded arrangements for the transfer of title to my name.

CHAPTER THIRTY-SEVEN

I'm afraid I've been guilty of picturing myself as a whip-cracking ringmaster of a three-ring circus.

In a sense it was, at the time, a fitting simile. The three corporate entities — Metaxis & Company, Metaxis y Cia. and the Kybernas Line — while separate companies, were closely linked and mutually supportive. I formulated broad policy for all three, but there any similarity between me and a ringmaster ceased.

Any man who believes he can control all aspects of far-flung corporate structures engaged in diverse activities such as agricultural pursuits, manufacturing, exporting, importing, distribution, marketing and maritime shipping is an idiot. I didn't try. As my interests expanded, I hand-picked qualified men to direct day-to-day operations and confined myself to financing and policymaking.

In Metaxis & Company, Gerry Welton, as executive vice president, was proving his worth. He displayed a genius for organization and surrounded himself with a Praetorian Guard of able young department heads. I appreciated that a time might come when his ambitions would conflict with my interests, yet, for now, I couldn't have asked for a more capable surrogate.

Panama-based Metaxis y Cia. was functioning smoothly under the direction of Alfredo Ruiz, the former managing director of the Colombian coffee exporting firm I'd taken over a few years earlier. I was well-satisfied with the regional managers Ruiz had appointed.

I must confess that my first love was the Kybernas Line, but, even there, I delegated the responsibility. Though all the ships were under Panamanian registry, the line was headquartered in the Metaxis Building in New York, where I'd appointed a retired Royal Navy commander, James Richardson, as marine superintendent. In time, I expected Enrique to fill that billet.

In 1938, on my return from Greece, I adopted a more cautious attitude toward corporate expansion. The Andros discussions were much on my mind. I was paying close attention to developments in Europe and was increasingly convinced the predictions of my shipowning colleagues that war was inevitable were well-founded.

I suppose that is why, when war erupted in Europe in September 1939, I was not particularly surprised.

I was in Guayaquil when news of Germany's invasion of Poland reached me. To most Ecuadorians a war in Europe seemed sufficiently remote to be of merely passing interest. Not to me. Though at that time I disliked flying, I booked passage on the first available flight to New York.

The United States had not followed the lead of France and Britain in declaring war on Nazi Germany. New Yorkers were cautiously optimistic. It was "business as usual." I could not bring myself to share this sanguine mood of detachment.

By late November the German *Wehrmacht* had achieved its objectives and annexed western Poland. Unopposed, Russian troops had marched into eastern Poland, demanding a division of the spoils. During those winter months, apart from a Russian invasion of Finland, it looked like hostilities in Europe had drawn to a close; that, with the annexation of Poland, Hitler's demands for territorial expansion had been satisfied. But, if my Greek shipowning colleagues had read the portents with any degree of accuracy, Poland was but the prelude.

On my visits to Washington during those winter months I voiced the opinion that the war in Europe could erupt anew at any moment. There were some who agreed with me, but most of my contacts in the Administration scoffed at my well-intended warning.

I'm not implying that I was wiser than the Allied leaders. I wasn't, but I had a gut feeling that trouble — big trouble — was brewing.

The dangerous illusion of "peace in our time" persisted through the winter. Then came April.

The Nazis launched their war in earnest. They took Norway with relative ease, occupied an unresisting Denmark, then turned their attention to conquest of the Low Countries. Unable to stand against the onslaught of a blitzkrieg, Belgium and Holland capitulated. What concerned me, and stunned most Americans, was the inability of French and British forces to halt, or even to delay, the advance of the fast-moving Panzer divisions. By late May the Allied forces had collapsed and were in disarray. At the end of May a minor miracle took place. A flotilla of every type of craft imaginable effected an evacuation of about three hundred fifty thousand British, French and Belgian troops from a rapidly shrinking beachhead at Dunkirk. The demoralized forces landed in England bereft of arms, armor, artillery and ammunition.

Britain stood naked and defenseless. What astonished me was my reaction to Britain's predicament. I had never had any particular love for the English, but in July, when France submitted and Britain stood defiantly alone, my sympathies underwent a subtle shift. At the outset of hostilities, I had applauded the Roosevelt Administration's actions in maintaining neutrality. To reject entanglement in a European conflict had appeared to be both a practical and reasonable course of action. Now, however, for America to remain neutral in Britain's hour of direst need smacked less of prudence that it did of cowardice.

I must confess that factors closer to home influenced my thinking. The Royal Navy recalled Commander Richardson to active duty in June and appointed him as merchant shipping control officer in St. John's, Newfoundland. The following month I was approached by the British Government, which wanted to charter the *Artemis*, the *Hebe* and the *Eos* for the duration of the hostilities.

The Kybernas Line, I thought wryly, was back where it started, reduced to its two smallest cargo vessels.

In the States, industry was gearing up to become, as the president termed it, the "Arsenal of Democracy." Welton and many of the bright young men with whom he'd surrounded himself were called upon to serve on various production, procurement and supply boards set up under the Roosevelt Administration. We found ourselves shorthanded in almost every department and had no option but to call a temporary halt to our proposed expansion.

Like the United States, Greece, under the leadership of King George II, had elected to remain neutral, though its sympathies were with the Allies. Good intentions notwithstanding, I thought, it would not be long before Greece found herself drawn into the conflict.

Inactivity didn't sit well with me. As the summer advanced, I grew increasingly restive. Often I found my thoughts turning toward my beloved homeland. Had it not been for circumstances beyond my control — a broken leg and my father's ill-timed stroke — I would have served my country in the First World War. Now, for the second time in a generation, Germany had plunged Europe into a bloody conflict. True, Greece was not yet involved, but I felt the day was not distant when it would be. At forty I certainly was not too old to volunteer my services in the Allied cause. I need not wait for Greece to become embroiled nor for the United States to declare its position openly. There were other avenues open to me.

The thought fathered the deed. Without disclosing my intentions to anyone, I traveled north to offer my services to the Royal Canadian Navy.

Armed with my Board of Trade master's certificate, I presented myself to a recruiting officer at Ottawa's reserve naval division. The officer was impressed with my credentials and sent me for a medical examination. I was told to return to my hotel and report to naval headquarters the following morning at 0900.

At 0700 the next morning I was advised by telephone that there would be a delay in my enrollment procedure. No further explanation was offered. For the next three days I was left cooling my heels in Ottawa's Chateau Laurier Hotel.

I chafed at the delay, and, as the days dragged on, I began to wonder if volunteering my services had been a mistake. Then, on the morning of the fourth day, two unannounced visitors, an admiral and a civilian, arrived at the door of my suite. They identified themselves as the Chief of Naval Staff and the Minister of External Affairs. Introductions dispensed with, the admiral opened the conversation.

"Your offer to serve with our naval forces, Mr. Sthanassis, is deeply appreciated. We are sending corvettes down the ways as rapidly as our shipbuilding industry can be expanded to cope with the desperate need for escort vessels, but, frankly, manning the ships is a problem not so readily resolved. A qualified sea captain such as yourself is a godsend but —"

"But," the cabinet minister said, "it has come to our attention that you are uniquely qualified in other respects. It has been suggested that these attributes could be exploited to better advantage in areas other than convoy duty."

"Such as?" I asked.

A frown shadowed the minister's features. "I'm afraid I don't know the answer to that question. The gentleman who does is anxious to meet with you. Our prime minister has directed that you be sent to Montreal for the meeting. A parlor-car seat has been booked for you on this afternoon's train, and accommodation has been reserved for you in the Windsor Hotel in Montreal."

"Who is this gentleman?" I asked.

The minister's frown deepened. "All I can tell you is that he will identify himself by the code name 'Intrepid.' Other than that, I cannot help you . . . except to assure you that you are under no obligation to accept any proposal he advances."

The admiral smiled. "Should Intrepid's proposals lack appeal, Mr. Sthanassis, our navy will be pleased to offer you an immediate commission in the naval reserve."

I registered at the Windsor, expecting there would be some sort of message awaiting my arrival. There wasn't. I dined alone and double-checked with the switchboard before retiring. Nothing.

Plagued by troubled dreams, I slept fitfully and rose early. Still no messages. Puzzled, and becoming more than a little annoyed, I breakfasted in the hotel dining room.

I hadn't been back in my suite more than a few minutes before there was a rap on the door. I opened it to admit a neatly dressed man of medium height and pleasant features. There was something vaguely familiar about him. Then it came to me. I'd met him a year or so earlier at a trade convention in New York. If memory served, he'd been a guest at a reception I'd hosted at the University Club. He was a Canadian industrialist, but for the life of me, I couldn't recall his name.

"I believe we met at a trade convention in New York," I said.

The man smiled and extended his name. "Indeed we did, Mr. Sthanassis. The name's Stevenson, William Stevenson . . . though in some circles I'm known by a whimsical code name — Intrepid."

Stevenson didn't waste time on pleasantries. He didn't bother to tell me how my application for naval service had come to his attention. By way of introduction, he disclosed that there was more high-level cooperation between William Lyon Mackenzie King, Franklin D. Roosevelt and Winston Churchill than was generally known — or even suspected. Then Stevenson came directly to the point.

I possessed valuable assets that could and should be exploited to the best advantage. I was a Greek national holding resident status in Ecuador, which, at least for the moment, was a neutral state. In addition to my native tongue, I was fluent in Spanish and English and had a more than adequate command of Italian and French. I had solid business connections and influential political contacts on both sides of the Atlantic and freedom of movement denied to most Allied nationals and sympathizers. Did I not think it would be tantamount to criminal waste to confine such attributes to naval service?

I hadn't considered my so-called assets in that light. I wanted to know how Stevenson viewed them as being of specific value to the Allied cause.

"On the face of it," Stevenson said, "you will be pursuing your commercial interests. There is no reason, in fact, why you should not do so in reality. However, from time to time you will be directed to perform certain functions specifically related to our overall objectives. For example, in Latin America you can exert economic and political pressures to keep the republics from espousing the Axis cause."

A thought struck me. "Won't it become known that I applied for entry in the Canadian navy? Won't that make my Allied sypathies self-evident?"

Stevenson chuckled. "As a matter of fact, that can work to our advantage. Your application *will* become common knowledge. There is nothing we can do to prevent it. However, by spreading the word that your application was rejected, it gives you good reason to appear somewhat disenchanted with Allied aims and objectives."

Stevenson must have wielded considerable influence if he was in a position to alter facts to serve his purpose. I regarded him with new respect. "If I agree to work with you, where and when do we start?"

"I'll arrange for you to go to England as a passenger with a convoy now being formed in Halifax. In England, you will confer directly with a member of Churchill's staff. The prime minister has in mind a mission of a delicate nature for which, in my estimation, you would be well-suited. But before you commit yourself, I must warn you of the possible consequences. This is a dangerous game involving a high degree of personal risk. There is no turning back. Your clandestine activities must be cloaked in utmost secrecy. If for any reason you were to land in inextricable trouble, we would disavow you. You would be entirely on your own. I trust that is clearly understood."

I nodded, then grinned. "When I came here to enlist in the navy, if anyone had suggested I'd end up being recruited as a spy I would've considered him a lunatic."

"Spy?" Stevenson's eyebrows inched fractionally upward. "I'd equate your clandestine employment with that of a diplomatic emissary or political broker. I wouldn't have called you a spy. But perhaps you're right. I guess, put simply, 'spy' would be a reasonably accurate term."

CHAPTER THIRTY-EIGHT

Truth is stranger than fiction!

I arrived in Halifax on August 3. The Halifax component of the convoy was due to form up and sail from Bedford Basin in the predawn hours of the fourth. I was met at the railroad station, whisked directly to the naval dockyard and thence by harbor craft to the basin.

As we neared the vessel aboard which I was to take passage, my heart skipped a beat. It couldn't be! But it was, even though she'd undergone some marked changes. A naval gun was mounted on a platform constructed on her stern. Her former bold colors of white and blue had been camouflaged with drab grays, blues and brown-greens, yet there was no mistaking her proud lines. It was none other than my erstwhile flagship, *Artemis*. I wondered if Stevenson had arranged it this way.

Enrique stood at the inboard end of the accommodation ladder, his eyes wide with surprise. I mounted toward him, grinning broadly.

"*¡Por Diós*, Kostas! What are *you* doing here?"

"You were expecting a passenger, weren't you?"

Enrique's expression was one of stunned disbelief. "You . . . *you're* our important passenger?"

I chuckled. "In the flesh, *mi hijo*, in the flesh. But believe me, it's as much a surprise to me as it is to you. I had no idea I'd be making the crossing on the *Artemis*. I doubt that the naval authorities who assigned me the billet knew I owned the ship. In fact, I hardly recognized her with her new paint job."

Enrique smiled. "She hasn't changed much below-decks. Welcome aboard, skipper." Then, his face clouding, he added, "But I'm afraid you won't be able to occupy your owner's suite."

"Why the hell not?"

"Your suite, along with most of the passenger accommodations, has been taken over by the convoy commodore and his naval staff."

"Shit! Suppose it can't be helped. Fit me in anywhere."

"You can take over my quarters."

"To hell with that. You're the captain of this ship. You must have a spare bunk *somewhere*. Where would you've put me if I'd been the important passenger you were expecting?"

"The second mate's cabin. The second is doubling up with the third mate."

"Okay. That'll do. Trust the navy to fuck everything up." No sooner were the words out of my mouth than I regretted them. But for a twist of fate, I'd have been a naval officer more than a week ago.

"Actually," Enrique said, "I think you and the convoy commodore will get along famously."

"Why should we?"

"He's a Newfoundland captain brought out of retirement. His name is Timothy Patrick Driscoll."

Shades of the *Pandora!* If only briefly, the three of us had been reunited by the vagrant winds of war.

It had been close to twelve years since I'd seen Driscoll, yet the crusty old sea dog had changed little. I had never known his age, but by now he must have been at the very least in his middle seventies. He didn't look it. I drew comfort from the fact that, as far as convoy discipline was concerned, we were in good hands. I could think of no man alive who was blessed with a more intimate knowledge of the North Atlantic and its moods and vagaries. Now, if the commander of the Canadian mid-ocean escort squadron was equally knowledgeable about Nazi *Unterseebooten* and Wolf Pack tactics, we should enjoy an uneventful crossing.

My confidence was not misplaced. The convoy ahead of us came under attack by U-boats south of Iceland. We took evasive action and completed the twenty-four-day crossing without incident.

Would you believe it? In the entire course of the voyage, Driscoll never once addressed either me or Enrique by our Christian names. He was affable and relaxed with us but would not permit himself the luxury of informality. We were, as we'd formerly been, "Mister Sthanassis" and "Mister Ramirez."

The *Artemis* docked at Liverpool. I had a farewell dinner with Driscoll and Enrique before disembarking to catch the night train to London. I told them only that I had business to attend to in London, which was essentially true, even if I'd yet to learn the nature of that business. I couldn't have told them I expected to meet with Winston Churchill even if I'd had a mind to do so.

In London, as directed by Stevenson, I checked into the Dorchester and found awaiting me at the reception desk an invitation to spend the weekend at Rockridge House, the Sussex country home of Sir Peter Crowther. Sir Peter was a mercantile banker with whom I'd had previous dealings, but, on this occasion, our business was of a different nature. It was at Rockridge during the course of that weekend that I was introduced to Colonel Malcolm Whitelaw.

In the privacy of Sir Peter's library, Whitelaw favored me with a synopsized version of the obstacles confronting Britain in the Mediterranean and the Middle East. The situation was grave. Italian naval, ground and air forces threatened the use of the Mediterranean as a maritime supply route for British forces in the Middle East and North Africa. Italian victories in East Africa and Italian-German initiatives in the Balkans clouded the issue even further. Spain, though not yet committed to the Axis, was an unknown factor in the equation. France, defeated and humiliated, was, under a puppet Vichy regime, collaborating — albeit unwillingly — in furthering Nazi ambitions. In Europe, Britain stood virtually alone in her resistance to the Axis powers. It was vital that her bastions in the Mediterranean, Gibraltar and Malta, be safeguarded and that the Suez Canal remain in British hands at all costs.

Colonel Whitelaw would be my sold link with the prime minister. In espionage parlance, I suppose he could be referred to as my "control."

When I arrived in London, the Nazi *Luftwaffe* was engaged in bombing assaults directed against British coastal shipping, coastal defenses and military airfields. A week later, in an attempt to shatter morale preceding a full-scale invasion, the air assault was concentrated on the city itself. The saturation bombing continued with unabated fury until mid-October. I can add nothing to the exhaustively documented story of the Battle of Britain except to recount how it affected me personally.

On September 3, I was a guest at a small dinner party at the Greek ambassador's residence. My dinner companion was a startlingly beautiful young woman named Beatrice Tocchi. Her face, framed softly in coppery red hair, was cameolike. Her skin was alabaster white. But what struck me immediately were her widely spaced blue-green eyes. Tocchi? An unusual surname. It struck a remote chord of memory. In the distant past Cephalonia had been ruled as a feudal fief by Venetian noblemen of that name. During the course of the dinner I asked the young lady about it.

The ghost of a smile played at the corner of her mouth. "My father tells me that some of our ancestors were merchant princes of Venice who dominated some of the Ionian isles . . . but that was some five centuries ago. I believe we were forcibly ejected by marauding Turks sometime in the fifteenth century. Why do you ask?"

"I'm a native of Cephalonia. I would like to think that one of your beauty laid claim to Greek blood."

She colored slightly, then laughed. "I will accept that as a compliment, Mr. Sthanassis, and admit to the distinct possibility that there is Greek blood in my family."

From that opening, she deftly turned the conversation to my commercial interests. She had heard, she said, that I was in shipping and involved in mining ventures. I said that my shipping interests were somewhat curtailed at the moment since most of my ships were leased to the British Government. With consummate skill, she steered the conversation into other channels. She had been told that I had recently arrived from the United States. What was life like in America? What were America's views on war in Europe? What was my opinion of European women in contrast to American women?

By the time she left, accompanied by the couple she'd come with, I realized I'd done most of the talking and knew very little about her.

At the conclusion of the evening, when I was sharing a nightcap with the ambassador, I asked him about Miss Tocchi.

From my host I learned that Beatrice Tocchi's father was Count Guglielmi Tocchi. The ambassador didn't know the whole story, but he did know that the count, on the death of his wife eight years earlier, had moved to London, bringing with him his daughter, who was then in her late teens. The ambassador understood there was a son four or five years older than Beatrice who had remained in Rome.

"I would have thought," I said, "that a woman of her singular beauty would be married . . . or at least engaged . . . yet I notice no rings to indicate either status. She mentioned no men in her life, other than her father."

The ambassador nodded. "Understandable. She was engaged to an Englishman, Evan, Viscount Broughton. They were to have been married next spring."

"You use the past tense. Did she break off the engagement?"

"Not exactly," the ambassador said. "Young Broughton was killed in Belgium nine months ago. He was a lieutenant with the British Expeditionary Force."

"But," I said, "that would have been in January. The BEF saw no action at that time."

"True. That's what makes it such a tragic waste. He was killed in a training exercise."

There was an undeniable physical attraction between us. Had Beatrice and I met at another time, in another place, we might have indulged in an affair and let it go at that. That would have been the wisest course to adopt. We were from very different backgrounds. Since I was some sixteen years her senior, I should have been the one to exercise caution. But I let passion override reason.

An air of fatalistic urgency pervaded wartime London. The tendency was to fly in the face of established mores by bending, if not breaking, the conventional rules of conduct. I should have allowed more time to elapse, but the day after the dinner party I sent a note around to the Tocchi flat in Lowndes Square, requesting the pleasure of Beatrice's company at dinner that very evening. She accepted my invitation.

I presented myself at the flat promptly at seven, which, by sun time, thanks to British double summer time, was five in the afternoon. While I waited for Beatrice, Count Tocchi served me a scotch and water. He sipped a Campari and soda and scrutinized me unsmilingly. He was courteous but distantly formal. I got the distinct impression that he didn't approve of me. To be perfectly honest, I can't say that I blamed him. He was a younger man than I'd anticipated, much closer to my age than I was to his daughter's. At the outside, I would have given him no more than fifty; I learned later that evening that he was, in fact, forty-seven.

It was memorable evening, one that I recall vividly to this day. After enjoying a leisurely dinner at the Savoy, we went to my suite at the Dorchester to continue our conversation over after-dinner drinks.

My intentions were anything but honorable, which I'm sure

Beatrice appreciated. She knew, however, that at this stage in our relationship it was highly unlikely that I would indulge in improper advances. Secure in that knowledge, she was coyly flirtatious.

It was at that point that Ares took a hand in the game.

When the sirens wailed, we guessed it to be a precautionary exercise until the hotel management telephoned to advise that an air attack was imminent. We were advised to proceed to the hotel basement. Ignoring the warning, we turned out the room lights, parting the heavy drapes and watching with morbid fascination as the frightening scenario unfolded.

Searchlights fanned the night sky with silvered tracery. Anti-aircraft guns thumped angrily. Then, as bombs rained down, the crash and rumble of near and distant explosions reverberated in our ears. The glare of explosions soon merged into the wavering, blood-red backdrop as fires gnawed voraciously at the tightly packed edifices of the East End.

A nearby explosion shook the Dorchester. Flakes of plaster sifted down on us. The blast momentarily deafened us. Trembling, Beatrice clung to me.

Drawing the drapes, I tried to switch on a lamp. Nothing happened. There must have been a temporary power failure. Opening the drapes once more to let in the ruddy glow of the burning city, I guided Beatrice into the bedroom. Wordlessly we undressed and crawled into bed. I held her slim, quivering body close to calm her terror.

I have never been able to explain it satisfactorily. I swear that sex was the farthest thing from my mind. But was it? There came a point where, unbidden, desire overrode fear. My first intimation of this was when her breathing became harsh and irregular and her nipples hardened. Seemingly of its own volition, my penis responded. Her mouth hungrily sought mine. With a whimpering moan, she moved to bring her body beneath mine and spread her legs wide to receive me.

There was a frenzied abandon to our lovemaking. She strained upward to meet my deep thrusts and raked my back with her nails. A strange sound, somewhere between a moan and a low growl, escaped from her parted lips. Then my own exultant shouts echoed in my ears as I exploded within her, and she wrapped her legs around me to keep me sheathed as she bucked and quivered in orgasm.

We didn't disengage. We clung tightly to each other and made love again, and yet again, as our sweat-slicked bodies responded to whatever drive possessed us.

When the "All Clear" sounded, I reached across the tangled sheets and tried the bedside lamp. It flooded the room with soft light. Grinning, I said, "It looks like the city's returned to normal."

Beatrice pushed herself to a sitting position and ran her fingers through her tousled hair. "The lifts will be running. I'd better shower and make myself presentable so you can get me home. Papa will be beside himself with worry."

My memory of the next two weeks is confused. Life was, to say the least, hectic. With but brief respite, bombs rained on London night and day. Sirens wailed; explosions crashed and rumbled. In an unequal struggle, firemen battled leaping flames, and, for the most part, the city's populace huddled in bomb shelters, basements and Underground stations. As intent as they were on survival, somehow Londoners managed to go about their daily chores. That, too, might have been termed "survival."

It was a time of near-exhaustion and heightened emotional responses. Time seemed compressed. When Beatrice and I could steal time to be together, we did little else but make love, though at a somewhat slower tempo than on our first night together. We didn't dwell on the past nor talk of the future. We were content to savor the present as though each moment might be our last.

Undoubtedly Churchill and his staff were occupied by weightier matters than whatever mission it was they had in mind for me. Though I expected to be summoned and briefed on a specific assignment, I wasn't contacted by Whitelaw for close to two weeks. On that occasion he looked haggard and seemed preoccupied. I got the impression that he didn't have a very clear idea about the exact nature of the tasks for which I'd been recruited.

The major concern of the moment appeared to be the preservation of Gibraltar as a naval base. I was to be sent to Spain, by way of Portugal, my mission to persuade the Spanish that it would be in their interests that Gibraltar remain a British possession and that Spain, if it could not actively side with Britain, should at least remain neutral. Arguments to support these contentions were left to my discretion. In short, I was to play it by ear.

On leaving Spain I was to proceed to Greece by whatever means of civilian transportation was available. In Greece I was simply to observe and report my findings on my return to London. I had the feeling that Greece had been an afterthought.

My preparation for this assignment was, to say the least, per-functory. I committed to memory the names and addresses of several pro-British Portuguese and Spanish officials. I was instructed in a book-code based on a 1938 edition of the *Michelin Guide to Spain and Portugal* and was given the address of a London customs broker, evidently a War Office cover, with whom I could communicate in the event of emergency — an eventuality, I was assured, that should not arise.

I didn't feel that much importance was attracted to my mission and wondered how in hell I'd allowed Stevenson to talk me into this predicament.

CHAPTER THIRTY-NINE

In Madrid and Barcelona I met with industrialists, bankers and exporters. My message was simple.

I said I'd come from New York with stops along the way in Montreal, London and Lisbon. In Portugal, I'd concluded agreements for expanded importations of Portuguese wines and fortified wines, a step made necessary by the loss of customary suppliers in France. I was anxious to ink similar agreements in Spain. Moreover, acting on behalf of American, Canadian and British importers, I was interested in other products in short supply such as olives, olive oil, cork and textiles.

In Barcelona I invited bids for the construction of two 20,000-ton, turbine-powered merchant vessels.

As was to be expected, my presence and the nature of my business caused quite a stir in both financial and political circles. I faced a barrage of questions.

Los Estados Unidos? Did I think America would declare war on Germany and Italy? I said that America, by supplying war material England and her Commonwealth allies sorely needed, was de facto already at war with the Axis powers. *Claro,* but could Britain, even with American support, hold out against the Nazi war machine? In spite of my innermost doubts on this score, I exuded confidence. To that often-asked question I would shrug eloquently and say that I'd just come from London, where I'd spent two weeks under Nazi saturation bombing designed to break England's will to resist. As far as I could determine, though, all the Nazis had achieved was a strengthening of British determination to fight on.

I generally concluded with a question of my own: "Would I be here negotiating on behalf of British importers if I thought England was on the verge of defeat?"

Whether implicit or explicit, my contention was that Generalissimo Franco, if he could not see his way clear to openly espouse the Allied cause, would be well-advised to insure that Spain remained neutral. I avoided bringing Gibraltar into the discussions. I didn't have to. Spain's neutrality maintained Gibraltar's status quo.

My business transacted, my point — I hoped — made, I went by train to Algeciras, crossed the straits to Tangier and took passage on a Libyan freighter bound for Piraeus.

In Greece I was simply to gather information. To that end I questioned shipping colleagues, politicians and military sources. My concern, in view of my shipping interests, was understandable.

During my week in Athens, I stayed with Georgiana and Penny in the suburb of Glifada. Discussions I had with my sisters and their friends were illuminating. Theirs was the viewpoint of the middle-class Greek. It proved to be one of cautious optimism. They were almost uniform in the belief that Greek neutrality would not be violated.

The politicians echoed that man-in-the street sentiment. The military sources, almost to a man, expressed every confidence that the Greek army was more than a match for the Italian forces likely to be arraigned against Greece. Only among the shipowning fraternity did I encounter opinions widely divergent from the generally accepted point of view.

Goulandris, Livanos, Embricos, Demitrios and other shipping magnates spoke as though with one voice. All of them agreed that the Greek forces were more than a match for the Italians, but they carried speculation one step further. It was their opinion that Germany wouldn't rely on Italy to protect the exposed flank and would intervene to transform Greece into a satellite state.

As the end of October, when I was on a Greek merchantman nearing Lisbon, the news reached us via ship's radio. The Italians had swarmed through Albanian passes in an assault on the Greek frontier. The attacks had been repulsed and the Italians sent reeling back into Albania.

The first thing I did after Whitelaw debriefed me was to place a call to the Tocchi flat. Actually, when Beatrice answered I was surprised. She had said in mid-September that she and her father would seek safety from the bombing by visiting friends in the country.

Beatrice seemed pleased to hear from me and said she was anxious to see me. She had, she said, something important to tell me. We agreed to meet that evening.

Once Beatrice was seated in the Dorchester's American Bar, I asked what it was she had to tell me.

She hesitated a moment, then said, "You were gone longer than you indicated. I thought you might return to London."

"I know," I said. "I had business in Portugal and Spain I had to attend to before I could go to Greece. I'd hoped to be able to go by air at least part of the way, but I had to travel by ship. Transportation poses a few problems these days."

She slowly twisted the stem of her sherry glass, then said, "There's something you should know. I'm pregnant."

I suppose I should have been stunned by this revelation, yet, oddly enough, I wasn't. I reached across the table and took her hand in mine. "Do you want to have the baby?"

"Yes . . . oh, yes."

"Then I suggest we get married."

She looked at me. "Are you sure that's what you want? You're not just asking me because you think it's the honorable thing to do?"

I smiled and squeezed her hand. "It's what I've wanted since we first met. I'd asked you to marry me before I went away, but I felt that was crowding things a little." Then, the smile leaving my lips, I added, "But it's up to you. I don't want to pressure you into something you might regret later."

Squeezing my hand in return, she leaned across and brushed my cheek with her lips. "I won't regret it . . . ever. I'm happy you've made me pregnant. We'll have a beautiful baby, darling."

"Does your father know about the baby?" I asked.

"Not yet. I'll tell him tomorrow. I'll also tell him you proposed to me before you left here in September."

"He isn't going to like it. He doesn't approve of me."

Beatrice laughed. "Don't worry about Papa. He didn't approve of Evan any more than he does of you."

Until that moment I'd forgotten about her engagement to Viscount Broughton.

With the Greek ambassador and his wife acting as witnesses, Beatrice and I were married in a registry office the following Friday. Count Tocchi showed his disapproval by not attending the ceremony.

It couldn't have been called a honeymoon. Beatrice and I spent a weekend at an inn in Walton-on-Thames and returned to our suite in the Dorchester on Monday morning. I promised her we'd take a long leisurely cruise later on. She said she didn't mind, declaring she was anxious to get back to make sure her father wasn't too annoyed with us. He would come around, she assured me, but it would take time.

On our return to the hotel, I received a message from Whitelaw suggesting that we meet without delay.

Whitelaw made no effort to hide his disapproval. "You should have let us know," he said, "and you shouldn't have left London without letting us know where you could be reached in the event of emergency."

I bridled. "I was only gone for a weekend. I don't consider that much of a honeymoon. *Is* there an emergency?"

"Well . . . no. But that's not the point. The Old Man was shocked when he learned of your marriage to an Italian. Consorting with the enemy and all that."

I snorted. "Balls! She's lived in London since she was a teenager. Until January of this year, she was betrothed to a peer of your precious realm. Besides, she knows nothing of my clandestine activities . . . nor will she."

"How did she react to the news that our naval fliers bombed the Italian fleet at Taranto?"

"She didn't seem unduly concerned."

"That's odd. She has a brother who's an officer in the Italian army."

"Mario? She rarely talks about him. I gather they don't communicate. He quarreled violently with his father some years back."

"The count? What was *his* reaction to the Taranto bombing?"

"I couldn't say. . . . We haven't discussed it."

Whitelaw's manner thawed. "We appreciate that Count Tocchi has resided here for eight years and doesn't appear to be at all well-disposed toward Mussolini's regime. The count has property holdings in Italy and, for some time now, has been unable to transfer his income to England."

"You seem remarkably well-informed about the count's affairs," I said.

"Well, he *is* Italian. We have to keep tabs on emeny aliens no matter how innocent they may appear. No need to get huffy about it, old boy."

At the end of November Beatrice and I moved into a flat on Pont Street within easy walking distance of Lowndes Square. Claiming the exercise did her good, Beatrice visited her father almost daily. At first I accompanied her on these excursions; however, since the count made no effort to disguise his dislike of me and wasted no opportunity to let me know it, I visited less and less frequently over the ensuing weeks.

There was encouraging news from the African theater early in December. British forces in Egypt, undaunted by the vastly superior numbers arraigned against them, launched attacks against Italian forces in Abyssinia and Libya. The British were spectacularly successful. In London spirits ran high.

Mindful of Whitelaw's assertions, I watched Beatrice and Guglielmi closely to judge their reactions to the news of ebbing Italian fortunes of war. If anything, the count seemed to derive pleasure from Il Duce's embarrassment in the field. Beatrice, on the other hand, was supremely indifferent to the Italian reverses. Except where it impinged on her personal life through the inconveniences of shortages and rationing, the war seemed to mean little to her. I noted that, at least in my presence, neither Beatrice nor the count mentioned Mario Tocchi.

A few days before Christmas, tragedy struck from a totally unexpected source. Count Tocchi, with typical disdain for rules and regulations, ignored the warning signs of a roped-off area and took a shortcut through a bomb-damaged section of the city. A wall of a building collapsed, burying him beneath a mass of falling masonry. It took workmen the better part of three hours to retrieve his battered corpse from the rubble.

I was not at home when the accident happened. I knew nothing about it until I returned to the flat late in the afternoon. The count's manservant had brought the news some hours earlier. Beatrice had collapsed in a state of shock. The doctor had been summoned and had ordered her sedated and confined to bed.

Long faces and hushed voices greeted me when I arrived home that afternoon. Still in attendance, the doctor told me confidentially that only a miracle had prevented Beatrice from the losing the baby. He prescribed rest and the avoidance of emotional stress. He had put in a call for a trained nurse to stay with Beatrice until he felt she had fully recovered.

It wasn't what one could term a festive season for those of us on Pont Street. Beatrice was deeply depressed. She seemed inconsolable and would break down at the slightest provocation.

Much of the time the nurse kept her under sedation. I stayed by her bed throughout her waking hours and slept on a cot in the adjoining dressing room lest she awake during the night. Until then, I hadn't appreciated how deeply attached Beatrice had been to her father.

At his request, I met with Whitelaw two days before the end of the year. He was in excellent spirits. He made no mention of Count Tocchi's death or Beatrice's infirmity, though I'm sure he knew of the situation. If he noticed my strained appearance, he ignored it. He said the prime minister wished him to congratulate me on the way I'd handled matters in Spain. Churchill had been particularly impressed by my solicitation of bids for ship construction in Spanish yards. The prime minister had thought it an inspired touch that displayed confidence in Britain during its darkest hour.

I was pleased — yet perplexed — that the prime minister was pleased. Inviting bids from Barcelona shipyards had been legitimate business that had had little or nothing to do with Britain's dilemma. Whichevr way the tide swung, the Kybernas Line needed new construction, and there were no yards in North America, and few in Europe, that could accept anything besides wartime contruction. My choice had been between Sweden and Spain. Surely Churchill had been aware of that.

Then Whitelaw veered to another subject, obviously the true purpose of our meeting. Intrepid had sent word that, if I was not desperately needed in Europe, my talents could be put to good use in Latin America. Accordingly, passage had been booked for my wife and I aboard the *Queen Mary* sailing eight days hence from Southampton to New York. Whitelaw added that a change of scene might benefit Beatrice.

When the colonel and I parted company a few moments later, I noted that Whitelaw had made no reference to my report on the situation in Greece.

Beatrice was no longer confined to her bed, but her depressed mood lingered on. She was listless and withdrawn. She received my news of our imminent departure for America without expression. I wasn't sure that she had grasped what I'd told her until later in the evening, when she asked me where we would live in the United States. I told her we would move into my penthouse apartment in New York and assured her she would not find the city too different from London — at least the London she had known in happier days.

Over the next week Beatrice became more animated as we prepared to leave. The idea that we were quitting London, which had been the scene of such grief, seemed to gain in appeal with each passing day.

The *Queen Mary,* in convoy parlance, was classed as a "monster." She would make the crossing alone and unescorted, relying on her speed to avoid or evade enemy submarines. We made the crossing without incident in five days.

CHAPTER FORTY

My meeting with Stevenson took place at the Waldorf-Astoria. On this occasion, Stevenson was accompanied by an American lawyer named William Donovan. Donovan did most of the talking.

The Nazis had introduced armed raiders into the South Atlantic, and there had been isolated reports of U-boat sightings in southern waters. The fear was that German naval activity might spill over into the South Pacific. My task was to do what I could in the South American republics facing on the Pacific to insure that Pacific bases were denied to the enemy. Up until now, most Latin American republics had been strictly neutral, but that wasn't enough. Neutrality would not deny German naval units refueling and resupply facilities and temporary haven if faced with difficulties. I was to exert what economic and political pressure I could to persuade the coastal republics to make formal commitments in favor of the Allied powers.

The *Pandora* was due to sail from Galveston to Barranquilla within the week. I was to join my ship there and begin the South American portion of my mission with Colombia.

"Should I take my wife with me?" I asked.

"Under normal circumstances," Stevenson said, "that would be an excellent idea. However, I understand she's now four months pregnant . . . and has not had a particularly easy time of it. In all, you will have five republics on your itinerary — Chile, Peru, Ecuador, Colombia and Panama. We're allowing one week in each republic, more if you consider it necessary. Therefore, including the traveling time, you should be absent a minimum of six weeks. Under those circumstances, we don't think it advisable that your wife accompany you." He paused briefly, then added, "Besides, should we need to recall you, your wife's condition provides us with the perfect excuse."

I left the meeting in a somber mood. My cab trip back to 94th Street gave me time for sober reflection.

I didn't like the idea of leaving Beatrice on her own. She was still given to prolonged bouts of depression. The servants could attend to her wants, but she needed companionship. I would have to ask Sofoclis and Aletha to keep an eye on her during my absence.

Two facts emerged with disturbing clarity from my meeting with Stevenson and Donovan. One: Stevenson, Donovan and Whitelaw were better-informed about my domestic affairs than I'd suspected. Two: If I thought my commitment to Stevenson left me a measure of freedom, I was sadly mistaken.

Still, I thought, what had I expected? I'd gone to Canada to enlist in the navy. Had I done so, I would've been subject to naval discipline and orders for the duration of hostilities. There was no reason for me to expect my commitment to Stevenson would be any less demanding. That I wasn't wearing a uniform and had continued to engage in commercial activities had created an illusion of independence. But Stevenson, as I'd just been reminded, was calling the shots.

Ruiz joined me in Panama City and accompanied me on my swing through the western South American republics. My opinions carried weight in financial and political circles in Colombia and Ecuador, where Metaxis y Cia. was firmly entrenched and an integral part of their economies. Where Metaxis y Cia.'s economic penetration was more recent, as was the case in Peru and Chile, the pressures I could exert were more limited. The pro-Allied arguments I presented were reinforced by the presence of Ruiz as managing director of Metaxis y Cia.

In Colombia and Ecuador I stated my case bluntly. The fortunes of Metaxis y Cia. were irrevocably tied to the economic health and well-being of Metaxis & Company. Accordingly, Colombian and Ecuadorian governments, in the best interests of their economies, would be well-advised to follow U.S. pro-Allied policies.

In Peru, and particularly in Chile, where pro-German sentiments were much in evidence, I was more circumspect but essentially advanced the same arguments and played on pro-British sympathies wherever I could.

How effective was the case Ruiz and I presented? Our arguments were weakened by the fact that America, while it made no secret of its sympathies, had not yet committed itself formally to the Allied cause. I firmly believe, however, that we helped swing official thinking toward a wait-and-see approach that ultimately, following the lead of the United States, led four of those South American republics to declare war against the Axis powers. The exception was Chile, which did not declare itself until 1944.

We followed the war news closely. In February, when Ruiz and I were in Quito, we learned that some four hundred Italian troops in East Africa and Libya had been decisively defeated by British forces. It was heartening news.

Much less heartening was the news that reached us in Panama City on the homeward leg of the trip. The Allied floodtide had peaked and was now ebbing. In the Atlantic, U-boats were taking an unprecedented toll. In the Balkans, Bulgaria yielded to Nazi demands that a German field army be based on Bulgarian soil; it was rumored that Yugoslavia had resisted a similar demand. In North Africa, General Erwin Rommel landed a crack armored division and support forces at Tripoli.

I don't want to give the impression that our trip was confined to promoting pro-Allied sentiments. The declared purpose of the trip — which Ruiz believed to be its sole purpose — was to call a temporary halt to plans for projected expansion and to bring exports into line with the reduced availability of shipping.

I took advantage of our brief stop in Guayaquil to attend to a personal matter. Retrieving the rough emerald from the safety deposit box in which it had lain for a decade, I took it to a jeweler. Then, returning from Lima and Santiago, I picked up the gemstone, which the jeweler had transformed into a necklace of spectacular beauty: a magnificent pendant set between two smaller stones and surrounded by sparkling diamonds. I would give it to Beatrice to celebrate the birth of our first child.

Two days after I returned to New York, I met with Donovan at the Yale Club.

"Where's Stevenson?" I asked.

"In London. Your report on Greece is causing a stir."

That surprised me. "No one seemed much interested when I submitted it."

"They sure as hell are now. You called the play right on the money. Looks like the Nazis are poised for an all-out assault on Yugoslavia and Greece. The Brits are rushing in seven or eight divisions from North Africa to back up the Greek forces."

"They should have been there and dug in months ago."

"Okay, so they weren't. At that time, Alexander was preoccupied with the Wops in Abyssinia and Libya. Now he's faced with Kraut panzer divisions all set to roll south out of Bulgaria, Rumania and Hungary *and* a buildup of Rommel's Afrika Korps in Libya."

"A two-pronged thrust aimed at Suez?"

"As a prelude, if we're reading the signs correctly, to a Nazi push into Russia."

I pondered the implications for a moment. Hitler's ambitions were vaulting. Could he be stopped? I seriously doubted that he could be — certainly not by the stopgap measures the British appeared to be taking. However, if Hitler were turning his gaze eastward, that should mean that England, if only for the moment, no longer faced the threat of invasion. But what I couldn't fathom was how I fitted into the picture. So I asked Donovan.

He shrugged. "Simple. Right now Greece is in the limelight. Since you called the play accurately, that makes you our Greek expert. They want you in London as rapidly as we can get you there."

"Hell, I only echoed the consensus of opinion of knowledgeable sources."

"So. Presumably those sources can be used again."

"Maybe. Maybe not. How long have I got in New York?"

"Three whole fun-filled days. Then you go to Canada and climb aboard a bomber being delivered to England."

Before calling the apartment to tell Beatrice I'd be home for dinner, I stopped off at the Metaxis Building to see Sofoclis.

It was the first time I'd seen him since my return from South America. The big ox embraced me affectionately and poured me a stiff drink.

"Want to thank you and Aletha for looking in on Beatrice while I was away," I said.

The smile left Sofie's face. "We didn't see much her her. She made it pretty clear that she neither needed nor welcomed our concern."

I frowned. I wondered if she'd had a falling out with Sofie and Aletha. "Sorry. It was an imposition. Shouldn't have asked you and Aletha to be nursemaids."

"No imposition, but she didn't need our attention. She's made friends in your building — a Broadway producer, a playwright, and a photographer and his wife — people a bit out of Aletha's and my league. It didn't help any that she's pissed off with you at the moment."

She had been noticeably cool toward me since my return. "Why? Because I didn't take her with me? In her condition she wouldn't have enjoyed the trip."

"I don't think that's the reason."

"Then what's eating her?"

Sofie opened a drawer in his desk, took out a folder and handed it to me.

The folder contained two sets of press clippings. One was from Los Angeles scandal sheet datelined Hollywood, December 29, 1940. The second, a reprint of the first, was clipped from a New York tabloid dated January 22, 1941.

Whoever had done the investigative reporting was almost as thorough as he or she was unprincipled.

Under the heading "The Golden Greek," the story covered lurid aspects of my life between 1924 and 1938. There were omissions during those periods where it would have been impossible to trace my movements or activities, but the story was reasonably accurate, though distorted. It was a muckraking smear.

The gist of the story was that I'd arrived in the United States a penniless Greek immigrant in the early twenties. Seizing on Prohibition as an avenue to riches, I'd engaged in bootlegging, then parlayed my illegal profits into ownership of a speakeasy. When my club was raided, I'd faced criminal charges and fled the country. Shortly thereafter I'd again come to the attention of the authorities as the rumrunning captain of a costal freighter.

Following the stock market crash of 1929, I'd dropped from sight then reappeared as a partner in an Ecuadorian exporting firm and soon thereafter had become the owner of a Panamanian conglomerate and a shipping company. When Prohibition was repealed, I had returned to the States and bought into one of the country's largest importing companies. It was estimated — a wildly speculative exaggeration — that by 1938 my net worth was in excess of three hundred million dollars.

To that point, the article contained facts that were largely a matter of record. The trouble was that the piece was slanted in a way that made me look like a speculative opportunist at best, at worst a crook.

The most damning part of the article noted that in 1932 and 1933 I'd lived in a palatial residence in Malibu Beach. During this period I'd taken as my mistress movie queen Tess Martin. The article that I'd financed her last film, "The Marriage Mill," then went on to say that, shortly after the film's release, Tess had drowned under suspicious circumstances and that an autopsy had revealed her to be two months pregnant at the time of her death.

That she'd been pregnant when she'd committed suicide was something I hadn't known until I read the article. I was shaken and seething. It implied that I'd fathered her unborn child. Worse, it implied that her death had not been suicide and that I, in some way, could have been responsible.

The article closed with a rehash of the Ecuadorian scandal involving Nadine Alvarez, without mentioning that I'd been cleared of all charges.

I closed the folder and slid it across the desk to Sofoclis. "Do you think Beatrice read this crap?" I asked.

At dinner that evening, Beatrice complained about the weather, her swollen belly and her lack of an adequate wardrobe. If she *had* read the defamatory article, why hadn't she raised the subject since my return two days ago? In another three days I'd have to leave again. Tonight seemed as good a time as any to bring matters to a head.

"I have to go away again a couple of days from now," I said.

Beatrice stopped talking in mid-sentence. Her features hardened. "Where this time?"

"Greece."

Her eyes narrowed as she said, "Why? Did you leave behind a pregnant actress on your last visit?"

"So you read that garbage."

"So you read that garbage," she mimicked. "Of course I read it. *Everyone* has. I suppose you're going to tell me it's a pack of lies."

"Part of it's fact. Most of it's utter crap."

"You *didn't* have an affair with Tess Martin?"

"Before she became a movie star, her name was Teresa Martinelli. I told you about her and her uncle. In Malibu, we had an off-again, on-again affair. I financed her comeback film. What the goddamned artilce omitted was that Tess and I parted company well before the film was released."

"But *not* before you made her pregnant."

"We broke up in March. I left for Europe in April and only

learned of her death that September on my way back from Europe. I hadn't laid eyes on her for six months and didn't know she was pregnant — if that's not also a lie — until I read about it in the article. If she *was* knocked up it sure as hell couldn't have been me."

"But the article made you out to be the father of her unborn child."

"It *implied* I was the father. If I thought it would do any good, I'd sue the ass off the papers that ran the story."

"Why don't you?"

"There were enough facts and half-truths in the piece to confuse the issue. All I could hope to get would be retractions, maybe an out-of-court settlement and, for certain, unwanted publicity . . . which I need like I need a dose of clap."

"Don't be crude," Beatrice said, then, almost as an afterthought, added, "Why *are* you going to Greece?"

I was prepared for the question. "Partly business. Mostly my sisters. I'm going to try and persuade them to return to the States before it's too late. I'm leaving now so I can get back before the baby's due."

CHAPTER FORTY-ONE

Upon my arrival in London I was greeted by shattering news. The *Artemis* had been torpedoed. Laden with the ammunition on an eastbound convoy, she'd been blown from the face of the ocean. There had been no survivors.

The loss of my erstwhile flagship was a staggering blow. Ships can be replaced, but not so men. Enrique was more than a friend. I'd come to think of him as a brother. In a sense, gruff old Timothy Driscoll had become my surrogate father, and I'd thought of him as being indestructible. Their deaths hit me like hammer blows.

I had little time to dwell on my loss. Following a short briefing by Whitelaw, I was driven to Portsmouth, where I boarded a Royal Navy H-Class destroyer as a civilian passenger. The destroyer was bound for Greece by way of Gibraltar and Crete.

Strange, is it not, how fabrications have a way of becoming fact? The story I'd given Beatrice about visiting my sisters in Greece had been an invention to explain what might become an extended absence. The last thing I'd expected was that I'd actually be sent to Greece.

What Whitelaw wanted was an objective appraisal of Greek reaction to, and the effectiveness of, the British units sent to bolster Greek forces in Crete and on the Greek mainland.

I could have been saved the trip. I disembarked at Piraeus in mid-April in time to witness what amounted to a scaled-down version of Dunkirk.

Earlier that month, in a lightning thrust from Bulgaria, the Germans overran Greece. From what I was told, resistance facing the advancing German forces simply collapsed. Of the approximately sixty thousand British combat troops committed to the defense of the Greek mainland, some two-thirds were evacuated in such haste that they left behind most of their heavy equipment.

With Greece facing Nazi occupation, I shouldn't have had difficulty persuading Georgiana and Penny to accompany me back to New York. To my astonishment, though, they rejected my offer. Penny pleaded a vaguely defined infirmity while Georgiana simply turned a deaf ear to my arguments. They stated confidently that, should life in Athens become too difficult, they would find some way of getting to Cephalonia where, in the remoteness of Drakopoulata, they should be able to live without molestation.

Time was running out. On April 23, the thoroughly demoralized government signed an armistice with the Germans. The following day I embarked on a Greek freighter bound for Milford Haven by way of Lisbon.

By leaving when I did I was spared the humiliating spectacle, described to me some years later by a still-outraged Georgiana, of German troops entering Athens.

Although I didn't learn of it until we reached Lisbon, there was a sequel to the debacle on the Greek mainland. In the closing ten days of May, the Germans wrapped up their conquest of Greece with an airborne invasion of Crete.

When I reached London, a preoccupied Colonel Whitelaw listened to my report, to which I could add nothing that he didn't already know. For the moment, Whitelaw had nothing in mind for me and arranged for me to be flown to Canada with a group of returning bomber ferry pilots.

Had Maria Veronica not arrived some three weeks behind schedule I wouldn't have made it back to New York in time for my daughter's birth. That auspicious event in June of 1941 overshadowed — at least I thought so — the crisis shaping up in Europe and North Africa.

I found Beatrice's reaction to the birth of our child not at all what I had expected. She was delighted that the ordeal of pregnancy was over and seemed inordinately relieved that the infant was sound in mind and limb. On the other hand, my assurances that it made absolutely no difference to me notwithstanding, she was obviously disappointed that she'd not given me a son. She seemed unaccountably nervous in the child's presence and steadfastly refused to breast-feed her.

Patently, however, there was at least one aspect of childbearing that appealed to Beatrice. Two days after the event she was holding court in her private suite in the hospital, accepting homage from her newly acquired circle of friends and admirers. Considering that she'd been a recluse during the latter months of her pregnancy, the number of well-wishers astonished me. Some, I noted with wry amusement, addressed her as "Countess." It shouldn't have amused me. I should have recognized it as harbinger of things to come.

I would have preferred to give her the necklace in private. I would have waited until she came home from the hospital to give it to her had I not been advised by Donovan that Stevenson wanted to meet with me in Toronto two days later. Since I had no idea what the assignment might develop, or when I was likely to see Beatrice again, I gave her the emerald pendant that evening.

Holding the slim, leather-covered box in my hand, I shouldered my way through the group around the bed and laid it on the coverlet. Beatrice broke off her conversation with an attractive young woman and looked up at me. Smiling, I nodded toward the jewel case.

Beatrice undid the clasp and lifted the lid. Nestled against black velvet, the necklace blazed with cold fire, the shimmering diamonds accentuating by contrast the cool green depths of the pendant emerald and its matching baguettes. Beatrice's eyes widened. The young woman with whom she'd been talking gasped in disbelief.

Graciously, to my discomfort, Beatrice allowed the necklace to circulate among her guests. Most of her following knew me by the reputation assigned me by unprincipled media scandalmongers, but otherwise I was an unknown quantity. To such people, the necklace represented an ostentatious display of wealth, confirming in their minds what they'd read or heard about "The Golden Greek." Allowing the necklace to be displayed in this manner must have compounded that opinion, a fact I felt Beatrice must have appreciated.

A woman's voice toward the rear of the room exclaimed, "My God, it must have cost a *fortune.*"

If she only knew, I thought grimly, at what cost that emerald had come into my possession. No price in dollars and cents could be placed on it. It had cost five lives, one, that of a man I had come to admire greatly, and another, that of a life more precious to me than my own. Over and above that fact, the uncut stone had been the collateral upon which my fortune was based.

The day might come when I would tell Beatrice the gemstone's history but not here. Not now.

Stevenson dropped a second cube of sugar into his coffee and replaced the tongs in the sugar bowl. Nodding his head in affirmation, he said, "I quite see how, as a man accustomed to action, you interpret your role up to now as passive. I can assure you, however, that your contributions in South America, Spain and Greece were appreciated."

"Greece? No action was taken on my recommendations."

"Your initial predictions were accurate. That was duly noted. Even had another ten British divisions been diverted to that theater, I doubt it would have altered the outcome. Hitler needed to secure his southern flank before attacking the Soviet Union. He would have done so even had he found it necessary to commit more troops to the Balkan assault."

"The Soviet Union? I wasn't aware they'd launched an attack against Russia."

"They haven't yet," Stevenson said, "but our intelligence sources assure us the attack is imminent. It could come at any time . . . in days, even hours."

"It would give Britain a breathing spell," I said.

"In Europe, perhaps, but in North Africa Rommel's Afrika Korps threatens Egypt and the Suez Canal, and Japan poses a grave threat to British possessions in Asia and Southeast Asia."

Global conflict? My thoughts winged back to Andros and the summer residence of Phil Demitrios. I recalled discussions between titans of the Greek shipping industry concerning just such an eventuality — and the key role crude oil and petroleum products would play in any such conflict. Their words now seemed prophetic.

Stevenson brought my straying thoughts sharply back to the present. "What we have in mind for you now," he said, "is a more active role, one that involves a good deal of personal risk. It is a far cry from the concept to which you originally agreed, and, for that reason, you are at liberty to withdraw from your earlier commitment without prejudice."

Stevenson read the resentment and displeasure that must have registered on my face. He held up his hand to silence, adding, "Your courage and resolve aren't questioned. You wouldn't have offered your services to the Canadian navy had you not been prepared to risk life and limb. But the terms of our unwritten agreement were that your employment would be more or less as an observer called upon to use influence and exert pressure where it could best serve our cause. As a Greek national with resident status in Ecuador, you enjoyed a measure of immunity. But what we now have in mind would substantially alter these ground rules. It would place you directly on the firing line. On the cutting edge, as it were. I felt it only fair that you be given the option of terminating our agreement."

"What exactly are you proposing?" I asked.

"A Nazi invasion of Russia will place enormous strains on German industry and tax her military and industrial manpower resources to the utmost. It is of paramount importance that we do everything possible to increase those difficulties by disrupting lines of communication, sabotage and pinning down occupation forces that could be used profitably on the front lines. To that end we have resistance movements operating in France, Norway, Denmark and the Low Countries. We're in the process of replicating such movements in the Balkans. Your role, if you accept the assignment would be to direct and coordinate resistance in Greece."

"Why me?"

"You've demonstrated talent for ogranization and a rare ability to delegate authority. In addition, your past experience in bootlegging and rumrunning should well suit you for clandestine coastal operations. I can think of no Greek better qualified to take on the task."

He had me. He knew he had me . . and he'd known it from the beginning. Giving me the option of terminating our unwritten agreement had been nothing but an opening gambit — window dressing. He'd presented me with a challenge he had known full well I wouldn't refuse. The only thing in our conversation that surprised me was his intimate knowledge of my background in the twenties, but that, too, I appreciated, had been thrown in for effect.

When I reached New York on June 22, I was greeted with the news that the Nazis had launched an all-out attack on the Soviet Union.

CHAPTER FORTY-TWO

Time was the governing factor. I was allowed three days in New York to put my affairs in order before I returned to Canada to report to a secluded estate in Quebec's Eastern Townships for a crash course in what Stevenson termed tradecraft — radio communications, codes and ciphers, commando tactics, unarmed combat and demolitions.

The story with which I explained the extended absences I anticipated was that the turn the war had taken necessitated a radical overhaul of my commercial activities geared to supplying wartime needs of the Soviet Union. I let it be known that I was going to Vladivostok to establish trade contacts. Since I had earned a reputation as a speculative opportunist, my intentions raised eyebrows but little else.

I had expected Beatrice to voice objections to another separation and was surprised when she accepted my announcement without comment. I was in New York just long enough to supervise her return from the hospital and the installation of a nurse for Maria Veronica.

Until subjected to Stevenson's training course in Quebec, I'd thought myself in reasonably good physical condition. For the most part my fellow trainees were young men and women in their twenties and thirties. But I found that, at forty-one, my reflexes had slowed perceptibly. Keeping up with my classmates in combat training made demands on me I wouldn't have believed possible.

Does it sound like I'm complaining? I'm not. I'm thankful for that training. On more than one occasion in the years that followed, the instruction I underwent in Quebec meant the difference between life and death.

During the six-week training period, as instructed, I grew a beard.

On completing the course, I was bomber-lifted to Scotland, flown to Gibraltar and boarded a light cruiser engaged in Mediterranean escort duty. I disembarked in Alexandria at the end of the first week in September.

My contact in Alexandria was Lieutenant Commander Livett-Jones, who knew me only by the code name assigned me, "Jason." Regionally, only one man — the officer in charge of Balkan and Middle East clandestine operations, Brigadier General Whitelaw — knew my true identity. His promotion from colonel to brigadier and his posting to Alexander's staff in Cairo had occurred while I'd been training in Canada.

Whitelaw briefed me in Cairo. As a first step in setting up an Alexandria-based headquarters from which to direct the Greek resistance movement, I was to establish lines of communication and supply depots at coastal points in western Greece and coordinate similar arrangements on the Adriatic coastline of Albania and in the Peloponniesos. Following that initial penetration, we would expand our operations to include the entire Greek mainland.

My approach to my mandate was, I believe, realistic. While I'd have to rely on subordinates for local knowlege, I needed on-the-ground familiarization in key areas and an opportunity to meet as many leaders of regional resistance groups as time and circumstances permitted. In addition, I wanted to assess for myself the strengths and weaknesses of both the Greek populace and the German occupying forces.

I've heard war described by front-line combatants as endless hours of numbing boredom interspersed by moments of sheer terror. That probably holds true for conventional warfare. As I quickly discovered, clandestine operations — at the "cutting edge," as Stevenson had said — are vastly different.

For one thing, if captured, servicemen are accorded a measure of protection by the Geneva Convention. Resistance fighters, under similar conditions, face summary execution normally preceded by days or weeks of torture.

For the agent provocateur, fear is a constant companion. Resistance workers live in dread of betrayal by the Judas within their ranks. Moments of complacency are rare. Coloring every waking moment and intruding into troubled sleep, fear is held at bay only by dedication to the common cause.

Nothing in my earlier employment by Stevenson prepared me for the shadowy world of clandestine activities in which I was now a prime mover. There were rewarding moments, but, on more than one occasion, I found myself wishing that my application for service in the Royal Canadian Navy had been accepted.

I don't intend to recount my wartime experiences in Greece in detail. While I'll never forget the heroism of Greek men, women and children who worked untiringly in the resistance movement and, in many cases, gave their lives in the cause of freedom, those were harrowing times I'd just as soon not think about.

Notwithstanding my resolve to let sleeping dogs lie, there are several incidents that refuse to remain decently interred and, sad to relate, political differences that detract from the Greek image of selfless heroics. I fear there is in the Greek temperament a contrariness that defies adequate description.

I launched my investigative field work in familiar terrain. Armed with forged papers identifying me as a fisherman, I traveled by fishing craft northward from Lefkas as far as the Albanian port of Durres, then returned by way of the Ionian islands. My initial stop was Corfu.

By prearrangement, I was met at the secluded cove of Analipsi and, having identified myself as "Jason," was escorted to Kerkyra where, in a two-room apartment in the old part of the city, I met with four leaders of the local resistance. One of these, a man accorded a good deal of respect, was introduced to me as Petros Koulouris, the owner of a fishing fleet operating out of Gouvia.

It came to me that he was the boat owner who had married Danai.

I listened to and noted requests for arms and ammunition and the temporary provision of instructors in demolitions and radio communications, but I must confess that Koulouris was the major focus of my attention. Now in his middle fifties, he was a ruggedly handsome man imbued with an air of quiet authority. I concluded, albeit reluctantly, that Danai had done well.

When the meeting ended, I engaged Koulouris in conversation. "Have you a family?" I asked.

"Seven children," he said. "Four sons and three daughters. My eldest son is twenty. Too bad you can't stay longer. My wife and I would be delighted to have you as our guest."

"Efcharistó," I said. "Perhaps on my next visit."

It is probably just as well there was no next visit. Had there been,

I fear I would've been tempted to accept Petros' invitation. More than two decades older and bearded, I wonder if Danai would've recognized me. I doubt it, but it would've been unwise to take the risk.

There was another reason, then and after the war, not to yield to the temptation to visit Petros' family. It is better to have Danai live in memory as I recall her, laughing and slim-waisted, rising glistening from the sea like a green-eyed Aphrodite.

It would have been a fatal error to underestimate the Gestapo. We gave them due credit. I'd not been in Greece a month before Whitelaw's coded radio messages advised me that the Germans knew that a British agent was operating in the Ionian isles, in all likelihood out of Lefkas or Cephalonia.

I wasn't particularly concerned. The only description collaborationist informers could have been given the Germans would be that of a bearded Greek of medium height in his middle years, a description fitting thousands of Greek fishermen. Moreover, I was about to shift my activities to the Peloponniesos and change my cover identity to that of a stevedore.

I was operating out of Patras when word of the Japanese sneak attack on Pearl Harbor and America's declaration of war against the Axis powers reached me. The war had become truly global, and, as I learned somewhat later, the fears Stevenson had expressed about British possessions in the Far East had been well-founded.

In the beginning, the only difference the entry of the United States into the war made for me was that the cover story I'd circulated in the States to explain my absence was altered to suit the situation. Beatrice, Sofoclis and Ruiz were advised that I'd volunteered to the newly instituted U.S. War Shipping Department and that I'd been assigned to the staff of a convoy commodore on the Murmansk run.

In January I moved my base of operations to Corinth. Three weeks later I traveled by rail to Argos with papers identifying me as a merchant seaman from Leonidio. From Leonidio I was taken by trawler to an offshore rendezvous with a submarine.

On my arrival in Alexandria I was gratified to find that Livett-Jones had carried out my instructions to the letter. During my absence he'd put together an administrative staff and assembled an impressive pool of Greek-speaking military and civilian specialists in commando tactics, communications, transportation, demolitions and psychological warfare. I'd already drawn on this pool of expert knowledge to provide the instructors the resistance leaders had requested. God alone knows where Livett-Jones found such talent on short notice. I didn't ask.

Whitelaw absently stroked his neatly trimmed mustache, a habit I'd come to recognize as signifying displeasure. "Through the sewer, you say. Dicey! Can't risk losing you. Leave heroics to less valuable members of your team."

I smiled. "I appreciate the compliment, but we weren't in any real danger."

"If you had to muck about in deep shit to make good an escape, it certainly *sounds* like you were in trouble."

"It does, but we weren't. The Germans must have homed in on our transmission. When we got word that the block was cordoned off, we had ample time to get to the basement, where a conduit gave us access to the sewer. That's one reason the building was chosen in the first place. I'll have to admit that sloshing through calf-deep sewage isn't my idea of fun, but it sure as hell gave us an effective escape route."

"All well and good, but you may not be so lucky next time. I suggest you direct future ops from Alex."

"After next month's meeting with regional leaders in Athens and an on-the-spot review of the situation in Macedonia, I'll give it serious consideration."

Whitelaw frowned. He could've tied me to a desk by ordering me to direct operations from Alexandria. He chose not to exercise that authority.

Had I told him the sequel, his reaction might have been different. I prudently withheld that part of the story.

When, under cover of darkness, we emerged from the sewer through a manhole six blocks from the building out of which we'd operated, we'd encountered a German patrol. Two of our number had been killed fighting as rear guard while the rest of us escaped.

In Greece, my vision was restricted by the immediacy of the ongoing struggle and the tactics needed to pursue our cause on a day-to-day basis. In Alexandria, I viewed the war in a broader context based on strategic, as opposed to tactical, considerations. In Greece, the conflict assaulted the senses. In Alexandria, while it was much in evidence, the war seemed curiously remote, abstract.

How was the war in Europe and North Africa progressing in 1942? How did these developments affect Greece and our continuing efforts to coordinate the activities of the various resistance groups?

If Hilter had expected an easy victory in Russia, he erred badly. Winter, Russia's age-old ally, saved both Leningrad and Moscow. Hitler's Operation Barbarossa ground to a halt as Nazi armies on the Eastern Front dug in to await the coming of spring.

As Stevenson had forseen, the dragged-out conflict was creating manpower problems for Germany. To relieve the shortfall, the Nazis turned to occupied Europe as a source of forced labor to keep German industry at peak production. Trainloads of forcefully conscripted Greek laborers rumbled northward daily.

The shortage was not only in laborers. With the coming of spring, as the Nazis prepared to resume their offensive, we learned that Rumanian, Hungarian and Italian divisions had been pressed into service on the Eastern Front.

In North Africa, Rommel's Afrika Korps went on the offensive at the end of May, racing eastward with alarming swiftness. Tobruk fell on June 21, and a week later Rommel was in Egypt, a mere sixty-five miles from Alexandria. At that point, his advance stalled. The reason, we learned later, was that he'd simply run out of fuel by outpacing his overextended supply lines.

Nazi objectives were readily discernible: In Russia they were the Caucasian oil fields and the Donets industrial basin; in North Africa, the Suez Canal and control of Middle East oil.

Allied fortunes seemed to be at their lowest ebb. In a disheartened Greece, it was said that *Moirai* — the Fates — had abandoned the Allies.

As summer drew to a close, the tide turned. When a resupplied Afrika Korps resumed its offensive at the end of August, it was stopped in its tracks in a series of hard-fought desert battles. In late October, at El Alamein, Montgomery took the initiative. On November 2 his British Eighth Army broke through the Italo-German lines and sent the Afrika Korps reeling in retreat toward Tunisia.

On November 8 an Anglo-American expeditionary force landed unopposed in Morocco and Algeria. In Alexandria, the immediate threat removed, we breathed a good deal easier.

In Russia, the Germans fared equally badly. The summer

offensive failed to achieve its objectives. In November the Russians went on the offensive, effecting a breakthrough on a broad front along the Don River. The German Sixth Army, besieging Stalingrad, was outflanked and ultimately surrendered in January 1943.

In looking back, I would say that November 1942 was the turning point in the European theater of conflict. The war was yet to witness some of its bitterest fighting, but it was in that winter that the initiative passed to the Allies who, from then on, never relinquished it.

CHAPTER FORTY-THREE

It was small consolation that millions of servicemen the world over were separated by great distances from their loved ones. The difference between their plight and mine lay in the realm of communication.

Letters between Beatrice and me were routed through London. Thanks to my job's peculiar nature, my letters were widely spaced and lacking in substance. I fell back on the excuse that my fictional employment on convoy duty precluded information of a factual nature that might prove useful to the enemy. In short, apart from expressions of abiding affection, my letters were virtually meaningless. Beatrice's responses, which grew less and less frequent as time progressed, were equally stilted. How could it have been otherwise? We had little by way of shared experiences to lend depth to our exchanges.

Beatrice's letters dealt in trivialities such as the weather and social engagements. They complained about annoyances such as gas rationing, shortages of imported delicacies and the difficulties of obtaining competent help. The names of friends paraded in her letters meant nothing to me, though a few from the world of arts and letters sounded vaguely familiar. I noted that Aletha and Sofoclis were never mentioned.

Her responses to my questions about Maria Veronica were distressingly vague. Early in our desultory exchange of letters, Beatrice advised me that she'd fired the nurse I'd hired and had had the good fortune to find as a replacement an English nanny. For factual information about my daughter, I would have done better had I directed my correspondence to the nanny, a Mrs. Brady.

About the only other piece of solid information I gathered from her letters was that she found my Fifth Avenue apartment too confining during the summer. Hence, in the summer of 1942, she'd leased a seaside house in Long Island's fashionable East Hampton.

To draw comparisons between the life Beatrice enjoyed in New York and the suffering endured by my countrymen would have been grossly unfair to her. Why should she not live in comparative luxury? Weren't my efforts directed toward preserving that way of life? There was absolutely no reason why Beatrice should be exposed to the war-inflicted miseries of others. She had survived the terror-bombing of London. Surely that was enough to ask of her.

What I tried to do was compartmentalize my thinking. I avoided comparisons by keeping New York and Greece neatly isolated from one another. For the most part, this worked admirably.

Nineteen forty-three was a fateful year for the Allies and for Greece.

Tunisia fell to General Eisenhower's Anglo-American forces in early May. Axis aggression in Africa was at an end, freeing the Allies to turn their attention to Fortress Europe. They wasted no time. On July 10 they launched the invasion of Sicily as a prelude to an assault on the Italian mainland. It would not have been strategically sound, but had that invasion been channeled through Greece and the Balkans, the situation that developed in Greece might have taken a very different turn.

Greece suffered cruelly during the war years, yet its suffering cannot be attributed solely to Nazi occupation.

From the beginning I'd encountered difficulties in my efforts to shape cohesive Greek resistance forces. There were marked political differences giving rise to mistrust and rivalry. At first these differences were submerged such that a more or less united front was presented to the common enemy. In 1943 the divergence resurfaced magnified out of all proportion.

By far the largest organized resistance force, claiming support from more than two-thirds of the populace, including most trade unionists, was the leftist *Ethnikon Apeleftheretikon Metopan,* or National Liberation Front. Organized along military lines, EAM fielded its own partisan army. EAM's conservative counterpart, *Ethnikos Demokratikos Ellenikos Syndesoms* — National Democratic Greek Union — proved less effective as a fighting force and, understandably, received less British financial and logistic support.

Until the summer of '43, while friction often surfaced between these ideologically opposed factions, they remained uneasy bedfellows dedicated to a common cause. Why, then, the violent rupture in the autumn of '43?

What I found particularly puzzling about the rift was its timing. The Germans, from the outset, had used harsh retaliatory measures against civilians suspected of aiding and abetting freedom fighters. Now, sensing impending defeat, the Germans turned to savage reprisals. There was scarcely a town or village where rotting corpses, turning slowly in the wind, did not hang from trees and lampposts in the market squares. Those grisly sights should have united the people against their Nazi oppressors. That didn't seem to be the case.

The spark that ignited what amounted to civil war in Greece was the Allied invasion of Italy. A leftist freedom fighter explained to me that, apparently, Greek Marxist leaders were acting on Comintern instructions. The aim was a communist takeover in advance of Allied victory. Already Stalin was greedily eyeing the spoils of war.

Whether that explanation was based on fact didn't concern me. All that mattered was that civil war was making my job more difficult with each passing day. The Germans desperately needed to divert men and equipment to Italy and the Eastern Front. My task was to destroy as much German war material as possible and to keep Nazi policing forces fully occupied in Greece. Civil strife notwithstanding, maximum pressure must be sustained. In the autumn of '43 the dilemma facing me was finding resistance groups I could rely on to carry out normal, let alone specific, disruptive operations.

By late autumn, additional developments had to be taken into consideration. The Nazis had systematically stripped Greece not only of able-bodied citizens but also of agricultural produce. When that continuing practice was coupled with Nazi reprisals and Greek fighting Greek in a bitter struggle for political ascendancy, there were few left to till fields and harvest crops. What resulted was famine aggravated by crippling inflation. This turn of events would have been — *should* have been — foreseen.

How bad was it? I'll content myself with one example of a classic foul-up. It took place in Macedonia, near the Yugoslavian border, in late November of '43.

For some months the SS had been rounding up Jews and Gypsies in Thrace, Thessaly and Macedonia. They were being taken under guard to Thessaloníki, where, daily, they were loaded into sealed boxcars and shipped north to Germany. We had yet to learn the tragic fate that awaited these hapless victims of Hitler's mania.

Our operation wasn't designed as a rescue mission, but, if it succeeded, at least one trainload of abductees would be released. The primary object of the plan was to disrupt rail traffic by simultaneously blowing up two railroad bridges southeast of Flórina.

These bridges had been individually damaged on several previous occasions and each time had been brought back into service. This was the first time we had attempted the coordinated demolition of the two bridges — an ambitious project. Two of my most experienced demolitions experts had been loaned to the rightist resistance groups that would actually blow up the targets.

Rescuing heavily guarded prisoners en route to Germany, while related to the bridge demolitions, was a secondary consideration. It called for an uninterrupted flow of information and coordinated timing. The armed force which would undertake this phase would have to be sufficiently strong to knock out any military escorts once the train was stalled between the blown-up bridges. The task was assigned to a well-equipped partisan force operating in and around Skopje.

At first the action went off without a hitch. The bridges were blown when the train was approximately midway along the ten-mile stretch separating them.

The second part of the action failed to materialize. We learned later that the SS guards had unloaded the boxcars and cold-bloodedly machine-gunned the prisoners.

Where was the partisan force? At least a portion of it had ambushed one of the resistance groups that had demolished the bridge. The partisans claimed confusion due to a mix-up in radio communciations.

When I learned what had happened, I was stunned. But as there are two or more sides to every issue, I was prepared to give the partisans the benefit of the doubt until I'd heard their side of the story. I set up a meeting in Thessaloníki with Josip Barcović, the military commander of the Skopje partisans.

Assuming the identity of a Greek Orthodox priest, I was airdropped near Kalamai and made my way by farm cart and on foot to Thessaloníki.

"I've been advised," I said, "that the message was received and acknowledged."

Barcović looked at me impassively. "If so, it didn't reach me."

I didn't believe him. It was a vital message they'd been expecting. No communication net could be *that* derelict. Patently, however, it was a lie from which Barcović had no intention of retreating. "With German garrisons in the region, why did your troops attack their own? You knew they were there. You knew *why* they were there."

"Yes," Barcović said noncommitally.

"Who *is* your enemy?" I asked. "Greeks or Germans?"

Barcović's flint-hard eyes didn't waver. "Our Soviet comrades drive steadily westward. Soon the Germans will leave Greece of their own accord. Our enemies — royalist sympathizers, capitalist reactionaries — will not have left. They must be liquidated."

There was no point in continuing the discussion. I reached for my conical, flat-topped black headgear and settled it firmly in place, signifying that the interview was over.

Soon after nightfall, I was rowed out to a waiting RN motor torpedo boat. In the small hours of the next morning, the MTB rendezvoused with a RN destroyer south of the Aegean island of Skiros.

When I disembarked at Alexandria, I traveled directly to Field Marshal Alexander's headquarters in Cairo.

Whitelaw nodded. "I sympathize with you, but we can't cut off funding and support just because one partisan leader is a militant Marxist."

"Barcović isn't an isolated case, and you damn well know it," I said. "I'm not suggesting that funding be cut off. What I recommended in my report was that support be transferred to the rightists . . . unless you *want* to see the country go communist."

"Not as easy as that, old boy," he said. "Can't just switch horses in midstream."

"Why the hell not? His Majesty's Government didn't appear to suffer qualms of conscience a few years ago when Mihajlović's Chetniks were dumped in favor of Tito's partisans in Yugoslavia."

The upshot of our discussion was that Whitelaw agreed to forward my report through proper channels to Churchill.

CHAPTER FORTY-FOUR

During 1943 there were some changes in my staff. For one, Teddy Livett-Jones was promoted to commander. Another was that, from early in the year, we'd had a modest influx of American servicemen, most of whom were Americans of Greek extraction, though only a few spoke Greek.

Two of those who stand out in my memory are Ensign Wade Stollings and Staff Sergeant Clifford Moran. I found it odd that Moran, a Negro, spoke Greek, until I learned that his father had been in the diplomatic service. Cliff Moran had spent his early years in Athens.

It was just as well that the number of specialist personnel at my disposal was expanded. From the summer of '43 onward, as Greece became increasingly immersed in bitter internecine conflict, I had to rely more and more on my own people for the execution of specific projects, and, as I did so, casualties mounted. The number killed or missing in action, which virtually amounted to the same thing, rose to fourteen during the course of the year.

Much as I resented being tied to administrative duties, I conceded that Whitelaw's point was well-taken. My rightful place was in Alexandria, the nerve-center of our ongoing operations. My strength lay in assessing intelligence reports, designating strategic targets and planning the execution of missions. I understood that and, accordingly, confined my on-the-ground fact-finding missions to a minimum. Nonetheless it was gut-wrenching to watch, as a bystander, my homeland being torn assunder by internal strife and Nazi atrocities.

Personal motivation did not justify my participation in the Patras operation. I excused myself on the grounds that I was familiar with the terrain and was known to the leaders of the Patras resistance fighters, and that we were shorhanded at the time, but I knew damn well I shouldn't have taken part in the misadventure.

It took place in late May of 1944. Our objective was the destruction of an oil storage depot and ammunition dump on the outskirts of Patras.

The twelve-man team of demolition specialists rehearsed each step of the operation near Alexandria on a scaled-down mock-up of the Patras tank farm and ammo dump. Ensign Stollings was in charge of the training. With Stollings as my second-in-command, I commanded the mission.

A destroyer was to put us ashore shortly after nightfall at a cove near the village of Manolás. There we were to be met by a group of resistance fighters whose job it was to lead us to our objective, create a diversion to allow us to gain access undetected and give us covering fire as we withdrew.

What went wrong? We never did find out, but we assume that collaborationists must have infiltrated the resistance group. We got no closer to Patras than the pebbled beach near Manolás. We stepped ashore into the waiting arms of a *Wehrmacht* welcoming committee.

What followed remains a jumble in my memory. There was a sharp exchange of gunfire. Moran and I became separated from the main body of the team. We were making for a scrub-mantled headland when I slipped on spray-slicked rocks at the water's edge. My handgun flew from my grasp. When I scrambled to my feet, I found myself face-to-face with a carbine-armed German soldier who seemed even more startled than I was.

I acted instinctively. Stepping forward, I swept the muzzle of his rifle to one side with my left arm as I pivoted and brought my right hand up in a sweeping arc. The edge of my palm made solid contact with his upper lip. I must confess I was astonished by the effectiveness of the maneuver. It happened as my unarmed combat instructor had said it would. The blow drove the cartilage of his septum upward into his brain. He dropped as if he'd been poleaxed. My one thought was to seek higher ground. A figure that I assumed was Moran was briefly outlined against the night sky before disappearing on the far side of the ridge. Heading in that direction, I'd almost reached the crest of the promontory when disaster overtook me.

I felt as though I'd been struck in the back by a giant fist. I staggered, regained my footing and somehow topped the rise. Then, sliding and stumbling, I careened down a steep slope to a rocky stretch of foreshore and then stopped, gasping.

I didn't see Moran until he stood over me. "Rowboat off the point!" he shouted. "C'mon, let's hit the water. The Krauts'll be all over us in a minute."

I tried to stand. A wave of dizziness engulfed me, and, coughing and gasping, I sank back onto the rocks. Moran bent down to help me, then exclaimed, "Shit, man, you been hit!"

Easing me back onto the rocks, he quickly assessed the situation. After a moment's silence, he said, "Can't swim — that's for damn sure — but you can float. If you don't struggle, man, I can get you to the boat, okay?"

I tried to answer, but liquid bubbled up into my mouth. The best I could do was nod my assent.

I'm damned if I know how Moran got me to the boat without drowning me. The crew must have seen us coming and rowed inshore to meet us. I have a hazy recollection of hearing firing from the shoreline and a babble of voices as I was lifted into the boat. After that, I must have passed out.

The next thing I remember is coming to in a bunk aboard ship with my chest wrapped in bandages. I wasn't alone. Stollings, smoking a cigarette, was on a bunk beside me.

"Where are we?" I asked.

Stollings glanced in my direction and grinned. "Glad to have you back among the living, sir. For a while there, when you were under the knife, it didn't look as though you were gonna make it."

"Under the knife?"

"Uh huh. We're back aboard HMS *Dragonfly* . . . in sick bay. You were operated on about an hour ago. Surgeon says the bullet was lodged so close to your heart that if it'd traveled another quarter of an inch, you'd have had it."

I noticed his leg was bandaged. "What happened to you?"

Stollings grimaced. "Copped one just above the knee. Nothing to write home about. Funny thing . . . don't know when it happened. Didn't feel a thing til the doc started probing."

"Moran?"

"Okay. Not a scratch."

"The others?"

Stollings sobered. "It was a four-star fuck-up. They even knew the password. We walked right into it. Six or seven of us fought our way back toward the beach. Only three of us got there: me, Barker, Sam Collins — ''

"What then?" I asked.

Stollings came out of his reverie. "The ship's whaler was standing by, about two cables to seaward. We skinned down and started to swim for it. They were shooting at us from the beach. Sam didn't make it — ''

Again Stollings lapsed into brooding silence. "And?" I prompted.

"Barker and I were hauled aboard and we took off. As we rounded the point, the cox'n spotted you and Moran in the water and closed the headland to pick you up. When we attracted fire from the point, one of the seamen was wounded and the cox'n promptly hauled ass."

"You, me, Barker, Moran? Who else made it out?"

"As far as I know, no one."

I closed my eyes. Eight good men written off in an abortive operation that had achieved nothing.

When we berthed at Alexandria, I was admitted to the military hospital. I was assured that the *Dragonfly's* surgeon had done an excellent job. Discharged from the hospital, I was confined to my residence for a two-week convalescence.

During the second week, Whitelaw journeyed from Cairo to Alexandria to visit me. He was in good form, exuding optimistic enthusiasm.

"I hope you're not blaming yourself for the failure of the Patras operation," Whitelaw said.

"I selected the target, planned the operation and commanded it. Who else can I blame?"

"Bad luck that you were part of the show. Tends to color your perspective. The operation was compromised through no fault of yours. It would have turned out as it did whether you'd been there or not."

"I know that, but it doesn't lessen my culpability."

"An unfortunate concomitant of command," Whitelaw said; then, adroitly switching the subject, "Rumor from London has it that your report deserves most of the credit for the government's change of heart. Did you know that reduced funding for EAM and stepped-up support of EDES was largely responsible for last month's uneasy coalition?"

"Suspected it."

"Unfortunately, it'll probably be a short honeymoon. Your friend Barcović hit the nail on the head. The Germans *will* pull out of the Balkans."

As he'd no doubt intended, he'd piqued my curiosity. "When?"

"Only a question of time. The Allied invasion of Normandy that took place four days ago is the beginning of the end for the Nazis. The outer defenses of Hilter's Fortress Europe have been breached in two places. Three — if you count the fact that the Red Army has overrun Bessarabia and Bukovina and is pushing into Rumania. The Germans are still hanging on to central and northern Italy. They're doing their damnedest to push Allied invasion forces back into the sea, so far with conspicuous lack of success. To withstand pressure on three fronts, the Nazis are going to need every man and boy they can lay their hands on. Therefore, it's only a question of time before they start pulling their occupation forces out of Greece and Yugoslavia."

"Where does that leave us?" I asked.

"Us?"

"You? Me? Your command structure controlling clandestine operations and resistance activities in the Balkans and Middle East?"

"Oh. I see what you mean. We can't relax just yet. However, when the Germans pull out of Greece *your* war will be over. Better start thinking in terms of closing up shop. It doesn't hurt to have a plan in place, old boy."

It annoyed me that Whitelaw seemed incapable of getting to the point without circumspection.

I found it difficult to believe that the Nazis would cling so tenaciously to conquered territories in the face of such devastating pressures. Surely, even if Hitler didn't, Germany's military leaders must have recognized the hopelessness of trying to wage war on three fronts. It didn't make sense, yet the *Wehrmacht* fought on with a ferocity born of desperation.

Not until September, following the formal surrender of Bulgaria and Rumania to the Soviets, did German forces begin a strategic withdrawal from Greece. The exodus was completed by mid-October.

It was as simple as that. Though war still raged unabated in the

Pacific Theater and was far from over in Europe, the obligation to which I'd committed myself was now discharged.

As Whitelaw had put it, *my* war was at an end.

CHAPTER FORTY-FIVE

It was peculiarly disorienting. Shaving off my beard was like discarding comfortable clothing. By a simple act of grooming I'd relegated "Jason" to history.

I wrote Beatrice to tell her that I had unfinished business to attend to in Greece and Spain, then I'd be coming home. That done, I boarded a RN destroyer transporting British troops to Athens. Now that I would no longer put them or me at risk, I was eager to visit my sisters.

Whitelaw's prediction had been accurate. The honeymoon had not lasted. Tensions ran high as Greece teetered on the brink of renewed civil war.

To my relief, I found that Georgiana and Penny had survived both the occupation and internal political strife without ill effects.

It was a poignant reunion. When I told them about my wartime employment, they were delighted; I basked shamelessly in their admiration. The only thing I found disappointing was their reaction when I suggested they visit New York at my expense. Penny said that her arthritis would keep her confined, for the time being, to Glifada. Georgiana's priority was to reopen her boutiques as soon as things settled down. They both assured me that they were eager to meet Beatrice and Maria Veronica and that they would visit New York in the near future.

Another long-overdue project demanded my attention. It was high time I did something about my property in Ithaca. Taking with me an Athenian estate agent, I went by hired launch from Piraeus to Vathí and was delighted to see that Ithaca had slumbered through the war virtually unscathed.

The agent and I inspected the dilapidated mansion and weed-choked grounds. I explained in detail how I wanted the house and grounds rehabilitated and left the hiring of a contractor to the agent's discretion. When the restoration was completed to his satisfaction, he was to hire a housekeeper, handyman and groundskeeper.

I returned to Piraeus and then Alexandria. In Alexandria I hitched a ride on a military aircraft to Gibraltar and proceeded by bus and rail to Barcelona.

To be perfectly candid, I don't think it was until I was installed in Barcelona's Ritz Hotel that I fully accepted my reversion to civilian status. I was back on familiar ground — as Constantine Sthanassis.

After conferring with shipbuilders, I gave the go-ahead for the long-delayed ship construction. That business finished, I journeyed by train to Lisbon, where I booked passage on the Pan American Airways clipper to New York. I cabled Beatrice the time and date of my expected arrival. On November 23, I boarded the flying boat.

As the aircraft droned eastward across the Atlantic, I had much to occupy my thoughts.

The war was behind me. What had I learned from it?

On more than one occasion, death had paused briefly at my elbow, yet passed me by. If nothing else, these near-misses had reminded me of my mortality. In five weeks I would be forty-five — well past the midpoint of life expectancy. It was a sobering thought. I had so much to do.

Greece? Exposure to my enemy-occupied homeland had wrought a subtle change in me. It had reawakened pride in my Greek heritage. Greeks are quick to love and equally quick to hate. Imbued with a passion for independence. Yet, as I could attest, having witnessed a disastrous political schism, their passions could be manipulated and misdirected to their detriment. It was a failing I must guard against.

I thought about the war in a broader context. As I had so often in the past, I speculated on how the war *might* have developed had Hitler exploited Rommel's desert victories to advantage. At the point where Rommel had been forced to halt his advance, he'd been within spitting distance of the Nile Delta with virtually nothing opposing him. He could have rolled up British defenses, handed Hitler control of the Suez Canal on a platter, swept through the Middle East and swung northeast to link up with German forces in the Caucasus. With Rommel to swing the tide in Axis favor, I firmly believe the Nazis would have attained their primary goal, Caucasian oil fields.

Oil was the key. Could the Allies have survived cut off from Middle East oil? Could the Russians have mounted their counter-offensive if they'd been deprived of oil from the Caucasus? How long could Hitler hold out now that the Red Army had robbed him of access to Rumania's Ploesti oil fields?

The global conflict was drawing to a close. In my estimation, it couldn't last another year. It would leave in its wake many countries with shattered economies. If access to a ready supply of oil had been the key to military victory, what influence would it exert on postwar reconstruction? I suspected it would play a crucial role, and it was a situation I intended to exploit to the fullest.

All of which steered my thinking toward future business. The war had taken a substantial chunk out of my life and, with the possible exception of Metaxis y Cia., put my commercial interests in limbo. I wouldn't know exactly where I stood until I'd had a chance to confer with Sofie and Ruiz, but certain basic changes suggested themselves.

Setting Metaxis y Cia., the exporter supplier, in motion as a subsidiary of Metaxis & Company had seemed logical at the time. The companies had been linked by mutual interests. Metaxis y Cia., however, from the outset, had been an autonomous entity. By no means was Metaxis & Company its sole customer. It was time the two companies were formally separated if for no other reason than tax purposes. The Latin American subsidiary should have been spun off before the war. No matter. It would be one of my first acts on my return.

The Kybernas Line? Although I hadn't learned of it until months afterward, the *Hebe* had shared the fate of the *Artemis*. Torpedoed in the spring of '43, the *Hebe,* unlike her sister ship, had not gone to the bottom with all hands. Only the third engineer, two firemen and one seaman had been killed. The rest of the officers and crew had been rescued.

When I learned of this, I'd made contact through the Admiralty with the *Hebe*'s surviving skipper, Sven Henningsen. I'd offered Henningsen the shore berth vacated by Richardson, the latter having indicated that he would not return to the line as marine superintendent at war's end. Henningsen had accepted my offer.

As acting marine superintendent of a shipping company consisting of only two aging vessels, with a third on loan to the Admiralty for the duration of hostilities, Henningsen had yet to prove his worth. I knew only that the Swede was a competent seaman. His mettle as an administrator was about to be put to the test.

The Kybernas Line was my true love. I intended it to grow and prosper. In the immediate postwar years there would be a demand for shipping. The vessels now under construction in Barcelona should give me a competitive edge but were only the beginning of what I had in mind. My plans went well beyond conventional freight handling. Vaulting projections? Probably, but not unrealistic, providing I didn't overextend myself in the process.

In charting my course, I couldn't overlook an important consideration. Where would I locate? My Ecuadorian resident status had lapsed. Renewing it would be a simple matter, but Ecuador no longer suited my purpose. I could apply for resident status in the United States and undoubtedly would be accepted. Before the war I'd considered such a move, but now I was not so sure it would be a wise choice. England? A possibility. From a shipowner's point of view, Greece offered distinct advantages — if political differences could be resolved.

There was no need for an immediate decision. Other factors would influence my choice. I had to consider what would be best for my family. Given a choice, I suspected Beatrice would opt for England.

When the flying boat touched down in Northumberland Straits and taxied to the fueling jetty at New Brunswick's Pointe-du-Chêne, my chain of thought was broken. When we lifted off and dipped one wing in a climbing turn, I looked down on a bleak, winter-gripped landscape and the smooth pewter-gray waters of the straits. The scenery complemented my thoughts. I suppose I'd been ducking the issue, but now that I was on the final leg of my flight my thoughts turned to Beatrice and our marriage.

Had I arrived in New York a week earlier, we would have celebrated an anniversary — our fourth — together for the first time. During those four years, how much time *had* we spent together? Less than five months. And during those months, Beatrice had been pregnant. Over and above that, since her father's fatal accident, shock and grief had frequently plunged her into severe depression.

Beatrice and I were virtual strangers. We'd had no chance to get to know each other. The war, the catalyst that had brought us together, had contrived to keep us apart. All we had in common was Maria Veronica, a child I knew only from the photographs Beatrice had sent in her infrequent letters.

Unique as the conditions surrounding my marriage were, in one respect mine certainly wasn't an isolated case. Tens of thousands of servicemen would be coming home to women they had parted from as brides, who were now strangers. And the husbands? War would have altered them mentally, if not physically as well.

As the aircraft droned southward, approaching New York, I appreciated that my marriage would be my biggest postwar adjustment. It called for understanding, tact and, above all, patience. It would be, after all, an accommodation as difficult for Beatrice as for me.

In the latter assumption, though it took me some time to accept it, I was off the mark.

The maître d'hôtel took our order and withdrew.

I subjected Sofoclis to thoughtful scrutiny. A trace of summer tan still lingered, but he didn't look at all well. I didn't comment on his appearance, but it worried me. I resolved to ask Aletha about his health.

"Beatrice celebrated my homecoming by tossing a star-studded extravaganza. Why weren't you and Aletha there? She said she invited you."

"She did, but Nicky was down with flu and Lettie didn't want to leave him . . . and I didn't want to go without her."

I couldn't help smiling. "You don't exactly care for Beatrice's friends."

Sofie looked at me and asked, "Do you?"

"No. Can't say that I do. Never been keen on socialites and the Broadway set. Prefer a less hectic life. In our Apollo Club days, you were the sport who ran with the fast set."

Sofie colored. "Okay, so I had a taste for showgirls in those days. Outgrew it."

"Is that collection of rich and restless freeloaders the norm for Beatrice?" I asked.

Sofie looked uncomfortable. "Lettie and I see very little of her. We exchange presents at Christmas. That's about the extent of it. But from what we read in society columns, that seems to be the crowd she favors."

"Has she never invited you to the summer place in East Hampton?"

"If she has, Lettie hasn't told me. Don't think so, though. She thinks of us as peasants. Only tolerates us because I'm your cousin."

It was my turn to be uncomfortable. "I suppose she was used to associating with theater people and royal hangers-on in London," I said, "but I didn't invite you to lunch to discuss Beatrice. We're here to establish the guidelines for our present and postwar actions."

Sofie didn't say anything. He sipped his dry martini and looked at me expectantly. Nothing had changed — he still looked to me for leadership.

I explained why I was splitting Metaxis y Cia. off from Metaxis & Company. I don't think Sofie ever had understood the intricacies of the corporate relationship or the tax bind that could face us if we continued on our present course. I said that my intention, once the severance was accomplished, was to take Ruiz on a fact-finding swing through Latin America and, on the basis of those findings, project a master plan for future development. When that was done, I'd leave the running of the company in Ruiz' competent hands.

It was at this point that Sofie's interest quickened. "Do you mean you're planning to retire from Metaxis y Cia.?"

"In a manner of speaking. Ruiz will run the show, but I'll still own the company. I plan to do much the same with Metaxis & Company."

As I'd expected, the latter statement drew a reaction. "What?" Sofie exploded. "For Chrissake, you're younger'n me. You *can't* retire."

"It's not retirement," I said. "I'm phasing myself out of active participation in both companies so that I can devote more time to my shipping interests. That doesn't constitute retirement."

"It does as far as Metaxis & Company is concerned. You're leaving me stranded!"

I could appreciate Sofie's concern. Since my takeover of the company twelve years ago, he'd deferred to me on all major decisions. "I'm not leaving you out on a limb," I said. "I'll still retain board membership even if I designate a proxy or proxies to vote my shares. They can only vote as I instruct them. Nothing will change."

Sofie still wasn't convinced I wouldn't be leaving him in the lurch. "But you're chairman of the board."

"So we vote in a replacement. So what? It won't alter the voting control we exercise. Anyway, I'll stay on as chairman until Welton and his whiz kids rejoin the firm."

Sofie's voice was edged with new anxiety. "You know he's now a two-star general. What makes you think he'll be content to come back as executive vice president?"

"I don't expect him to return to the position he vacated. We'll have to sweeten the pot. We'll vote *you* in as chairman of the board and offer Welton president and chief executive officer — at a substantial increase of salary. We may have to throw in added incentives such as bonuses and stock options, but don't worry about it. If we make it attractive enough, Welton will accept. After all, he's not likely to throw more than a decade of seniority down the drain."

Sofie brightened. "I hadn't thought of that." Then, changing tacks, he asked, "What are your plans for your shipping company?"

"Ambitious," I said. "When the war in Europe ends, the Brits will return the *Eos,* suitably refitted. I should receive adequate compensation for the *Artemis* and the *Hebe.* Construction is already underway on two seventeen-thousand tonners in Barcelona. When they come on line, the *Pandora,* then the *Galatea,* will go on the block. And next month I'm sending Henningsen to Sweden to negotiate for the construction of two tankships."

"Tankships?"

"Oil tankers . . . forerunners of a fleet of tankers I intend to operate. Only the tankers won't operate under Kybernas colors. They will be Greek-registered and leased to British and American oil companies. It probably will mean I'll have to set up a base in Greece. I own property on the island of Ithaca."

Sofie's face was a study in bewilderment. "What is it with you Greeks? Lettie talks incessantly of taking the kids to visit Lefkas after the war. Now you. How does the thought of living on an island in the Ionian Sea appeal to Beatrice?"

"I haven't mentioned it to her, but I know what her reaction will be. Ithaca is far too rustic and isolated to suit her. I suppose I'll have to work out a trade-off between Ithaca and New York — or London — to keep peace in the family."

CHAPTER FORTY-SIX

Beatrice didn't entertain, she held court. With regal aplomb she graciously condescended to mingle with her adoring subjects. Somehow *contessa* didn't seem at all out of place when applied to her.

I'll have to admit that I couldn't have returned at a worse time of year — the holiday season. Scarcely a night went by that we weren't entertaining or being entertained. And wherever we went, Beatrice, poised and breathtakingly beautiful, was the center of attention. I, on the other hand, was treated more like an interloper than a royal consort.

While I recognized some of the names and faces of the famous and infamous among Beatrice's guests, most were total strangers. I had no desire to become better acquainted with any of them, but then I was prejudiced and guilty, I fear, of inverted snobbery. There were among them a fair sprinkling of uniforms, rear-echelon brass strutting like pouter pigeons. It was a source of amusement to me that, when I'd left Alexander's staff, I'd held rank equivalent to General Whitelaw's.

Unfortunately there was a different side to Beatric. In private, she was withdrawn and listless. It seemed as though she fed off adulation, needed fawning supplication as a plant needs sunlight. Without it she was like an empty shell.

Although she used a number of subterfuges to reduce their frequency, she did not deny me my conjugal rights. She might as well have. Her lack of response to my lovemaking robbed the act of meaning or pleasure. It was like coupling — or at any rate trying to couple — with a marble statue.

Where had the fire gone? One of my mother's oft-repeated sayings sprang to mind: "Absence makes the heart grow fonder — but rarely for the absent party." During my absence, had Beatrice taken a lover? Or lovers? Certainly she wouldn't have lacked for opportunity. Men of all ages were attracted to her as moths to a guttering flame.

Yet, as I watched her, that explanation seemed to lack substance. While she *appeared* to flirt outrageously, she did so from behind a protective barrier. I'd yet to see her lower her defenses either to me or anyone else. I could find no one, male or female, among her acquaintances that I regarded as her intimate friend.

What I found especially disturbing was Beatrice's attitude toward Maria Veronica. She seemed to consider the child an encumbrance. There was little or no warmth between her and our daughter.

Maria Veronica sensed and was bewildered by her mother's rejection. In consequence, the three-and-a-half-old tot turned to Mrs. Brady for love and affection. It was love returned in kind. Manifestly, the nanny adored her small charge and, though she masked it in civility, cordially disliked Beatrice.

Unfortunately, Mrs. Brady extended that mistrust to me. Overly protective, she resented the time I spent with Maria Veronica, attempting to win the child's trust and affection. I must admit that those overtures singularly lacked success. I suppose it hardly could have been otherwise. To Maria Veronica, long shielded from male influence, I must have seemed frightening.

My resolve to use forebearance notwithstanding, my patience was being tried to the utmost. What made matters even more difficult was that Beatrice seemed oblivious to my growing discomfort. Resentment I could have understood. Rejection I could have coped with. But how does one combat indifference?

I didn't give up on Beatrice, but, in at least one aspect of our relationship, I arrived at an accommodation. I lay no claim to sainthood. If Beatrice found intercourse distasteful, I'd seek gratification, as I'd done during our wartime separation, elsewhere.

That decision didn't mean I was promiscuous. If there was one thing I'd learned from experience, it was that a man in my position had to use caution. I avoided my extramarital activities far from New York — and then only when pressures demanded release. For that reason I probably spent more time traveling than I would have had my home life been different.

Ruiz and I were in Lima when news of Roosevelt's death reached us. I was shaken. It was difficult to imagine the United States without FDR at the helm. Moreover, I felt a bond existed between us. My financial success had been indirectly linked to his political fortunes. My one regret was that I'd never met him.

At the end of April, Ruiz and I parted company in Valparaíso, he to return to Panama City by sea and I to go overland by rail to Buenos Aires and then by ship to Rio de Janeiro. On May 9, as I neared Rio, the long-awaited news crackled over the ship's radio. Germany had surrendered unconditionally.

This turn of events altered the picture considerably. It meant that, before long, European shipyards would be swamped with orders. It meant as well that the shipping business was about to emerge from its war-imposed holding pattern. I stopped in Rio only long enough to book a northbound flight and to cable New York my anticipated time of arrival.

The last two weeks of May and the months of June and July were hectic. Henningsen, I was pleased to note, met the challenge and passed the test with flying colors.

We were notified that the *Eos* was being returned to us and arranged for her to go into a Brooklyn yard for overhaul and repainting — at the Admiralty's expense. In London an Admiralty court awarded us compensation for the *Artemis* and the *Hebe.*

The Barcelona shipyard notified us that construction of the first of our vessels, to be christened the *Athena,* was ahead of schedule and that she would be ready to undergo sea trials in July. The second vessel, the *Demeter,* would follow three or four weeks later. Crews for the two vessels were signed on and flown to Spain to accept delivery.

In the last week of June, resplendent in blue-trimmed gleaming white, the *Eos* came out of refit and steamed south toward the Panama Canal. Four days later, Henningsen flew to Spain to be on hand for the *Athena*'s sea trials.

I wasn't kidding myself. All I'd done was return the Kybernas Line close to its status quo in shipping circles in 1940. I'd speedily made the transition to a peacetime stance, which should put me marginally ahead of my competitors, but to retain that advantage I would have to expand the line dramatically. Therein lay the snag. Chartering would have bridged the interim gap, but the war in Europe had exacted a heavy toll in torpedoed tonnage. Other than rust-laden relics that had long since outlived their usefulness, there were simply no vessels available for charter.

I'd promised myself I wouldn't allow myself to get overextended, but there comes a time when one *must* gamble or settle for second best. I'd empowered Henningsen, when he took delivery of the *Athena,* to order immediate construction of two additional vessels of the same design. Then, unbeknownst to Henningsen, I cabled Stockholm and placed on order two more forty-thousand-ton tankships. No one knew better than I that I was taking one hell of a chance. If the postwar economic boom I anticipated failed to materialize, I stood to lose everything.

Beatrice's phone call from the East Hampton estate, where she'd taken up residence for the summer, took me completely by surprise, more so because the call came not to the apartment but to the Kybernas Line office. It was out of character for her. My initial reaction was that Maria Veronica must have had an accident. Thank God that was not the case.

Beatrice had received a letter — forwarded to East Hampton by our apartment building's doorman, according to her instructions — from her London solicitor. The letter advised her that her solicitors had been contacted by the Rome law firm charged with the administration of her late father's estate. Apparently confusion had arisen.

The reason she'd called me was to find out whether I'd be able to meet her at the apartment that evening. She wanted to drive in from Long Island and discuss with me the contents of the letter.

Never had I seen Beatrice in a rage. Normally her emotional responses were at best tepid. Not so this time. I'd known that she harbored no affection for her brother, but I hadn't expected the rancor she now displayed. To her, it was unconscionable that Mario should profit from their father's death. Oh, the title was Mario's, but had she been able to deny him that, she would have. In the matter of inheritance, however, Count Guglielmi had willed Beatrice his entire property holdings.

At issue were the years between Count Gugliemi's death in 1940 and the present. During this period of disrupted communications — and for some years prior to that if I correctly understood her solicitor's letter — Mario had administered many of his father's properties. In return for this service, Mario had retained revenues from, and now laid claim to, some of the holdings.

Beatrice was adamant. Her brother was not entitled to one square centimeter of their father's holdings. Moreover, she claimed, income from these properties was rightfully hers, and if Mario had pocketed so much as a lira, she vowed she would get it back.

She railed against the London solicitors and the law firm in Rome. Then her uncharacteristic tirade culminated in a demand to which I submitted since it meshed with my plans. I would accompany her to Rome to see that justice was done.

Privately I was skeptical about the merits of her case. I had not seen her father's will. There could well be differences between British and Italian laws of inheritance. It struck me that her brother, Count Mario, must have had sound advice and might be within his legal rights.

We flew to Rome and settled into a suite in the Excelsior Hotel on July 10.

There *were* legal complications. Had Count Guglielmi legally disinherited his son, a precaution the late count had neglected to take, he could then have bequeathed all of his properties to Beatrice. As matters now stood, Mario had inherited, along with the title, ancestral lands and properties, namely an estate in Lombardy and a crumbling old palace in Venice. Beatrice had to accept those claims as valid. But Mario hadn't stopped there. By right of tenure, he was claiming vineyards, a winery and a country mansion in Tuscany as well as a *palazzo* in Florence. And, though he wasn't claiming title to the properties, he'd pocketed rentals from two blocks of apartments in Naples as compensation for management and upkeep. In fact, the only property belonging to his late father to which Mario had *not* laid claim was a palatial residence in a fashionable quarter of Rome, the erstwhile residence of their mother, Guglielmi's deceased wife, Countess Lavinia Tocchi. Since the countess' death a decade earlier, the mansion had been tended by family retainers but otherwise had remained unoccupied.

Mario's claims were not without justification. When, accompanied by his teenage daughter, Count Guglielmi had moved to England, he'd entrusted the management of his affairs to stewards, agents and lawyers. Yet there had been times, notably during the war, when Mario had found it necessary to step in in order to protect family interests. In my opinion, he was entitled to compensation for the performance of those services.

With regard to the landholdings in Tuscany and the *palazzo* in Florence, Mario contended that, while there was no legal documentation to support his claim, these had been deeded to his mother and were rightfully his. A will left by the countess supported this contention.

The entire matter could have been settled without litigation had Beatrice been willing to compromise. This she refused to do. She refused to meet with Mario. Any dealings between them had to be conducted by their respective legal counsels. Beatrice wouldn't consider anything less than Mario's eviction from the Tuscan estate and the restitution in full of any and all income derived from holdings she believed to be rightfully hers.

As far as I could tell, a lengthy and contentious court battle seemed inevitable. I was seeing a side of Beatrice I hadn't known existed. I knew her to be spoiled and totally self-centered, but the vindictiveness she now displayed both puzzled and disturbed me. I thought her intransigence bordered on aberrant behavior. Nor was that the only aspect of her behavior I found difficult to comprehend, let alone explain.

Take, for example, her attitude toward the house in Rome in which she'd been raised. It was located within easy walking distance of the Excelsior. No doubt she would have remembered many of the family retainers still living there. Yet she flatly refused to set foot on the premises.

She intended, she said, to liquidate the property as rapidly as possible. Explaining to her that now was not a good time to unload assets was difficult. Reluctantly, she agreed to wait for more favorable market conditions.

I don't suppose the reaction of Rome's hedonistic socialites to Beatrice's presence should have surprised me. She was young, beautiful, of impeccable Italian bloodline and had the added cachet of wealth. Her reputation as a patroness of the performing arts had preceded her. To her delight, and much to my annoyance, we were inundated with so many invitations that, when it came time for us to leave, she was reluctant to do so.

I had arranged for us to take passage on the *Demeter* on her maiden voyage from Barcelona to New York. Much as she would have liked to, Beatrice had no reason to stay in Rome.

The Italian courts were clogged with pending cases. It would be months before her litigation came to trial and many more months before settlement could be expected. This she had been advised by her lawyers, who told her she would be alerted well in advance when, or if, her presence would be required.

When we boarded the flight to Spain, Beatrice was ill-tempered and, throughout most of the trip, uncommunicative. As we neared Barcelona, she advised me that she'd given it considerable thought and had decided to live in Rome. She did not, she assured me, intend to relinquish her United States resident status, but would commute between Rome and New York.

To support this decision, she argued that she *was* after all an Italian and felt she had lived as an expatriate far too long. She also said that, in her opinion, Maria Veronica would receive a better education in Europe than in America.

To be perfectly truthful, I was elated. Her move would suit my purpose admirably. I'd yet to tell her I had decided to settle in Greece once the restoration of my estate in Ithaca was completed. I didn't do so now, but I decided I'd tell her of that decision during the sea voyage. For the moment, I raised counterarguments yet allowed myself to appear swayed by her logic.

When we deplaned in Barcelona, Beatrice was in good spirits.

CHAPTER FORTY-SEVEN

The owner's suite on board the *Demeter* was spacious and luxuriously appointed. Quarters for the twelve other passengers she was licensed to carry were on an equal par in furnishings and fittings.

Our fellow passengers on the maiden voyage were Sven and Monica Henningsen, the Spanish ambassador-designate to Mexico and his wife and their two teenage daughters, two Spanish industrialists and their wives, and a young Swiss banker. With the exception of Henningsen, who was overly conscious of his position as marine superintendent and the decorum he felt it demanded, it was a lively group Beatrice found entertaining. Both the passengers and crew went out of their way to please her. I don't think it occurred to her that this might, in part, be because she was the wife of the owner of the shipping company.

This was the second sea voyage Beatrice and I had made together, although I wouldn't have called the first, aboard the *Queen Mary*, an enjoyable experience. Beatrice had been pregnant and grief-stricken; I had been too concerned about her physical condition and state of mind to pay attention to much else. Accordingly, our crossing on the *Demeter* could be considered our first *shared* voyage.

We couldn't have had more ideal conditions. The summer weather favored us with calm seas and sun-drenched days. Our shipboard companions were convivial. The cuisine and service were nothing short of superlative. It should have been an enjoyable and memorable trip. If it was less than that, neither the *Demeter* nor her crew can be blamed.

Ocean voyages are supposed to heighten women's romantic responses. Not Beatrice's.

On our first night out of Barcelona, she blamed her lack of desire on overindulgence in champagne. It was a claim that had some foundation. Normally Beatrice drank sparingly, but she *had* consumed more champagne than usual both prior to and following our late-afternoon sailing.

The second night at sea we made love. To be more accurate, though, *I* made love. Beatrice merely went through the motions.

Nothing cools a man's ardor more effectively than an unresponsive sexual partner. With Beatrice, my performance had suffered, but I'd been unwilling, until that fateful night, to accept the cold, hard fact.

Leaving Beatrice soundly asleep, I slip quietly from bed, put on slacks, a polo shirt and loafers and made my way to the ship's bridge. Absently greeting the second officer, I walked out onto the starboard wing and stood, elbows resting on the rail capping, gazing into the blackness of the moonless night.

I'd run out of excuses. It was time to face the issue. It went deeper than cultural and attitudinal differences. The simple truth was that my beautiful wife and I were sexually mismatched.

Absently, I rubbed the thin line of my facial scar. The question was, what, if anything, were we going to do about it? Beatrice was a practicing Roman Catholic; I, at least in theory, was Greek Orthodox. Both creeds were opposed in principle to divorce.

Legal separation? It was a possibility, but how would Maria Veronica be affected by such an arrangement?

Was I jumping the gun on this issue? Beatrice hadn't indicated that she wanted any change in marital status. I concluded that things could not continue as they were without causing increasing frustration and tension. The short-term solution was to accept the fact that, barring some miracle, Beatrice would not — or *could* not — give me sexual gratification and to continue to seek such pleasures elsewhere. The long-range solution — ?

During those predawn deliberations I came to no conclusions other than to maintain the status quo. It was a dilemma I'd have to approach with caution. I'd have to carefully consider all aspects of the situation before embarking on any course of action from which there could be no retreat.

I would say the voyage, while I didn't particularly enjoy it, was certainly memorable.

The staggering news made my personal trials pale into insignificance. On August 6, an atomic bomb had been dropped on Hiroshima in Japan, and shortly thereafter a second such device had rained death and destruction on Nagasaki.

For good or bad, the world had entered the Nuclear Age.

As though to compensate for my fouled-up domestic affairs, the Fates smiled on my postwar business dealings. I must confess, however, that at first their smiles looked suspiciously grimacelike.

The conclusion of the war in the Pacific dramatically changed the shipping business. Suddenly there were more vessels of wartime construction available — American Liberty and Victory ships and Canadian Park ships — than existing shipping companies could absorb. Astute operators with good connections in Washington and Ottawa could pick up surplus merchant ships for a song.

Though I was in the process of mending political fences in Washington that had fallen into disrepair during the war, I lacked the clout other shipowners enjoyed. In dismay, I learned that Aristotle Onassis had concluded a deal whereby he'd acquired five Liberty ships at a price — if rumors could be believed — so negligible it amounted to stealing.

Perhaps it is just as well that I didn't pick up Liberty ships in like manner. First, the ten-thousand-ton Liberty ships were of welded construction and, in the opinion of many shipowners, not seaworthy in excessively heavy seas. Second, the Onassis deal, once its details leaked out, generated a howl of protest, not the least of which because Onassis wasn't an American citizen. Neither was I.

Fortunately, due to Stevenson's leverage, I enjoyed enviable status in Ottawa. I entered a bid on four ten-thousand-ton Park ships, vessels having the advantage of riveted-plate construction. Admittedly my deal couldn't compare with the one Onassis reputedly had made, but it provided me stopgap bottoms that enabled me to get my foot in the door of Pacific trading.

I could handle the terms of the Park ship acquisitions. The catch was that the ships had to operate under Canadian registry for a minimum four-year period. To offset that operating cost disadvantage, I was allowed to depreciate the vessels at the rate of 25 percent per annum for tax purposes. Under those conditions, it paid me to set up a Canadian subsidiary, Kybernas-Dominion Line, for the time I would have to operate out of Canadian home ports.

Had I not spent time in Ottawa negotiating the terms and conditions of the Park ship acquisition, the matter of surplus Canadian-built warships would not have come to my attention. In a government-to-government arrangement, Canada was making a number of frigates available to the Greek navy on very attractive terms. I was able, by pulling a few strings in Greece, to have one of those frigates consigned to me.

In 1946-47, the *Heracles* and the *Theseus* came down the ways in Barcelona to join their sister ships, the *Athena* and the *Demeter*. In addition, during that same period, two of the four tankships I had on order were delivered, placed under Greek registry and put into service on long-term leasing arrangements with a consortium known as Arabian American Oil Company, or Aramco. But to meet the demand for freighters and oil tankers I was certain lay in the offing, I needed more ships — many more ships.

When hostilities had ended in the autumn of 1945, the economies of Europe and the Far East were in a shambles. The only countries to emerge from the war with healthy economies were noncombatant states, the United States and Canada. As I saw it, the United States, if it wished to protect its trading interests, would be obliged to financially assist both Europe and Asia. I was banking on American monetary intervention, which, if *not* forthcoming, would place me in a difficult, if not impossible, position.

My gamble paid off. Japan, under U.S. military occupation, was making economic recovery as early as 1946. In 1947-48, the European Recovery Program — familiarly known as the Marshall Plan — was initiated to bolster the economies of Western Europe.

The Kybernas Line, together with its wholly owned subsidiary, Kybernas-Dominion, certainly wasn't an industry giant, but, operating a total of nine vessels, four of them newly constructed seventeen-thousand-ton reefer ships, it was making its presence felt in shipping circles. The Greek-registered, leased-out tankships were operated separately by Sthanassis Shipping and, while not yet paid for, were paying their way.

Nineteen forty-eight was the critical make-or-break year. I was mortgaged to the hilt. My Metaxis holdings were escrowed as collateral against outstanding loans. I had ships under construction in Sweden, Norway, Scotland, Spain and Japan. As I said earlier, that was the year I sold off my Bolivian shareholdings to meet interest payments and defray mounting operating costs. I don't believe I was in danger of foundering, but dark storm clouds did loom large on the horizon. Fortunately the storm brushed past, and by the latter part of the year my shipping companies steamed into less troubled waters.

But I'm getting ahead of myself. Nineteen forty-eight was also a memorable year for a reason unrelated to business. It was during that summer that I met Olivia Cappellari.

CHAPTER FORTY-EIGHT

Saying she'd no desire to suffer through another New York winter, Beatrice informed me early in January 1946 that she intended to move to Rome. I raised no objection. It was then that I told her of my plan to take up residence in Greece, on the property I owned on the island of Ithaca.

Beatrice eyed me suspiciously. "Why haven't you mentioned this until now?"

"I didn't make up my mind until a week ago."

"This property you speak of? A family landholding? An inheritance?"

"No. It's an abandoned estate I bought before the war. Two years ago, before leaving Greece, I contracted to have it restored. I had in mind using it as a summer retreat. I've not seen it since and am eager to do so."

"How big is it?"

I could read her thoughts. She was wondering if the estate, like the one she rented in East Hampton, would be suitable for entertaining summertime guests. "Big enough. Fifty hectares. The manor house has six bedrooms, and I had a swimming pool installed. The property also has beach frontage." What I *didn't* add was that no way in the world could Ithaca be compared to Long Island.

With Maria Veronica and Mrs. Brady, Beatrice left for Rome the last week in January. I was involved in setting up the Kybernas-Dominion Line in Montreal, so I didn't go with them. I planned to join them later. As things developed, I didn't arrive in Rome until summer, by which time Beatrice was vacationing in Cannes.

After a brief stopover in Cannes to see Maria Veronica, I flew to Athens, then, accompanied by the estate agent, went to Vathí.

The estate agent was justifiably proud of how the contractor he'd chosen had handled the restoration. I must say I, too, was pleased. Workmen had added such appropriate touches as a pergola-shaded bar and barbecue pit next to the poolside changing rooms. There were, however, a number of changes I wanted made if, as I now did, I wanted the manor house to serve as my base of operations.

For example, I needed a consistent supply of electricity. Behind the stables, I ordered a generating plant installed to supplement Vathí's erratic power supply. Also, to the yacht basin I'd had built on my sea frontage, I ordered a breakwater equipped with a lighted beacon constructed. The stone jetty was to be extended and supplied with fresh water, electrical outlets and telephone connections.

On that visit I stayed at Vathí a mere six days, wishing I could do so for much longer. The following year I did much better, extending my stay to nearly four months.

The summer of 1947 was a landmark of sorts. By then I'd added a fourth vessel to Sthanassis Shipping's growing fleet of tankships and two diesel-powered cargo vessels to the Kybernas Line's roster. In shipping circles it was generally conceded that I was becoming a power to be reckoned with, though many of my colleagues thought I was getting in over my head.

That summer, at my invitation, Sofoclis, Aletha and their two young sons, Nicholas and Peter, came to visit and stayed six weeks. They used Ithaca as a hub from which to explore the Ionian isles, mainland Greece, Crete and the Aegean Islands. They added luster to the proudest moment of my summer, the christening and delivery of the *Veronica*.

Built in a Quebec City shipyard, she had started life as HMCS *Coquitlam* and served with distinction on convoy escort duty in the North Atlantic before becoming surplus at war's end. She was the frigate turned over to the Greek navy in 1946 that I'd arranged to take off their hands in return for reimbursement of the original purchase price.

Before turning her over to me, the Greek navy had stripped her of armament, navigational aides, above- and below-deck fittings and antisubmarine detection equipment. What I had gotten was a three-hundred-foot hull of thirty-seven-foot beam fitted with twin screws and two triple-expansion engines — and little else.

I'd had the hull towed to Patras and put her in shipyard hands. I'd spared no expense in converting her to a luxury yacht fitted out with the latest in navigational aids and telecommunications equipment. Painted gleaming white, brass fittings glistening in the sunlight, she was my pride and joy.

Leaving Patras in mid-August, our first port of call was Piraeus to pick up Georgiana and Penny before embarking on a cruise of the Ionian isles. In Corfu we were to be joined by Beatrice, Maria Veronica, Mrs. Brady, a small party of Beatrice's friends and Georgiana's so-called business associate, Umberto Bartonelli.

As Piraeus, I watched in dismay as Penny was trundled aboard in a wheelchair. Privately, I asked Georgiana what was wrong.

After making me promise that I'd say nothing about it to Penny, Georgiana told me Penny had multiple sclerosis, not arthritis, as Penny had led me to believe. There was nothing that could be done about Penny's affliction that doctors in Athens weren't already doing.

Unfortunately, that disturbing news wasn't the only thing to cast a pall over the *Veronica*'s maiden voyage. En route to Corfu, I received a cable advising me that, due to an unexpected minor ailment, Maria Veronica was too ill to travel. In consequence, Beatrice and her party would not be joining us in Kerkyra.

The fact that Beatrice and her friends wouldn't be coming aboard didn't particularly concern me. Indeed, I'm sure they would've found Georgiana and Penny provincial. But I'd been eager for Sofie, Aletha and the boys to see how Maria Veronica had grown and for Georgiana and Penny to meet their young niece.

It couldn't be helped. They would have to meet their niece *next* summer. I vowed that, whether or not Beatrice condescended to favor us with her presence, Maria Veronica would spend the better part of next summer's vacation with me in Ithaca.

As August drew to a close, Sofie and his family, Umberto, Georgiana and Penny disembarked at Piraeus. Sofie and his family had to return to the States for the beginning of school, Georgiana and Umberto had business to attend to and Penny, though unfailingly cheerful, must have been tired by all the unaccustomed activity.

When the *Veronica* was safely secured alongside in her berth at my yacht harbor in Ithaca, I returned by launch to Piraeus and flew from Athens to Rome.

Beyond a vague reference to a "virus," Beatrice failed to mention Maria Veronica's supposed illness. Mrs. Brady, who had evidently been cautioned to say nothing about it, was equally closemouthed.

I spent only four days in Rome before continuing on to Paris, Rotterdam, Stockholm, London and finally New York. A long weekend with Beatrice and her friends was about all I could stand. Had I not been eager to spend some time with Maria Veronica, I'd have bypassed Rome altogether.

To my shame, I hadn't seen Maria Veronica since the previous Christmas — and would not see her again until Beatrice made her annual visit to New York during the coming holiday season. The six-year-old child and I were strangers to each other.

Each time I saw her, I was struck by some unexpected aspect of her development. This time I discovered she'd sprouted up a full two inches and had lost two of her front teeth since our last meeting. Yet there was another, more subtle, change. In the past, the child had been painfully shy in my presence. This time I sensed toward me a hostility I found impossible to explain.

I think it had something to do with my relationship with Beatrice. Outwardly the relationship was cordial, yet the child seemed to sense the undercurrent of antipathy. It was as though my daughter held me personally responsible for the alienation between her mother and me.

Although Beatrice adopted a proprietory attitude toward Maria Veronica, she spent little time with her and, when with her, was openly critical. Yet paradoxically the child adored her mother and tried pathetically hard to win her approval. It was an anomaly that defied logic.

At this point I should backtrack a little.

The lawsuit Beatrice initiated against her brother in the summer of 1945 dragged on for months. In the final analysis, she succeeded in having Mario evicted from the Tuscan properties and wrested from his control the income-producing properties in Naples. On the other hand — rightly, I thought — the court ruled that she was entitled only to token compensation for monies she claimed Mario had misappropriated. She should have accepted my recommendation and settled the matter out of court. As so often happens, the only ones to profit from the litigation were the law firms involved.

Heeding my advice about her property in Rome, she didn't put it on the market until Italy's economy took an upswing. On her return to Rome in 1946, she took advantage of the buyer's market and bought a residential property at a fraction of its actual worth. She did not, in fact, sell the old family homestead until early in the fifties and then at a handsome profit. I've been told that not once from the time she returned to Rome in 1946 did she so much as set foot in what had been her childhood home or contact any of her family's former retainers. Estate agents handled the entire sale.

CHAPTER FORTY-NINE

Nineteen forty-eight was only a few hours old when I brought matters to a head.

We were attending a New Year's Eve party at the New York Yacht Club. I took Beatrice to one side and told her that, a few hours later, I'd be flying to the West Coast where I'd join one of my Park ships, the *Dominion Navigator*. I expected to be gone four or five months, calling at Asian, Southeast Asian, Indian and Persian Gulf ports. Beatrice smiled sweetly, said she hoped I'd enjoy the trip and turned to leave.

Grasping her by the elbow, I turned her to face me. "When I return," I said, "I'll go directly to Ithaca. By then you'll either be in Rome or vacationing somewhere on the French Riviera."

Eyes narrowing, Beatrice said, "A reasonable assumption."

"I'll send the *Veronica* to collect you and Maria Veronica in late June or early July."

She colored. "You'll do no such thing," she said.

Ignoring her outburst, I continued, "Maria Veronica will spend the summer with me. I'll expect you to stay a minimum of two weeks. You can, if you like, bring along some of your friends."

"I've been told Ithaca offers nothing but scenery," Beatrice said. "Do you think I'd subject my friends to that social *graveyard*?"

"I don't give a damn whether you come along or with the whole tribe. The point is you *will* come and stay at least two weeks."

"And if I refuse?"

"Then you'd better to learn to live within your lira income."

She knew by the look on my face and tone of voice that I meant it.

Accompanied by a party of ten friends, Beatrice, with Maria Veronica and Mrs. Brady, boarded the *Veronica* at St. Tropez. The yacht tied up alongside my jetty on July 7.

I'll agree that Ithaca isn't exactly a vacationer's mecca. On the other hand, it wasn't quite the morgue Beatrice and her friends expected.

True, after one visit to a *taverna* in Vathí she and her companions unanimously condemned the food as inedible and the wine as abominable. Thereafter they confined their activities to the estate, where they could find no fault with either the cuisine or my well-stocked wine cellar.

The trouble with Beatrice and her companions was that they were night people. Swimming, sunbathing, sailing and water-skiing, all daytime pleasures, didn't interest them. By the end of the first week, they were unmistakably bored.

I welcomed Beatrice's suggestion that we take the *Veronica* and go to Corfu for a few days. Pleading a backlog of paperwork, I declined. And, since a seven-year-old child would undoubtedly have hampered their activities, Maria Veronica and her nanny were also left behind.

On the morning of the yacht's departure, I discovered that another of Beatrice's guests had stayed in Ithaca as well.

Wearing swimming trunks and a bathrobe, I descended the stone steps toward the flagged terrace and swimming pool. On the third step from the top, I paused in surprise. Evidently, I was mistaken that all of Beatrice's guests had joined her on the expedition to Corfu. A scantily clad young woman lay stretched out on a lounge chair at the side of the pool.

At first I didn't recognize her, though I should have. She'd been introduced to me as Beatrice's cousin, but, for the life of me, I couldn't recall her name.

From my vantage point, I surveyed her critically. Facially, I wouldn't have called her beautiful. Attractive, even arresting, but certainly not beautiful. However, now that she was displayed in seminudity, I revised my opinion. Her lithe young body was nothing short of magnificent.

She was lying on her back, the skimpy wisp of her bikini bottom her sole concession to propriety. The twin globes of her full breasts thrust proudly upward. She was a large-boned young woman, but there was nothing even remotely angular about her smoothly curved figure.

An involuntary surge of warmth flooded my groin. Hell, I thought wryly, you're old enough to be her father. The warmth in my crotch persisted nonetheless.

Descending the remaining steps, I walked toward the reclining figure, clearing my throat to alert her of my presence. She opened her eyes and turned her face in my direction.

"Hello," she said. "I thought you'd gone with the others."

I smiled. "No. I've some paperwork to take care of. What about you?"

Sitting up, she slid her legs off the lounge chair. Facing me, she smiled impishly. "The only time I find Corfu bearable is at the end of the season when the tourists leave and most Corfiotes have gone into hibernation. In the summer, it's like a zoo." Her smile widened as she nodded toward an umbrella-shaded table. "If you'll pass me my bikini bra, I'll make myself a bit more presentable. I don't think your servants approve of my immodest attire."

Chuckling, I handed her the bra. She was right about the servants. They had said nothing, but their tight-lipped faces were mute testimony to their disapproval of Beatrice's guests.

Watching her deftly don the bra, a thought struck me. If she disliked Corfu, she need not have gone ashore. "You could have gone along for the ride and sunned yourself on the foredeck," I said, then, recalling her surname, I added, "Signorina Cappellari."

Her smile vanished. "I'm sorry. I didn't mean to intrude."

I hadn't meant it to sound the way she'd taken it. "You're not intruding," I said. "On the contrary."

The smile returned. "Then please don't be so formal. My name's Olivia. My friends call me Livy."

Her smile was infectious. I smiled in response. "*My* friends call me Kostas."

"Good. That's settled. But you wanted to know why, since I *am* Beatrice's guest, I didn't join her yachting party. If I don't like Corfu, I didn't have to go ashore. Is that what you meant?"

"Well . . . yes."

"Two reasons. First, I find most of Beatrice's friends a bit hard to take. I think the only reason she invited me was to balance the male-female mix. But the most important reason is that I have to be in Milan no later than Monday."

"Couldn't you have flown there from Corfu?"

"Flights are solidly booked until the end of August."

"So how do you intend to get there?"

"Fly from Cephalonia. I've arranged for one of your boatmen to take me to Sami on Friday. From there I'll take a taxi cross-island to the airport. My flight's booked for Sunday afternoon. No problem."

"Why is it so important that you be in Milan on Monday?"

"I'm a member of La Scala opera company."

That took me by surprise. I'd been of the opinion that few, if any, of Beatrice's guests were gainfully employed. More to the point, I wasn't sure, but I'd thought La Scala closed down for the summer months. "Do they perform during the summer?" I asked.

Olivia laughed. "Not in Milan. But the training doesn't let up . . . especially for those of us on the bottom rungs of the ladder. I really shouldn't have let Beatrice talk me into this trip. When I become a diva I'll allow myself the luxury of long summer vacations."

I noted with inner amusement that there seemed to be no question in her mind that she was destined for stardom. I regarded her with awakening respect. The fact that she was attached to a prestigious opera company like *Teatro alla Scala* spoke volumes. She had to have talent, or they wouldn't have accepted her.

She'd aroused my curiosity. I would have questioned her further had not a distraction intervened.

Maria Veronica, followed sedately by Mrs. Brady, ran toward us from the far end of the terrace. Excitedly, she came directly to Olivia. "Auntie Livy," she exclaimed breathlessly, "come see them! You *must* come! They're beautiful!"

Olivia laughed delightedly, smoothed Maria Veronica's copper-bright hair and kissed her on the tip of her freckle-dusted nose. "Slow down, Ronnie. What is it I *must* see . . . and where?"

"Puppies! A mama and four puppies! They're behind the house, by the horses. Can I have one of them, Auntie Livy? *Please*?"

I knew the blessed event we'd been expecting must have happened. Chloe, my pregnant mongrel bitch, had dropped her litter behind the stables.

What baffled me was the intimacy that appeared to exist between Olivia and Maria Veronica. "Ronnie"? I hadn't heard that affectionate diminutive applied by anyone other than Olivia. If Olivia lived in Milan, how had the relationship developed? Surely, given the fact that Maria Veronica was painfully shy, such rapport could not have grown from a mere week's exposure.

Glancing in my direction, Olivia said, "They're not mine to give, dear. You'll have to ask your father."

Maria Veronica stiffened. Turning slowly to face me, eyes downcast, she asked in a barely audible voice, "Can I have one of the puppies?"

"Yes . . . but not for a few days. They're still too young to leave their mother. This afternoon, after your nap, your Aunt Olivia and I will help you choose one."

Mrs. Brady joined us and led Maria Veronica off to wash up before lunch. We watched them climb the steps toward the patio.

Olivia broke the growing silence. "Why did you include me in the selection of a puppy?"

"Because," I said, "she seems more at ease with you than she does with me."

Olivia brushed an errant strand of dark hair from her brow and looked at me solemnly. "Is she always like that with you? Is she afraid of you?"

Her bluntness annoyed me. I frowned. "I don't think she fears me . . . but it's a possibility. I've spent so little time with her over the past few years and I'm pretty much a stranger to her. With me, she retreats into a shell."

Olivia nodded. "I can understand that. She doesn't take easily to strangers. It took me almost a month of being with her every day to win her confidence."

"Oh? When was that?"

"Last summer . . . when Mrs. Brady had the flu. Beatrice was tied up in Cannes and Monaco and left Ronnie with me for six weeks."

"Where?"

"Milan."

That must have been about the time Beatrice had cabled that she couldn't join us due to Maria Veronica's illness. I would gain nothing by disclosing that deception to Olivia, so I withheld comment. My expression, however, must have given me away.

Olivia looked at me uncertainly. "Was there something wrong with her being with me in Milan?"

I smiled reassuringly. "Not at all. Was I scowling?"

"Ferociously."

"Forgive me. Mention of Milan brought to mind a business deal that soured."

Untying the sash of my bathrobe, I shrugged out of it, draped it across a chair, then headed toward the pool. I'd taken only a couple of steps when an idea came to me, and I turned and asked Olivia, "Do you water-ski?"

"Yes."

"Can you drive a ski boat?"

"If it's an outboard."

"Good. After lunch, if you like, we'll go skiing."

She grinned mischievously. "I thought you were swamped with paperwork."

I laughed. "Touché. That was *my* excuse for not going to Corfu."

That evening, Olivia dined with me on the patio. She proved to be a delightful dinner companion even though, as I'd discovered earlier in the day, she asked some penetrating, disconcerting questions.

Over before-dinner drinks, during the course of the meal and while we lingered over coffee and liqueurs, I learned a good deal about Olivia — family background, education, aspirations. For the most part, since she spoke little Greek and my Italian was at best labored, we conducted our conversation in English, a tongue in which she was surprisingly fluent.

Her mother was a Tocchi, the youngest sister of the late Count Guglielmi. Her father, Dr. Niccolo Cappellari, practiced medicine in the Piedmont in and around the town of Nizza Monferrato. The family was not wealthy but was comfortably well off. Olivia had been educated at a girl's school in Lugano, Switzerland, where her closest friend had been an American girl who undoubtedly had contributed to Olivia's familiarity with English. After graduating at eighteen, Olivia had taken voice lessons and continued her language studies. She had been with La Scala for the past five years. She was twenty-six, a few years older than I had originally estimated.

The exchange of background information wasn't one-sided. To my surprise, I found myself telling her of my early years in Drakopoulata and of my youthful labors as a fisherman in Corfu. I told her how I'd learned English — from reading, tutoring, practicing conversational exchanges with English tourists in Kerkyra and night school in New York — and how I'd acquired a reasonable command of Spanish from exposure to Latin American shipmates and through business dealings in Colombia, Ecuador and Cuba.

To my even greater surprise, toward the end of the meal, I made a spur-of-the-moment decision and asked a favor of Olivia.

"It's too bad you can't stay a few days longer. My sisters, Georgiana and Penelope, are coming over from Athens to spend a week with me. Georgie is fluent in Italian, and Penny, whose late husband was Greek-American, speaks English. I think you'd have liked them."

"I'm sure I would have."

"This will be their first meeting with either Beatrice or Maria Veronica. I thought it would be a good time to take Veronica and, with my sisters, visit Drakopoulata. I want to show Veronica — Ronnie — the village where I was born and raised and the old graveyard in Aghia Efimia where my father and grandparents are buried. But I've just now changed my mind."

"Why? It sounds like a worthwhile trip to me."

"Oh, I'll go there with my sisters. We've quite a few relatives and old friends in the village. Might even take Ronnie along if she wants to go a second time . . . but I think it would be better to take her for her first visit tomorrow. If you've nothing else planned, would you come with us?"

"I'd be delighted. But why me?"

"Ronnie likes you. Trusts you. I think she'd enjoy the outing more if she shared it with you instead of strangers."

CHAPTER FIFTY

In corporate climate predictions, the degree of warmth in bankers'
smiles probably provides the most accurate form of measurement.
In the autumn of 1948, while I wouldn't say my bankers were
beaming, their smiles were a good deal less frosty.

The financial crisis the Kybernas Line and Sthanassis Shipping
had faced was behind us. Now that the patients were on the road
to recovery, I should have been able to relax. Far from it. I now
faced the *real* challenge — the transformation of my loosely related
shipping interests into a cohesive shipping empire.

Anyone who says a shipping empire comes into being by chance
isn't playing with a full deck. There *is* an element of chance. Luck
takes a hand in the game. But the chief, the indispensible, ingredient
is hard work.

We had cargo vessels, oil tankers and bulk carriers coming off
the ways in six countries. They had to start paying their way almost
from the moment of acceptance. In fact, I made it a practice with
tankships to conclude leasing arrangements before the keels were
laid. If I was late in delivering, I faced hefty penalties. The agents
appointed to serve the Kybernas Line and, for its limited lifespan,
Dominion-Kybernas Line had to pursue cargoes aggressively. A ship
in ballast costs, not earns, money. And, on top of that, we had to
find buyers for our now fully depreciated Park ships and negotiate
construction contracts for additional tonnage.

My intention was to make Ithaca the nerve-center and base of
operations for my far-flung shipping interests, but, before that could
happen, the gossamer threads of the expanding web had to be made
stronger. *Much* stronger. From the autumn of 1948 until the summer
of 1950, I spent little time in Ithaca.

It was a hectic time for both Captain Henningsen and me. It seemed as though we had to be in two or three places at the same time. Yet somehow I managed to squeeze in a few days, weekends and weeks with Maria Veronica during that period. The last thing I wanted to do was lose ground I'd gained in Ithaca during the summer of 1948.

I don't mean to imply that I'd gained Maria Veronica's confidence. I didn't expect miracles. But she no longer retreated behind an impenetrable barrier in my presence. Now there was a guarded emergence, an indication of willingness to meet me part way. As a concession to our changing relationship, she now called me "Papa." An encouraging sign. And even more encouraging was that Mrs. Brady's glacial attitude toward me seemed to be thawing.

I owed Olivia a debt of gratitude for the catalytic role she'd played at Drakopoulata and in the four days that followed. At first I led myself to believe that was all there was to it. It explained why she was so often in my thoughts. But it was an explanation that didn't hold water.

From the first day we'd met, I'd been attracted to Olivia. She exhibited qualities I admired — ambition, lack of pretense, a pragmatic turn of mind and a delightfully earthy sense of humor. I'd enjoyed the time I'd spent with her, and, thinking back on it, I realized I'd told her more about myself and *my* ambitions than I'd told anyone in decades.

If I denied that I was physically attracted to her, I'd be lying. I down-played that aspect of the relationship due to the difference in our ages — and to the fact that, patently, it was one-sided.

I didn't see Olivia until the spring of 1949 and wouldn't have seen her then had I not invented an excuse to visit Milan.

My timing was bad. Not only were Olivia's days devoted to language, voice and music lessons, but also her evenings were occupied with rehearsals for La Scala's forthcoming presentation of Verdi's *Il Trovatore*, in which she had a demanding role. She skipped some of her daytime lessons in order to spend time with me but dared not miss any of the rehearsals. Opening night was but two days away.

When I told her that Maria Veronica now called me Papa, Olivia clapped her hands and laughingly warned me to watch my step. Ronnie was at an impressionable age. In the near future, Olivia said, when Ronnie's hormones started to churn about in earnest, the child-woman was more than likely to switch her emotional attachment from Beatrice to me. I'd better be prepared to be a role model for future suitors.

The morning following Olivia's opening night, I was due in Geneva for an important meeting with a Swiss banker. I pushed it to the limit by attending the opening night performance.

I had assumed Olivia was gifted, but I was ill-prepared for the revelation of the extent of her talent. I know a good deal more about operatically trained voices now than I did then, but, still, I recognized that her voice had a special quality and that her belief that she was destined to be a prima donna was by no means wishful thinking.

On the program she was listed as a mezzo-soprano, a register that meant little or nothing to me then. All I knew was that her voice had a richness and clarity that brought a lump to my throat and gave me gooseflesh.

After the performance, I hosted a late supper for Olivia and a few of her close friends from the ensemble. The group, after weeks of exhausting rehearsal, knew that their performance had been praiseworthy and, from the applause and number of curtain calls, that it had been well-received by a critical audience. In a festive mood, they showed little inclination to make it an early night and welcomed Olivia's suggestion that we continue the party at her apartment. Not wishing to dampen their enthusiasm, I went along but, after a nightcap, took leave of them on the valid excuse that I had to catch an early flight to Geneva.

I attributed the fervor of Olivia's parting kiss to the mood of the evening — and to the champagne.

I spent Christmas and New Year's in New York with my family. When Beatrice left for Rome in late January, I went to Panama City for business discussions with Ruiz. While there, I received a letter from Olivia that had been forwarded through my Genoa shipping agent.

The letter had been written on the eve of the opera company's departure for London, where they were to perform at Covent Garden, following which they were to appear in Paris, Frankfurt and Vienna before returning to Milan.

The big news, which she reserved until late in her letter, was that the Fates had favored her. Her good fortune was that the entourage's leading mezzo-soprano had suffered an accident just prior to the company's departure on its Continental tour. And, to her surprise,

Olivia had been selected to take over the roles assigned to the injured singer. When the company opened in Covent Garden, its initial presentation was to be Verdi's *Aida,* with Olivia cast in the role of Amneris.

At the conclusion of her letter, Olivia listd the dates the company would appear in each city before returning to Milan early in May. She expressed the hope that business might bring me to one or more of the cities listed.

As things worked out, I didn't have to invent an excuse to fly to London. Devaluation of the British pound was causing havoc in shipping circles, necessitating the rescheduling of cargo bookings. Unfortunately, I wasn't in time for her Covent Garden debut. Instead, I rendezvoused with her in Paris.

I suppose there would have been nothing wrong with my putting in an appearance in Paris — and nothing improper with entertaining my wife's cousin — yet I felt that it *could* generate unwanted publicity. I was too well-known on the international scene to escape attention. While I would have considered it an honor to have my name linked with Olivia's, the attention we attracted could well have worked to her disadvantage. At this stage of her career, she could ill-afford unfavorable publicity. Accordingly, for public consumption, the raison d'être for my being in Paris was negotiations with the Compagnie Française de Pétrole concerning leasing arrangements for two new tankships then undergoing construction in Oslo.

In the afternoons we visited points of interest like the Louvre, the Tuileries and the Basilica of Sacré Coeur in Montmartre. After the evening performances we dined at out-of-the-way restaurants and bistros. At a respectable hour, I returned her to the hotel just off the Place de l'Opéra, where her touring company was quartered. Our partings were chaste; our conduct above reproach.

To be truthful, the role of a kindly uncle was a part for which I was ill-suited. As Olivia later confessed, playing the part of a dutiful niece was not at all what she'd had in mind. Thinking back it seems like a ludicrous way to have played out the scene in Paris, a city renowned the world over for romance. Happily, before we parted, we had sense enough to plan a return engagement.

In mid-July, she planned to take a month's vacation. We arranged that I would have the *Veronica* pick her up at either Genoa or Venice so we could spend at least part of her holiday together.

On June 27, the *Veronica* embarked Beatrice, a party of her vacationing friends and Maria Veronica — together with Mrs. Brady, now referred to as Veronica's "governess" — at Naples to transport them to St. Tropez. Beatrice, as I'd anticipated, curtly declined my invitation to spend part of the summer in Ithaca, but she agreed to let me take Maria Veronica to the estate for the latter part of August. At St. Tropez, I stayed aboard the yacht and steamed southeastward the following day.

A word of explanation is in order. In effect, the yacht was an extension of my Ithaca base of operations. Along with her captain and crew, the *Veronica* carried an administrative staff of two executive assistants and six communications specialists.

That spring there had been an important addition to the staff, a helicopter pilot. I'd had a helipad constructed on the after-superstructure of the *Veronica* and another one installed at the Ithaca estate. Not only was I kept informed at all times, whether in Ithaca or on board the yacht, of ship movements, but, if the need arose, I now was in a position to be helicopter-lifted to a major international airport at a moment's notice.

As we steamed toward the toe of Italy in the early days of July 1950, the incoming news was disturbing.

Three days before I dropped Beatrice and her party at St. Tropez, Soviet-armed North Korean forces invaded South Korea. On the very day Beatrice disembarked at St. Tropez, Seoul, the South Korean capital, fell to the North Koreans. A hastily convened UN Security Council meeting, boycotted by the Soviet Union, voted to send troops to beleaguered South Korea to restore order. These troops, under the overall command of General Douglas MacArthur, had landed at Pusan and were facing determined North Korean resistance.

How did this concern me? Shipping was needed to supply these ground, air and naval forces. I had diverted cargo vessels in the vicinity to the theater of action and had more ships on standby. As we rounded the heel of Italy's boot and steamed north into the Adriatic Sea, I followed the war news closely.

On July 14, Olivia boarded the *Veronica* at Venice. My concern for UN forces holding a defensive position based on Pusan became less compelling. I had other matters of a more personal and pressing nature to think about.

That evening, steaming south on a glass-smooth sea, we dined alone in the saloon. Olivia had much to tell me about the ensemble's triumphs and tragedies since Paris and after its return to Milan. I talked mostly about my business dealings in the Far East and the impact hostilities in Korea were likely to have on the American economy in general and the shipping business in particular.

Olivia's contributions to the discussion were perceptive. She was a remarkable young woman in many ways and, as I was soon to learn, in more ways than I imagined.

The hour grew late. Before we knew it, it was midnight. Leaving the saloon, we made our way out onto the deck. Hand in hand, we stood by the starboard rail, drinking in the magic of the soft summer night.

"You love the sea," Olivia said.

"Love? She can be a cruel mistress . . . but yes, I love her. At sea, I feel an affinity with the elements — and close to God."

With her free hand, Olivia pulled her shawl up to cover her bare shoulders. Releasing her other hand, I circled her shoulder and drew her close. "It's turned cool," I said. "We'd better go inside. Would you like a nightcap before you turn in?"

"Not unless you've liquor in your cabin."

"There's a bar in my stateroom but — " At that moment, the implication of what she'd just said struck me, and I stopped abruptly.

Within the circle of my arm she turned to face me and said, "I think it's time we made love."

Morning sunlight slanted through the porthole, forming a wavering pattern on the deckhead. Bemusedly, I watched the play of light and shadow on the overhead paneling before lifting myself onto one elbow and gazing down at Olivia's sleeping form.

Her face, partially screened by dark hair in disarray, was turned toward me. In repose, her expression was one of childlike innocence. I leaned over and gently pushed a few strands of hair from her cheek. There had been nothing remotely childlike about the uninhibited passion she'd displayed a few hours earlier.

She stirred. Her eyelids fluttered, then opened. Looking up at me, she sighed contentedly and stretched. The coverlet slid down, provocatively exposing one breast. "Mmmm," she murmured. "Been awake long?"

"No."

"You look pensive. Something troubling you? Pangs of conscience?"

I grinned. "God knows, I *should* have a guilty conscience . . . but I don't. I was lying here thinking that I'd almost forgotten how good it is to make love to someone I truly care for. It was great. You were wonderful."

Her smile was radiant. She snuggled against me. "I'm glad," she said, "and happy you don't think me a shameless slut. Dammit, I got tired of waiting for you to proposition me. Would you *ever* have gotten around to it?"

"Without a lot of encouragement, I doubt it."

CHAPTER FIFTY-ONE

The days sped by.

We sailed, water skied, swam in the pool and sea and roamed the hills and mountains near the manor house. We made love whenever the spirit moved us.

It was a time for exploration — of the sun-dappled countryside, of each other's bodies and of our innermost thoughts and feelings. It was a wondrous time of sharing.

All too soon the day came when Olivia had to leave. On August 11, we boarded the *Veronica* for Naples. Beatrice had telephoned from Nice that Maria Veronica and Mrs. Brady would meet us there.

When she saw Aunt Livy at the top of the accommodation ladder, waiting to welcome her aboard, Veronica practically flew up the steps and into her arms. In Maria Veronica's wake, Mrs. Brady picked her way up the ladder with due caution. Pausing on the upper grating, Mrs. Brady looked at her nine-year-old charge wrapped in her aunt's embrace. Swinging her gaze to me, Mrs. Brady's normally austere countenance softened into something suspiciously resembling a look of approval.

We steamed north to Genoa to disembark Olivia.

When I told Olivia that I wasn't plagued by a guilty conscience I'd spoken the truth, yet that didn't mean that our dramatically altered relationship didn't give rise to complications. It would only be a question of time before Beatrice learned of our liaison. I preferred that she hear the news from me rather than from someone else.

When at the end of August it was time for Maria Veronica to return to Rome and school, we sailed west from Ithaca. When the *Veronica* nosed into Naples Bay, I casually suggested that we complete our journey by helicopter. Maria Veronica bounced with excitement, while Mrs. Brady approached the ordeal with a magnificent show of indifference.

Fortunately — or unfortunately, depending on how it's viewed — Beatrice had returned from the French Riviera early and was at her villa in Rome when a hired limousine deposited us at its baroque porte cochere.

Despite the fact that the helicopter was standing by at the airport, I stayed to dine with Beatrice and Maria Veronica. I waited until Veronica went off to bed before broaching the subject uppermost in my mind.

Eyes glinting dangerously, Beatrice heard me out in thin-lipped silence. When I finished my unadorned, unapologetic confession, Beatrice said, "I've never objected to your sleeping around . . . providing it was done discreetly. Openly taking a mistress is a different matter — *especially* when she's related to me. I should never have trusted that bitch. Damn you, Kostas, I will *not* be humiliated by your actions . . . or hers."

Suppressing my anger, I said, "We'll not flaunt the affair, but neither will we meet furtively in back alleys and cheap hotels. If you find that humiliating, I suggest you consider divorce."

"You *know* that's out of the question," she said.

"The hell I do. We haven't made love in five years. On the strength of that, you could be granted a Vatican divorce."

"I've never denied you my bed."

"For Chrissake!" I exploded. "There's more to sex than flopping on your back and spreading your legs."

Beatrice colored. "If you think I'll give you your freedom, you're sadly mistaken. We're married. We're going to *stay* married!"

It was October before Olivia and I met again in Milan. When I told her how Beatrice reacted to my disclosure, Olivia nodded. "You didn't say you were going to, but I'm glad you told her. I wonder, considering what I know about her, if she'd have had the guts to call me a bitch to my face."

"What you know about her?"

Olivia looked uncomfortable. "I shouldn't have said that. It's knowledge based on hearsay. But if what I suspect is only halfway close to the truth, you're the one with grounds for divorce."

"I don't follow you."

"What has she told you about her childhood?"

I thought for a moment. What *had* she told me about her formative years? Precious little. She neither invited nor gave confidences. In truth, I was abysmally ignorant about Beatrice's past — and not much more knowledgeable about her present. The simple fact was that I'd long since ceased to care one way or the other. "A topic she avoided," I said. "I didn't press her, particularly after her father died. But it works both ways. She knows next to nothing about my early years or, for that matter, my more recent activities."

Olivia regarded me pensively. "I suppose there's fault on both sides . . . but more on hers than yours. She had the most to hide. There's something you should know, but I shouldn't be the one to tell you."

"If not you, who?"

"Your brother-in-law, Mario."

"I've never even met the man."

" I know. If it were up to Beatrice you never would. I'll arrange for you to meet him."

Olivia was as good as her word, but my meeting with Count Mario Tocchi didn't materialize until the spring of 1951. The fault was neither Mario's nor Olivia's.

In late October 1950, Chinese "volunteers" had flooded into North Korea, adding an entirely new dimension to that undeclared war. Would China go all the way and make it a declared war? Which way would the Soviet Union jump?

Those were worrisome questions. We had four vessels under construction in Japanese shipyards. I felt it best to be close to the action and spent December and the better part of January in the Far East before returning via the States and Europe. I arrived back in Ithaca in late April.

Three days later I arrived in Milan. The following weekend, Olivia drove me to Verona to meet my brother-in-law.

During our drive, Olivia supplied me with background information. Mario's military career had been short-lived. An army captain, he'd been with the Italian forces invading Greece in 1940. Wounded in action, he'd been hospitalized in Trieste, where he'd had his left arm amputated below the elbow.

While now financially secure because of his lucrative Mercedes-Benz agency covering the two populous and prosperous northern regions of Lombardy and Veneto, in the years immediately following the war Mario had had to struggle to make ends meet. Compounding his problems during those lean years had been his sister's vindictive lawsuit.

I wouldn't have blamed Mario for harboring deep-seated resentment against Beatrice and, by extension, me. I fully expected to be greeted with reserve, if not hostility, and was surprised by the warmth of his welcome.

We arrived at the count's spacious yet unpretentious villa shortly before noon on Saturday and were met by Mario, his charming wife Lucia, his two sons and his infant daughter. The weather was pleasantly warm. Luncheon was served on the terrace.

Directly following the meal, the boys excused themselves, and Olivia went with Lucia to help put the baby down for her afternoon nap. I smiled inwardly. It was patently obvious that Mario and I had been left to ourselves by design.

Leaning across the table to refill my wineglass, Mario began the conversation without preamble. "We're all very fond of Livy. Reluctant as I am to do so, she has persuaded me to speak frankly to you about my sister. Livy is convinced you were coerced into marriage. Knowing what I do about Beatrice's background supports that contention. At the time of your marriage, she claimed to be pregnant, did she not?"

Initially I was annoyed. "Yes," I said. "Under such circumstances, what would *you* have done?"

Mario smiled faintly. "Probably just what you did, marry the girl. But if Beatrice *was* pregnant, I suspect it was by design, not accident, and she used her condition as leverage."

My annoyance was rapidly approaching anger. "Beatrice is an uncommonly beautiful woman. What makes you think she used coercive tactics? My concern was that she might accept me on the rebound from an earlier romance simply because she *was* pregnant."

Mario's eyebrows inched upward. "An earlier romance?"

"Before I met her, she was engaged to a young English army officer who was killed in Belgium early in 1940."

"Was he wealthy?"

The question took me by surprise. "I suppose so. He was heir to an earldom."

Mario grinned broadly. "Nobility doesn't always indicate wealth, but I assume he must have been well-off . . . and that her reason for getting engaged to him was identical to that for which she snared you. Money. Only by the time you entered the picture the need must have been more pressing."

Anger flared briefly, then subsided. "To be told you were married for money isn't flattering. It didn't seem to matter to Beatrice."

"It was of paramount concern to my father. He'd been cut off from his source of income for about a year when you met Beatrice. By then, he must have been not just penniless but heavily in debt to tradesmen. Even had he been employable, the thought of working for a living wouldn't have entered his mind. His only marketable commodity was his daughter."

"You make him sound like a pimp," I said.

"He wouldn't have thought of it in that light ... but the description fits. It's more apt than you imagine. They were lovers."

When what he'd said registered, I didn't believe I'd heard him correctly. "What do you mean?"

"That their relationship was incestuous."

It was a monstrous accusation to level against one's father and sister. "Do you realize what you're saying? You can't be serious."

"But I am. Dead serious." Mario lapsed into silence. Slowly he twisted the stem of his wineglass between his thumb and forefinger, studying its contents reflectively. Finally he looked up and said, "It's not something I like to think about, let alone talk about, but it's the truth. I'd hoped this skeleton in our closet had been interred with my father. Had Livy not persuaded me otherwise, it would have been. Listen closely to what I'm about to tell you ... and judge for yourself."

It was an incredible story. I listened to his graphic account, torn between indignation and revulsion.

He'd been nineteen at the time, and, as he pointed out, Beatrice had just turned fourteen. He'd been to England attending Cambridge.

Over the Easter break, he'd had no intention of going home but had gone instead to Paris, where he'd met friends who were motoring to Italy. He'd joined their party. Accordingly, he'd arrived in Rome unannounced.

He'd arrived home in mid-afternoon and, finding no one other than servants on hand to greet him, had gone directly to his room to unpack. While doing so, he'd been distracted by moans and gasps coming from Beatrice's adjoining bedroom. Alarmed by what he though were sounds of distress, Mario had knocked lightly on the door connecting the bedrooms. When there was no response, and the moaning was increasing in volume, Mario tried the door and, finding it unlocked, opened it. He had been confronted by a spectacle that, from that day onward, he'd been unable to erase from his memory.

On Beatrice's bed were two writhing figures. One, his younger sister, sat astride the other. To an accompaniment of her bedmate's rasping grunts and her own whimpering moans, Beatrice was gyrating frantically in orgiastic abandon. Horrified, Mario saw that the figure upon whom she was rutting was their father.

Blinded by rage, Mario burst into the bedroom, knocked Beatrice aside and attacked his astonished father. His intention, Mario freely admitted, had been to kill his father, and if he'd had a weapon, he would have done so.

Recovering from his initial shock, Guglielmi fought back desparately. Beatrice added to the commotion by screaming shrilly.

Count Guglielmi was in the prime of life and no weakling. What the outcome of the struggle would have been, Mario could not say, but he admitted that it had not been going in his favor. Fortunately, the butler and the head gardener, attracted by the ruckus, converged on the scene to separate the combatants.

The count and his daughter packed a few belongings and left the villa that very afternoon. That was the last Mario had seen of either of them.

Countess Lavinia returned later that evening. Without doubt, the butler told her of the incident. Mario was summoned to her dressing room to account for his presence and actions.

His mother revealed that she had known of the shameful relationship for some years — as had most of the servants. She couldn't say when Guglielmi had first seduced his daughter, but she assumed it was well before Beatrice reached puberty. Lavinia had hoped and prayed that Mario would never learn of his father's and sister's incestuous relationship. The servants had joined the countess in a conspiracy of silence.

Paradoxically, the countess excused her husband's aberrant behavior, taking much of the blame on herself.

Theirs had been an arranged marriage. Guglielmi had been eighteen, too young, Countess Lavinia contended, to assume marital responsibilities. Lavinia was seven years her husband's senior and admitted that Guglielmi had never been sexually attracted to her. Mario's conception had resulted from the consummation of their marriage bonds; five years later, Beatrice had been conceived during one of Guglielmi's inebriated lapses.

Nothing his mother said, no excuse she put forward for Guglielmi's behavior, altered Mario's opinion; there was no way he could condone incest. The sexual act he had witnessed, he said, was as vivid in his memory now as it was the day it had occurred.

I cleared my throat and said that twenty years had passed since the incident. I contended that the relationship was unlikely to have continued unchanged as Beatrice grew into adulthood.

Mario looked at me bleakly. "I've every reason to think it did," he said. "Although we never saw nor heard from them, we knew where they were. Bank drafts were forwarded to my father on a regular basis. They stayed in Paris for about two years. They were there when my mother died in 1932. They were notified of her death, yet neither of them attended her funeral. Shortly afterward they moved to London."

I failed to see what bearing that disclosure had on my suggestion that their relationship could have altered, but I held my tongue.

Mario wiped beads of perspiration from his brow with the back of his right hand, then continued. "In summer of 1937, Aunt Claudia — Livy's mother — was in London. Before leaving, she got her brother's address from his lawyer and looked then up. When she returned, she came to see me and asked my about the way she'd been received in London. She was understandably confused. You see, she knew nothing about their incestuous relationship, though she *did* know that some scandal had been responsible for the rift in the family."

When Mario once again fell silent, I said, "And? How did they receive her?"

"Coldly. She felt unwelcome and stayed at their flat no longer than was courteous. What Aunt Claudia found puzzling was their unseemly conduct. As she put it, they behaved more like husband and wife than father and daughter. And by then, Beatrice was no longer a teenager. She was twenty-one."

"Did you tell your aunt what you've just told me?"

"No. Couldn't bring myself to do so. I put her off with a vague reference to an unfortunate incident that had happened some years earlier . . . an event I didn't want to discuss. I suppose I should hve been more specific. All I succeeded in doing was to arouse her curiosity and give rise to speculation. When Livy came to me for clarification some months ago, all she knew was that Beatrice had some dark secret in her past — a secret that had bearing on your unhappy marriage."

"Does Livy know all the details?"

"She does now."

CHAPTER FIFTY-TWO

Olivia at the wheel, we drove west toward Genoa, where the *Veronica* was tied alongside awaiting my arrival. I sat, absorbed in thought, slouched in the bucket seat beside her. Mario had given me much to think about.

Olivia glanced sideways at me. "Did I do the right thing?"

"Huh?"

"Persuading Mario to tell you about Beatrice?"

"It sure as hell wasn't pleasant . . . but yes, you did the right thing. It answers many questions that have baffled me, but, unfortunately, it also brings up new questions."

"Such as?"

"According to Mario, money was her only motive for marrying me. She doesn't love me. Never did. Now that she has income-producing property — and could have any amount of money from me as a settlement — why does she want to cling to a loveless marriage?"

"I don't think it has anything to do with money. At least not now. In the beginning, maybe. But not now."

"Why, then? Maria Veronica?"

"No. It's sort of like she's performing an emotional high-wire balancing act and needs your marriage as a safety net in case she stumbles and falls."

I nodded reflectively. "Perhaps. I never realized the extent of her instability. Frankly, I still don't. Funny, I thought Mario was going to tell me that she'd exhibited lesbian tendencies at an early age . . . had a traumatic love affair with a housemaid or classmate. That wouldn't have surprised me. But *this* threw me for a loss."

"It's true, you know," Olivia said, "she *is* a discreetly practicing lesbian. Most of her emotionally warped friends are either dykes or fags. Those approaching normalcy are bisexual. When I was first introduced to you, darling, I thought you were some kind of wierdo."

"When did you change your mind?"

"The afternoon you took Ronnie and me to Drakopoulata."

"Tell me," I asked, changing the subject, "when did you begin to suspect that Beatrice's behavior was more abnormal than you'd originally thought? Last October, when you raised the subject, did you know about her incestuous relationship with her father?"

"No, though I suspected it had something to do with Uncle Guglielmi. Mummy often hinted that there was some dreadful scandal involving him and Beatrice. It wasn't until I met you, and started to fall in love with you, that I badgered her unmercifully for details. Eventually, she admitted that she had no concrete proof of wrongdoing, just suspicions based on something that happened before the war when she'd visited them in London. She told me that Mario, if he chose to, could provide me with answers."

"So you went to see Mario?"

"Yes. Last September. But he told me very little except to confirm that whatever had taken place did involve Uncle Guglielmi. It wasn't until last Christmas, when I spent a week with Mario and Lucia, that he told me the whole story."

For a few moments we talked about Mario, Lucia and their children, then I retreated once more into my thoughts while Olivia drove on in silence.

Mario's suggestion that Beatrice's pregnancy could have been faked to pressure me into proposing prodded me into darkly disturbing channels. Suppose, for the sake of argument, it hadn't been a contrived pregnancy. Suppose I hadn't fathered her child. If not me, who? Beatrice was the only one who could answer that question, and I wasn't at all sure I wanted to know the answer.

Maria Veronica? I'd never been able to see any of the Sthanassis hereditary traits in the child. I'd paid this little heed, dismissing it as one of the unfathomable mysteries of genetics. I had, that is, until now. And there was another point to consider. If Beatrice had conceived during the blitz, as she claimed, she should have gone to term in early June of 1941. The baby had arrived later that month, two or three weeks behind schedule. I'd been assured that was not uncommon in a first pregnancy and had given it no thought — again until now.

Suppose, again just for the sake of argument, that Guglielmi had fathered the child. Could that possibly have bearing on the antipathy Beatrice displayed toward Veronica? Logic told me that the reverse should have been the case; she should have adored the seed of his loins. Or should she? Perhaps if she'd borne a son — ? Did she look upon a daughter as some sort of punishment? Or did it have roots in her Catholic faith — the sins of the father being visited on succeeding generations? In her mind, was Beatrice convinced that Maria Veronica harbored some congenital defect?

Dammit, I thought angrily, why was I allowing myself to think such morbid thoughts? It didn't really matter who had sired Maria Veronica. She was *my* daughter, and, even if her mother didn't, I loved her dearly. Her well-being was my responsibility. Mine alone.

I focused my thoughts on Beatrice. That she'd taken it upon herself to judge my past or present conduct with Olivia was a supreme irony. Mario's disclosures had provided me with all the ammunition I needed to force the issue of divorce. That I would do so immediately had been my first reaction. Now, on more sober reflection, I wasn't so sure.

How was she likely to react if I pressed the issue? She was more unbalanced that I'd suspected. How close to the edge was she operating? What would it take to push her over the edge? Our lives had followed divergent paths for such a long time that I felt I no longer knew her — if, in fact, I ever had. To the world she presented a façade of control. What seethed just below the surface?

I'd seen her mask slip but once, and that example had been anything but reassuring. Deep-seated animosity had eaten away inside her like a cancer for more than a decade. When it had surfaced, it had blinded her to reason. Against advice, and despite the shakiness of her legal position, she had pressed the issue to its limits and beyond, vindictively intent on ruining her brother.

My concern was not for myself but that, if pushed into a corner, Beatrice was capable of savagely lashing out at Olivia, or Maria Veronica, or both.

I decided it wouldn't be politic to reveal my hold card unless, or until, Beatrice called the hand. I might not even have to show the card. A bluff might suffice. Given an indication of the strength of my position, if reason prevailed, I felt she would back down rather than risk open confrontation. But would reason prevail? That was the catch. For the moment, it might be prudent to lower my sights and shoot for a legal separation as a prelude to a Vatican divorce. It was a fallback position that didn't appeal to me, but it was one that I felt I should discuss with Olivia.

My initial reaction to Mario's disclosures had been disgust and anger. Now I recognized that a good deal of my bitterness had stemmed from self-pity. I'd been wronged! Cheated!

On closer scrutiny, Beatrice's conduct in 1940 seemed less deserving of reproof. All the evidence pointed to the fact that her warped love for her father had strengthened, not lessened, with the passage of time. There must have come a time when she recognized that their actions were affronts to religious doctrine and man-made laws. Sins in the eyes of church and state. Yet somehow she'd been able to reach an accommodation between principles and practice.

To shield her father from financial distress, she'd set out to sell her body to the highest bidder. In that light, contracting a loveless marriage took on the trappings of self-sacrifice. Had I not been the victim, I might have grudgingly admitted that her motives could be considered praiseworthy.

The culpability was not hers but her father's. The truly sad feature was that Guglielmi had not lived to answer for his crimes against God and Nature.

I voiced those sentiments. "Hell of a thing, being seduced by your own father. Can't help feeling sorry for her."

"Don't waste pity on Beatrice," Olivia said. "What do you think she'd have done if Guglielmi had lived? Once the war ended, and he regained access to his money, she would have left you like a shot. Godammit, she was in *love* with him. She'd have sacrificed everything — you, Ronnie, social position, religious convictions — to be with him."

As it turned out, I was spared the necessity of making an immediate decision on how I would handle things with Beatrice. I was greeted with the jolting news the minute I stepped on board the *Veronica* in Genoa.

At ten o'clock Eastern Standard time that morning, Sofoclis had suffered a massive coronary while golfing near his home in Charlotte, North Carolina. He'd been rushed to the hospital but had been declared dead on arrival.

It was a shattering blow. True, my cousin and I hadn't spent much time with each other over the past few years, yet he'd been an integral part of my life for more than three decades, and I'd grown inordinately fond of him. I was going to find it hard to adjust to a world without him.

Although I tried to contain my grief, Olivia sensed it. Appreciating that I would have to attend the funeral and do what I could to console Sofie's family, she said she would return to Milan, cancel her upcoming June performances and book a flight so that she could join me in the States within a few days.

I was chopper-lifted to Rome and from there flew to New York, where I made a connection for Charlotte. I arrived in time for the funeral.

CHAPTER FIFTY-THREE

Gerry Welton didn't waste any time. At the reception following Sofie's interment, he approached Aletha and made a generous purchase offer for the family's corporate shareholdings. It was so generous, in fact, that it aroused my suspicion.

When Aletha sought my advice, I asked her, "Did Sofie make any harebrained investments . . . suffer any losses lately? You and the boys aren't hurting for money, are you?"

"You should know better," Aletha said. "He never invested without first consulting you. When the doctor advised him to take it easy three years ago, we moved here from Queens, and Sofie practically divorced himself from the business world. He went up to New York no more than once a month to attend meetings of the board. Since the business was flourishing under Gerry's direction, those meetings weren't a strain on Sofie. I know, since I always went with him in case he needed me. As for Metaxis & Company, its profits mounted steadily."

"Evidently," I said. "As for your Metaxis shares, you can't dispose of them until the will is probated and they're transferred to your names. Gerry knows that. I strongly suspect that his attractive offer was aimed more at me than at you."

"Do you mean it wasn't genuine?"

"Hell, no. It was kosher. But you don't have to commit yourselves in any hurry . . . which gives me time to check out the situation."

I gave a good deal of thought to Welton's offer. I'd been expecting him to make a bid for corporate control for so long that I was more than half-convinced he'd seized on Sofoclis' death as the opportunity he'd been waiting for. He'd know that Aletha, providing I attended the funeral, would seek my advice. I don't believe he would have made the offer had I not been there. It was only logical to assume that I would check into the state of corporate affairs following on the heels of Aletha's request for advice. He'd fully expected I would do so, which could only mean one thing. My investigation would reveal that Metaxis & Company was in robust health. It was. Under Welton's stewardship, the corporation had moved from strength to strength. What did Welton hope to achieve?

I carried my investigation a step further by having a firm of investigators check on Welton's activities over the past year. I wanted to know if he'd had any meetings in private or begun any outside negotiations of any significance. As far as I could determine, Welton had done none of those things. He'd been grooming his son, twenty-five-year-old Cyrus Welton, to take over eventually as executive vice president, a projection I considered only natural. Moreover, over the last three or four years, both he and Cyrus had quietly acquired substantial holdings in Metaxis common stock. I saw nothing untoward in those acquisitions; they simply displayed confidence in the corporation. Reluctantly, I concluded that my suspicions were unfounded. I overreacted.

After all, Sofie's death had been totally unexpected, and, even if he'd been hatching a takeover plan, Welton couldn't possibly have put it into effect on such short notice. Besides, even though my votes were exercised by proxies, I still retained a 52-percent controlling interest. I'd only to put in an appearance, rescind my proxies and exercise my vote to forestall anything Welton contemplated. Or so I thought until the first week in October, when something happened to radically alter my point of view.

Aletha came up to New York to do some shopping and stayed overnight with Olivia and me at my penthouse apartment. During dinner that evening, we reminisced about Sofoclis.

"It's such a shame he died when he did," Aletha said. "Next year, when he retired, we were planning to book passage on one of your ships and spend a year or so seeing the world at a leisurely pace. Peter is old enough now to be left on his own. Sofie was so looking forward to it."

"Retired. My God, Aletha, fifty-two was too early for him to retire. He never mentioned retirement to me."

"He didn't want to worry you. He'd known for some time that he had a bad heart and was at risk. It was all arranged. Gerry would be voted in as chairman of the board, and Cyrus would take over as president and chief executive officer. Sofie intended to turn over his preferred share to you."

Sweet Mother of Jesus! I'd been investigating the wrong Welton!

The next day, I swung into action and switched the private investigation to Cyrus Welton. Within ten days, a report was on my desk at my Kybernas Line office in the Metaxis Building.

Gerry Welton might not have done much traveling during the past year, but the same could not be said for his son. Cyrus had been almost constantly on the move. Since he was being groomed for the presidency, this was understandable. He would have had to familiarize himself with all phases of the operation — exactly what he appeared to have been doing.

There was only one puzzling aspect to the report. While he'd visited most locations only once, Cyrus had made three trips to Minneapolis during the year. Why? Was Metaxis & Company experiencing difficulties in the Midwest? There was nothing in the corporate records to indicate this.

Two days later I received clarification in the form of a slim confidential report. A few days earlier, Cyrus had made yet another trip to Minneapolis, only this time, unbeknownst to him, under close surveillance. As before, Cyrus had made a brief visit to the Metaxis & Company offices in the morning and cursorily inspected the warehouses during the afternoon. That evening, he'd gone by taxi to an out-of-the-way restaurant in St. Paul where he'd dined with a middle-aged gentleman. Cyrus' dinner companion had been identified as Jason Dangerfield, president of Metaxis & Company's major competitor, Minneapolis-based National Foods, Incorporated.

The pieces started to fall into place. There was either a takeover or merger in the wind. Considering National Foods' corporate size, a merger was the more likely. Negotiations, conducted secretly by Cyrus Welton, had been underway for the better part of a year, or longer. They could only have been conducted with Gerry Welton's approval, and, in all likelihood, he'd initiated them. Then why had he gone to such pains to conceal his involvement?

When it came to me, the answer was simple. The entire operation had been carefully cloaked in secrecy for the sole purpose of keeping me in the dark until the Weltons could present me with a fait accompli. And that meant, of course, that Sofie couldn't know or suspect what was going on because he would have alerted me, either advertently or inadvertently. Accordingly, Gerry had kept up a façade of normalcy. He hadn't gone anywhere out of the ordinary and had remained in almost daily contact with Sofie. It had been Cyrus, using familiarization as a convenient excuse, who had done the legwork. But why go to such lengths to keep from me the possibility of a merger that couldn't help but be beneficial to both corporations involved? The answer to that was equally simple. I was the only person who could block the merger.

And why, if it would benefit both parties, should I want to block a merger? A merger would entail a stockholding restructuring, during the process of which the restriction that tied voting rights to preferred shares would no longer be applicable. I'd have to relinquish control. Apart from its being a precondition that must have been imposed by National Foods, it was Gerry Welton's major objective.

Since Sofie hadn't commanded enough votes to block actions, why had Welton considered it necessary to ease him out of the picture? To prevent Sofie from alerting me to what was going on. The last thing Welton wanted was to have me appear at a crucial board meeting, rescind my proxies and vote my shares. To that end, if he hadn't actually been its architect, Welton had encouraged Sofie's plan to retire early.

As I visualized it, the scenario would have gone something like this: Following Sofie's retirement, a board meeting would have been called to confirm Gerry as the incoming chairman of the board and Cyrus as the president-elect. At the meeting — while it wouldn't be indicated as an agenda item and accordingly would be brought up as "other business" — the proposed merger with National Foods would be tabled by the new chairman. On some pretext demanding immediacy, Welton would rush it to a vote. The outcome would have been predictable. The merger would be approved without a dissenting vote.

It had been five years since I'd taken an active part, or even displayed much interest, in the corporate affairs of Metaxis & Company. I'd left everything to the discretion of the three board members who held my proxies. By now they must have full confidence in Gerry Welton's direction and decisions. It would be assumed that I had been advised of the proposed merger, and, in the absence of direction to the contrary, my proxy holders would support him. Logically, so they should. Shareholders of the confluent corporations would profit from the merger.

Sofie's untimely death necessitated only minor changes in Welton's scenario. I needed to be given assurance that Metaxis & Company's position was sound and healthy — and that I would leave the country secure in that knowledge. Once I was safely out of the way, the farce could be played out as originally scripted.

I admitted to grudging admiration. The Weltons had laid the groundwork with consummate skill. Had it not been for Aletha's opportunely timed observations about the executive positions Gerry and young Cyrus would fill, my suspicions would not have been rekindled.

The one question remaining was, what was I going to do about the situation now that I'd figured it out?

I pondered that question at some length before placing a call to Aletha in North Carolina. At the end of our conversation, I cradled the phone and smiled broadly.

Whistling tunelessly, I rode the elevator down four floors to the executive offices of Metaxis & Company. Striding unannounced into Gerry Welton's office, I sank into an easy chair opposite his big desk. "Well, Gerry," I said, "four days from now I'll be heading back to Greece . . . by way of Italy."

Only Welton's eyes betrayed relief, and something akin to triumph. "Everything at this end concluded to your satisfaction?" he asked.

"Just about. I'll have to visit Japan, but that trip can wait until early next year. But that's not why I dropped by. I talked to Aletha a few moments ago about Sofie's Metaxis shareholdings. At the time of his death, she asked my advice about their disposition. She told me about your generous offer to take them off her hands."

Welton's eyes became wary, but otherwise his expression didn't change. "I see. What advice did you give her?"

"That she hang onto them. Considering the healthy state of the stateside economy — and other factors — they should appreciate in value. Sofie left her and the boys well-taken-care-of. There's no immediate need for cash. As for the boys, I've already underwritten their college education. So, while your generosity was appreciated, I thought it best that she retain Sofie's portfolio intact for at least the next few years."

"What about his Metaxis preferred shares? Does she know enough about the business to vote them intelligently?"

I laughed. "No . . . and the same might have been said of Sofie, which is why I took the precaution of retaining control. In any event, as you must know, I have first call on those preferred shares. I decided, for the moment, not to exercise that option. My advice to her was to give you the voting proxy. You're in the best position to know what's good for the company."

Welton's eyebrows inched upward, and he permitted himself a thin smile. "Thank you, Kostas. I'll see to it that her interests are protected."

I savored the moment. Rising to my feet, smiling genially, I said, "I'm sure you will." I turned toward the door, hesitated as though struck by an afterthought, then turned back to face Welton. "Oh, one last item of interest. Since I will undoubtedly be otherwise occupied when it comes up, I'm giving the directors holding *my* proxies written instructions about how they're to vote when you table your proposed merger with National Foods."

Presumably intending to escort me to the door, Welton had half-risen from his chair. When what I'd just said sank in, he sat down abruptly as if his legs had given way beneath him. For a moment his features registered dazed incredulity. But, to his credit, Gerry didn't spook easily. He regained his composure quickly; only a twitching muscle in his cheek betrayed his agitation. He didn't waste time on denials or ask how I'd come by my knowledge. When he regained his speech, he came directly to the point. "You must appreciate the need for absolute secrecy in negotiations of this nature. You would have been brought fully into the picture before it came to a vote. How did you instruct your proxy representatives to vote?"

He was right about the need for secrecy, but I knew — and he knew I knew — that I would've been the last one to be advised of the pending merger. I said mildly, "In the best interests of all concerned, to vote conditionally in favor of the merger."

Welton's brow furrowed in a puzzled frown. If only as a matter of pride, he expected me to fight to retain corporate control. "Conditionally?" he asked.

"Two conditions," I said. "The first is a trifling concession prompted by sentiment. Aletha would like to see the Metaxis name perpetuated. The stipulation is that 'Metaxis' be a part of whatever name you settle on for the merged companies."

"And the second condition?" Gerry asked.

"Again prompted purely by sentiment. The Metaxis voting shares now held by Aletha, me and a handful of others are to be converted to nonvoting preferred shares in the merged corporation at an equitable rate of exchange."

"What do you consider *equitable*?"

"Ten to one would sound reasonable, wouldn't it? That's the figure I've stipulated to my proxies."

Welton inhaled sharply. After a moment's silence, he said, "National Foods won't accept that condition."

"If they want the merger, they will. It's up to you and Cyrus to sell Dangerfield."

"And if *I* don't agree to those conditions?"

My voice went hard and flat. "In that case, someone else will present them to National Foods, and I'll expect your resignation by five o'clock this evening. It'd be a shame to lose you after all these years, Gerry. The choice is yours. The conditions stay — and are implemented to the letter — or you go."

CHAPTER FIFTY-FOUR

Olivia and I did not fly to Europe; instead we went by sea, installed in a stateroom on one of my newest cargo-passenger vessels, the *Hera*. After discharging and loading cargo at Montreal, Southampton, Le Havre, Lisbon and Marseilles, we proceeded to Naples, where Olivia and I disembarked in early July.

I'd cabled ahead. The *Veronica* rode at anchor in the outer harbor, awaiting our arrival.

The program was that Olivia would go with me as far as Genoa, whence the helicopter would take her to Milan. Since Beatrice would already have been at St. Tropez for more than a month, I'd stay on board the *Veronica* and go there to embark Maria Veronica and Mrs. Brady, who were to spend six weeks with me in Ithaca. Olivia was to join us for the final two weeks of Maria Veronica's vacation.

That, at any rate, was the plan. It didn't work out that way.

"Veronica will not be joining you," Beatrice said.

"Why not?"

Her answer wasn't what I'd expected. "Because Mrs. Brady is retiring."

"Retiring? Why?"

"She is sixty-six, well past retirement age. She wishes to return to England. Besides, lately she's become insufferable."

I suspected there was a good deal more to it than Beatrice was telling me. An uneasy truce had characterized Beatrice's relationship with Mrs. Brady from the beginning. If it had flared into open defiance on Mrs. Brady's part, it would not have surprised me.

The hiring or firing of a nanny was Beatrice's province, but Mrs. Brady was not a governess. The termination of her employment should have been a joint responsibility — I should have been consulted. "If she's set on retirement, we can't stop her," I said, "but I'll try to talk her out of it . . . at least till we find a suitable replacement."

"That won't be possible," Beatrice said. "She left three weeks ago. I've already interviewed a number of applicants and settled on a replacement, a young woman whose approach to child education is more advanced than the old-fashioned methods Mrs. Brady favored."

My heart sank. "I'll be the judge of that," I said. "When can I interview her?"

"Her name is Signorina Petucci. I'm sure you'll find her well-qualified in every respect. I've already hired her."

As best I could, I held my temper in check. "Maria Veronica? What does *she* think of the new governess . . . or is that of no importance?"

"Of course it's important," Beatrice said. "They'll get along beautifully once they get to know each other. Veronica is spending the summer with her in Rome so they can become better acquainted before Veronica's tutors return from vacation."

I disembarked at Nice and caught a commercial flight to Rome. The yacht proceeded on to Naples, where it would ride at anchor until I needed it.

I had formulated no clear plan of action. Essentially it was a scouting expedition. I wanted to see Maria Veronica's reaction to Mrs. Brady's retirement and to assess Signorina Petucci's qualifications as a governess.

I could have stayed, but didn't, at Beatrice's residence. Instead I put up at the Excelsior and visited the house daily. If Signorina Petucci was trying to get to know the child and work out a routine to follow during the fall and winter months, I didn't want to unduly interfere.

It didn't take me more than a day to discover that, of the two of them, Signorina Petucci was the more deserving of sympathy. Maria Veronica was hugely enjoying her new found freedom. Intuitively appreciating that she had the governess at a disadvantage, Veronica was exploiting the situation to the fullest. In turn willful, petulant and imperious, she was behaving like a spoiled brat. I'm sure the young governess was grateful for the break when I took Veronica off her hands for shopping expeditions.

On the drive into town from Milan's domestic airport, I gave Olivia an abbreviated rundown of the latest developments.

"How's Ronnie taking it? Beautifully! She's having the time of her life. The only fly in her ointment is that she won't see her Auntie Livy this summer," I said.

"Doesn't she miss Mrs. Brady?"

"She does — but she doesn't yet realize how much. The dear old soul was a zealous watchdog and a strict disciplinarian. In Ronnie's eyes, she was someone to be both loved and feared . . . a beloved ogress. Just how much she misses Mrs. Brady won't hit Ronnie for a few weeks, or months. For the moment, she's enjoying her freedom."

"Mrs. Brady?"

"When I tried to get through to her, she was visiting relatives in Ireland and couldn't be reached. Only managed to make contact with her yesterday morning. She's pretty broken up about the dismissal."

"Dismissal? I thought you said she'd resigned."

"That was Beatrice's version. She was canned. The hell of it is, Beatrice was within her rights because of Mrs. Brady's age and the fact that she hasn't been in the best of health over the last few years. But you and I were the real reason for her dismissal."

"You? Me? What have *we* done? Dammit, darling, I haven't even *seen* Beatrice in over a year."

I laughed mirthlessly. "The unfortunate thing, m'love, is that it's becoming next to impossible for us to avoid publicity. Your adoring public has taken you to its heart and affectionately dubbed you 'La Cappa.' Can't say I blame them. You're young, beautiful and blessed with a voice that comes along once in a century — if then. On top of that, your escort of late has been an excessively wealthy Greek shipowner. We've become what's known in media circles as 'an item.' "

"But what's that got to do with Mrs. Brady's dismissal?"

"Everything. Some well-meaning friend sent Beatrice a clipping and photo of us from a New York tabloid. She blew her stack and said that under no circumstances would Maria Veronica spend any part of her vacation with me . . . especially if *that* woman would be in Ithaca. Mrs. Brady made the mistake of rallying to our defense. Exit Mrs. Brady."

"How unfair!"

"No one ever said life was fair," I said, "but Beatrice *did* give her a generous termination settlement — to which I'll add an equally generous pension."

"The new governess? What's she like?"

"Educationally qualified. Young, plain, intense . . . and no match for either Beatrice *or* Ronnie. Feel sorry for her. She's just a pawn. So, unhappily, is Ronnie. Beatrice's game is depriving Ronnie of our company, and vice versa. I'm damned if I'm going to let her get away with whipsawing the child."

"What can you do about it?"

"Is ten too early an age for boarding school?"

"I was thirteen when my parents bundled me off to Sacred Heart in Lugano, but there were a number of girls younger than me there. I wouldn't say ten was too young. Is boarding school what you have in mind?"

"Yes. Will I have difficulty getting her into Sacred Heart? Lugano is close enough to Milan that you could sort of keep an eye on her and let me know how she's doing."

"You shouldn't have any trouble. The convent welcomes contributions. But what about Beatrice? Won't she object?"

"I expect her to."

Olivia's autumn schedule was a busy one. After our visit to Lugano to arrange for Maria Veronica's enrollment in Sacred Heart Convent School, Olivia and I had less than a week together in Ithaca before she had to return to Milan for rehearsals. The company would be performing in Eastern European capitals from mid-September to mid-October. Then it would perform in Berne, Switzerland, before returning to Milan at the end of October.

Tentatively I would join Olivia in Berne for the closing performances, after which we would motor south to Milan, stopping off in Lugano to spend a weekend with Maria Veronica.

At the end of August, the *Veronica* dropped us off at Venice. Olivia proceeded westward to Milan; I flew south to Rome to await Beatrice's return from the French Riviera.

I didn't relish what faced me, but I could postpone a confrontation with Beatrice no longer.

There was no way I could broach the subject diplomatically. I bluntly put it to Beatrice that our marriage in name only could not continue. Moreover, I'd given the question of Maria Veronica careful consideration and had arrived at the following conclusions: One, her interests would best be served by supervised schooling; to that end I'd enrolled her at the Ursuline-operated Sacred Heart

Convent School in Lugano. Two, while I would not oppose joint custody in principle, Maria Veronica was to spend her summer vacations with me in Ithaca. In return for those considerations, I would not oppose a Vatican divorce.

Not for a moment had I expected Beatrice to accede to my ultimatum without demur, yet I was surprised by the violence of her reaction. She was beside herself with rage, trembling and nearly incoherent. Finally sputtering, face contorted, she said, "How *dare* you presume to dictate to *me*, you Greek oaf. If you think I'll let her spend so much as a minute with you and your — your *whore* — you're out of your mind."

"In that case," I said, "you leave me no choice. I'll sue for divorce in civil court, petition for sole custody and — "

"You'll *WHAT!*?" she screamed.

Ignoring her interruption, I continued," — and call on your brother to testify on my behalf."

It took a moment for what I'd said to register. When it did, the effect was incredible. One minute, cheeks flushed and eyes flashing angrily, she'd raged at me; then, abruptly, the color drained from her face, her mouth went slack and the fire went out of her eyes, leaving them dull, glazed and oddly out of focus.

It was a truly startling transformation. She stared at me blankly. Taking her by the shoulders, I shook her none too gently. I realized that, in an instant, she'd been transported some two decades back in time and was reliving in memory a devastating scene from her childhood — a dread chimera she'd thought safely put to rest.

"Did you understand what I just said?" I asked.

Gradually, her eyes came back in focus. Her lips worked, but no words issued from them. Her head bobbed weakly in what I took to be acknowledgment.

I'd not put into words what had passed between me and Mario. There'd been no need to. The mere threat of disclosure had been enough to trigger her dramatic response.

At the time I was uneasy, yet I can say in all honesty that I had no premonition of the tragedy that would result from that confrontation.

CHAPTER FIFTY-FIVE

Signorina Petucci seemed relieved when I told her that her services would no longer be required. When I wrote out a check for a year's salary in severance, she was delighted and helped me pack the few things I thought Maria Veronica would need for the short trip to Milan.

Beatrice did not put in an appearance when Maria Veronica and I left to drive to the airport.

In Milan, Olivia helped us buy clothes and supplies Ronnie would need at the convent school, then drove north with us to Lugano to get Maria Veronica safely settled. The Ursuline mother superior assured us that Ronnie would be well-looked-after.

As we drove south toward Milan, Olivia raised a subject she'd purposely avoided until now. "How did you get Beatrice to agree to boarding school?"

"I put it on the line . . . a Vatican divorce, or a civil action with a custody battle. Threatened with the public disclosure of her relationship with her father, she caved in."

"Would you have followed through with a civil action?"

"Yes . . . if she forced my hand."

"Do you think Mario would have supported you?"

"Frankly, of his own free will, no. To be perfectly honest, Liv, I wouldn't have tried to persuade him to act against his conscience."

"Then you were bluffing."

"Yes . . . and no. Mario's testimony was a bluff. The civil action wasn't. If she hasn't petitioned the Vatican by December, I'll bring suit against her."

"Can you win?"

"Divorce, yes. Custody will be tougher." I grinned sourly and added, "I'm counting heavily on the old adage that there's a law for the rich and a law for the poor. If there was ever a case where my money can be put to good use, it'll be if I'm forced into civil action."

Olivia brought her hand to rest lightly on my right forearm. "I just hope, darling, that we're doing the right thing."

"So do I, Liv . . . so do I. I hope you appreciate the position in which this places you."

She smiled. "Of course I do. Whichever route we go, I'm branded as an adultress."

In October, in Berne, we dined with the stage manager and several members of the cast before retiring to my suite in the hotel. When the door closed behind us, Olivia kicked off her shoes and smiled up at me. Turning, she murmured "Unzip me, lover."

When I'd done so, she shrugged out of the shoulder straps, and the gown whispered as it slid to the floor. Stepping from the discarded garment, clad only in filmy panties, she turned to face me. Arms encircling my neck, firm breasts pressed against my chest, she gently pulled my head down and kissed me hungrily. I responded with equal fervor and, as the tip of her tongue probed seductively, felt fire flooding my loins.

Her thrusting pelvis still pressed provocatively against me, she withdrew sufficiently from my embrace to start unbuttoning my shirt. "Darling," she said, "I've something to tell you."

"Mmmm . . . what?"

"It was confirmed in Sofia. Your 'other woman' is with child."

In Lugano, the mother superior and Veronica's teachers told us that she had adjusted readily to her new environment. Her grades were above average and, in fact, thanks to tutoring, were well above average in history, geography and languages. Moreover, she was popular with her classmates. Any lingering doubts Olivia and I had harbored evaporated.

The three of us dined in a cosy restaurant off Lugano's main square. Olivia was radiantly beautiful. Veronica, face aglow and eyes dancing, ate everything put before her, yet somehow managed to chatter incessantly. We heard all about her closest friend, especially an English girl named Felicia whom we simply *must* meet, and about Veronica's favorite teacher, Sister Anna. We learned that the mother superior was *very* strict and didn't take kindly to practical jokes.

As I watched Veronica laughing and talking animatedly, relief flooded me. It was comforting to know that we *had* done the right thing. She had never looked better. Her copper-colored hair, which had been neatly groomed when she had been handed into our custody, was now engagingly untidy. Her tan nearly, but not quite, masked her facial freckles. In her navy-blue blazer with the school crest on its breast pocket, she was the picture of health and innocence.

We returned Veronica to the school promptly at eight o'clock. As we drove southward toward Milan, Olivia asked, "Well, what do you think? What's your impression of the school . . . of Ronnie?"

"Favorable. More than that, I'm highly pleased. The school seems to be doing wonders for her. Never seen her livelier, or looking better."

"Have you given thought to her Christmas holidays?"

"I was hoping you and she could spend the holidays with me in Ithaca."

"What about Beatrice? If Ronnie's going to spend her summers with you, won't Beatrice expect to have her at Christmas and Easter?"

"I doubt it. Beatrice has spent every holiday season for the past ten years in New York. It's an established pattern she's unlikely to break now. Without a governess to take care of Veronica, I don't think Beatrice will want to take her to the States. The truth is, I think she'll be happy to have me relieve her of the responsibility."

"Maybe," Olivia said. "Hadn't you better check with her just to make sure?"

"Yes, I'll do that. I'll go by way of Rome and discuss it with her."

"Good. But instead of spending both Christmas and New Year's in Ithaca, I'd hoped you and Ronnie could come with me to Nizza Monferrato and spend Christmas with my folks. We could go on to Ithaca to see the new year in."

I rubbed my chin. "Don't know whether that's a good idea, Liv. Your parents don't approve of our relationship."

Olivia smiled. "They're getting used to the idea. Daddy still has reservations, but Mummy finds our affair romantically appealing. They can't judge fairly until they get to know you better, darling. It's high time they did, considering we're about to make them grandparents. Besides they've never met Ronnie. They'll adore her."

Her response surprised me. "Do your parents *know* you're

pregnant?''

"As soon as I was sure, I wrote Mummy the news. She'll be delighted. She has two months to work on Daddy. Believe me, that's more than enough time to bring him around to her way of thinking."

I was far from convinced. How would *I* react ten or so years down the road if Maria Veronica came to me announcing she was about to become an unwed mother? I don't think I'd have been delighted. Nonetheless, I didn't voice the doubts that plagued me. Olivia was right — it was high time her parents, for good or ill, got to know me better.

I was as good as my word. I returned to Ithaca via Rome and called on Beatrice. It was not what I would call a pleasant encounter.

She kept me waiting the better part of an hour before appearing. Despite the fact that she received me with an outward show of civility, the atmosphere was strained.

She wasn't hostile, which rather surprised me. She seemed withdrawn, much as she'd been following the death of her father. To get a response I had to repeat my questions several times.

Yes, she *thought* she'd be going to New York for Christmas. No, she hadn't been planning to take Maria Veronica with her. She raised no objection to my taking her to meet her great-aunt and great-uncle. In fact, from the listlessness of her response, I got the impression that Beatrice didn't connect Claudia and Niccolo with Olivia.

It was an oddly disquieting meeting. It wasn't until after I'd left that I realized she'd made no reference to divorce. Mentally I kicked myself. I should've introduced that subject.

Maria Veronica's last day of school was December 19. Those students leaving for the holidays would be free to do so on the twentieth and were not expected back until January 3.

Olivia, either driving with friends or by taxi, planned to go to Lugano on the eighteenth for the term's closing ceremonies on the nineteenth. I would fly to Milan the following day, hire a car and drive up to meet her and Maria Veronica. All three of us would spend the night of the twentieth in a hotel and leave early the next morning to drive to Nizza Monferrato. On the twenty-seventh we would drive to Genoa, where we would be met by the *Veronica*.

On December 18, in the early evening, Olivia phoned me from Lugano. Her voice sounded oddly strained.

"Is something wrong?" I asked.

"Not wrong, exactly, but there's been a change of plans."

"What sort of change?"

"Friends driving through to Geneva dropped me off here a couple of hours ago. Beatrice was here ahead of me."

"What? What the hell's *she* doing in Lugano? She's supposed to be in New York!"

"I know, darling. She says she's booked on a flight leaving Rome the day after tomorrow. She explained that she was at her place in Florence and, wanting to see Ronnie for a day or two before she left, decided on impulse to drive here."

"I don't get it. She knew I was supposed to collect Veronica on the twentieth. She knew we were going to Nizza Monferrato to spend Christmas with your family."

"Yes. She said she knew that. She was going to phone you to save you the trip."

"What do you mean . . . save me the trip?"

"She was going to pick up Ronnie tomorrow — after the ceremony at noon — and drive her to Nizza Monferratto. She said it would give her a full day with Ronnie and, at the same time, allow her to pay long-overdue respects to Mummy and Daddy. After she dropped Ronnie off, she'd drive to Genoa, leave the car there to be picked up later and catch a flight to Rome in time to make her connection for her flight to New York."

"And what was I supposed to do?"

"Skip Milan and come directly to Nizza Monferrato by way of Genoa."

"And you? When we discussed my plans two months ago I purposely didn't mention you. Did she expect to see you in Lugano?"

"I don't think so. She seemed surprised to see me. I must say, though, she's been pleasant. Very civilized. She's invited me to join her and Ronnie on the drive to Nizza Monferrato."

"There's no way I can make it up there by morning. Dammit, Liv, I don't like it — I don't trust her."

Olivia's question was only half-bantering. "What do you expect her to do . . . kidnap Ronnie?"

"No! Yes! Hell, I don't know what goes on in her mixed-up mind. Just don't leave them alone together."

"Don't worry, darling, I'll stick to them like glue."

Cradling the phone, I glared at the offending instrument irritably. Damn Beatrice. I didn't believe for a second that she'd acted on a sudden impulse — or a burning desire to spend time with Maria Veronica.

No, Beatrice's drive to Lugano had been planned well in advance. But to what purpose?

I didn't really believe she would kidnap Maria Veronica, although it was a possibility I couldn't rule out entirely. A more likely explanation was that she planned to put in an appearance in Nizza Monferrato with Maria Veronica dutifully in tow and make a bid for sympathy as the injured wife and mother. As I well knew, Beatrice, when she chose to exercise the talent, was a consummate actress. Why else, after all these years, would contact with her aunt and uncle be so vitally important?

Had Beatrice expected Olivia to be on hand in Lugano? I suspected that Beatrice had known she would be. How? It would not have been difficult for Beatrice to phone the school and get the details of our plans in advance. Arriving in Nizza Monferrato as the wronged party, yet manifesting forgiveness for the "other woman," would be a neat touch.

I turned from the telephone in disgust. I had never understood Beatrice. Trying to fathom her motives and thought patterns at this late date was an exercise in futility. There was only one thing of which I *was* sure. Whatever she had in mind, it boded ill for Olivia and me.

CHAPTER FIFTY-SIX

The call came through at 3:47 p.m. on December 19. The caller identified himself as a commander of police attached to the Swiss canton of Ticino. Tersely, he informed me that a vehicle registered in my name had been involved in an automobile accident.

Cold fingers of fear clutched at my heart. "What happened? Was anyone injured?"

"A head-on collision with a truck. The truck driver is in the hospital in serious condition. The occupants of your vehicle, two adult females and one female child, were also taken to the hospital. One of the adults was declared dead on arrival. The other adult and the child sustained grave injuries and are in critical condition."

Swallowing to relieve the constriction of my throat and chest, I asked, "Which woman died?"

It seemed to me there was a moment of hesitation before the answer came. "We have not yet made positive identifications."

I was convinced the commandant knew more than he'd told me. As it happened, my assumption was correct. I would have saved a good deal of needless agony had I framed the question differently.

I don't recall the exact time, but it must have been close to midnight of the nineteenth that I arrived in Lugano. I went directly to the hospital, where I was told that neither of the accident victims of whom I inquired had regained consciousness. A nurse steered me to a waiting room.

The minute I was ushered into the waiting room, I felt as though a nearly intolerable burden had been lifted from my shoulders. Indirectly, the question that had weighed most heavily on me was answered. Dr. Cappellari was seated in one corner of the room. His presence could mean but one thing. Olivia was the one who had survived the accident.

My surging hope was quickly dampened by one look at Dr. Cappellari's craggy countenance. He regarded me darkly, accusingly, as though whatever had happened to his only daughter was my doing. And, in a sense, I suppose his attitude was justified.

The short-lived feeling of relief ebbed for another reason. Dr. Cappellari's presence in the waiting room augured ill. It meant that Olivia was still in grave danger. That undoubtedly held true for Maria Veronica as well, though my daughter's well-being could hardly be expected to be Dr. Cappellari's major concern.

Clearing my throat, I asked, "They would tell me nothing at the desk. Do you know their condition?"

Dr. Cappellari looked at me fixedly for a moment before answering, "I've seen neither patient, but the fact that they're still unconscious isn't good. Unless they rally soon, one or both could die." He retreated into silence for a moment before adding, almost as an afterthought, "They've told you, I presume, that your wife is dead."

I nodded dumbly. They, whoever "they" were, had told me nothing. I noted that he'd not used Beatrice's name, or called her his niece. He'd referred to her as "your wife." Wittingly or unwittingly, he was distancing himself and his daughter from me and my family.

A question I'd not thought to ask suggested itself. "How did you learn of the accident?"

"The police phoned me. They'd identified your daughter as a student from Sacred Heart by the blazer she was wearing. When the mother superior was called in to make a positive identification, she recognized Olivia."

That, for the moment, marked the end of our exchange. We sat slumped in chairs at opposite ends of the waiting room absorbed in private thoughts neither of us wanted to share with the other.

I've no way of knowing how long we sat there. It seemed like an eternity but was probably less than an hour. We both looked up expectantly as a gowned doctor entered the waiting room.

"Mr. Sthanassis?" the doctor asked. I nodded mutely. "I'm sorry, sir, but your daughter died a few moments ago."

The grief welling up in me prevented me from speaking. The doctor looked at me sympathetically and added, "She did not suffer. She did not regain consciousness. If it's any consolation, it may be for the best. She suffered massive brain damage and, had she lived, would have been a vegetable for the rest of her life."

Turning from me, the physician spoke briefly to Dr. Cappellari in a low voice, then turned and left the room. Dr. Cappellari rose from his chair and followed the physician.

How long I sat there, elbows on my knees, face cradled in my cupped hands, I don't know. It couldn't have been long. I was roused from my introspective grief by a gentle touch on my shoulder. I looked up into Dr. Cappellari's face.

His expression had softened. His tone was kindly. "My condolence and sincere sympathy, Kostas. We share your loss."

"Thank you."

"Olivia has emerged from her coma. She is asking for you."

I was allowed only a few minutes at her bedside. Her head and much of her face were swathed in bandages.

She motioned me to her side and grasped my hand. A tear slid down her cheek as she drew me down and said in a voice that was little more than a whisper, "It wasn't an accident. She tried to kill us . . . all of us."

Olivia's injuries were extensive. She had suffered a severe concussion, serious facial lacerations, broken and cracked ribs, multiple fractures of her right femur *and* a crushed pelvis. By some miracle, her unborn child appeared to have survived the ordeal intact.

As soon as it was safe to do so, she was taken by helicopter from Lugano to a private hospital in Geneva where she was attended by specialists in obstetrics and orthopedic and cosmetic surgery.

Of course, what I've mentioned took place over the course of long and anxious months. I should return now to the days I spent in Lugano immediately after the accident.

I reported to the police station and was taken to the morgue to identify Beatrice. It was an experience I've no wish to remember.

The attendant pulled back the sheet. I gazed down on her face. It was drained of color but otherwise was unmarked and readily recognizable. In death, her face retained its compelling beauty. What a waste. What a goddamn waste! In whatever netherworld to which he'd been assigned, Count Guglielmi had much to answer for.

The morgue attendant next conducted me to a second slab on which lay a pitifully small sheet-draped form. When the attendant reached down to pull back the sheet, I stopped him with a gesture. In Maria Veronica's case, further identification was unnecessary, the mother superior having already attended to that formality. I wanted to remember my child as I'd last seen her.

Closing my eyes to fight back tears, plunging my hands into my trouser pockets to hide their trembling, I turned away from Maria Veronica's sheet-covered body. Too long had I left her upbringing in Mrs. Brady's hands; too late had I stepped in with efforts to shield her from harmful influence. My belated efforts had come to naught. Life had held such promise for her, yet she'd not lived long enough to fulfill that promise.

I made arrangements for both bodies to be shipped to Rome, where separate Requiem Masses would be sung, followed by Beatrice's interment in the family mausoleum in Florence. I would have Maria Veronica cremated, and I would take the urn containing her ashes with me to Ithaca.

What about Olivia's contention that the crash had been no accident? When she'd leveled that accusation, she'd been coming out of a coma and still in a state of shock. At that time, I hadn't taken the accusation seriously. It was not until I received a copy of the police report that I began to piece things together and concluded that Olivia had indeed spoken nothing but the unvarnished truth.

When the events became clearer in her mind, Olivia not only stuck to her story but also amplified it with remembered details.

It had rained that morning, but it had cleared by noon, and driving conditions had been excellent. The road south from Lugano, while scenic, is hazardous at the best of times. The highway follows the contour of mountainous terrain skirting Lake Lugano and in places is cut into the face of sheer-sided cliffs. According to both Olivia and the accident report, the fatal collision had occurred on an outward curve of a precipitous outcropping some fifteen kilometers south of Lugano.

The blind curve had a history of accidents. It was not considered unusual by the police that it had chalked up yet another victim, particularly since Beatrice was unfamiliar with the tortuous route.

There were a number of factors, however, that supported Olivia's contention that it was not an accident. For one thing, Beatrice had been driving recklessly and at high speed. Olivia, in the rear seat, had twice told Beatrice to slow down. Beatrice had only shrugged and laughed disdainfully. Maria Veronica, in the front seat beside her mother, had been enjoying the wild ride.

Beatrice had taken the curve at high speed, swinging wide to do so. She must have seen the approaching truck but had made no attempt to avoid it. Had she simply panicked and frozen at the wheel, or had she deliberately driven into the oncoming truck?

The puzzling thing about the so-called accident was that Beatrice had a distinct aversion to driving. Normally, wherever she went, she was chauffered. On those infrequent occasions when she took the wheel herself she was cautious. Why, in this instance, had she been driving? Why had she thrown caution to the wind?

The most damning part of the accident report was the statement given the police by the truck driver. According to his testimony, the Mercedes had suddenly appeared, bearing down on him at excessive speed in the northbound traffic lane. He'd hit the brakes and sounded a warning blast on his air-horn. There had been nothing else he *could* do. On his right, the roadway fell away in a sheer drop to the rock-bound lakeshore. On his left towered the cliff face. The Mercedes had neither slowed nor swerved. The collision had followed moments later.

The trucker had not been seriously injured. As the Mercedes slowed on impact, Maria Veronica had been thrown violently forward against the windshield. Olivia had been catapulted onto the back of the front seat before being tossed sideways against a shattered rear window. The steering column had been driven backward into Beatrice's chest.

When removed from the twisted wreckage, Maria Veronica and Olivia had been unconscious. Beatrice, despite her chest injury, had been conscious. The ambulance report stated that nothing could have been done to save her; she drowned in her own blood on the way to the hospital.

The inescapable conclusion I reached was that Beatrice had come to Lugano with one purpose in mind, *a deliberate act of self-destruction — suicide — and the willful murder of the two people in all the world who were nearest and dearest to me.*

It had not been an act of vengeance aimed at Maria Veronica or Olivia — but at me.

CHAPTER FIFTY-SEVEN

I did not mourn Beatrice's passing. My grief was reserved for Maria Veronica. Still, no amount of grieving will restore life to the dead. Maria Veronica was beyond pain. I consoled myself with that thought as I concentrated my attention on problems of the moment.

My chief concern was for Olivia, yet, beyond insuring that she had the best medical attention money could provide, there was little I could do for her in the early days of her convalescence. Before leaving for Rome with Maria Veronica's ashes, I placed my helicopter at the disposal of Niccolo Cappellari.

Beatrice had drawn up a last will and testament leaving everything to Maria Veronica — which, for all the good it did now that Maria Veronica was dead, meant that Beatrice might as well have died intestate. In due course, everything, once the estate was settled and death duties paid, would come to me. There were, however, some outstanding matters to be attended to before her estate could be settled. One of these was to open the wall-safe in the master bedroom of her Rome residence. The catch was that no one but Beatrice had known the safe's combination.

As a last resort, I could have gotten a safecracker. Before doing that, I went through the drawers of her bedside table and writing desk, thinking she could have written down the combination rather than trust to memory. That is exactly what she had done. I found the combination taped to the bottom of her desk drawer.

The contents of the safe surprised me. While she had spent *my* money freely, Beatrice, as documents within the safe testified, had been much less profligate with income derived from her own landholdings. I smiled wryly. She seemed to have operated on the principle that what was mine was hers — and what was hers was none of my goddamned business.

Along with stacks of Italian, British and American banknotes, the safe contained statements of accounts from her income-producing properties and passbooks indicating substantial balances in savings accounts in Italian, French, British, Swiss and American banks. There was also an envelope containing a key to a safety deposit box in a Rome bank.

There was one other item in the bottom of the safe. Beneath some documents was a flat leather jewel case I recognized immediately. I opened the case and looked down at the emerald necklace nestling in its velvet bed. Why, I wondered, was it here and not in the safety deposit box where, evidently, she kept most of her valuable jewelry?

The necklace sent my thoughts back to the summer afternoon I'd given Olivia an abbreviated version of my adventures and misadventures in Colombia.

Olivia had asked two questions. First, she asked whether I'd told Beatrice about Pepita. I'd said no, that I'd meant to, but that Beatrice had never been interested in anything that had happened to me prior to our marriage. As it was, Olivia was the *only* person to whom I'd confided the story of Pepita's tragic death.

Second, Olivia had asked what had become of the emerald. I'd told her that, years later, I'd had it cut and made into a necklace that I'd given to Beatrice when Maria Veronica was born. Olivia had observed that, though she'd attended a number of formal functions with Beatrice in Rome, she'd never seen Beatrice wear the necklace. I confessed that neither had I, in Rome or elsewhere.

But here it was. I was about to return it to the wall-safe when I changed my mind. What the hell — it would be mine soon enough. On impulse, I closed the case and slipped it into the inside pocket of my tweed jacket.

The January sky was leaden. A thin rain was falling, which softened the earth. Had it not been for a tangle of roots at the base of the ancient olive tree, the digging would have been relatively easy. The hole wasn't large, but I dug down several feet and was sweating profusely by the time I finished. Placing the urn with Maria Veronica's ashes at its bottom, I refilled the hole and carefully tamped down the earth.

It was a solemn moment. I stood there in the rain, head bowed in silent prayer.

I looked up, took a deep breath and exhaled slowly. The simple ceremony was over. It was fitting, I thought, that her ashes should rest here in Ithaca, the one place where she had enjoyed happiness and freedom during her all-too-short life.

I raised my eyes to the rain-shrouded mountain that formed a backdrop for my estate. My thoughts went back through the years to that summer day when first I'd seen the abandoned manor house and its forlorn garden. Both had undergone considerable change in the intervening years. So had I.

Fifteen years! So much had happened. I was now in my fifty-second year. How, in balance, did my record stand?

A loveless marriage that had ended in tragedy topped the list in the debit column. On the credit side were the facts that I'd carved out a fortune in the cutthroat world of commerce and put together a shipping empire of which I was justifiably proud. That I had recovered from a serious chest wound and lived through a war was on the plus side of the ledger, yet that probably was balanced by the fact that the war, like most wars, had resolved nothing. That Olivia and our unborn child had survived a near-fatal car crash was definitely in the credit column but that tally couldn't be properly evaluated until Olivia had recovered and it could be determined that her fetus had sustained no damage.

My errant thoughts veered to another channel. As though spoken yesterday, I recalled the words of the long-dead oldster I'd met that first day in Ithaca: ". . . *don't stay away too long. It is here, where the sea and sky are clean and clear, that one finds peace of soul.*"

Well, I'd heeded the old man's counsel, hadn't I? I had, like Odysseus, returned to Ithaca, yet peace of soul eluded me.

There was finality involved in my ritual act of burying Maria Veronica's ashes beneath the spreading branches of a venerable olive tree. She would live in memory for as long as I lived, but I was no longer a slave to that memory. I could now devote my undivided energies to tasks at hand.

As it often had in the past, the *Veronica* served as an extension of my Ithaca base of operations. Until Olivia recovered, the yacht, anchored off Venice within easy commuting range of Geneva, was to be my headquarters. Actually, over the winter and spring months of 1952, I spent much more time in Geneva than I did aboard the *Veronica*.

Olivia made a truly remarkable recovery. Her physical strength and unflagging optimism were contributing factors.

Her orthopedic surgeon was pleased with her progress. He advised us that her pinned and wired thighbone and pelvis were knitting satisfactorily and even quicker than he had anticipated. While she would require physiotherapy to rebuild her muscles, he assured us she would walk with only a trace of a limp.

The cosmetic surgeon was equally optimistic and pleased with his handiwork. He said that, once the bandages were removed, she would be delighted with the results. When, eventually, the bandages *were* removed, we found he was as good as his word.

Despite her obstetrician's assurances that the child in her womb had come through the accident unscathed, it was a subject Olivia and I studiously avoided. I think, despite the confidence Olivia expressed, we both had reservations.

In mid-February I moved Olivia from the hospital to a suite in a hotel overlooking Lake Geneva. From the picture window, cloud-cover permitting, we enjoyed a spectacular view of Mont Blanc.

Olivia progressed from wheelchair, to crutches, to a cane. Throughout this period of transition, either with me or with a nurse, Olivia enjoyed daily outings along the broad promenade fronting the lake. Her unfailing good humor endeared her to her nurse, the hotel staff and all who met her. It was gratifying to her that La Cappa's devoted following had not deserted her.

During our outings and in the confines of our hotel suite we talked of many things — of the resumption of her singing career, of my plans to establish a Geneva-based Sthanassis Foundation and of our pending nuptials. By unspoken agreement, we avoided discussing the blessed event due to take place as spring drew to a close.

Father Schaub officiating, we exchanged marriage vows in the hospital chapel on March 5, 1952. It was a ceremony attended by a small group of our friends and relatives. It hardly could have been otherwise since Olivia was by then more than six months pregnant and still on crutches. I feared the event would tire her unduly.

The captain of the *Veronica* acted as my best man. One of Olivia's closest friends from the opera company served as her maid of honor. Also present at the ceremony were Niccolo and Claudia Cappellari, Mario and Lucia Tocchi, Georgiana and wheelchair-confined Penny — and Aletha, who had flown in from the States.

The ceremony was followed by a reception at the hotel. By this stage of the evening, Olivia, like Penny, was confined to a wheelchair. No formal invitations had been issued. News of the event had spread by word of mouth. I'd left all the reception arrangements in the competent hands of the *Veronica*'s chief steward and the hotel's catering manager. I presumed they had some idea of the number of guests. I assumed these would include most of the off-duty crew and administrative staff of the *Veronica*, many of Olivia's friends from La Scala and a number of doctors and nurses who'd attended Olivia. Beyond those, I had no idea who might put in an appearance. I was in for some pleasant — and a few astonishing — surprises.

Along with those verbally invited guests, Olivia and I were warmly congratulated by Irving and Phoebe Goldman, Alfredo and Consuelo Ruiz, Sven and Monica Henningsen, a beaming though tearful Mrs. Brady — and last, but by no means least, by Gerry and Cyrus Welton and their respective wives.

It was gratifying to know that, differences notwithstanding, if I hand't earned Gerry's affection over the course of our many years of association, at least I had gained his respect.

CHAPTER FIFTY-EIGHT

Squalling lustily, Stefano Niccolo Sthanassis made his debut on life's stage at 2:17 a.m. on May 19, 1952. He was delivered by Caesarean section and, as the Swiss obstetrician had contended, was sound in mind and limb.

On June 10, at 0800 hours, mother and child safely installed in the owner's stateroom, the *Veronica* weighed anchor and set course for the Ionian islands.

The day had dawned overcast and blustery. By mid-morning, though the scudding clouds were breaking, the wind had freshened and backed to the southeast. The *Veronica* pitched and shuddered as she knifed into rising, foam-crested seas.

At 1045 hours I made my way from the operations room, where I'd been reviewing reports clattering in on teleprinters, up to the bridge. The third officer greeted me and commented that the glass appeared to have steadied and that the blow should be of relatively short duration. I nodded in agreement, turned and left the bridge. Descending the ladder, I proceeded aft along the companionway to my quarters.

Entering the carpeted stateroom, I greeted the steward affably, "Morning, Andreas."

"Good morning, sir."

"Everything under control?"

"Yes, sir."

"Where's Mrs. Sthanassis?"

"In there, sir," the steward answered, nodding toward the master bedroom, "feeding the baby."

Pushing the sliding door until the catch clicked, I parted the curtain and entered the bedroom. Olivia was seated on the outsized bunk, her left breast bared, suckling our infant son. She glanced up on my entrance and smiled.

"You're bound and determined to make a sailor out of Stefie," she said. "Couldn't we have waited until the weather improved?"

"There wasn't any indication of heavy weather," I said. "The glass is steady. I don't think we'll get gale-force winds. A summer duster. Sky appears to be clearing."

Olivia laughed. Looking down at little Stefano, his mouth glued to her nipple, she said, "Do you hear that, Stefie? Your father, Captain Sthanassis, predicts fair winds and following seas. You'd think the very *least* he could do would be to produce a full-fledged storm for your initiation to a seafarer's life." Pushing a stray strand of black hair back from his brow, she added, "Look at him. Just like his father. He'd sooner drink than engage in polite conversation. Greedy little bastard, isn't he?"

I grinned. "How dare you, madame, refer to my son and heir as a bastard."

"Well," she said, "you'll have to admit he was conceived in sin . . . even though you *did* go to some pains to make an honest woman of his mother."

Normally untroubled by the *Veronica*'s skittish behavior in response to wind and wave, Olivia was an excellent sailor. This, however, was her first voyage encumbered by a walking stick, and she was finding it difficult to maintain her balance. In consequence, we did not join the captain and ship's officers in the saloon for lunch but had it served in our stateroom.

My casual comment that the stalemated Korean War was going nowhere, that peace talks in North Korea's Kaesong were still hopelessly bogged down in semantic quibbling and that the continuing ideological struggle in French Indochina appeared to be equally inconclusive drew a surprisingly spirited response from Olivia.

The Truman Administration's policy of containment of militant communist expansion was not a new topic of discussion between us. Since the preceding autumn, when the opera company had returned from its tour of Eastern European capitals, Olivia's concepts had altered significantly. She'd found Soviet-inspired Marxist repression repugnant. She'd been in sympathy with the stirrings of revolt she'd heard cautiously expressed in artistic circles in Warsaw, Prague and Budapest.

Prior to that trip, Olivia's views were apolitical. On her return, she was openly critical of the Italian Communist Party and decidedly pro-free enterprise in her sentiments. We'd been in agreement on that score, and, during her convalescence in Geneva, I'd taken it upon myself to broaden her political horizons to include ideological confrontations in Asia, South-east Asia, the Middle East, Africa and Latin America. As a shipowner with global contacts on a day-by-day basis, I was in an excellent position to undertake this tutelage. I must confess, however, that my views were not always in accord with American policy. In my estimation, the American approach, while well-intentioned, was tinged with naïveté.

That day, at lunch, the views Olivia expressed had an added dimension. Not surprisingly, they were speculative and focused inward. What bearing would events shaping in Korea and French Indochina have on our lives? What sort of a world would Stefano face as he approached maturity? Did the Atomic Age, which now was upon us, spell eventual doom for mankind?

Questions for which I could supply no satisfactory answers.

Following lunch, Olivia retired to the bedroom to take a nap. The questions she'd posed still troubling me, I restlessly paced the stateroom.

Little Stefano was less than a month old. I'll admit that, when told that Olivia had borne me a son, my thoughts had turned to a distant day when I could bequeath him the shipping empire I'd nursed through a turbulent adolescence to solid maturity. But that had been a nebulous concept. I really hadn't thought in terms of his maturity.

Sweet Mother of Jesus! When he turned twenty, assuming I lived that long, I'd be well into my seventy-third year. What sort of world *would* he inherit?

Suddenly I found the stateroom oppressively confining. I felt the need to be on deck and let my thoughts take wing on the gale-force winds. Balancing myself against the roll and pitch, I went to the adjoining cabin I'd fitted out as a study-cum-library to find suitable wet-weather gear. Rummaging through the cupboard in search of an oilskin slicker, my hand rested momentarily on my tweed jacket.

Memory flooded in on me. I recalled the last time I'd worn the jacket. On that occasion, I'd pocketed the jewel case. I hadn't left it in the jacket. On my return to the *Veronica,* I'd locked it in the drawer of my desk and promptly forgotten about it — until this very minute.

Shrugging into my slicker, I turned, then hesitated. Walking unsteadily over to the desk, I unlocked the drawer and took out the jewel case. Then, case in hand, I left the stateroom and made my way onto the afterdeck.

Shielded from wind and spray by the superstructure, I stood with my elbows resting on the teak rail-capping, staring pensively at the foam-flecked wash sliding astern. It's been said that, throughout the course of human history, each generation has had its war. Without doubt, Stefano's generation would have its share of conflict. But, if sanity prevailed, his war would not be global. The world could not survive another global war, particularly if nuclear weapons were used tactically or strategically. No, sanity *must* prevail.

My gaze fell on the jewel case in my hand. I opened the case and looked at the necklace. Lifting the necklace from the case, I held it up and stared moodily into the large pendant emerald's green depths.

I wondered if Beatrice had ever had the necklace appraised. I decided she had not, that she was ignorant of its true value. Why had she never, at least to my knowledge, worn the necklace? By some peculiar thought process, had she associated the necklace with the birth of Maria Veronica, an event that evoked unhappy memories?

In its uncut state, I had considered the gemstone a talisman. True, it had been the cornerstone of my subsequent good fortune. I recalled how, fancifully, I had once imagined that Pepita had smiled encouragingly at me from within the stone.

It was strange, but I hadn't thought of the emerald as the embodiment of good fortune once I'd had it cut into its present form. Come to think of it, the necklace had ceased to have meaning for me one way or the other since the day I'd given it to Beatrice.

I don't think Pepita would have approved of Beatrice. I do think, however, that she would have approved of Olivia. It was a shame I hadn't waited until Olivia entered my life to have the gemstone cut and mounted.

I let go of the necklace and watched it tumble down and disappear in the frothing wash. At that moment, the sun broke through the scudding clouds to flood the *Veronica*'s afterdeck in golden light.

I laughed aloud and fancied that the gods laughed with me. Had my offering to Poseidon released Prometheus from his confining chains?

A link with the past was severed.

The future beckoned.

HERE IS YOUR CHANCE TO ORDER SOME OF OUR BEST

HISTORICAL ROMANCES

BY SOME OF YOUR FAVORITE AUTHORS

____ **BELOVED OUTCAST** — Lorena Dureau   7701-0508-4/$3.95

____ **DARK WINDS** — Virginia Coffman   7701-0405-3/$3.95

____ **KISS OF GOLD** — Samantha Harte   7701-0529-7/$3.50

____ **MISTRESS OF MOON HILL** — Jill Downie
7701-0424-X/$3.95

____ **SWEET WHISPERS** — Samantha Harte
7701-0496-7/$3.50

____ **TIMBERS AND GOLD LACE**— Patricia Werner
7701-0600-5/$3.95

____ **TIME TO LOVE** — Helen McCullough
7701-0560-2/$3.95

____ **WAYWARD LADY**— Nan Ryan   7701-0605-6/$3.95

Available at your local bookstore or return this coupon to:

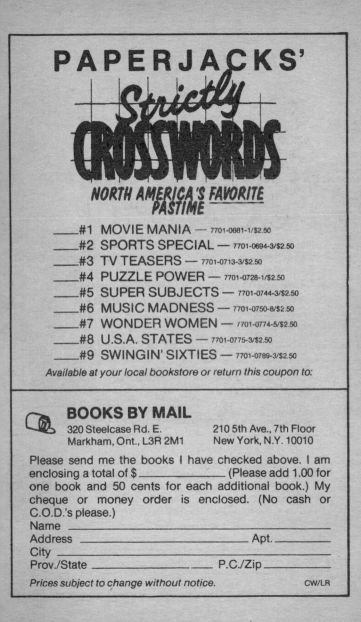

FREE!!
BOOKS BY MAIL
CATALOGUE

BOOKS BY MAIL will share with you our current bestselling books as well as hard to find specialty titles in areas that will match your interests. You will be updated on what's new in books at no cost to you. Just fill in the coupon below and discover the convenience of having books delivered to your home.

PLEASE ADD $1.00 TO COVER THE COST OF POSTAGE & HANDLING.

BOOKS BY MAIL

320 Steelcase Road E.,
Markham, Ontario L3R 2M1

210 5th Ave., 7th Floor
New York, N.Y., 10010

Please send Books By Mail catalogue to:

Name _____
(please print)

Address _____

City _____

Prov./State _____ P.C./Zip _____

(BBM1)